The Wish
I Wish Tonight

Barbara Elliott Carpenter

Barbara Elliott Carpenter
April 2015

authorHOUSE®

AuthorHouse™
1663 Liberty Drive, Suite 200
Bloomington, IN 47403
www.authorhouse.com
Phone: 1-800-839-8640

First published by AuthorHouse 10/31/2007

ISBN: 978-1-4343-4230-0 (sc)
ISBN: 978-1-4343-4231-7 (hc)

Library of Congress Control Number: 2007907503

Printed in the United States of America
Bloomington, Indiana

This book is printed on acid-free paper.

Dedication

This book is lovingly dedicated to the memory of my husband's mother, Alice Barbara Bailey Carpenter, and to her father, John Bailey, both of whom were born and lived near Charleston, West Virginia. At the age of eighty-eight, Alice Carpenter died on November 3rd, 2002, shortly before the first book of the Starlight Trilogy was published, in 2003. She read most of the first book's chapters, and she always read the ending first, to assure that it was a happy one.

I mentioned her briefly in the dedication of the first book, but she deserves more than a mention. She was a source of support and encouragement to me from the time I first met her, more years ago than I care to admit. She was my best friend.

John Bailey worked in a West Virginia coal mine, decades before all the safety measures were implemented. He and his wife, Callie, reared seven children on those hillsides. John lived to be well over ninety, and I was privileged to know him for a few years before he passed away. I could not end this series without basing a character on him. Stories my mother-in-law told me about him alone would fill a book. My husband, Glenn, looks like John Bailey; and it is my pleasure to dedicate this final Starlight book to his mother and grandfather. God bless them all.

~ Barbara Elliott Carpenter

Acknowledgement

While working on the chapter titled LUCINDA BARNES, in Starlight, Starbright..., I met, online, **James Loewen**, author of several books, one of which became a best seller, **LIES MY TEACHERS TOLD ME**. He went on to write **LIES ACROSS AMERICA**, as well as other publications.

At the time we met, Professor Loewen was involved with massive research for another book. He traveled literally from coast to coast for several years, collecting and documenting information on so-called "sundown towns." Coincidentally, the chapter I was working on contained a segment about that very subject.

I shared with him what little I knew and could learn, locally, about sundown towns in my area. When I received an autographed copy of his book, **SUNDOWN TOWNS**, it was quite a pleasant surprise to discover that he had footnoted both my book and a bit of information I had passed on to him.

James Loewen has graciously granted me permission to use as much of his research for SUNDOWN TOWNS as I needed. The only specific circumstances I used in this book are ones I discovered myself, but I borrowed a lot of background and general information from his book.

SUNDOWN TOWNS is a magnificent book. I think it should be placed in every library and high school classroom in America. It details a true account of what life in most American towns was like for well over a hundred years, and in some instances, still is. The book is available online and through major bookstores. Autographed copies can be obtained by contacting him at jloewen@zoo.uvm.edu.

James Loewen holds several titles, among them **Visiting Professor of Sociology at the Catholic University of America** and **Emeritus Professor of Sociology at the University of Vermont**. He continues to write, and he is a sought-after speaker at universities, colleges, historical societies and organizations across the country. His web site lists his current speaking schedules. If you know of information confirming a community as a sundown town in the past (or present), do let him know at his email address.

His web site is: http://www.uvm.edu/~jloewen/sundowntowns.php

Contents

Prologue

The years my family lived in Redbud Grove, Illinois, have taken on the idyllic hue distance sometimes lends to actual events. In memory, that time shimmers with the aura of golden days and starlit evenings, interlaced with summer showers and winter-y marshmallow mounds of snow.

Vivid, yet softened, images fill my mind: long shadows cast upon late afternoon's sidewalks beside the park, where I spent the summers of my childhood; the creak of rusty cables on the swings; sunlight glinting off the harness of Frank Thompson's horse; the soft smile that greeted me when Mrs. East opened her screened door to me; sticky Tootsie Roll grins on the faces of my seven-year-old friends; glorious spring blossoms on the ancient magnolia tree in the Monahan's front yard, visible from our front step.

The yellow house on South Pine Street, our home for seven and a half years, has become to me an icon of my own innocence and youth. The patina of time has softened the images in my mind. They have taken on the hues and tones of oil paintings on canvasses the brush of memory will not allow to age.

Unaware how precious was that fleeting era, I lavishly, even wantonly, spent the hours as they spun into years, not knowing how transient the seconds were. Childhood traumas have dwindled to trifles, brushed away with my own careless adult hand. Despite the passage of decades, memory allows the faces of schoolmates to remain as fresh and young in my mind as they were so many years ago.

Even from such a distance, I have not forgotten how painful it was to move away from Redbud Grove. I hated to leave my friends and the house beside the park, but it didn't take long for me to fall in love with our new home in Dixon, West Virginia. The house was larger than the little bungalow, and my family enjoyed the additional room and privacy.

From the time I was in the first grade, I had known only prairie land. The wide vistas of flat fields that surrounded the little town in Central Illinois, broken by farm houses and an occasional stand of trees, were completely different from the West Virginia terrain.

Wooded mountains and hills surrounded Dixon, and they were spectacular in all seasons. The city nestled between two ancient peaks. It spread upward, covering the hills and slopes in all directions. Except for Main Street, which meandered along the flattest part of the city, scarcely a street lay flat for any distance.

Friendships and ties formed during my high school and college years in Dixon became as binding and strong, some even stronger, than those in Redbud Grove. My love of classical music came from the years spent under the influence of Mrs. Grimes, the high school music director. In my paintings I see the influence of Willow Thornhill and Greg Boudroux, her unacknowledged grandson, as well as Dixon High's art instructor.

Plaintive mountain music transports me back to the evening I sat with Mark Watson, when we listened to his extensive family sing melodies passed down for generations. The sight of a German shepherd still brings back the stories told to me by Diane Anderson. While Redbud Grove remained my fantasyland of childhood, Dixon became my home, the place where I grew up.

During the first few years in Dixon, my mother fulfilled her long-held dream of becoming a nurse. With a lot of hard work and perseverance, she obtained an LPN license. She continued to study; and eventually she became a registered nurse, which led to promotions and increased salaries.

Her determination proved to be more beneficial than she could have imagined. At the age of forty-one, my father, along with several other local men, was killed in a tragic coalmine explosion, a turn of events that changed all our lives. My mother was forced into the role of sole provider for her family. Materially secure, her life was shattered emotionally.

Our father's death affected my brother, my sister and me in different ways. Bill and I were young adults when he died. However, our little sister, Beth, was deprived of a strong, loving father, the protector, the good, solid male influence that children need long past childhood.

I was almost twenty years old when Dad died, and I had come to view him as a separate person, someone who had an identity aside from being our father. Beth would never have that perspective. To her, he would always be the daddy who was taken from her long before she outgrew the need of his love and care. I think Beth felt the loss her whole life. Perhaps we never outgrow that need.

Even before the death of our father, my life had taken a new direction. I became engaged to Jackson McCoy, the handsome boy who had declared his love for me when we were teenagers. Jack and I were married the summer after my dad died. Had I listened to my own intuitive doubts, the marriage would never have taken place. Years of heartache and pain for both of us could have been avoided.

Hidden within the wealthy, talented, charming Jackson McCoy was a terrible flaw. Jack's controlling nature, ugly in itself, became worse as his love of alcohol turned him into someone I scarcely recognized. He physically abused me, the woman he had vowed to love and cherish for as long as we lived. When his plane was shot down over Viet Nam in nineteen sixty-eight, I felt more reprieve and guilt than grief.

In time, the guilt dissipated. I took my Journalism degree in hand and pursued a career as a writer in Sumter, South Carolina, near Shaw Air Force Base, where Jack had been stationed. I learned that the independence I had nurtured as a girl would serve me well as an adult.

My mother remarried. My brother married his red-haired Lainie, and my sister moved to California, where she met and married a suitable young man. There was no one to object when I moved to the city of New York. There I forged a new life, found new friends, and made a name for myself in the field of journalism. I made some unwise decisions, and it didn't happen overnight; but it happened.

After a time, restlessness settled upon me like an uncomfortable, scratchy wool blanket. I sought assignments that called for hours of research, and I especially liked those that took me to different parts of the country, even sometimes beyond the country's borders. What I found during those times not only affected my articles, it affected me and the way I related to life and those with whom I came in contact, both professionally and personally.

Work held the restlessness at bay; but a simple, innocent desire, followed by a decision to reconnect with my past, destroyed that scratchy blanket. Fortunately, instead of ignoring it, I listened to the inner voice when it spoke. It led me onto a convoluted path, one with unexpected turns and through emotional upheavals such as I could not have imagined. Not for anything in this world would I have missed the wonder and joy that were to come from following that instinct.

There is a saying: *Be careful what you wish for.* It's possible that what we think we want, what we hope to attain, or what we reach out to grasp is not the thing that will bring us happiness. Pyrite ore, fool's gold, sparkles when we first see it; but it has only flash and no value. True gold takes more effort to locate and is refined by fire.

There is a vast difference from having an acceptable life, a good life, to having one filled with passion and joy, one that makes a good cup of coffee in the morning just the first of many remarkable events of every day. Passion without joy can be tiresome, but joy without passion is impossible. Passion and Joy--two sides of only one of many precious coins of life.

How fortunate are those who find that coin.

PART ONE
NEW YORK

My Neighbor's Keeper

Two years after my husband died in Viet Nam, I sent resumes to every newspaper and magazine whose address in New York City I could find. Several offers came my way, but most of them were less than spectacular. When the editor of Streetside offered me the job as copy editor, I accepted. It was a small "about town" type of news magazine with a fair-sized readership. The salary was not impressive, but it would at least pay my rent. I had saved enough to carry me until I could find a better job or get a promotion, whichever came first.

Neither The Wall Street Journal nor The New York Times had responded to my resume, but I told myself that it was just a matter of time. I didn't specify how *much* time. I was content to wait until an offer came from one or the other of them. Optimistic by nature, I still lived in the reality of what is, not in what I fantasized.

I loved the city. From my first night, which I spent in a less than luxurious hotel, I loved the bustle, the busy-ness, and the people. Arms folded beneath my head, I lay in the double bed and contemplated the cracks in the plastered ceiling. I left the lamp beside the bed lit, not from fear, but in order to convince myself that I really was in New York.

As I lay there, I numbered the relocations that had taken place in my life, only one of which had been by my choice. I couldn't call this change of address a disruption, as the moves to Redbud Grove and Dixon had been. Although I had considered both of those moves disastrous, they had provided opportunities to make new friends and to benefit from new experiences. I counted my marriage as one, and I skipped over all the transfers to various bases with Jack.

Sleep was long in coming and fitful when it came. The unfamiliar jangle of intermittent sirens brought me straight up in bed more than once. Near dawn, I dozed, only to be wakened by delivery trucks outside the hotel. I thought I would get up at an early hour, eager to begin a new life in a new town. Instead, I slept until nearly noon.

I explored my new surroundings and looked for an apartment the first week. There were many available, but only a few met my requirements: affordable, clean, and a reasonable walk to my place of employment. I leased space for the Corvette and rarely drove it.

At last I found an adequate two-room apartment five blocks from the building that housed Streetside's offices. Bellamy Apartments had once been a hotel. Eight stories high, built of red brick blackened by age and soot, it was still an impressive structure. Original mosaic tile covered the lobby, and marble panels reached halfway up the walls. A few cracks showed here and there, but the dark-veined green stone lent a touch of class.

From the apartment's bedroom window, a sliver of the East River sometimes glistened in the morning light; and the bathroom had new plumbing. There were no windows in the living room/kitchen, but the space compensated nicely. Since I was rarely there during daytime hours, the lack of a window didn't bother me.

The walls were not thoroughly insulated, and I was sometimes privy to conversations and other interesting communications that occurred on either side of my little domain. Instead of finding the activity bothersome, I was reminded of my childhood in Redbud Grove. I couldn't number the nights I had listened to my parents in the bedroom below my attic room. Totally unaware that their pillow chats and exchanges floated upward through the air vents, my mom and dad kept me abreast of everything I did or did not need to know. I smiled at the memories.

I spent my second week in bargain-priced furniture stores. I asked the building's manager to remove everything from the apartment except the small refrigerator and range. I didn't trust or want to know the history of the upholstered things, including the bed. I bought an inexpensive bed frame, but I splurged on a brand new mattress and springs. Within a week, I managed to turn the unattractive suite into a bright, cheerful space; and I was happy with my choices of color and accessories.

On one wall I placed Willow Thornhill's paintings. They were so beautiful they needed nothing to accent them. They added a special touch to the apartment and reminded me of a fantastic woman. Occasionally I used the painting of Eagle's Landing as Willow had suggested: a place of quiet retreat after a hectic day.

Among the items I bought was a thick spiral notebook. I scrawled "First Apartment" across the front of it. I hadn't asked to be an observer of my neighbors' lives; but since I was, I decided to make a journal of the experiences. Sometimes I scrawled little cartoons around the edges. After I learned the names and relationships of the occupants on either side, the cartoon characters I drew became recognizable. Just to be on the safe side, I carried the notebook with me. It would prove to be one of my most prized possessions.

"You good-for-nothing slob! When are you going to get off that couch and find a job! The least you could do is pick up after yourself while I'm working!" The strident voice pierced through the adjoining wall as effectively as an arrow shot from William Tell's bow. I could only imagine how it grated when heard up close and personal.

"Yeah, yeah, yeah! If you don't like it, there's the door!"

"I'm not going *anywhere!* I pay the rent for this place, remember?"

I looked at the clock on the bedside table. One-thirty a.m. I closed my eyes and placed my hands over my ears. It was the same conversation that took place, with varying insults, nearly every evening from apartment Four-twenty-one. The bout was much later than usual. I clicked on the radio beside my bed and turned up the volume. The Beach Boys sang to me of California girls; and at the moment, California was where I wished to be.

The argument on the west side of me dwindled to barely discernible murmurs, and I drifted off to sleep. Just as the first glow of dawn arrived, I became aware of music that didn't come from the radio I had neglected to silence in the night. I turned down the volume. From apartment Four-twenty-five, on the other side of mine, came soft strains of a violin, a well-played violin. I recognized the melody as the sweet sound of Schubert's "Serenade."

I lay there, eyes closed, and listened to the music. What a wonderful beginning to the day, especially after hearing an ugly, late night argument. Faint strains of the morning concert filtered through the walls while I showered and enjoyed my two cups of coffee.

I had four days to fill before I reported to the newspaper office. The shops would not be open for a couple of hours, so I was in no hurry to venture into the streets. I would listen to the music until the virtuoso next door grew tired of playing.

I imagined different personalities for the musician. Perhaps a woman drew the bow across the strings, not extremely young, but reed-slender and pale, with long, dark hair and limpid brown eyes. On the other hand, it could be a strong, ruggedly handsome man with sharp blue eyes and shaggy blond hair, a bohemian with no sense of responsibility except to his music.

A rousing rendition of a blue grass melody made me smile. From Rachmaninov to grass roots! The violinist was certainly versatile. I puttered quietly while the music continued. I opened the bedroom window and discovered that the melodies could be heard even better, for the windows in the violinist's apartment were also open.

Even from where I sat in my bedroom, I could hear the sudden banging on the musician's door. "Cut out that noise, would ya!? Some of us would like to sleep around here!" The music stopped. I recognized the voice as that of the man who lived on the other side of me, the one who evidently had no job. I couldn't understand how the music would have disturbed him, soft as it had to be through the buffer of my apartment. Angry mumbles accompanied my neighbor back to his apartment, and the music did not resume.

I waited until lunchtime before I ventured onto the busy sidewalks. A wonderful little deli, called Luigi's, was housed in a hole-in-the-wall shop only a few blocks from my office building, a good long walk from my apartment, but worth it. Huge sandwiches, stuffed with luscious meats, cheeses and vegetables, were reasonably priced there; and the clientele were nothing if not loyal.

The sandwiches were so big I was unable to eat both halves; so I not only enjoyed a great lunch, there was usually enough left for my evening meal. I wasn't exactly tight, just careful with my money.

I spent most of the afternoon riding bus after bus around the city, only half-heartedly trying not to look like a tourist. There I was, thirty years old, widowed, self-reliant; and I felt as if I had just arrived, fresh off the farm, smack in the middle of the largest city in the country. It was one of the most intriguing times of my life; but even in the midst of my excitement, I felt a pang of loneliness. It would have been nice to share it with someone. The feeling passed.

I returned to my building late that afternoon, tired, but satisfied with my day. The bags I carried, one filled with throw pillows and the other with groceries, grew heavier by the moment. I looked forward to placing them on the kitchen table.

With my elbow, I hit the UP elevator button and waited for the approaching "ding." When the doors opened, a burly, stubble-faced man of about forty-five lunged from the elevator. Before I could move aside, he clipped my left arm; and my bags dropped to the floor.

"Watch where you're going!" he snarled. Dismayed, I stared after him, then down at the scattered remains of my foodstuffs, where broken eggs mingled with romaine and smashed tomatoes. I didn't know whether to laugh or cry. I dropped to one knee and tried to gather the mess into the other intact paper bag.

"Oh, my! Let me help you!"

I glanced up and met a pair of sweet blue eyes. For a moment I felt as if I were looking at the model for the granny in the Sylvester/Tweety cartoons. The short little woman actually wore granny glasses, the kind that perch low on the nose. Snowy white hair, fluffed into fullness around her wrinkled face, formed a soft bun on the back of her head.

The woman wore a high necked white blouse, trimmed with a ruffled collar and cuffs on the long sleeves. A black and white cameo brooch nestled among the ruffles on her chest, and an ankle length black skirt completed her attire. She tucked her skirt between her knees and bent agilely to the floor.

"Dear, dear," she muttered. "So many people just seem to have no sense of decency these days. My papa, rest his soul, would have dispatched that bully right away." She shook her head. "It's just a shame to see the niceties of civilization diminish in such a rude manner."

Together we scooped the mess into one bag and transferred salvageable items into the other. Tsk-tsking away, my Good Samaritan rummaged in her crocheted handbag and brought out a large white handkerchief. With it, she wiped away all evidence of the impromptu raw egg-romaine-lettuce salad.

"Thank you so much," I said.

"Think nothing of it, Dearie. Ta-ta."

"Wait! I don't know your…name." Before the last word was out of my mouth, the little lady bustled across the lobby and exited onto the busy street. I shook my head and walked into the elevator. With my elbow I again pushed my floor's number. I was fairly certain that I had just met my ugly-mouthed neighbor, but I had no clue as to the identity of the granny lady.

The rest of the week passed in much the same way as the previous days, with one exception. There was no repeat performance of the violin concerto. I could only assume that the artist practiced during the hours I was out of the building. While silence prevailed on one side of me, the mutterings and arguments continued, at various levels, on the other. I learned to turn up the volume on the radio and television just enough to mask the voices.

By Sunday, my apartment looked cozy and habitable. Mementos from every period of my life dotted the rooms: little pottery pieces, paintings, books and photographs. I had no idea how long it would be my home; but while I was in that small space, it would reflect who I was and what I liked. I already felt settled.

Shouts and thuds, intermingled with oaths and swearing such as I had never heard, woke me from a sound sleep the next morning. Disoriented for a moment, I sat up and glanced quickly around my apartment. Diffused light came through the closed curtains, and I could hear the sounds of early morning activity on the street below. I shrugged into a robe and hurried to the door, where I placed one ear against the painted surface.

"You crazy old woman, get away from me!" I recognized the voice of the brute from the apartment in Four Twenty-one. "Ow! Cut it out!" Carefully, I opened the door a slit. I covered my mouth to stop the laughter that threatened to erupt at the scene before me. Dressed in a soft, flowing negligee right out of a thirties movie, marched the little granny lady who had helped me at the elevator. In one hand she grasped her robe. In the other, she wielded a long, black umbrella, using the tip as a sword against the fleshy middle of the man who had knocked my groceries onto the lobby floor.

"You will cease banging on my door for any reason. You will cease your unseemly behavior to other residents and patrons of this building. You will cease using foul, rude language. In short, Mr. Kelly, you will behave as a man of your age should; or I will ram the point of this umbrella up your ample posterior." The soft, genteel voice that delivered those ultimatums didn't raise one iota from the conversational tone the little lady had used outside the elevator.

Mr. Kelly managed to open the door of his apartment and escape into the safety of its walls. I stepped into the hall. A couple of curious neighbors peered from behind their doors briefly, but no one else seemed interested. The granny-lady turned toward me.

"Good morning," she smiled sweetly. "I hope you slept well last night."

"Uh, yes, I did," I replied. "Are you all right?"

"Oh, yes, perfectly, Dearie." She extended her free hand to me. "Permit me to introduce myself. My name is Mrs. Genevieve McLaughlin, and it appears that we are neighbors."

"Sissy Bannister," I told her. "It's a pleasure to meet you—again."

"Yes, indeed," Mrs. McLaughlin replied. "I hope you have a pleasant day." She smiled sweetly and entered apartment Four Twenty-five, the one where the lovely music originated. I had no idea she lived next door. Intrigued, I could only stand with open mouth and stare after her.

Once again the fourth floor of the Bellamy Apartment Building was filled with the sound of melody, and no one banged upon the door in protest. I smiled happily, not just at the music, but at the thought of Mrs. McLaughlin doing what she had threatened to do to Mr. Kelly.

During those first weeks, I saw as many landmarks as possible. Like dozens of other tourists, I went to the top of the Empire State Building and peered over the railing at people and vehicles that looked like ants on the street below. I spent several afternoons in Greenwich Village, notebook in hand.

I sketched and made notes about some of the people I saw, about the music and the poetry. I learned how to nurse non-alcoholic drinks for a long time at a sidewalk table. It was a time of double-knit leisure suits, bohemian looseness and splendor, flared jeans, midi tops, strands of beads and long hair on everyone.

During the liberated times of free love and drugs and "if it feels good, do it" sixties, I was married and never stayed in one place for any length of time. Life in the air bases was anything but liberated.

I'm glad my conservative inhibitions of right and wrong had become ingrained, but I found those without said inhibitions, fascinating creatures. Sometimes it was like watching otherworldly creatures in a psychedelic-colored zoo.

I learned anew how to laugh, how to dance and how to have fun. I was too young to get married when I did, both in years and in experience. Except for the two years in college, during which I still lived in my mother's house, there had been no personal time to learn who I was and of what I was capable.

One of the places that offered the most laughs was a coffee house in the Village that scheduled poetry readings. Anyone could read anything and call it poetry. Ruthee, a young woman from Streetside, invited me to join her there one evening after work.

"You'll love it," she told me. "There are these way-out guys that get up and read pure trash, so in love with their own voice, they don't know people are laughing at them. Some of them are so stoned, it's a wonder they can read anything."

"Sounds like real literary stuff," I said.

The sound of bongo drums greeted us at the beaded door. A blue haze of smoke (I was afraid to ask what kind) hovered in the air, enhanced by the slow-circling blue lights on the ceiling. A man, so thin he could nearly hide behind the microphone stand, staggered onto the stage and propped his skinny behind on a stool. His hair fell in long, stringy strands over his shoulders and dropped over much of his face.

Occasionally, he attempted to brush it away from one eye, so he could see the paper in his hand. I recorded his words in my notebook, simply to remind myself never to think that what I wrote was automatically brilliant. No matter how good I thought it might be, someone else could consider it pure drivel.

"Life crawls over the planet like ants on a dung heap, Man. People fill their claws with green stuff called money, but all they have is a handful of shit, Man. Someone ought'a step on all of 'em."

People at the front tables clapped listlessly. Ruthee and I looked at each other. She choked on her drink, and I had to cover my mouth to keep from howling with laughter. The reader on stage actually bowed before he stumbled to the floor. He shaded his eyes against the glare of the blue lights with his hands, so he could find his seat.

We laughed all the way to the bus stop. At work the next day, we chuckled every time our eyes met; and we promised each other that we would never, ever get on stage to read our poetry. It was an easily kept promise for both of us.

My life fell into a pleasant pattern of work and sleep and tourism. I became more in love with the hypnotic city of New York. On weekends, I sometimes met with new acquaintances, male and female, for dinner or a movie. When we could afford it, which wasn't often, we attended shows on Broadway.

I sent long, descriptive letters to my mother. I wrote to Penny Olson, happily married to the boy who had lived on the farm next to hers in Nebraska. Together they had produced five strapping, blond boys, currently between the ages of eight and one. Penny described herself and her husband as "carelessly prolific." She sounded obscenely happy.

My mother kept me up to date with news of the hospital and her life with Russell. Sometimes she threw in tidbits about my classmates who had remained in Dixon. She told me that Mark Watson, the handsome, pleasant boy who had taken me to a family picnic, which now seemed like ages ago, had married one of the Lancaster twins—she wasn't sure which one—and they also had twin daughters.

I pictured Mark taking his little girls up to the cider barrel on the hill above his grandfather's house. It should have been a happy image, but something about it made me sad. If things had been different... Oh well, I had learned not to dwell on things in the past that could not be changed.

Still, sometimes I wondered what my life might have been, had I not married Jack McCoy. I might have stayed in Dixon, perhaps married a classmate, perhaps even Mark Watson. I thought about that possibility for a moment before I laughed at my silly "what ifs?" and got on with the business of my real life.

I liked my job. I was amazed at the easy camaraderie between the office staff and editor, Dirk Warneke, who seemed more like a benevolent daycare manager than a newspaper editor. Dirk, often referred to as Quirky-Dirky by his underlings, more than filled the swivel chair behind his desk.

His jowls flowed onto his neck, in much the same manner as his belly flowed onto his thighs. A mane of thick, black hair, slicked back and caught with a rubber band, grew below his shoulders. Eyebrows as thick and dark as his hair framed bright eyes that were an incredible shade of violet-blue, Liz Taylor eyes.

For a man of his size, Dirk Warneke moved with a smooth grace that defied the pull of gravity. He could dance with the same élan and dexterity as his hundred-pound-lighter peers, which I learned at the first Christmas party he hosted. He was never without an eager dancing partner.

Within a few months, I rose from copy editor to assistant editor, which resulted in a salary increase and my name on the door of my own little cubical office. Though small, the space was mine, and it felt good.

It was the last of February, and I had just turned thirty-one. The new title didn't prevent me from finding and covering stories that appealed to me. Dirk seemed pleased to give me a by-line and feature my work when a particular story piqued his interest.

Meanwhile, the early morning concerts continued to fill my apartment with beautiful music. Arguments on the other side of me could still be heard, but at a lower volume. Occasionally I met Mrs. McLaughlin in the corridor. Always pleasant, she sometimes patted my cheek with a touch of grandmotherly concern.

On the days when the elevators didn't work, which seemed to be many, we sometimes walked down the four flights of stairs together. One morning I summoned enough courage to ask about the music that came from her apartment. I told her how pleasant it was to start my day with a serenade.

"Why, thank you, Dearie," she said. "My son plays the violin. Poor boy, it's the only pleasure he has left in life. I'm so glad you like his music." I thought about that information for a bit. The woman had to be in her late seventies, quite possibly a few years older. Calculating the age difference between my parents and me, Mrs. McLaughlin's son would have to be in his fifties. I wondered why I had never seen him. It was on the tip of tongue to ask more questions, but we had reached the lobby.

"Do avoid strangers, Dearie," she told me. "You never know what dark, troublesome things they may be concocting." I told her that I would most certainly follow her advice, but doing so was impossible on the busy street that led to the newspaper office. I saw very few familiar faces on my way to work.

✳ ✳ ✳

One glorious late spring afternoon, I arrived at Bellamy Apartments to discover three police cars double-parked on the street. A uniformed officer stopped me at the front door and demanded to know what my business was there.

"I live here," I told him. He asked my name and my apartment number, which he checked against a clipboard in his hands.

"I'm sorry, Miss; but you'll have to wait in the lobby until the scene of an accident on that floor has been investigated."

"What kind of accident," I asked. "Has someone been hurt?"

"Yes, Miss. One of the occupants fell down an elevator shaft," he replied. I felt the blood leave my face.

"Can you tell me who?"

"It was a man, but I can't tell you his name. He's being brought out now." An enormous sense of relief swept through me. There were many men and women in the building, but I had only nodding acquaintance with most of them. The one male resident I actively disliked was Mr. Kelly. I told myself that his demise wouldn't be a tragedy, then promptly felt guilty at the thought. I stood with the crowd of other residents and curiosity seekers who had gathered along the sidewalk.

"Move back! Give them room!" One of the officers yelled. Two other uniformed policemen cleared a path from the main doors to an ambulance that waited on the street. The attendants emerged from the building with a gurney that held Mr. Kelly, who lay very still. The small gathering of onlookers grew quiet.

As soon as the ambulance drove away, the policemen departed. The curiosity seekers wandered away. I was amazed how smoothly the waters of life on our street flowed back together, leaving not even a ripple in the stream.

I took the four flights of stairs up to my floor and passed the elevators with their yellow strips taped across the doors. At Mrs. McLaughlin's apartment, I stopped. Hesitantly, I knocked. It was several seconds before she answered.

"Oh, do come in, Dearie," she said. The sweet smile on her face showed no hint of distress at the accident.

"I don't mean to disturb you," I told her. "I just want to be sure you are all right."

"Of course, Sissy. Is it okay if I call you that?" I nodded. "We are fine." She turned to the shadowy figure hunched deeply into the corner of an overstuffed sofa. "Lawrence, say hello to Miss Bannister." Lawrence gave no indication that he heard his mother's voice. "He's just a bit shy, you know," Mrs. McLaughlin told me.

"Hello, Lawrence," I said. The dark-haired man stared straight ahead. I guessed his age around fifty, perhaps fifty-five. Lamplight touched only the edges of his profile, giving him a dramatic, even theatrical appearance. "I'll look forward to your music tomorrow morning." Lawrence turned his face slightly away from me, and I felt as if I had been dismissed.

"I'm afraid he won't be playing for awhile," Mrs. McLaughlin said. "His violin has been broken, and I think it is beyond repair. I do, however, think a new one will be forthcoming. Thank you for stopping by." She placed a hand beneath my elbow and ushered me to the door. I found myself standing in the corridor, amazed how she had managed to get me out of her apartment so quickly without appearing rude or inhospitable.

The next morning I woke to the sterile sound of my radio. Nothing came through the open balcony window except a brisk autumn breeze and sounds of the waking city.

A few weeks passed, and one morning the strains of violin music again gently woke me. I lay beneath the covers and listened as the muted melodies seeped through the walls. It was much too cold now to open the balcony window. As unlearned as I was about violins, I could distinguish a difference in the tone and resonance. While still wonderful, the music was less pure—not flawed, just not as rich and full toned.

Later that day I learned that Mr. Kelly had returned home from his long hospital stay. His broken bones were mending, and his internal injuries had apparently healed. I wondered if his attitude had undergone a transformation, as well; but I wouldn't have given a nickel for the chances.

That evening I decided it couldn't hurt to make a neighborly overture, so I took a deep breath and knocked on their door. I had not yet met Mrs. Kelly, so I was surprised when a very attractive woman, not much older than I, opened the door. I explained that I lived in the adjoining apartment and that I hoped Mr. Kelly was recovering.

"He'll be okay," she said with a shrug. "God must take care of drunks and fools, for he's both. He says he wasn't drinking that day, but he doesn't remember how he came to fall down the shaft. He must have been drunk, or he wouldn't have fallen. Crazy fool." I told her I hoped her husband made a full recovery, and then I made a more than hasty retreat to the serenity of my own little space.

The days turned colder, and preparations for the holidays blazed from every department store window. On the Monday before Thanksgiving, my mother called to ask if I were coming home for the holiday. Apparently, Beth and her husband could not come; and Bill would be having dinner with his wife's family. I hesitated.

"I'm really swamped with work, Mom," I told her. A deafening silence nearly froze the telephone lines. *Uh oh*, I thought. It had been a long time since I'd been the recipient of my mother's icy quiet, but I still recognized its potency. "Why don't you and Russell come to New York and spend the holiday with me?" I asked. As soon as the words were out of my mouth, I wished them back. *Where would they stay?* My first frantic thought filled me with panic.

"Oh, I don't know, Sissy," my mother said. "It's a long drive, and the weather could turn bad." I grinned ruefully. The distance was just as long for me, and the red Corvette, which I drove occasionally, was not very ice and snow hardy. "Let me talk to Russ, and I'll get back to you. Okay?" Was there a hint of excitement in her voice when she hung up the phone? She had never been to New York, and it occurred to me that perhaps she had been waiting for an invitation. I felt chastised.

My eyes darted around the room. I bit my lip in concentration. With some rearranging, accommodations would be possible. I could sleep on the sofa, and my mother and her husband could have the bedroom. The folding carved screen I had found in a second-hand furniture store could be placed discreetly along the couch. It would provide a modicum of privacy for me. I sighed.

It turned out that Russell would be delighted to come to New York, which meant I had two days to find a turkey and all the stuff that went with one. I was certain my mom would insist upon cooking, and I was equally certain I would let her.

They arrived on Tuesday afternoon. The weather could not have been more cooperative. New Yorkers carried their jackets and sweaters, instead of wearing them. It was a perfect, extra-late Indian summer day, with near balmy temperatures.

I couldn't believe how happy I was to see my mother. I even welcomed my stepfather's reticent hug, and I hugged him back. I blinked back tears as I embraced my mom. It was the first time she had been in any residence of mine since I married Jack

They ooh-ed and ah-ed appropriately when I showed them around the apartment. Russell pointed out areas that could be enhanced with shelves. I could see the wheels turn in Mom's head while she examined the upholstered pieces. I would bet that new throw pillows and other decorative touches would be in place before she went back to Dixon. I didn't mind.

My mother approved of the turkey, but she shook her head over the absence of needed ingredients in my pantry. She made a list, and the three of us walked to a grocery store not far from my building. Twilight had begun to settle on the city on our way back, and a November chill returned to claim its territory.

We chatted and laughed and bumped into each other in the elevator, especially when we tried to exit at the same time. I jostled the bags in my arms and finally placed them on the floor while I fumbled through my purse for my keys.

"How merry you sound." Mrs. McLaughlin smiled at us from the open door of her apartment. I pointed to my guests.

"Mrs. McLaughlin, this is my mother and her husband." I made introductions all around and was pleased that the three seemed happy to meet each other.

"Well, this is just wonderful. Family should be together for holidays," said my neighbor. I thought I detected a hint of wistfulness in her voice.

"Would you and your son like to come to Thanksgiving dinner? There will be more than enough food," I told her.

"Well, well, now, I just don't know," Mrs. McLaughlin replied. She blinked rapidly. "That would be so lovely. Let me see how Lawrence feels about it."

"Wonderful," I said. I opened my door. "Hope to see you Thursday!"

Mom and I chatted and laughed while we tried to find storage for the additional groceries in my less than ample cabinet space. I sat at the kitchen table with her while she wrote down her menu. I knew what the dishes would be before she listed them. Russell, seemingly content to watch television on my small screen, asked only for one thing: whipped cream to go with the pumpkin pie. In that, he was like my dad.

They insisted I go to work the next day. My mother and Russell planned to see as much of the city as possible. Before I left, I went through a litany of warnings, until Mom laughed and told me not to worry and to go to work. So I did.

Thanksgiving morning, I woke to the sounds of my mother happily at reign in front of the kitchen stove. The aroma of strong coffee roused my nose before full consciousness opened my eyes. I smiled and pretended, just for a moment, that I was in my bedroom back in Dixon, that my dad would shake the furnace stoker, and I could run downstairs to find him and my mother having coffee at the kitchen table.

"Good morning, Jackie." The sound of Russell's loud kiss on Mom's cheek burst my fantasy bubble. I threw my robe over sensible pajamas, a concession to my mother's presence, and folded up the bedding. I pushed the screen back to its original place and greeted my guests.

"What smells so good?" I asked. The three of us danced around each other in the small space of the kitchen while Russell and I filled our coffee cups.

"Excuse me."

"Oops, I'm sorry!"

"Sorry!"

"I put muffins in the oven to bake while I get the turkey ready," Mom said. She had cut and chopped celery and onions the previous evening, and the bosom-y turkey already rested in the roaster, purchased at the grocery just for this occasion. In spite of such close quarters, I enjoyed breakfast and the company of my guests.

Mid-morning I answered the doorbell to find Mrs. McLaughlin. "If the invitation still stands, we would be happy to take Thanksgiving dinner with you," she said.

"Of course!" I turned to my mother. "What time is dinner, Mom?"

"Two o'clock," she stated.

"We'll look forward to having you," I told my neighbor. Graciously, Mrs. McLaughlin nodded her head.

"I'll bring something," she said. I drew in my breath to tell her it wasn't necessary, but she seemed excited at the thought.

"See you then," I told her.

Promptly at two o'clock, I opened the discreet knock at the door. It was impossible not to stare. Mrs. McLaughlin, dressed in a somewhat dated two-pieced dress of gray silk, looked as elegant as royalty.

Soft pearls lay beneath the collar, and matching earrings glowed at her ears. Her usual bun hairstyle had become an upswept mass of silvery curls. My family and I were painfully underdressed. She extended a covered crystal bowl filled with dried fruit and nuts.

Lawrence stood beside his mother. Hands at his sides, military-straight, he gazed above our heads. I had not realized he was so tall, for I had only seen him seated. He stood a couple inches taller than Russell. Freshly shaved, dressed in a black suit, white shirt and gray tie, he looked like a statesman.

Heads would have turned twice to look at him. His pale blue eyes glistened beneath thick brows, and the few silvery streaks at his temples contrasted beautifully against his dark hair. Worn longer than most men his age, his hair looked thick and heavy. It lay against his collar and curled at the ends.

Dinner progressed with pleasant conversation, except for the silence of Lawrence. He ate, with apparent relish, what his mother served to him; but he spoke not one word. It seemed to me an occasional phrase or sentence caught his attention, and his eyes focused momentarily on the speaker.

"Ahhh, pumpkin pie," my stepfather practically purred at the sight of the plate my mother placed before him. "Whipped cream?" he asked, hopefully. My mother smiled as she placed a perfect dollop of the forbidden substance on the pie.

"Don't get used to it," she warned. Rich coffee accompanied the pie, and conversation lagged while we enjoyed the spicy, traditional treat.

"Mother, this pie is as good as you used to make."

Four forks stopped in mid-air. Lawrence could speak. He continued to eat as if he had not rendered his mother and the rest of us speechless. My mother recovered first.

"I'm glad you like the pie, Lawrence. Do you want another piece?" Our guest continued to eat as if no one had spoken. Mrs. McLaughlin patted his shoulder.

Later, after our guests left and we cleaned up the kitchen, I told my mother and Russell all I knew about the McLaughlins, which wasn't much. Intrigued by the son, his music and his mother's protective hovering, my writer/reporter curiosity had kicked into gear. I would unravel the mystery of my unconventional neighbors.

By Sunday, the weather had become cold and cloudy, typically late November in New York. Mom and Russell departed with promises and admonitions—promises to return and admonitions to me about traffic, strangers and locked doors. With the last hug and a final wave, I retreated to my quiet haven, collapsed on the sofa and heaved a huge sigh.

I spent the rest of the day reclaiming my territory before I took a long, hot bubble bath. By nine o'clock, I had put on pajamas, eaten a sandwich made from turkey scraps, brushed my teeth and crawled into bed. The outside noises no longer bothered me, and I soon went to sleep with thoughts of the McLaughlins trailing into my slumber.

The five Ws of good reporting gave me the questions. I needed to find the answers to: WHO, WHAT, WHERE, WHEN and WHY. I already knew the who: Lawrence McLaughlin. I wanted to know what a man with his talent was doing in a nondescript apartment, where he had been, when he had been there and many, many whys. I began my search from the offices at Streetside.

"Does the name 'Lawrence McLaughlin' mean anything to you?" I asked Samantha Irons, society editor, as well as head of advertising. Samantha frowned, drawing her dark brows together in concentration. I watched the thought processes on her lined face. Her blue eyes narrowed into a quizzical squint, and she bit the inside of her lower right lip before she spoke.

Short and thin, Samantha, dubbed "Sam" at the office, could have been anywhere between forty and sixty. While her face was sun tanned and full of lines, she had the athletic build of a younger woman. She wore little makeup, and her salt and pepper hair fell around her face in a boyish, no-nonsense cut. It suited her, without taking away from her femininity.

"You know, that name sounds familiar. Lawrence McLaughlin.... I know I've seen or heard something...." Her words trailed away. She opened the middle drawer of a tall filing cabinet, one of several in her cubical. There was barely room enough for her, tiny as she was, to walk around her desk. She mumbled bits of names and phrases as she fingered through the dozens of files. "Here we go." She pulled a folder and slammed the drawer closed. She glanced at me. "Sit down." I looked around for a chair, but my only option was to unfold a metal one from the two that leaned against one of the file cabinets.

"What do you have?" I asked.

"It's old," Sam told me. "I knew the name was familiar; but it's been so long since I'd heard it, I wasn't sure. Here's a picture." I reached for the slick black and white publicity photo she extended across the desk. Staring up at me was the image of a striking, handsome man, a younger, debonair, Lawrence McLaughlin.

With one hand, Lawrence held a violin loosely against his left shoulder, not tucked beneath his chin, as I would have expected. The bow dangled from his right hand, and he appeared to have begun to raise it. A smile barely touched his full mouth. One slightly raised eyebrow gave his expression a hint of challenge, as if to ask, "Are you ready to hear the music?"

"What happened to him?" I asked Sam.

"I'm not sure," she replied. "I think there was an accident or something...in Europe or somewhere out of the States. Gosh, it's been at least twenty years ago, maybe longer."

"Was he famous?"

"Oh, yeah. 'Bout as famous as a violinist can get. Too bad...."

"Do you mind if I keep this?" I waved the picture. Sam shrugged.

"Keep it. What's the story here? Why are you asking about him?"

"He lives in my building," I told her.

"No! You've seen him?"

I stood up and headed out the door. "He had Thanksgiving dinner with my folks and me. Thanks, Sam." When I walked away, she was staring after me, mouth slightly ajar.

Streetside had not been in business long enough to have carried a story about Lawrence McLaughlin. Their archives went back a mere eleven years, so I used the nearest library to research the story. Without a specific date, I had to look at a lot of newspaper film in the library's basement. Computers were not yet standard equipment in any public facility.

On my third Saturday at the library, I found the first article about my musical neighbor. It was simply a notice that in the Austrian Alps, on October tenth, 1948, renowned American violinist, Lawrence McLaughlin, had been seriously injured in an automobile accident. An edition dated two days later carried a photo and a more detailed account of the traffic collision that had seriously injured the musician and killed his wife, Theresa McLauglin, who was also his accompanist.

The article gave a brief history, describing Lawrence as a child prodigy who had performed before heads of state all over Europe before the war. He and his wife had just successfully completed their first European tour following that war and were enjoying a brief vacation in the Alps before their return to the United States. That's when the accident occurred.

Although Lawrence had been a well-known violinist, there were only a couple of follow-up articles about him after he returned to New York. The presidential campaigns of Harry S. Truman and Thomas Dewey, followed by the upset election of Mr. Truman, dominated the news that autumn. I was in the third grade that year, and I remembered the election and bits of conversation between teachers in the halls. Some had been jubilant, but most had been surprised.

I entered a few pertinent notes to my joined-at-the-hip notebook. My theory, passed on from a journalism instructor, was that one never knew what information might be useful some day.

My next course of action would be to attempt an interview with Mrs. McLaughlin. It was a toss-up what her reaction would be: either an open dialogue about her son or a swift and final edict to mind my own business.

A few days passed before my neighbor and I met in the corridor, both of us headed for the elevator. I thought she looked tired, even weary.

"Are you feeling all right, Mrs. McLaughlin?" I asked. She smiled sweetly and rubbed her forehead.

"I just have a headache," she replied. "Lawrence had a restless night; and I don't sleep much when he's, well, indisposed, so to speak." We stepped into the elevator. We both held onto the rail as the device shuddered and groaned its way downward until it jolted to a stop on the ground floor.

Someone had draped garlands of evergreens around the front double doors, and a small artificial Christmas tree blinked near the wall of mailboxes. I had been so occupied with assignments and moonlighting at the library, I had scarcely noticed that another Christmas season was in full array.

Three or four snowfalls had kept the streets alternately white and dingy gray, and decorations filled the storefronts; but it had all somehow gone over my head. Less than two weeks remained before the commercial holiday windfall for the department stores. I had not even begun to think of shopping.

"Will you be spending the holiday with your delightful mother and step-father?" she asked. Although I had not yet thought about it, I nodded.

"Yes, I think so. My sister and brother are planning to come home this year. I haven't seen them since last Christmas." I was surprised by the sudden wave of longing to see my siblings. It was almost a physical pain.

"That will be lovely for all of you, I'm sure." The wistfulness in the woman's voice added a touch of guilt to my longing.

"Do you have other family?" I asked. "Other children, perhaps?" She shook her head.

"No, I fear not. My husband died during the war, in one of those nasty bombings in England, don't you know." She looked thoughtful. "It was actually one of the first. He was there in regards to a tour for...." She stopped. "I'm so sorry, Sissy. Here I am prattling on, and you must be in a hurry. I have errands to run, too. You have a wonderful day."

I held open the door for her, and she scurried out and along the busy, snowy sidewalk. Speculatively, I watched her small, busy body, her silver hair covered with a black shawl against the cold. I was more intrigued than ever, but my anticipated interview with her would probably have to wait until after Christmas. Quirky Dirky had dumped more work onto my already overloaded desk; and completion of it would take all my time and concentration if I intended to make that trip home to Dixon.

The evening before I left, I made a batch of peanut butter cookies and a pan of brownies. I placed several on a plate, covered them with foil and a stick-on bow and knocked on the McLaughlins' door. I waited several moments before I knocked again.

"Hello? Mrs. McLaughlin, it's Sissy. I have some warm cookies for you." After a few seconds, I turned to leave, turned back when the door opened. "Hi, I..." Lawrence stood beside the open door, looking straight at me. I didn't know what to say. "Uh, uh, hello, Lawrence." I held out the plate. "Merry Christmas. I, uh, hope you like peanut butter cookies and chocolate brownies. Well, uh, Merry Christmas." *Dolt, you already said that!* I thought.

Without taking his eyes from mine, Lawrence took the plate. He inclined his head in a polite nod. "Thank you very much," he said and carefully closed the door. I stood there with my hands at my sides, my heart beating so hard I could hear it. I didn't know where the man's mother was, but I wished she could have heard him. I grinned at the thought that perhaps desserts were the trigger to the speech center in his brain.

Darkness had settled on Dixon by the time I arrived at my mother's house on Christmas Eve. My stepfather had put up the usual decorations. Glowing holiday lights outlined the porch roof, railing and all the windows along the front of the house, as well as the evergreens and shrubbery.

I got out of the Corvette and glanced upward at the sky above the mountains, where stars twinkled against a vast, cloudless expanse of indigo. I listened to the quiet of a hill town, so different from the constant noise of a city.

"You're here!" The front door burst open, and Beth ran to me, arms extended in welcome.

"You're pregnant!" I held my little sister at arms length before I enveloped her in a bear hug. "Oh, I'm sorry! Is it okay to hug you?"

My question was late, considering that I had already squashed her burgeoning belly against my flat one. Beth laughed.

"You can't hurt me, Sissy. I'm healthy as a cow in clover!"

"Nearly as round as one, too," her husband, Eric Malone, quipped. He followed closely on Beth's heels. "How are you, Sissy? It's good to see you." We hugged warmly before he placed a protective arm around Beth's shoulders. Handsome to a disgusting degree, Eric's brown eyes and sun-touched brown hair went well with his California tanned skin.

Beth and I carried in a few packages while Eric took the bulk of them, along with my bulging overnight bag. I exchanged hugs with my mother and Russell, less than a month after our goodbyes at Thanksgiving. Familiar aromas of Christmases past filled the house, as they had every Christmas I could remember from the time I was seven.

As I shrugged out of my coat, I took a quick glance into the living room. A new sofa and glass-topped coffee table had replaced the old ones since my visit last Christmas. I made a cursory examination of the dining room, where everything seemed much the same. *Stop it. Mom has every right to change anything she desires. It's her house, for Pete's sake!* The adult that occasionally reigned inside my head condemned my unbidden childish rebellion against changes in the house. I told myself it was normal to still think of the house as belonging to my dad, but another voice thought not.

I missed Dad. Nine years had softened the sharp edge of painful loss; but I would have given anything to smell his Aqua Velva after shave, as well as the aged scent of his pipe. For me, the house would always be filled with the absence of my dad.

After a light supper, my sister and I watched Russell and Eric assemble and set up toys for our brother's little boys, Willie, David and John, ages five, three and eighteen months. I looked forward to another Christmas with children in the house. I watched Beth's happy face as she told me about her pregnancy, and I understood the cliché about the radiance of motherhood. In her fifth month, she assured me that there were no problems and she felt wonderful.

Over dessert on Christmas afternoon, Bill, Beth and I played "remember when." Bill's wife, Lainie, and Eric were gracious enough not to object when we talked about events that occurred before they were part of the family. Together we laughed about Bill's Christmas sledding accident that landed him in the hospital and put him at the mercy of the fanatical preacher, Dewey Snodgrass.

"I don't know who or what scared me the most," Bill said, "Dad's anger or the preacher's praying. I was only twelve; but by the time the nurse came in and ran him off, I just knew the floor was going to open up and drop me into the hell he kept yelling about." I smiled at Bill's soft West Virginia drawl. I had been away long enough to be aware once again of the difference in geographical nuances of speech. New York's broad dialects seemed far away from the cozy West Virginia dining room.

We touched briefly on the year we thought Beth had been kidnapped, but we moved quickly to more pleasant memories of times and people we all knew. Although Beth had fewer memories of Redbud Grove, we spent some time reminiscing about the little yellow house and good times we had shared there as a family. Talk dwindled, heads nodded and Beth opted to take a nap. The children already slept; so while the other adults sought comfortable spots to snooze, I put on a jacket and went out the front door.

I missed Sophie. The little Schnauzer had been gone for a few years, leaving an empty spot my mother had not yet attempted to fill with another pet. I took a deep breath of mountain air, less polluted now than when we first came to Dixon. Attempts had been made to restrict at least some of the coal dust.

Sunny skies softened the chill that moved through the streets on a capricious breeze. Snow had skipped across the mountains, leaving white streaks on the tops, but sparing the valley. I walked down the switchbacks and turns to Main Street, seeing only a few people along the way. Decorations blinked in the store windows, but none of them were open.

On a whim, instead of turning back, I walked the familiar streets to Dooby's in the late afternoon light. I hadn't expected it to be open, but it was. I was surprised at the number of cars parked along the sides. The jukebox played, not artists from the fifties, with the exception of Elvis, but Fleetwood Mac and The Mamas and the Papas.

I sat down at the counter and ordered a cup of coffee. Teenagers still gathered around the tables, as when I was younger. Menus, faces and the music had changed; but the atmosphere was the same: youthful exuberance and the belief that it would never age.

"Sissy? Sissy Bannister?" The soft, deep voice was one I had once known; but it wasn't until I looked into the speaker's blue eyes that I recognized Mark Watson. "It's really you!" Memories of a family picnic, sipping cider from a rusty cup and moonlight music echoed in Mark's warm greeting. I slipped from the stool, and we exchanged a hug.

"It's wonderful to see you," I said.

"Daddy?"

I looked down, and on each side of Mark stood a little girl, images of each other. They both had their father's eyes, but soft blond curls framed their beautiful faces.

"Sissy, these are my daughters, Alyssa and Clarice. Girls, this is an old friend of mine, Sissy Bannister." Mark knelt between the children. " Say 'Hello' to her." Shyly the girls looked up. No more than four or five years old, they were absolutely breathtaking. I extended my hand.

"I'm so glad to meet you," I said. They each shyly offered little hands, and I was captivated. "Oh, Mark, they are lovely." He laughed.

"They are, aren't they? They just woke up from naps and wanted ice cream. We had everything else in the house, except…" He paused.

"Ice cream!" The girls spoke as one. I laughed. Mark picked up the girls and placed them on stools beside mine. He gave his order for ice cream, and we chatted while he waited. Within minutes the waitress brought out the carton of hand dipped ice cream. I paid the waitress for my coffee and stood. It looked dark through the windows, and I wasn't looking forward to the long walk back up the hill.

"It was great seeing you again, Mark. I'd better get back before my family sends out a search party. Give my best to…I'm sorry. I don't know which Lancaster twin you married." He laughed.

"I married Terri in nineteen sixty-five. Her sister, Twila, married a guy she met in college; and they live in Ohio."

"Tell Terri I think her daughters are beautiful. 'Bye."

" 'Bye, Sissy. Take care." Mark waved to me, and I walked out the door. I had gone no more than half a block in the deepening twilight when a car pulled along beside me. "Did you walk all the way from your house? Why didn't you say so? Hop in and we'll take you home!"

"Your ice cream will melt," I told him.

"No, it won't. I'll have you home in a few minutes." It was much colder and later than I anticipated, so without further hesitation I got into Mark's car. "Did you forget how cold it gets here in the winter when the sun goes down?"

"I guess I did." I shivered, grateful for the warmth from the heater and the company, as well. "I didn't intend to go so far, but I enjoyed walking along the old paths again."

"Do you walk much in the city?" he asked.

"Most of the time. Occasionally I take the car out, but not often. It's just not practical, and local transit is more convenient in bad weather."

"So you have become a bona fide big city girl, huh? Do you enjoy it?" Mark teased.

"I do," I replied. "I love my job, and I have friends where I work."

"Daddy, are we almost home?"

"Daddy, I want some ice cream." The voices from the back seat were as identical as the faces.

"It won't be long," Mark assured his daughters. He turned onto Symington and pulled up the driveway. "Looks like your folks welcomed you home with lots of lights," he said.

"My step-father hangs them, but I don't think it was done in my honor," I told him. "Thanks so much, Mark." I shivered. "It's *cold* out here!" I waved and hurried into the house where I had to explain my long absence.

"Didn't you date him?" Lainie asked. "Seems I remember you and Mark went out about the time Bill and I connected." Her little pixie face beneath her red hair was all innocence.

"Not really," I replied. "After Jack and I broke up, I went out with Mark a few times right after high school. He was going away to college. He was a nice boy, and we were good friends."

"Too bad you went back to Jack," Lainie stated. There was an uncomfortable pause. I couldn't say aloud that I agreed with her, although I had felt the same way many times. It was my own private regret and not up for discussion, not even with family. Much as I loved my sister-in-law, I wanted to shake her.

"Did your walk give you room for more pie?" Bill asked.

"Sure," I replied. "Why not? It's Christmas." There was a nearly audible sigh of relief that an uncomfortable moment had passed. The pecan pie was delicious and worth the extra calories. "Mom, I learned something about my neighbors, the McLaughlins. Lawrence was a violinist, known around the world. He hasn't played publicly for a long time, but some twenty-two or three years or so ago he was quite famous. Do you remember anything about him?" My mother shook her head.

"I do," Russell said. Surprised, I looked at him. "Some of his concerts were broadcast over the radio, and my mother loved to hear him play. That was, oh, probably in the late nineteen thirties."

"Do you remember hearing about the accident that killed his wife and injured him?"

"Seems like I do, but it was a long time ago."

I nodded. "Nineteen forty-eight," I told him. "I'm going to look further into his history. I think there may be a story there."

"They might not want you to do that," my mother said. "They seem like nice people. You wouldn't want to hurt them."

"I have no intention of hurting them." Sometimes words and intentions can come back to haunt you. The next day, I hugged all my relatives again before I threw my bag into my car and pointed it toward New York.

New Year's Eve saw the end of the relatively mild autumn. The first days of nineteen seventy-two brought snow that lingered well into the third week of January. I continued to walk to and from work, shopping occasionally for items I needed; but I stayed home most evenings. The morning concerts from the McLaughlins' apartment were muted through the walls and closed windows; and there was a difference in

Lawrence's music, a melancholy that I had not heard before. I thought perhaps the gray days of winter affected him.

I found and read everything possible about Lawrence McLaughlin, from his parents, his birth, his childhood and subsequent rise as one of the foremost masters of classical music in his time. I found a faded newspaper announcement of his engagement to the lovely Theresa Forth, along with a formal photograph of the bride-to-be. Prominent papers carried their wedding picture in the social pages.

Following the fatal accident, a couple of the papers suggested, without outright reporting it, that Lawrence McLaughlin could have been intoxicated at the time of the tragedy. Aside from those articles in the two publications, there was no further mention of the possibility that Lawrence contributed to the death of his wife. It seemed to have been ruled a tragic accident.

It took a long time to put my notes in order. By the time I had completed the task, I realized I had the makings of a good story. By mid-February, a full first draft was complete; and I felt good about my work. I edited the piece in my apartment after my evening meal, which was never formal enough to call dinner or normal enough to call supper. Totally immersed in the story, I usually ate a sandwich of some sort at the typewriter.

Spring arrived on the same day I took the Lawrence McLaughlin article to Dirk Warneke. I don't know what I expected from him. Occasionally he ran a short human interest story or a biographical piece on a well-known New Yorker. Sometimes an Associated Press article caught his eye, and he ran that; but most of the content centered on social and current events, a "news about town" periodical that targeted the up-and-coming twenty-five to forty age groups.

"What is it?" my boss asked when I placed the manuscript on his desk.

"An article I've been working on for awhile. If you have time, I'd like to get your opinion."

"Free lancing on me, are you?" Dirk raised his Liz-blue eyes to my face, a mock scowl on his. "Been writing on my time?"

I shook my head. "Of course not! I wrote this totally on my own."

"Okay, I'll look at it. Everyone thinks he's a Putlizer candidate," he grumbled. He raised one eyebrow and cocked his head to one side. "Or *she*," he amended. He was still mumbling when I left his office; but when I looked back, he had already picked up my story.

After supper that evening, I knocked on my neighbor's door. It had been some time since I'd seen her, either in the corridor, the elevator or the lobby. Lawrence played to invisible audiences virtually daily, so I assumed he and his mother were well. There was no answer. I knocked again.

"Mrs. McLaughlin? It's Sissy. Are you okay?" I placed my ear against the door, and I nearly fell when it opened. "Oh, Lawrence," I laughed, embarrassed and a little unnerved at his sudden appearance. He took my hand and drew me inside. Now that *really* made me nervous! "Lawrence, where is your mother?" I asked. He didn't reply; he just pulled me along behind him until I nearly tripped on a rug.

"Mother." Lawrence pointed toward the open door of another room. He dropped my hand and went into the bedroom. Carefully, I followed.

"Oh, Mrs. McLaughlin!" I cried. I hurried to the bedside of the elderly woman. Her eyes were closed, and the sound of each struggling breath indicated how ill she was. I picked up the phone beside her bed and called emergency services as quickly as I could before I turned back to her. "Mrs. McLaughlin, can you hear me?" There was no response.

"Lawrence, how long has she been sick?" Lawrence stared silently at his mother. "Lawrence, bring me a wet cloth from the bathroom. Now, Lawrence!" I yelled at him. Slowly he turned his eyes toward me, blinked and left the room. I propped pillows behind the poor woman's head and brushed her uncombed hair from her face. A cold, dripping cloth appeared over my shoulder. Well, I hadn't specified that the water should be wrung from it; so what did I expect?

I squeezed excess water into a nearby waste can and gently washed Mrs. McLaughlin's face. I slipped my arms beneath her shoulders and sat down, cradling her against my side. Her skin was dry and very hot. Lawrence stood quietly beside the bed. He didn't move when the paramedics banged on the door. He seemed transfixed.

"Come in!" I called. The two attendants began to work with the gentle lady. The slim, sandy-haired man immediately strapped an oxygen mask onto her still, pale face. His companion, a younger, heavier man with Oriental features, began to talk to the ER staff via a static-y mouthpiece. I touched Lawrence's arm, and he allowed me to guide him away from the bed.

"How long has she been like this?" one of the men asked.

"I don't know. I haven't seen her for a few days, which is unusual; so I dropped by to check on her. What's wrong with her?"

"It sounds like pneumonia to me. We have her on oxygen to help her breathe." He withdrew a thermometer from beneath her arm. "Her temp is a hundred-four. We'll have to take her to the nearest hospital. Are you a relative?" I shook my head.

"No, I'm her neighbor." I nodded toward Lawrence. "He is her son, but he doesn't communicate well."

"We'll take her to New York General, but we'll need someone to fill out forms and sign for treatment as soon as possible." The man looked from me to Lawrence, who remained motionless.

"I'll take care of it," I said. The man nodded, and as effortlessly as if she were a doll, the two of them lifted the little woman onto a stretcher and wheeled her from the room. I closed the door and turned to Lawrence. Without acknowledging me, he opened a case and withdrew his violin. He went to the window, tucked the instrument under his chin and began to play.

A melody, unknown to me, flowed from the strings like rivers of crystal tears. Heartbreak has a melody without words, and Lawrence McLaughlin found it on his violin. I felt my own tears course down my cheeks while he played. It seemed that the whole apartment was filled with the sadness of the world, with bereavement felt at some point by every person who ever lived, every love lost, every broken heart. The last strain faded away to silence.

As mute as Lawrence, I stood watching him. I didn't know what to do or say, and I was totally unprepared for the violence that followed the music. With both hands, Lawrence grasped the neck of the violin and swung it against the window. The fragile wood shattered with the first blow, but he continued to beat what was left of it until there were only splinters.

"Lawrence, don't!" It was too late, of course; but I didn't know what else to say. And then the man looked at me.

"They all die," he said, as matter-of-factly as if he'd remarked on the weather. He shrugged. He sat down on the sofa as if he were weary to the core. He rested his head against the back cushion and closed his eyes.

"Lawrence, I should go to the hospital to be with your mother. Are you going to be all right while I do that?" After a moment, he answered, without opening his eyes.

"Of course," he said.

This is too weird, I thought. *Lawrence and I are having a conversation. His mother may be dying and we're having a crazy conversation!*

"I'll be back as soon as I can," I told him.

I took a taxi to the hospital and discovered that Mrs. McLaughlin had been admitted. She did, indeed, have pneumonia and would have to remain there for a few days. Her temperature had dropped a couple degrees. The doctor felt that the antibiotics had begun to take affect and the prognosis was good. "She must be one tough lady," he told me.

By the time I returned to my apartment building, it was well after midnight. There was no answer when I knocked at Lawrence's door. I listened, but could hear nothing. I was too tired to pursue him, so I unlocked my own door. Within twenty minutes, I was undressed and in bed; and in less time than that, I was asleep.

The next morning I called my boss and explained my concern for my neighbors. In a pseudo gruff voice, he told me to take as much time as I needed, but not to overdo it. I spent some time gathering Mrs. McLaughlin's personal effects: her handbag, a frilly bed jacket and robe from her closet, and toiletries.

Lawrence ignored me. A plate and a cereal bowl were in the sink, so I knew he had eaten. I explained to him what I had learned about his mother. He seemed to listen, but he didn't speak.

At the hospital I found the spunky lady awake and upset. "Really, Sissy, there is no need for such a fuss. I feel much better, and I believe I should go home. Lawrence needs me, you know."

"Lawrence is fine," I told her. I omitted the part about the shattered violin and my tiny conversation with him. "He has eaten, and I'll look in on him until you come home." That seemed to appease her somewhat, so I undertook the task of combing out her long, white hair. I combed it up and tried to use the long pins as she did, but there was no guarantee how long it would stay. She looked much better, and I felt relieved that she breathed on her own.

The next three days I fell into the routine of looking in on Lawrence before I went to the hospital, followed by three or four hours at Streetside. Dirk told me he would run my story about Lawrence, and it would appear in the following Sunday issue. I was gratified that he liked the article. I decided to save the news as a surprise for Mrs. McLaughlin, for she was being discharged on Saturday. It seemed as if life in the Bellamy Building would return to normal.

"Sissy, what have you done?!" Dismay bordering on hysteria was not the reaction I expected when I presented the newspaper to Mrs. McLaughlin. "Oh, dear, dear me! What have you done? How will I ever be able to protect him?" She stared at the old photograph of her son, the last professional copy I could find to head the story. I thought it looked good.

I dropped to my knees beside her chair and tried to calm her. It wouldn't do for her to have a relapse. "I don't understand," I said. The distraught woman's shoulders slumped.

"I know you don't," she said. She steadied her hands and began to read quickly down the page. "Oh thank the dear Lord," she whispered. "You didn't print our address."

"Of course not. That would be an invasion of your privacy, and that wasn't my intention. I think many in the music world still remember Lawrence and his wonderful talent. I'm sure they would like to know that he still lives and plays beautifully." I thought of the broken instrument. "Well, before he broke his new violin, that is." Briefly I relayed to her Lawrence's reaction after the paramedics had taken her from the apartment.

She glanced at her son. Lawrence stared out the window. He had not moved from the chair or indicated he was aware of my presence since I had entered the room.

"He can get…excited, sometimes," the woman told me. "Sissy, I must ask you not to speak of us to anyone. We have lived here for six years now, and I was hoping that we could remain unnoticed." She sadly shook her head.

"Mrs. McLaughlin, why are you afraid? I'm sure no one would hurt you or Lawrence. If anything, people would be thrilled to know…"

"Sissy, no one can know where we are!"

"Okay, okay, I promise not to tell a soul; but you need to stay calm. You've been very sick. Let me make you something to drink. Coffee? Hot tea? What would you like?"

"Nothing, nothing." She looked into my eyes, as if she were searching for something. "Sissy, can I trust you with a great secret? Before you answer, you must know that it's a burdensome secret." I placed my hands over hers, clasped on her lap.

"I promise to keep whatever you tell me."

"Even if it would be a great story for you?"

"Even then," I told her. I didn't know what I was saying.

"Lawrence. Lawrence, it's time for you to take a nap, Dear Boy." At his name, Lawrence dutifully rose, went into his room and closed the door. "Now, Sissy, if you don't mind, I really would like a cup of tea." As responsive to her suggestion as Lawrence had been, I put water on the stove for tea.

Slowly, Mrs. McLaughlin rose and held onto furniture as she made her way to a bookshelf stuffed with books and periodicals. She seemed weak, even frail; but without hesitation, she took down a folder that had been wedged between heavy volumes. I watched carefully, ready to assist her should she stumble or begin to fall.

"Thank you so much," she sighed when I brought her a mug filled with tea, laced with milk and a spoonful of sugar. She didn't complain at the taste, so I sat on the floor at her feet and waited for her to speak.

Her hands shook when she unfolded the faded clippings she withdrew from the folder. With just a glance, I knew the papers were not written in English.

"These articles contain reports of the accident that injured Lawrence and killed his wife so long ago," she began. "Remember your promise, Sissy, to keep to yourself what I am about to share with you." I nodded.

33

"Lawrence has always been a sensitive boy, don't you know. He was never able to bear disappointments, and he often reacted to obstacles in ways that were, well, some might say irrational.

"Theresa was a beautiful girl, but she didn't understand my Lawrence, not at all, you see. He was devoted to her, not like to his music, of course; but he did love her. After awhile, she apparently tired of sharing him with the world; and she sought... comfort... elsewhere." Mrs. McLaughlin's lips tightened with disgust, and she shook her head. The sweet granny image slipped a bit.

"My Dear, do you read German? No? Then I'll just tell you what this account says about the accident. Someone on the tour told the authorities that Theresa was going to divorce my son and that Lawrence had insisted they take a trip to Austria to discuss reconciliation. They said Theresa was afraid of Lawrence, afraid of his temper, said that he was sometimes violent, which, of course, was untrue. He was just... disappointed." She sipped her tea before she continued.

"Lawrence was in a hospital for many weeks, and the officials were relentless. Rumors spread that my son had tried to kill himself and his wife by running their vehicle down a steep ravine. Sheer nonsense. He would never have tried to destroy his talent." I frowned. "Nor himself or Theresa, of course," she quickly added.

"Why did the police force think so?" I asked.

"Some woman," she waved her hand in the air, "said Theresa had given a note to her, stating that Lawrence had threatened to harm her. A fabrication, don't you know? And then there was all that disruption, with the war beginning and all; so I quietly brought Lawrence home. We have lived in many places, you see. We have adequate funds." From nowhere, a question popped into my head.

"Mrs. McLaughlin, how was Lawrence's other violin broken?"

"Oh, that terrible Kelly person knocked on the door one morning while Lawrence was playing. When I opened the door, he pushed past me, grabbed the violin and smashed it, right in front of my poor son. The violin was priceless, and that—that *Philistine* smashed it to bits! He is not a good man, not at all." Another thought, a frightening one, would not be stilled.

"Did Lawrence push Mr. Kelly down the elevator shaft?" I asked.

"Oh, now, My Dear! You really shouldn't jump to conclusions. Lawrence was…disappointed, of course, but he could never…" She blinked rapidly and her words trailed away to nothing. I patted her hands. There was no doubt in my mind that Lawrence could and had done so. "You really should go now, Sissy." I stood to my feet and took the mug to the sink. A slight movement caught my eye, and I turned just in time to see Lawrence's door silently close. I felt a chill.

"You get some rest, and I'll check in on you later this evening," I told Mrs. McLaughlin.

"Thank you so much, Sissy." I gave her a brief hug and let myself out the door.

I wrestled with my quandary for the rest of the day and into the night. I had made a promise that I would keep secret anything the woman told me. At eight o'clock I knocked on her door. I waited and knocked several times, but there was no answer. I told myself they were sleeping and did not hear me.

The next morning, I tried again. Still no answer. Really worried, I went down to the super's office and asked him to check on the McLaughlins. "They moved out," the man told me. "The old lady called me last night and said that someone would come for their things in a few days." I was stunned.

"Did she say where they were going?"

"No. She left the remainder of their lease money on the kitchen table, and they took off. No forwarding address, either."

"Thank you," I said. I went to the newspaper office and tried to concentrate on my work; but all I could do was mull over the McLaughlin story possibilities. The woman was nearly eighty, ill and not strong. Lawrence, on the other hand, appeared to be perfectly healthy, physically. The more I thought about him, I was fairly certain that his mental capabilities, while sometimes possibly murderous, were also in tact.

I wondered how he could have fooled his mother for so many years. She obviously doted upon him and believed he could do no wrong. Perhaps she saw only what she wished to see, and she had devoted her life to his care. He made her feel needed.

For several days I pondered what to do. It finally occurred to me there was nothing I *could* do. If Lawrence had been instrumental in the death of his wife, in a foreign country, over twenty years ago, who was going to care? As far as Mr. Kelly's trip down the elevator shaft, he didn't remember; and there was no proof that it was anything other than an accident. Besides, I knew nothing of the McLaughlins' destination.

After a time, my biggest regret was the promise I had made not to reveal any part of their secrets, which had the components to provide what every good journalist desires above all else, a great story.

And a byline.

The Brotherhood

L unchtime found me at Luigi's Deli two or three times a week. Only minutes from my office, the restaurant served superb submarine and Italian beef sandwiches, as well as pizza and desserts. I became acquainted with the servers; and, in time, I was treated to a bit of the colorful clan's history, along with my lunch. Luigi's lyrical accent delighted me, and his ebullient personality swung from teasing to belligerent with no warning. He delivered insults to his customers that should have made them furious, but the sometimes-stinging barbs brought only laughter.

One day I took a late lunch just as the only woman server was about to go on break. "May I sit with you?" she asked. Delighted with the prospect, I nodded.

"Of course," I told her. She came around the counter, and we sat at a small glass-topped, sidewalk table. It was my second spring in New York, and I felt less like a tourist, although there was still more to see than I would probably ever explore.

"Ahhhh." The woman leaned against the back of her chair and sighed with relief.

"Except for one bathroom break, I haven't been off my feet all day. It's bagels, sweet breads and rolls they want from six until eleven, and then the lunch crowd begins." She held out her hand and indicated the embroidered name on her shirt. "I'm Carmen Smith," she told me. We shook hands, and I liked her immediately.

"I'm C.C. Bannister, but please call me 'Sissy.'"

Carmen moved with the efficiency of a pared down bulldozer, able to make a wide swath with a minimum of collateral damage. She probably could have served the dozens of daily lunch customers by herself. She maneuvered around five counter servers, three of whom were dark-haired sons of Luigi, much as a golden finch would flit around a flock of plodding turkeys.

Carmen took a bite of her thick Rueben, closed her dark eyes in appreciation and, with her tongue, retrieved a bit of dressing from the corner of her mouth. I bit into a zesty pepper that accompanied my Italian beef. "It's crowded every time I come here," I told her. "Do you serve evening meals? I live the opposite direction from my office, so I've never come this way after work."

"No, Luigi closes at three. We clean up and restock and get ready for breakfast. Luigi and the boys start making breads at three in the morning, and I come to work at seven. Luigi would like for me to come earlier, but I tell him I won't. You know what? I'm forty-five years old, and I work for him only because he is like an uncle to me. He and my dad have been friends ever since he came here from Sicily. He used to say he wanted me to be his daughter-in-law."

"I take it you didn't marry his son?" I asked.

With her left arm, Carmen tossed a dismissive gesture into the air and laughed. "None of them were old enough. I married Donald Smith, a nice American boy, when I was seventeen. You would think I'd done something worthy of excommunication. Luigi and my papa carried on as if I'd betrayed, them, the Pope and all of Sicily!" She laughed, remembering.

"Are any of Luigi's sons married?" I asked. She shot a glance at me.

"Are you interested?"

"No, no!" I laughed and shook my head. "I'm just curious. They are such friendly, pleasant men. Carlo is very handsome."

"Ahhhhhh, that Carlo!" Carmen wagged her finger at me. "He is a ladies' man. Many, many women have pursued him; and he allows some of them to catch him for a while. He tires of them easily." She cast a speculative glance at me. "Are you sure you are not interested, maybe just a *little*? Ricci is married, and Johnnie is engaged. How old are you?"

"I'm thirty-two, but..."

"Carlo is forty-one, only nine years older. You could be the one to tame him." Again, I shook my head.

"No, thank you. I don't have time for men these days."

"Where do you work? I've seen you many times, but behind the counter, there is no time to talk." Carmen seemed as curious about me as I was about her. Briefly I told her about Streetside. "Ah, yes, I have seen your paper. Maybe Luigi would advertise with you." While she sounded like most residents in the area, the sound of Italy came from her lips.

"My boss would appreciate that," I assured her. "How long have you lived in New York?"

"I was born here. My parents came to America following the first war. Luigi brought his family here a few years before the second war began. I think there was some kind of vendetta against his wife's family. My parents said that Luigi had already felt there wasn't enough land for him and his brother to make a good living in the family vineyards, so he came here.

"There was a terrible depression in America. I don't know how they survived those first few years. I remember how my father took any odd job he could find to put food on the table. I think they might all have returned to Sicily if the war had not begun.

"What about you, Sissy? How long have you been in New York?"

"Two years," I told her. "I worked at a newspaper in South Carolina before I came to Streetside. I haven't seen as much of the city as I would like, but I love it here."

While we ate, I studied Carmen. Her eyes were a beautiful Italian black; but her hair, a golden, natural blond made me wonder about her genetic heritage. Her olive skin was as smooth as a much younger woman's. She looked nowhere near the forty-five years she claimed. Perhaps, in time, I would know her well enough to ask the questions that hovered in my thoughts.

"Carmen, are you going to sit out there the rest of the day?" bellowed Luigi through the open door. *"Mama mia!* I don't pay you to sit!"

"You old donkey, you don't pay me much to do anything!" Carmen shot back. She stood and gathered our napkins and glasses. "It's been nice talking with you," she told me. "Maybe we can visit another time."

"I'll look forward to it. I've got to run, or my boss will be yelling at me, too."

He yelled anyway, something he rarely did. He was in full voice when I opened the door, so I wasn't the cause of his anger. That did not, however, keep me from being a target. That honor fell upon Mort Cassidy, Streetside's photographer; but the fallout filtered onto everyone in the office.

"How could you not know the mayor was coming to this building? Every other photographer in New York knew it! There he was, His Honor in person, ten floors up; and you're out taking pictures of trees in bloom in Central Park!" I don't know how the man made such simple, innocent words sound as profane as utterances from the most proficient, obscene gutter-mouth in the city. It wasn't the words; it was the way he said them.

"It was a perfect photo-op, a scoop right here under our noses!" Dirk raved on and on. Mort stood, a hand on his left hip, wordless until Dirk paused for a breath.

"Well, Boss, did you know the mayor was coming?"

Dirk narrowed his violet-blue eyes and pulled up his pants, which had slipped beneath his ponderous belly. "That comes under the list of things I pay *you* to know!" He glared at us: me, reporters, staff, clerks, receptionist, everyone. "And the rest of you, as well!" With that, he stomped into his office and slammed the door. There was a collective sigh of relief.

"Why was the mayor here today?" I asked of anyone who wanted to tell me.

"Our illustrious dignitary delivered news of a grant approved by the city for restoration of this building. The Historical Society has discovered a picture of Theodore Roosevelt standing in front of it. Seems Teddy was here visiting with the Rockefellers about some important matter...don't know what, but I'm sure it was connected to money in some way. Dirk didn't stop foaming at the mouth long enough to get to that part." Mort took his camera from his desktop and headed for the door. "Tell Moby Dick I'm out taking more bloomin' pictures," he threw over his shoulder.

By late afternoon, Dirk was his usual pleasant self. It was as if he had never lost his temper, so I felt safe enough to question him. I tapped on the glass of his door, and he readily invited me to come inside. "May I ask you something?"

"Shoot."

"I've been here almost two years, and I've never heard you swear. Even when you're angry," I grinned, "like this afternoon, you never swear. A lot of men curse in simple conversation; and most men, my dad included, swear in anger." Dirk grinned.

"When I was in high school, the principal was a short, dignified man with silver hair, horn-rimmed glasses, a stern face and a soft voice." Dirk leaned back in his big chair and locked his hands behind his head. I could see memories soften his eyes. "That old man held control of the school with just his presence. When he wanted us to really listen, he nearly whispered into the microphone at assemblies.

"He caught some of the boys cursing like sailors one day. Of course, we...uh, *they* hadn't heard him approach. He ordered, uh...the boys to his office and gave them a dressing down you wouldn't believe, all without raising his voice. He told us...uh, them that cursing, swearing, and speech laden with vulgarities were all marks of extreme ignorance. He said that men who lose themselves in such habits are fools, ignorant fools. I, that is, the *boys* never forgot what he said." His wry grin would have given him away if his slips-of-the-tongue had not.

"I'll remember that," I told him. "It's another good criteria for judging character. Thanks for telling me."

"However, I haven't mastered the soft voice part yet," he added with a chuckle.

"I noticed."

✳ ✳ ✳

I met diverse segments of Streetside's subscribers and advertisers, to say nothing of its subjects, during my tenure on Dirk Warneke's payroll. When I look back at that time, a few individuals stand out; but none more memorably than Guiseppe Donatelli. I couldn't know, when I met him, how his story would change my life.

After my lunch with Carmen Smith, I decided to try the freshly baked breakfast breads the deli/bakery offered. I left my apartment early one morning and took a bus, instead of walking. As Carmen had told me, a line of people waited along the front of the shop. The aroma of good bread, spicy and sweet, filled the warm, late spring morning.

At one of the outdoor tables sat an old man, well over eighty. His hands, folded atop a weathered cane, were brown and gnarled like small, twisted tree branches. Baggy trousers, a faded merlot hue, draped across his knees and fell onto corduroy house slippers. A white undershirt peeked from beneath his gray cardigan, so unraveled at the cuffs they looked fringed.

A black, beret-type cap sat on his head. The small visor, tipped downward, could not hide the man's bushy, salt-and-pepper eyebrows. A lush, matching mustache drooped along both sides of his mouth like parentheses; and black eyes glittered like little black marbles in his weathered face.

When the line moved enough to put me across from him, I nodded my head and spoke. "Good morning."

Beneath the mustache, the old man's mouth lifted in a near flirtatious grin. "Good morning, Young Lady." His accent was wonderful, just like all the Italian characters I'd ever seen in old movies...*Good-a morning-a Young-a Lady.* His eyes fairly sparkled with appreciation of a female presence, and I suspect they would have sparkled for any female. I smiled.

"I don't remember seeing you before," he continued. "I always remember beautiful young women. Is this your first visit to Luigi's?"

"I come for lunch several times a week," I told him. The line shifted, and I moved closer to the door. "I'm Sissy McCoy."

"Ah, yes. Carmen spoke of you." The man took off his cap and bowed from his chair. "Guiseppe Donatelli, at your service, Lady McCoy. Perhaps one day you will have the lunch with me, no?" I laughed.

"I would be delighted, Mr. Donatelli." The line pushed me forward, and I entered the Mecca for Italian bread lovers. Before I left the deli, I had purchased a tall container of strong, amazing coffee and enough rolls and biscotti to feed the whole crew at Streetside.

Thereafter, I tried to be more than caught up with my daily assignments by lunchtime, whenever possible. I became addicted to lunches at Luigi's, and I soon learned it was better to lunch late. The crowd had dispersed by then, and it wasn't always Carmen who sat with me.

One sunny afternoon, the handsome Carlo approached my sidewalk table, confidence and a cola in hand. Through the window, I caught a glimpse of Carmen and the broad grin plastered on her face. I knew, as surely as sunrise, she had sent this lothario to check me out, or possibly, for me to check *him* out.

"May I join you?" he asked. I looked up at him, but didn't answer right away.

"If you wish." Practiced, old world charm emanated from him. He didn't have to work at it. His dark, curly hair grew low on his neck, and there was a hint of dark beard shadow on his face. I knew he must have shaved early in the day. If he were seeing a woman in the evening, he would need to shave again. I could imagine the beard burn a woman's cheeks would have after necking with him.

"My name is Carlo Donatelli." He offered his hand and I allowed him to take mine. His grip was firm, but not crushing. "My father is Luigi, and my grandfather is Guiseppe. You met him the other day, I understand."

"Yes, I did; and he is delightful. I'd love to talk with him again. Does he come outdoors often?" Carlo sat down and shifted his chair around the table, closer to mine.

"He comes out more when the sun shines. He says the warmth feels good on his bones. Carmen tells me that you are called 'Sissy,' but I think you must have another name, a beautiful one, perhaps, to accompany such a lovely face?" Carlo's smile was dazzling.

"Yes, I have another name; and no, it isn't beautiful. I prefer Sissy." He laughed, a charming laugh, of course.

"Well, Miss Sissy, I assume it is 'Miss'?" I nodded, and he continued. "Would you permit me to show you some of the sights of New York? Carmen said you have not lived here a very long time." Wow, he didn't even wait for the introduction to cool off!

"Thank you, Carlo; but I see a lot of the city, connected to my job. I don't have much time of my own these days. Speaking of which, I really need to get back to work." I stood and picked up my napkin and paper cup, tossed them into the large bin under the window and started to walk away. "Oh, and please tell your grandfather that I would love to spend some time with him." Carlo was still half-standing at the table. I grinned all the way back to the office.

I don't know if my near-aversion to charming, handsome men was caused by my experience with Jackson McCoy, or if I simply had a perverse streak. I enjoyed looking at handsome faces and good bodies. I was young, unattached and as human as any woman my age. I missed the touching, the closeness I had loved with Jack during the first few years of our marriage.

The opportunities to date were always present, and I had accepted several, even a second and third date a time or two; but I always pulled away when I sensed a man's growing interest. Sometimes I wondered if I could ever again be drawn to someone, could fall in love for real some day, perhaps even have a family. It wasn't a thing I dwelt on, just an occasional pondering, usually at holidays and on rainy weekends.

During that summer, I spent many late afternoons at a sidewalk table with Guiseppe. I became so engrossed with his memories and stories that I finally asked if I could record our conversations. After each of our talks, I took as many notes as I could remember, but it wasn't the same as being able to transcribe from his voice.

"Sure, sure," he agreed. "Why don't you come upstairs to the apartment, where we can sit on something soft?" He shifted uncomfortably in the wrought iron chair. I looked at my watch. It was already past five, and I had errands to run.

"Could I come tomorrow evening?" I asked.

"Sure, sure." He nodded. "Carlo, come help me up!" he called. Carlo hurried from the deli, leaning a broom against the doorframe. He smiled and nodded to me as he helped his grandfather stand. He supported the old man, who took a moment to get his balance before he shuffled toward the door.

"Carlo, don't scare her off. *La bella* and I have a date tomorrow night. Tell her where to come. I have to go to the bathroom now. I have to start to the bathroom early, or it will be late when I get there." Carlo grinned at me and shrugged his broad shoulders. He seemed different from our first encounter, friendly instead of flirtatious.

"I enjoy your grandfather very much," I told him. Carlo's grin became a smile, and I looked more closely at his face. Black lashes framed replicas of his grandfather's black eyes beneath the same dark brows. Odds were he would resemble Guiseppe as he aged. Odds were also that I could like him.

"Grandpapa is a character," he told me. "When I was a little boy, I followed him around like a shadow, sometimes even standing on his feet while he walked. He was my hero, still is, I guess."

"He has agreed to let me record his memoirs."

"I'm glad," Carlo replied. "After the war, my parents sent me to him for visits every couple of years. He told me stories then, and it would be great to have those memories on tape. Wish I'd thought of it years ago." He told me which buzzer to ring and how to reach the apartment above the store.

"Does he live alone?" I asked.

"No, my father still lives in the apartment. He tried to get Grandpapa to come to America three years ago, after my mother died; but he refused to leave Sicily. Except for distant cousins, there are no other relatives left in Italy to see to him. He fought leaving his home for as long as he could. He finally came last year, but he says he is only visiting. He wants to go back home."

"He has no other children?"

"My Uncle Marcus, the younger son, was killed in the war. He worked with the underground against Mussolini."

"Did your grandfather sell his home?" Carlo laughed

"Oh, no. He would never sell it. He's still hoping that one of his grandsons will take it and raise children there. Actually, I have thought about it. The house is on a hillside in vineyard country, small, but as picturesque as any artist's painting. Grandpapa lived through two world wars on that little piece of Sicily, and he loves it. Who knows? Maybe one day I'll live there." He turned back to the doorway and retrieved his broom.

"Thank you for telling me about your grandfather." I waved and hurried toward the bus stop. If I missed the next bus, the little grocery store where I shopped would be closed before I could pick up what I needed.

The next evening, shortly before seven, I pushed the buzzer Carlo had indicated. Immediately the lock opened, and I let myself inside. A staircase led straight up from the small entrance. A bare bulb hung above the outer door, and another above the stairs, providing enough light to see the worn carpet on the treads.

Two doors opened off the landing, one near the top of the stairs and another at the end of a fairly long hall. Uncertain on which to knock, I opted for the nearer one. It opened inward as I raised my hand.

"Ah, come in, come in." Guiseppe stood aside, and I felt as if I had stepped back in time. The room was large. It stretched the width of the shop and was filled with wonderful things: overstuffed mohair furniture; ornate lamps with bright scarves draped across tasseled shades; carved tables laden with porcelain statuettes and glassware; portraits and dark paintings set in ornate frames; and shelves stacked with volumes of leather and cloth bound books.

I didn't know where to look first. Everything in the room belonged to another era and atmosphere, certainly not to an apartment in New York, above an Italian deli.

"Welcome." Guiseppe bowed slightly, took my hand and kissed it. His lush mustached tickled.

"Thank you. Your furnishings are beautiful. Did you bring all this with you from Italy?"

"No, no. I brought very little." He waved his hand around the room. "Most of these things belonged to the family of my daughter-in-law, Francesca. They shipped as much as they could to America with her and Luigi, before the war. Her family was quite wealthy at that time." Thoughtfully, he ran his fingers through his iron-gray hair. "Perhaps they had a premonition.... Sit, sit and be comfortable," Guiseppe told me. He indicated that I should take the brown, overstuffed chair. Covered in tapestry so worn that some individual frayed threads lay broken, the chair seemed to envelope me with old world comfort. I wondered how many people had settled into its depth.

"Ummmm, this would be a great place to take a nap," I told him.

"It is," Guiseppe agreed. "It's one of Luigi's favorites. Most evenings he falls asleep there, and I doze on that sofa. May I offer you something to drink? Coffee? Wine, perhaps?"

"Coffee would be nice, thank you. May I help?"

"Yes, please." Guiseppe shuffled through a wide archway into a kitchen, which was nearly as wide as the living room. Updates showed in the cabinets, countertops and appliances; but the center of the room was filled with a large, old-fashioned, round table. I didn't know much about woods, but I thought it might be made of mahogany.

Although many nicks, cuts and scratches were apparent on the table, it glowed with the soft patina of years. Ten, possibly twelve, could easily sit at dinner there. The double pedestal, thick and carved with deep designs, was so large that a child could have, and probably had, hidden between the posts.

Instead of a porcelain service, a chunky terra cotta teapot and thick pottery mugs in other earthy colors sat in the middle of the table. They spoke to me of sunny days, bread baked in clay ovens and the wine-y aroma of grapes. My imagination raced with colorful scenarios, none based upon experience.

My host seemed more than happy for me to make the coffee. He told me where to find the grounds, how many scoops to use and how to operate the stained coffee maker. "Twelve scoops?" I asked. "For six cups?"

"Yes, yes," Guiseppe insisted. "Luigi never makes it strong enough."

"Where is your son? I hope he didn't leave because of me. I could meet with you on a weekend, any place that's convenient for you."

"No, no. Luigi goes with his friends to a tavern in Little Italy every Friday night. Carmen opens the deli on Saturday, but they don't make breads on the weekends. Luigi doesn't return until very late, so you can enjoy your coffee and stay as long as you wish."

After one cup, I felt as if my hair had lifted a couple inches off my head. My eyes were open so wide, I thought I might never blink again. I had tasted espresso; but Guiseppe's brew was the thickest, strongest, most bitter concoction ever to reach my stomach, where it seemed to set up it's own caffeine distribution line straight to my brain.

While Guiseppe sipped multiple cups of the coffee concentrate, he talked to me. The tape recorder did not bother him in the least. He had told me some family history during our previous chats, of his wife, Anna, the mother of his two sons, and how she drowned off the coast of Messina. On that first night of taped memoirs he took me into a world

I could not have imagined. Only when the massive grandfather clock chimed ten times did I realize I had been unaware of hours eight and nine.

"Mr. Donatelli, I am so sorry for keeping you up this late," I apologized. The old man chuckled.

"I will be awake and asleep many times tonight. Sleep comes when it wants. At my age, I take what you call 'cat naps.' Sometimes the cat stays away until morning, and then I sleep most of a day." He shrugged one shoulder. "What does it matter? My dreams can be better than waking, for then I am able to see my Maria." He smiled at me. "Another time I may tell you about Maria."

"I thought your wife's name was Anna," I said, sure that he had misspoken.

"It was," he smiled and pointed to the telephone. "Call a taxi, *Bella*; and we will speak more another evening." I did as he said. When the cab arrived, I impulsively kissed Guiseppi's weathered cheek. He smelled of strong coffee, a hint of wine, age and something else—something of the earth. He patted my back, and I let myself out of the apartment.

✳ ✳ ✳

Spring turned into early summer, and I amassed a stack of cassette tapes that contained the memories and stories of the Italian gentleman. On one of those chatty Friday evenings, Carlo joined us. He brought sweet cannoli; and he made the coffee, a much milder version of his grandfather's.

"Grandpapa, do you ever turn the tables on your guest and ask questions about her?" Carlo's black eyes smiled at me above his coffee mug.

"No, I have not," Guiseppe answered, "an old man's vanity, I suppose. Why don't you ask her?"

"I'm not the one being interviewed," I told him. "Nothing in my life has been remarkable; but your family, your Sicilian heritage and your survival of two world wars are all sources of material for good stories."

"What are you going to write?" Guiseppe gestured toward the tape recorder. "Are you going to put me in a book?"

"I don't know about a book; but it you don't object, I would love to write an extensive story of you and your family."

"Who would read it?" he demanded, a look of comic disbelief on his face. "I am just an old immigrant, no longer able to live where I want or go where I want, except for my many trips to the bathroom at all hours of the days and nights. Who wants to read about me? And who would print it?"

"Any number of people would love to read about you. As for the printing, I'm not yet sure. I would probably freelance it around the publishing community. We already have enough material to start sending queries, if it's all right with you."

Guiseppe shrugged, a movement that expressed his attitude toward much of his life, a careless, dismissive gesture. "Do with it what you want," he told me. "If you make me famous, maybe the young ladies will smile at me more often on the street."

"Do you mind if I listen to some of the tapes?" Carlo asked. He had grown quiet as Guiseppe and I talked.

"Of course not. Your grandfather has taken us through his life during the first war, and he's just begun to talk about the pre-World War II years. We must be pretty close to the time you were born."

"Grandpapa, are you sure? You and Papa have told me stories about those times, and I wonder if all of it should be reopened." Carlo sounded concerned. "There are still," he hesitated, "...factions, people, who might strongly object to...."

"Hah!" Guiseppe shouted. "Cowards, all of them! I didn't care what any of them thought forty years ago, and I don't care now!" A torrent of angry Sicilian/Italian poured from his mouth, and his face grew red.

"Okay, okay, Grandpapa," Carlo soothed. "Don't be upset. Calm down, now." Carlo stood behind his grandfather and patted his shoulder. He said something in the same language, a beautiful sound; and soon Guiseppe heaved a great sigh.

"Forgive me, *Bella*," he said. "I think I am very tired. Remembering some things...." He waved his hand in the air again. "Next time I will try not to become so angry. Carlo, see Miss Sissy home." Guiseppe bowed and moved slowly from the kitchen into a hallway, where I could see four other doors. I assumed they opened onto bedrooms and a bath.

"We can go down the back stairs. My car's in the service street," Carlo told me.

"I took a taxi here, so I can just call another one. It's such a beautiful evening, I'd walk, if it weren't so late."

"Let's do that. I'll walk you home, and then I'll take a cab back here to get my car." I didn't argue with him. I loved the busy night streets, especially Friday nights. Residents lingered on the sidewalks later as the days lengthened. Even so, I wasn't foolish enough to walk alone after stores and shops closed.

Luigi's deli was four blocks from Streetside's office; and it was another six blocks from there to my apartment, just a nice spring evening's stroll. The background hum of the city was punctuated with music from open shop doors, conversations among the pedestrians, and occasional impatient honking from cabs and cars.

Carlo carried my canvas bag with the recorder and cassettes inside, and we strolled comfortably together, close, but not touching. I looked up, although I knew no stars would be visible, even on such a clear night. The millions of lights below outshone the constellations.

"Do you ever see the stars?" I asked. Carlo glanced upward, too.

"Not in the city," he said. "They were so bright where we lived when I was a boy. I didn't remember how brilliant they could be until I moved back to the country." Surprised, I stared at him.

"You don't live here? How can you live so far away and still work at the deli—and be there so early?"

Carlo laughed. "The deli is not my full time job," he told me. "I show up now and then, just to keep my father happy; and to tell the truth, I enjoy being there. My brothers and I grew up in the apartment above the restaurant, so it's still home to me. It's not the same since my mother died. My father seems more content with Grandpapa here."

"Where do you work, besides the deli?" I asked.

"I import Italian tile. I own a display and design suite in an interior design complex in White Plains; but I live outside the town."

"How long have you worked with tile?"

"Several years. On a trip back to Sicily, when I was in my late twenties, I became intrigued with the craftsmanship of a local tile maker. I brought some of his tiles back with me and showed them to a couple of interior designers, who both loved the tile. So I took a chance and contracted several designs." Carlo shrugged in the same manner as his grandfather. "I now import from Italy, as well as Sicily. The rest, so they say, is history. What about you? How long have you worked at Streetside?"

"I'm into my second year." I related a short, dispassionate account of my last few years. Carlo was appropriately sympathetic in the right places, to which I murmured brief thanks. "Streetside has a great staff, and I like my boss; but I don't want to stay there forever. In fact, I have articles being considered in several magazines, and three have been accepted. When I have enough material in my resume, I'm going to approach some big name papers, before long, I hope."

"Is my grandfather's story one of your possible submissions?" Carlo's tone changed.

"Not without his permission, of course; but I think it has great potential. You know, it just occurred to me who he reminds me of," I laughed. "It's Anthony Quinn, one of my favorite actors. Without his mustache, your grandfather could be Anthony's brother." I laughed again. "I know it's silly, but I've always compared peoples' likenesses to movie stars." Carlo remained quiet for several moments.

"Sissy, my grandfather is not an actor; and his life is not a movie. At various times in the old country, he was involved in dangerous...," he paused, "let's just say there are some aspects of his past life best left alone. He's an old man now, but he has an extended family that could be affected."

My heart accelerated, and my mind jumped from one possibility to another. War intrigue? Nazi collaboration? Allies collaboration? Spying for either side? Omigosh! Mafia connection? Vendettas? What had I stumbled upon? I stopped on the sidewalk.

"Carlo, you can't just dump a statement like that on me and expect me not to ask questions! What?!" I couldn't hide my excitement.

"You sound like a little girl wanting hints about a gift!" Carlo exclaimed. He shook his head, reluctant laughter in his voice. "I have a feeling I've just further whetted the blade of your curiosity. I'm not going to say another word. It's between you and Grandpapa."

Too quickly we arrived at the Bellamy Apartments. "I'll carry this up for you," Carlo said. There was a tone in his voice that allowed no argument. I unlocked the outer door, and he followed me to the elevator. At my door, he waited until I inserted the key before he handed the heavy bag to me. I turned to him, words of thanks on my lips. With his hands in his pants pockets, he leaned down and planted a warm, sweet kiss on my mouth. Even as off guard as I was, there was only one possible response. I kissed him back.

"Call me a taxi?" he murmured.

"What?"

"A taxi," he repeated, his mouth only a breath from mine.

"You're a taxi," I whispered. Carlo burst into laughter. I pushed open the door and smiled at him over my shoulder. "I'll call one right away. You can wait in the lobby. Good night."

The last thing I saw before I closed the door was his handsome face, black eyes a-twinkle with mirth. Hmmmm...I didn't know black eyes could twinkle. I thought they only glittered. I leaned against the door and sighed, a deep sigh, filled with contentment and regret, an oxymoron, if I ever thought one.

✳ ✳ ✳

Summer passed quickly. Much to my delight, every article I submitted to various magazines was accepted. A couple of them paid well and led to proposals for more stories. Further sessions with Guiseppe had to be postponed while I worked feverishly on additional articles and juggled my work at Streetside. I could feel the welcome presence of an impressive resume hovering above my career.

When I was able to meet again with Guiseppe on Friday evenings, I often took a sandwich to work or found somewhere closer to the office than Luigi's for lunch. Carlo did not come again to my meetings with his grandfather. At first, I had expected him; then I was both relieved and disappointed. I thought about his kiss, more than I intended; but I told myself I had no time to develop a serious relationship. I wanted to concentrate on the Donatelli chronicles.

Guiseppe told me he was born in Sicily in eighteen eighty-four, one of five children. His father owned a small vineyard that had been passed down to him from his father. Guiseppe and his two brothers had taken care of the vineyard in the same manner as their parents and grandparents before them, until World War I. The two brothers were both killed in that carnage, which left the eldest son, Guiseppe, in charge of the fertile land. His sisters married and moved to Northern Italy.

"It was a hard time," Guiseppe said. "My sons, Luigi and Marcus, were only boys when the war began; but they knew how to care for the vines and how to harvest the grapes. We sold our grapes to a good winery, even during the war. The Kaiser enjoyed fine Sicilian wine, too."

"What about your wife, Anna?" I asked.

"Ah, you want to go backward?"

"I would like to know about your wife. I'm sure it was a very bad time for her, as well." Guiseppe nodded.

"It was, it was. Anna was a good woman, a good wife. Our parents arranged our marriage when Anna was fifteen, and I was twenty. Her family lived in another village. A mutual acquaintance introduced our parents to each other, and the wedding contract was signed before Anna and I met."

"You had no say in it at all?" I had read of arranged marriages, but I had never known anyone who had become engaged before meeting their perspective spouse. Guiseppe grinned at my expression.

"None. We had a few weeks to become acquainted, but we were never without a chaperone. The day of our wedding was the first time I kissed Anna."

"Who was Maria?" I tossed the question at him casually, but I watched Guiseppe's face for any sign of guilty reaction. There was none.

"Ah, Maria," he sighed. His dark eyes softened, and he rested his head against the back of his overstuffed chair. "Now you want to go forward? You skip around like an impatient child. I will tell you all, but in my way." He pointed to the recorder. "Is that machine loaded?" I nodded. "Then tonight I will tell you about the second war, how we survived it and about Maria...."

Stately and tall, the lighthouse stretched high above the water, as it had stood for many, many years, a sure beacon to warn sea-faring vessels of the dangerous rocks along the coast. Not far from the rocks, an aged fishing boat bobbed like a cork on the deep blue water of the strait between Sicily and the tip of Italy's boot. Choppy whitecaps of the Mediterranean tossed it from side-to-side, but the sturdy craft was not deterred from its course.

The sun bounced brilliant beams off the crested waves. Two sailors, one very young, one some fifty years older, shaded their eyes with their hands. The six-year-old boy, as brown as his grandfather, laughed with the sheer joy of youth, no trace of fear on his countenance.

Guiseppe Donatelli gazed with pride at his grandson. "Would you like to take her in, Carlo?" he asked.

"Yes!"

"Sit here beside the engine." The two exchanged places, and Guiseppe took his hand from the rudder. "Take her, Boy!" With a grin as wide as his face, young Carlo Donatelli guided the small craft toward the rocky coast. To the untrained eye, a safe haven was not visible; but Carlo steered the small craft as surely as if he had done it many times. From the age of three, he had gone fishing with his grandfather. As the boat neared the shore, Guiseppe's hand hovered close to the control, not touching, but ready, should the need arise.

"Good!" proclaimed the older man. The boy grabbed a rope and jumped onto a flat rock. "I think you are not quite big enough to pull in the boat and me, too!" Guiseppe laughed. He stepped upon the rock and pulled the boat along the shore for several feet before he guided it into a narrow inlet, where he secured it to a weathered pole, securely wedged between two massive boulders.

"Take the fish, Carlo." Guiseppe pulled up their catch and passed it to the boy. "Your mother will make a fine meal tonight, no?" He roughed up the child's hair and let his hand rest briefly on his grandson's shoulder. He loved all three of his son's boys; but this one, the eldest, was special to him.

Guiseppe gazed around the countryside he had known all his life. To his left, the outline of Messina glistened in the warm light of a late afternoon. To his right, across the water, he could see the dim coast of Italy, less than three miles away. He grasped the boy's hand, and together they followed a worn path to a patch of wind-blown, scrubby bushes and trees where they had left their bicycles.

From the deep pocket of his trousers, Guiseppe took a large piece of folded oiled paper and wrapped it around the fish, which he then placed in the beat-up basket attached to the handlebars. Whistling as if no war loomed over them, they pedaled three miles to the village where they lived, outside Messina.

There they got off their bicycles and pushed them up the hillside, above the town, to the small stone villa where Guiseppe and his parents, as well as his children and grandchildren, had been born. "Mama, we caught many fish!" Carlo threw open the heavy gate and entered the courtyard.

Guiseppe stood outside the gate and looked down at the village. One side of the bleached stone and aged, yellowed brick walls of the houses glowed softly in the sunlight, casting long shadows upon the dirt and cobblestone-packed streets.

Terracotta and red tiles formed bright splashes of color among the older faded rooftops. Tall fig and olive trees, many of them ancient and gnarled, provided shady places for children to hide, as well as a buffer against the midday sun. The scene had changed very little since his childhood, and he enjoyed the view even more as he grew older.

Guiseppe followed Carlo into the courtyard. Off to one side, a short distance from the house, Francesca Donatelli turned from the round, clay oven, where she had just placed three long loaves of raised bread to bake. Blackened from the fires of decades, the oven itself smelled of good bread and flaky pastries.

"Wonderful," Francesca proclaimed. "I made fettucini, and we have fresh zucchini and tomatoes from the market. I brought home unsold sweets from the shop." She took the fish from her father-in-law. "Carlo, go play with Ricci until it's time to eat, but don't wake Giovanni." Carlo disappeared around the house. "I'll ring the bell when dinner is ready," she called after him.

Francesca leaned backward and rubbed tired muscles that ached from her long day's work. Every morning she rose before the sun and walked down the hill to the village, where she opened the bakery, a niche in the wall of stone buildings that lined the market street.

From the beginning of her marriage to Luigi, she had helped her mother-in-law, Anna, make the breads and pastries sold in the shop. Anna had drowned in the strait shortly before the birth of Giovanni, and most of the work had become Francesca's responsibility. When the vineyard didn't require his presence, Marcus, Luigi's nineteen-year-old brother, helped make the breads that people came from as far away as Messina to buy. People said that Donatelli breads were better.

Guiseppe bent over a low trough and splashed water upon his head and neck. "What did you hear in the market?" he asked. His daughter-in-law's mouth tightened.

"There is talk that Mussolini will join Germany and that a war is coming. Some say it is nothing." She paused. "People are talking about my father and the Grazias again," she said. "They still want to buy his land down by the sea, but he won't sell. My mother says to sell it before something bad happens, but Papa is too stubborn. He doesn't use the property, but he doesn't want Vincenzo to have it."

"I don't blame him," Guiseppe replied. "I would not sell, either."

Dinner at the Donatelli table was sober that night. Oil sconces on the rough walls cast shadows that moved with the soft air from open windows, while scents from the hillside and the sea mingled with the savory aromas of good food. Even so, the mood was as dark as the shadows.

Carlo and his four-year-old brother, Ricci, watched their parents and grandfather exchange heated opinions. One-year-old Giovanni slept peacefully in the heavy baby bed that had held, not only his brothers, but his father and grandfather, as well.

"People must stand against those animals!" Guiseppe stated. "They can't have something just because they want it!"

"Papa, the next offer might come after one of Francesca's brothers has his throat slit." Luigi pointed his fork to emphasize his words.

"Luigi!" Francesca nodded at the children. He ignored her.

"It's true, Francesca. They have murdered before, and they will do it again." None of them knew how portentous were his words.

Six days later, Mario, the youngest son of Dominic Corelli, Francesca's father, was found on the plot of coastal property desired by Don Luciana. No marks were apparent on the boy's body, but it was determined by his blue lips that he had been suffocated. Francesca was devastated.

"I want to leave this place!" she screamed at her husband. "They could come for my boys, too!" She gave Luigi no peace. After days and days of Francesca's arguments, desperate for peaceful sleep and the safety of his sons, he agreed to take his family to America. Guiseppe was enraged.

"How can you even consider such a thing?" he demanded of his son. "You are my heir! You and your brother must continue to work the vineyard and keep this house, just as I have done! You *cannot* leave! We are not cowards! We will avenge Francesca's brother, and we will stay here!"

"No, Papa. What will it gain us to avenge the boy? We kill one of them, and they kill two of us; and then we kill some more? If you do that, it will never end! We're going to America, if only for awhile."

"Then your portion of the vineyards and this house and the shop will go to Marcus!"

Luigi shrugged. "Papa, there is not enough to keep three families, as it is. I have three boys. Marcus will marry one day and have children, too. Even if I stayed here, I would have to find another way to make a living. No one wants to sell land, so I would have to find other vineyard work, or perhaps move to the mainland. We could not remain here forever. Besides, there are rumors of war...."

"Then go! Go!"

"Papa..."

"Go!"

Luigi kept his promise to his wife. By month's end, he had booked passage on a ship; and his branch of the Donatelli family sailed for New York Harbor, United States of America. With them they took the dowry and furniture given to Francesca when she married Luigi.

Guiseppe did not go to the ship to bid them goodbye; but on the day they left the harbor, he stood high on a rocky slope and watched the vessel pull away from Sicily. He watched until the ship became a tiny speck. Even after it disappeared, he stood and stared at the empty horizon.

Tears ran down his brown, weathered cheeks, the only tears he would shed for his son, for Carlo, the grandson he adored, and for the other little boys who would not know him, would not walk on the tops of his feet, as Carlo had done. Despair for the loss outweighed his anger.

A year passed. Guiseppe and Marcus worked the vineyard together during the seasons of the grapes. His anger at the Grazias festered until it became a righteous vendetta in his mind. No one had been arrested for the murder of his daughter-in-law's young brother, but the whole community knew who was responsible.

By the same token, no one was surprised when a cousin of Vincenzo Grazia drowned in the rough waters off the rocky coast. His widow and children mourned long and loudly and declared in the village that the Corellis had murdered the man. Again, there was no proof. Anyone could slip from the treacherous rocks and drown in the sea, as Anna Donatelli had done.

Within the next two years, four more apparently accidental deaths afflicted the two families, who reacted with tears followed by raging stoicism. Guiseppe and Marcus Donatelli kept their own counsel. The encroaching war seemed not to disturb them. Some twenty years earlier, Sicilians had survived what some people called "The Great War." It seemed to Guiseppe that a war was always in progress somewhere, even in the surrounding hills of his village.

At fifty-seven years of age, Guiseppe worked doggedly when it was required, drank his share of red wine with his friends in the village and tried not to dream of his lost loved ones. Marcus found a girl he wanted to marry, and Guiseppe was glad for his son, glad for himself. He was happy not to participate in another arranged marriage. Perhaps there would be children in the villa once more.

As suddenly as a Mediterranean gale, the Mussolini government sided with Adolph Hitler, the land-hungry lunatic in charge of Germany. The appearance of thousands of Italian and German troops throughout the land and along the coastal harbors had not personally affected Guiseppe until he learned that the villa of a prominent Messina official had been overtaken by a German general. The general had taken not only the beautiful, hillside home, he had taken the official's young daughter.

From that moment, Guiseppe had a new enemy, someone to hate other than the Grazias. When he heard that America had been drawn into the war, his heart pounded with a new resolve. He was invigorated, more alive than he had been since his Anna died.

Guiseppe listened with new ears to the talk in the village. He heard what was said and what was not said. He learned to read a man's eyes as well as his words, and it wasn't long before he became a part of the resistance, the growing number of Sicilians dissatisfied with the dictatorship of Benito Mussolini and the arrogant, German and Italian soldiers who seemed to be everywhere.

The Resistance, well-entrenched and responsible for disruption of supply lines, sabotage of ammunition stores, even the simple act of draining gasoline from officers vehicles, screened and tested new recruits. After a time, Guiseppe was welcomed as a comrade; and it was only then that he discovered how long Marcus had been an active, un-uniformed soldier in the movement.

Regular letters arrived from Luigi in America. They told of the bakery he and Francesca operated in New York, of the hundreds of Italians and Sicilians in the community, of the wonderful school the two older boys attended and how they wished their father and brother would follow them. They wrote little of the depression that sometimes forced them to give away bread that could not be sold.

Guiseppe read each letter several times before he folded it and placed it in a small, strapped trunk. He would not allow himself to dwell on his missing loved ones. America was far away from the war that raged in his country and other parts of the world. Much as he missed his beloved family, he felt relief that they were safe from the German forces. His focus remained on his part in deliverance from that force.

The first week of July, nineteen forty-three, resistance members filtered singly or in pairs into a catacomb-like cave that meandered beneath a hillside, northwest of Guiseppe's village. Many of the arrivals were unknown to him. Surnames were not divulged; nor were addresses of the newcomers.

The leader stood in deep shadow. The only light came from a few oil lanterns, held high. They provided just enough light for safety in movement, and only well into the recesses of the passage to avoid detection from outside.

"We've learned that an invasion will begin within a few days. English and American troops are coming, but Italian and German forces are waiting for them. We don't know exactly where they will land, but we know they'll come by air and sea." A murmur, although subdued, gave evidence of excited expectation among the men and women of all ages in the cave.

"There will probably be paratroopers, so watch for them and be ready to help any way you can. Don't put yourself at risk, but watch. Remember that others will be watching, too; so don't take any foolish chances. Don't think that your neighbors will assist you. Contact only those you're positive will be sympathetic."

Without identifying themselves, people spoke of pilfered hand grenades from supply trucks, of ammunition stores blown up, of tainted foods being delivered to officers, and numerous, ingenious ways of distraction, aggravation, and mayhem to the enemy. Any act of sabotage, carefully carried out, kept the enemy off balance.

"Do you know where the paratroopers will drop?" Guiseppe searched in the dim light for the woman with the low, throaty voice. Something stirred in his chest at the sound.

"No. Our source said only that there may be multiple landings, on all coasts. Any more questions?"

"How many of us can speak or have an understanding of English? I know enough to communicate." Again the husky voice spoke. Only a few acknowledged at least some ability. Guiseppe edged through his comrades, driven to see the woman whose voice intrigued him. "If some wish to stay a few minutes longer, I'll give you a few phrases. It might make a difference in how we could help."

A lantern focused on the face of the speaker. Guiseppe drew in his breath. Long, curly black hair framed a face of classic beauty. Even in the dimness, Guiseppe could detect dark eyes and lashes that cast shadows on her cheeks. Her face reflected the passion in her voice; and for the first time in his life, Guiseppe fell helplessly, hopelessly in love.

While most of the supporters filed out in staggered numbers, Guiseppe stayed with those who wanted to learn the English phrases. He couldn't have left, even had he not desired to know the foreign words. His eyes did not leave the woman's face while she asked her eager pupils to parrot simple phrases after her: *I will take you to safety. I am a Resistance Fighter. I will help you. Follow me.*

Guiseppe stared at her as she spoke. She glanced back at him after her eyes had passed over him. He smiled faintly, his lips pursed in self-derision. His breath caught in his throat at the beauty of her tentative smile. With quick presence of mind, he inclined his head in a slow nod, which she returned. On his solitary, careful walk back to his home, he thought of nothing but the woman; and he repeated to himself the meaningless English phrases.

Marcus came into the house much later than his father. Each made it a practice to stay alert until the other had returned safely. The two men had grown used to living only with each other, but they were both lonely for a feminine presence in the house. Guiseppe waited in an easy chair, a glass of wine in his hand. When he heard the back door open, he got up and poured a glass for Marcus, who took it gratefully.

"Who is the woman who taught the English?" Guiseppe asked his son.

"I know her only as Maria. She lives in the country, to the west of Messina."

Guiseppe cleared his throat. "Does she have a family?" he asked.

"Not anymore," Marcus told him. "Her husband was killed two years ago by a soldier."

"German?"

"No, Italian," Marcus answered. "The only difference in some of them is the color of the uniform."

"She has no children?" Guiseppe pressed.

"No, no one. I'm going to bed, Papa. Good night."

"Good night."

Marcus turned back to his father. "Papa, I almost forgot. These are for you." From a leather pouch, he took two weapons and extended them to Guiseppe. "Both came from the body of a German officer. No, Papa, don't ask how I came by them. Just take them and keep them on you every time you go out." Guiseppe took the cased luger and a two-edged dagger, snapped into its leather scabbard. He and Marcus looked long into each other's eyes before Marcus went to his room.

Past midnight, Guiseppe lay awake in his bed. His heart pounded with excitement at the approaching conflict, and blood rushed in his veins at the thought of the woman called Maria. He chided himself for his foolishness. He was fifty-seven years old, a grandfather three times; and the woman could not possibly be over forty, perhaps younger.

Guiseppe's hair, still thick and dark, showed no silver. Years of work on the sunny hillside had burnished his skin to a coppery hue, but the lines in his face spoke more of experience than age. His body remained firm; his arms and legs, long and muscular, were strong and supple.

Black eyes and a full mustache that matched his hair suggested the look of a pirate. Lately, he was given to an occasional quirk of his eyebrows at the mirror, in mockery of his infatuation with the lovely Maria.

Guiseppe sighed. Fear for Marcus, Maria and all those who stood in peril hovered over him. Still, his last thought before sleep overtook him was of the way her lashes cast shadows on her face and the sparkle in Maria's eyes when she smiled.

On the night of July ninth the Allies began their invasion of Sicily, on the south and east coasts of the island. Neither the winds nor the waters were cooperative with the invading forces. Some of the gliders were blown off course in the darkness, and many of the English paratroopers were dropped far from their targeted areas. A number of the planes were lost at sea.

Even though most of the scattered English soldiers were not where they had planned to be, they were effective in interrupting some communications lines, while others attacked patrols and created disruption in any way they could. While they were unable to provide a front line for the incoming soldiers on the beaches as planned, they did everything possible to create diversions.

Resistance to the invaders was little more than half-hearted at the beginning of the landing. Much of the Italian forces along the coast laid down their arms, and the British entered Syracuse with brief opposition. The American troops were confronted with only a bit more conflict in that area. By the end of the first day of the operation, the tenth of July, a beachhead was established. The invasion of Sicily had begun.

The sound of artillery could be heard for miles along the coast and inland, announcing the arrival of, depending upon the perspective, invaders or liberators. In Messina and the surrounding countryside, German and Italian forces came down hard on suspected resisters. Many were detained, some were taken prisoner and some were executed. Again, rumors abounded.

Word came to Guiseppe and Marcus to go to the cave late on the night of July twelfth, but to use extreme caution. Grateful for the hard work that kept him strong, Guiseppe arrived before Marcus. Only four of their number waited inside the cavern.

The same spokesman from the previous gathering spoke softly in the darkness. "We have rescued two paratroopers," he whispered. "They landed less than a mile apart, one on the farm of Pietro, the sheepherder. The other landed near the quarry closer to Etna. They are hidden in Pietro's sheepcote, not very pleasant, but safe for the moment."

"How long can we hide them?" Maria asked.

"Hopefully until their units come north or we can smuggle them south to the advancing line."

"Marcus and I could bring them into our home on the hillside," Guiseppe volunteered. He felt the presence of his son.

"Papa, are you sure?"

"We are above the village, and our house is surrounded by the vineyard and many trees and bushes that grow a good kilometer up the hill behind it."

"There are patrols and people who are more afraid of the Germans than of the English and Americans. They would turn you in without a qualm," the leader told them.

"If you can bring them to us, we will keep them safe," Guiseppe stated.

"Let's do it." Maria's voice rang with confidence. "I will bring them, but it will take at least two nights. Neither of them speaks Italian. I cannot claim them as relatives and risk having them questioned."

"How long before the Allies reach Messina?" Marcus asked.

"Several weeks. The British are coming up from Augusta on the east coast, and the Americans are advancing upward from Gela. The Hermann Goering division is hitting them hard, but they can't stop them." Satisfaction filled the voice of the unnamed Resistance leader.

At three o'clock in the morning, two nights later, Guiseppe opened the back door of his house and allowed four shadowy figures to come inside. All the windows were covered, and the only light was a single oil lamp that glowed softly in a back hallway. Quickly, Guiseppe pulled up a door in the kitchen floor and led the two English soldiers down stairs carved from stone, to the cellar.

He located a lamp and lit it before he extended his hand to his guests. Dressed in clothing supplied by their first host, the men could have blended well in a local crowd. Nothing about them would have drawn attention. An abrasion discolored the cheek of the taller man, but a three-day's growth of beard already partially covered it.

Guiseppe indicated two cots against a wall. A table along another wall held a wooden water bucket and dipper. A cloth covered a loaf of sliced bread and a wedge of cheese. Behind a makeshift curtain was a chamber pot, since, like most houses in the community, the Donatelli residence had no plumbing.

"*Grazi, grazi,*" whispered both men. Apparently they had picked up a few Italian words and phrases. Guiseppe nodded his head and went upstairs, where Maria and her companion waited.

"We must go," Maria whispered. "We have no reason to be here, and our presence tomorrow would make people wonder." She held out her hand to Guiseppe, who covered it with both of his. Only inches shorter than he, she looked into his eyes. Before he could stop himself, Guiseppe brought her close to his body and kissed one smooth cheek, then the other.

Shocked at his own audacity, he expected her to stiffen and pull away, but she did not. She brought up her arms and wrapped them briefly around his waist before she stepped away. Again she looked into his eyes, and she smiled. She and the other man slipped from the house and disappeared into the early morning darkness.

Guiseppe spent the rest of the night in a chair, for he could not sleep. Every natural night noise was a challenge to his heightened awareness of danger to himself and his guests, but the main reason for his sleeplessness was the memory of Maria's warm body, so tantalizingly close to his own.

In the days that followed, additional British and American soldiers were found and rescued by the underground. Not all were so fortunate. Others were captured and interrogated by German patrols. They fared better than the four Sicilians intercepted on a mission from the hills of Messina to the advancing line of Americans near Catania. Questioned and tortured, they were summarily executed, as an example.

Guiseppe continued to work his vineyards by day, carrying on his normal routine. He managed to spend an hour or so a few evenings every week at the tavern with his friends. The only discordant note he could discern was the appearance of Vincenzo Grazia, who often sat at a table with his son, Mario.

The self-proclaimed land baron still coveted the coastal land owned by Dominic Corelli, Luigi's father-in-law. Since the death of Dominic's son, Vincenzo had rarely socialized with the people of the village. Rather, he kept company with the more affluent residents of Messina, affecting a higher social status than he possessed.

His sudden overtures of apparent friendliness couldn't hide the disdain he felt toward the men in the tavern. With the first appearance of the man, Guiseppe suspected he was an informer, for in his heart, he knew that Vincenzo was a murderer.

On the paratroopers' seventh night in Guiseppe's cellar, Maria rapped softly three times, paused and rapped twice more on the back door. It was late, near midnight, but neither Guiseppe nor Marcus slept. Quickly they took Maria inside. She removed her dark shawl and shook out her hair. She didn't smile.

"We've got to move the men tonight," she said. "The Americans are nearing Palermo, and the English are advancing on either side of Etna. We have people waiting a few miles west of the caves. They will guide the men to the west of Etna and leave them with others, nearer the front lines.

"The fighting is brutal there now, and they'll need every able-bodied man they can find. Our contacts tell us there are hundreds of casualties on both sides."

"Marcus, bring them up," Guiseppe ordered. "Be sure they take with them everything they brought." He shoved aside the woven rug and pulled up the cellar door. He and Maria gathered and wrapped bread, cheese and roasted lamb in two packets. "How much time will it take to reach the first post?" he asked.

"Three hours, possibly four, if patrols are diligent," she replied.

"I'm coming with you," Guiseppe told her.

"No." Maria shook her head.

"I'm coming with you."

Maria shook her head again and opened her mouth to protest. Guisepped leaned toward her and stopped her words with an unplanned, passionate kiss. "I'm coming with you." Stunned, Maria stared into his eyes. She took a deep breath.

"It will be dangerous," she whispered.

"I know. It will be nearing dawn before you reach your people. I cannot let you go alone." Amazed at himself, Guiseppe touched her cheek. She turned her face into his hand, lightly touched his fingers with her mouth. She moved away as Marcus and the two soldiers came up the stairs and into the kitchen. Still dressed as rural Sicilians, they pulled the soft caps low on their foreheads and expressed thanks in both languages.

"Be careful, Papa," Marcus whispered. Guiseppe opened his jacket enough to display the gun and the dagger, both of which he carried with him constantly. He closed the door, and the four stepped into darkness.

No moon touched the sky, but the blackness was dotted with millions of stars. Guiseppe led the way upward, through the massive olive trees, along the edge of the vineyard and well above the sight of houses below before he relaxed, even a little. No one spoke, and every eye was vigilant.

Near the caves, Maria veered west, bent slightly to the south. After two hours, they stopped to rest in a wooded area, where a trickle of water fell down a rocky slope and splashed softly into a small pool. Brush and saplings grew over lava beds, some ancient and crumbled, some newer but still old, remnants of eruptions from Mount Etna, many miles away.

After a brief rest, the travelers continued their wary way. Already in the foothills of the Caronie Mountains, the path became more rugged and hazardous as they progressed. For another hour they trudged upward.

At the sound of a birdcall, Maria stopped and listened for several moments. She cupped her hands around her mouth and echoed the sound once, twice. Two figures emerged silently from the shadows and indicated that the paratroopers should follow them.

"Go quietly," one whispered to Maria. "Civilian spies are in the hills, and there are scattered patrols. If we hurry, we can reach the next stop before dawn." He shifted the rifle, slung on one shoulder. With a slight wave of his hand, he turned. Guiseppe and Maria watched the night swallow their British charges.

As one, they turned; but instead of retracing their steps, Maria moved north of their previous route. Guiseppe knew the woman had to be tired, but she crossed the rugged terrain as if she had not already walked over three hours.

"Halt!" The harsh, Italian command came from slightly above them.

Adrenalin surged through Guiseppe's body in a painful rush. The hair on the back of his neck lifted, and he knew the primal fear and lust for survival. He sensed Maria stiffen beside him. In the darkness, he moved slightly forward, hoping to put himself between Maria and the gunman.

"Where are the others?" the voice demanded.

"There are no others," Guiseppe answered, "just my wife and myself."

"Imbecile! We saw you and two others on the track just south of here not half-an-hour ago!" Against the subtle change of light before dawn, Guiseppe could see the single man and his rifle, aimed at Maria and himself.

Feeling with his foot for solid rock, Guiseppe, shifted his weight a fraction. Close to his side, Maria moved her revolver into position. Guiseppe clutched her wrist in warning, tightly enough to stop her from raising the weapon.

"You must have seen someone else," Guiseppe contined. "My wife and I rose early to go to market in Messina. Sir, we still have a long way to go, with your permission." He released Maria's wrist and extended both his hands in apparent supplication. The soldier laughed, and he dropped the barrel of his rifle a few inches.

It was enough. Guiseppe hurled the German dagger and struck the man in the center of his chest. In slow motion, with only the sound of falling rock, the soldier fell. Guiseppe grabbed the rifle in midair and scurried down the slope where the man's body came to rest against a huge boulder.

Carefully, he ascertained that the man was dead. He pulled his dagger from the lifeless body. He looked for and took possession of additional ammunition before he wiped the bloody blade on the man's uniform.

"Let's go," he whispered.

"There's a cave about a kilometer ahead," she told Guiseppe. "We can hide there." They moved as quickly as they dared, constantly on guard against the possibility of additional patrol, who would be looking for their comrade.

They were upon the cave before Guiseppe saw the slit in the rocks. On first glance, it appeared to be nothing but a shadow cast by a tall pillar in the rosy haze of dawn. Maria slipped through easily, but it was a tighter squeeze for Guiseppe.

Maria led the way deeper into the cave. She didn't stop until she rounded a bend that hid them from the entrance. With a long sigh, she dropped her canvas bag and coat to the earthen floor. "We can rest for awhile, until the sun is higher in the sky." Without another word, she curled upon the coat, draped her heavy shawl across her shoulders and closed her eyes. Guiseppe peered into the depths beyond, but it was impossible to see in the narrow, dark interior.

He leaned against the hard surface, near Maria, and slipped the Luger from its case. He slid down the wall and placed the gun near his right hand. He shifted his body into as comfortable a position as possible. Alternately, he watched Maria and the faint light from the cave's entrance, until his eyes grew so heavy he could no longer hold them open.

"Guiseppe. Guiseppe, wake up." Although Maria whispered, Guiseppe woke instantly. "It's later than I hoped. We should go."

Guiseppe had never felt more awake or more alive. He could smell the tangle of aromas that was Maria: the outdoorsy, clean sweat; the lingering fragrance of newly washed hair; the woman scent, uniquely her own. Other than of the war and their work, they had exchanged no words. No endearments or passionate phrases had passed their lips. Yet, no words were needed to describe what hovered in the air between them.

Later, Guiseppe could not say who moved first or if they moved upon the same thought. He knew only that Maria was suddenly in his arms, and their mouths clung together, as if they drew life from each other. He knew he was a man, more of a man than he had ever been; and the woman beneath, over and around him was the only woman in the world. There was no yesterday or tomorrow; there was only now, the cave and Maria....

They woke in each other's arms. Maria's head fit perfectly beneath Guiseppe's chin, her cheek against his chest; his right arm protectively around her body. Neither knew whose heart they heard beating. With his right hand, Guiseppe drew Maria's shawl around them. Sunlight streamed into the cave's narrow opening, but an underground chill lingered in the air.

"We must go," Maria repeated; but she didn't move.

"I know." Guiseppe agreed.

"It must be noon or later," she said.

"I know. What is your name?" he asked.

"Maria Paglia."

"Guiseppe?" Maria raised her head and looked into his eyes.

"Yes?"

"Nothing," she whispered, "just Guiseppe." She sighed his name.

A rush of tenderness, such as he had never known, swept through him. His soul sang with love for the woman who fit so perfectly in his arms. She tightened her hold on him, and he felt her tears on his chest. He understood them.

When they finally left the haven of the cave, twilight approached. Guiseppe tenderly removed a small twig from Maria's hair. Hand in hand, they headed east, toward Messina and the completion of their dangerous mission. They did not speak of their encounter with the enemy.

They held hands as they left behind them the maze of caves high above Guiseppe's village. A faint light flickered in one window of his house. Other lights dotted the lower slopes that led to the main thoroughfare. The quietude and apparent calm of the valley belied the battles that raged only miles away.

The sound of a single gunshot shattered the peaceful night and echoed from hillside to hillside. Stunned, Guiseppe and Maria froze, not knowing the source of the gunfire.

Guiseppe stared across the vineyard at his house, and he saw someone run from the front courtyard. He tore along the rows of grapevines, down the slanting path toward the back of his house. He saw no one.

"Marcus!" he called. Maria reached his side as he pushed open the back door. "Marcus!" In a crumpled, bloody heap near the kitchen door lay Guiseppe's younger son. "Marcus! Marcus!" he cried. He gathered him into his arms and cradled him as he had done when the young man was a boy.

"Papa?" Marcus seemed bewildered. "Papa? I thought—it was you—at the door. Papa? Papa?" He struggled for breath.

"Shhhh, Marcus. Don't talk. Maria, go get help!" Maria turned toward the door.

"No, Papa. He knows—Papa, he knows."

"Who knows, My Son?" Guiseppe was unaware of the tears that fell down his face.

"Vincenzo knows—the resistance—Papa, he meant to—kill you. Papa—Papa, Grazia—shot me. Vincenzo—Grazia..." A long, gentle sigh followed the boy's last words.

"No-o-o-o!" Guiseppe cried. "Marcus! Marcus, my son!" He clutched Marcus fiercely to his chest and rocked back and forth in agony. Maria dropped beside him and wrapped her arms around both of them. The blood of the man on the rocky slopes and the blood of the boy on the stone floor mingled with the spilled blood and the millions of tears shed upon the island of Sicily. Such was the day and the night that began Guiseppe's personal war.

A Mass of Christian Burial for Marcus was held in the church where, for generations, the Donatelli's had been baptized, wed and eulogized. Stoic and grim, Guiseppe witnessed the ritual with no other family member present. The war prevented Luigi and his family from returning to Sicily, for which Guiseppe was grateful. He could not let himself be distracted from the task ahead of him.

He forbade Maria to attend. She was unknown in the town, and Guiseppe wanted to prevent any idle talk or speculation about the two of them. She followed his wishes, but she came to him in the darkness two weeks after Marcus was killed.

"What are you going to do, Guiseppe?"

"I'm going to kill the bastard that murdered my son." Guiseppe's words, spoken softly and matter-of-factly, were as solemn as any vow. "I've told no one what Marcus said before he died. Vincenzo has no idea we are aware of his collaboration with the Germans. Let him watch me and think he toys with me."

"I will help you," Maria told him. "Together we will bring him and his supporters down." Guiseppe did not try to dissuade her.

Life continued much as it had. The British approached Messina, and the Americans pushed through western and central Sicily. Guiseppe and Maria were able to slip away from the watchful eyes of Grazia's spies to aid three more airmen, one via the previous route, the other two through the more treacherous, populated area south of Messina.

To Guiseppe's dismay, he returned to learn that his daughter-in-law's family had been arrested and taken away from their villa, in a beautiful section of Messina. No one seemed to know what had become of them, but it was soon learned that Vincenzo Grazia had been deeded their city holdings and the coastal property he had coveted for so many years. The cold rage inside Guiseppe burned icy hot.

During the first week of August, fierce battles continued between the two forces. The final assault on Messina drew near. Guiseppe's comrades took outrageous chances, seemingly fearless in their efforts to steal more ammunitions and explosives from German supply depots throughout the city.

Often disguised as a boy, Maria moved through the shops and bakeries where Germans patrolled. Under their very noses, she managed to lift clothing, food and whatever she saw that would assist her cause. She didn't enter the same place twice, so she never raised suspicion.

Toward the end of that final week, frantic Italians and many Germans, who were of the opinion that discretion is the better part of valor, took any means of crossing the strait onto the mainland of Italy. Some Italian troops laid down their weapons and surrendered to the Allies, disheartened by the defection of many German troops and officers.

On the final day of the Battle for Sicily, Allied tanks and trucks preceded the hundreds of foot soldiers into the streets of Messina. For the most part they were greeted with cheers and shouts of joyful liberation and victory. That night, Guiseppe and Maria entered the town, openly together. A curfew had been announced, but evasion was no problem for the two freedom fighters.

Carrying the gun and dagger that had been his constant companions for weeks, Guiseppe led the way to the home of Vincenzo Grazia. The wrought iron gate that connected the high fence around the grounds had been destroyed, but lights shown in the upper windows of the impressive villa. Not everyone had deserted the house.

Getting inside was no problem for Guiseppe and Maria. Silently they determined that the lower floor was empty. They mounted the winding staircase to the upper story and followed the sounds of occupancy that came from a single room. Guiseppe peered around the open door.

Frantically throwing items into a large bag, Vincenzo Grazia, a thin, swarthy-skinned man with graying hair and stooped shoulders took no notice of the shadow that crossed the doorway. "I'm not quite ready," he said, without looking up. "I'll ring when I want you."

Guiseppe, gun in hand, stood full in the doorway. "That won't be necessary. I'm already here." Vincenzo's head jerked upward, and his face paled. Guiseppe entered the room, Maria slightly behind him. The little man's eyes darted from side to side, as if looking for assistance.

"No one is coming, Vincenzo. Your man ran when he saw me, almost as if he knew why I'm here." Guiseppe stepped into the room; and in the same moment, Grazia reached into the bag. The sound of the discharging Luger reverberated around the room.

With a scream of pain, Grazia dropped his weapon onto the desk, grabbed his left shoulder and staggered against the wall. "Don't kill me! There! There's a bag full of money, not just paper, but gold and silver! Take it! Take it all! Just don't kill me!" Guiseppe took two more steps into the room, Maria at his side.

"You killed my son. You destroyed the Corelli family. You surely don't think I will let you live." There was no mistaking Guiseppe's intent. Grazia slowly dropped his right arm, in apparent defeat. He dropped his head, and Guiseppe lowered his gun just a fraction.

"Look out!" Maria cried. In a split second, Grazia picked up his fallen pistol and fired in the same instant as Guiseppe. Grazia fell across the desk, a bullet in his head.

"I made it too easy for him," Guiseppe said. He stepped closer to the desk. "Look, Maria. The fool really thought he could pay for my son with money." There was no answer. "Maria?" He turned. "Maria!" She slid slowly down the wall, leaving a trail of blood as she fell.

"I think he shot me, Guiseppe," she said. Maria held her hand over her left side "Perhaps you should find a doctor."

The next few days were glorious for some, tragic for others, memorable for all of Messina and the people of Sicily. The battle for the island was over, and the Allies were victorious. They followed the retreating Germans and sporadic Italians across the strait and into Italy, where battles would rage for many months to come.

Guiseppe managed to get Maria to a hospital, where she remained for several days, slowly recovering from the gunshot wound. He would never forget the paralyzing terror he felt when he saw her on the floor of Vincenzo's bedroom. It haunted his dreams while she recovered.

He tried to pick up his life without Marcus. The sweet girl the boy had planned to marry grieved with Guiseppe, until he told her to get on with her life. As youth does, she did. Guiseppe worked in his vineyard from dawn until the sun faded, counting the days until Maria could be with him.

On the day she was to be released, he hired a car to pick her up. They had to park behind the hospital and wait for clearance before he could go to her room, which he found empty. He stopped one of the long-gowned nuns and asked where he would find Maria Paglia.

"Are you Mr. Donatelli?" she asked.

"I am."

"She asked me to give this to you. She said you would understand." The woman nodded to him, folded her hands inside her long sleeves and walked away. Guiseppe dropped onto a hard bench in the hallway and opened the envelope. Inside was a single page. His hands shook as he opened it.

"My Darling,

There is still much to be done before our part of the world is free. You are a man of honor, and you have a fine home and vineyard to care for. Sicily is free now, and so are you. You have another son who may come home someday, so you need to stay safe for him and for your grandsons.

I have no one who depends on me, Guiseppe. I know you will understand why I have to go where I can still aid the Resistance. One day we will win, and I will come to you, if God wills and I am able. Stay well, my darling Guiseppe. I thank God for you and I thank Him that you have loved me, if only for a little while.

Think of me and say a prayer for your
Maria."

The war raged on for another two years. Three letters from Maria came to Guiseppe in those years, and then there were no more. In his heart, he knew that she could never return to him. He worked hard, as he had always done. There were many widows who wanted to make a home with him, but Guiseppe's heart belonged to only one woman.

Her name was Maria....

✳ ✳ ✳

When Guiseppe stopped talking the last night we recorded, I sat, stunned, while tears ran down my face. I could hardly bear to look at the man, afraid that I would find him in tears, too. I shouldn't have worried.

"Oh, Guiseppe, I'm so sorry you lost your Maria," I told him. The old man smiled at me.

"Dear Child, I did not lose her. She is always here," he tapped his chest, "in my heart. It took me awhile to understand that she didn't leave *me*. She left to follow her destiny, to help assure that freedom would come to all of Italy, not just our island. She gave to me the most precious thing I ever had, aside from my sons. She gave me herself."

While I looked at the old man in his chair, something seemed to shimmer around him. For a moment I saw him as Maria must have seen him: strong, virile, ruggedly handsome in the autumn of his life, with black eyes that sparkled and strong arms to hold her. The illusion faded. I stood and collected the recorder and tapes.

"What are you going to do with my life?" he asked.

"It will take me some time to compile and correlate everything," I told him. "I'll let you read it before I sign a contract for it. I'll share with you whatever I am paid."

Guiseppe waved his hand, a gesture I had come to know. "Nonsense," he said. "I lived it. I need nothing for that. If you can sell any of it, take the payment with my blessing. Wait! I have photographs to show you." He gestured toward a heavy, tall cabinet. "Bring to me the things in the second drawer."

I did as he said. Inside the drawer were some very old albums and envelopes stuffed with faded pictures. Guiseppe took the albums from me and spread them across his knees. He scattered the loose pictures over the albums, selected one and handed it to me.

A small boy stood in front of what looked like a heavy stone or marble building in the background. His hand reached upwards to touch the mane of a stone lion that rested on a platform, also made of stone. I peered at it closely. Impossibly, the background and lion seemed familiar to me.

"Where was this taken?" I asked, "and who is the boy?"

"I am the boy. The picture was taken in Naples, when my father took me there to visit relatives, all long dead now. I forget the name of the building, but it was a huge thing, built hundreds of years ago. Here are others."

Guiseppe handed more pictures to me. They were very old, but remarkably sharp in detail. Beside the same lion, the little boy, Guiseppe, stood in front of an older man. "My papa," he said. Again, I had a sense of having seen the lion before. Excitement flooded through me.

"I've seen this lion!" I told him. "My father sent home pictures from Italy when he was in the war. There are some of him and his buddies sitting on this lion or one similar to it. No, I'm sure it's the same one!" I shuffled through the photographs, and I found more of the building, taken from different angles. Additional stone lions guarded the front steps of the tall, ornamented edifice. Again, I picked up the picture of the boy, Guiseppe.

"You may take that one, if you wish," he told me. My eyes flew to his face.

"Really? You would let me take it? What about your family? Shouldn't they have it?"

He shrugged. "There are many," he said. "They will not miss one."

I leaned across the albums on his lap and hugged him. I would never forget how he smelled, how frail his shoulders felt beneath my arms or how he wrapped his arms around me and hugged me back.

It was several weeks before I completed Guiseppe's story. When it was finished, I looked at the stack of typed pages and knew it was the best writing I had ever done. I submitted it to the top newspapers in the city; and when an acceptance came from the New York Times, I was elated, but not surprised. I *knew* that the story was good. They wanted to run it in the Features section.

After work the next evening, I went by Luigi's to tell him my wonderful news. Autumn approached the city, and a chill lingered in the air. I pressed the buzzer twice, but no one responded. The restaurant was closed and deserted. Disappointed, I hailed a cab, suddenly cold in the late afternoon.

The next morning, instead of walking to work, I again took a taxi to Luigi's. It was only the middle of September, but I could see my breath in the early morning air. From inside the cab, it was apparent that Luigi's was not open. On the door was a large white poster with black letters: DEATH IN THE FAMILY – CLOSED UNTIL FURTHER NOTICE.

I told the driver to take me to Streetside. I felt such a sense of loss; for in my heart, I knew that Guiseppe would never see his beloved hillside winery again. I had grown to care about him. His strong sense of family, of loyalty to his native country and his constant devotion to a woman long gone had captured my imagination and my heart.

From the office, I made some calls; and I learned that Guiseppe Donatelli had passed away peacefully in his sleep two nights previously. There would be no wake locally. Guiseppe's body would be returned to Sicily for burial next to his wife, Anna, and Marcus, their younger son.

In the phonebook, I found Carlo's business, Italian Custom Tile and Marble. I called and was told that Carlo had left the country on family business. Dejected, I gave up. I would be unable to contact the family to offer my condolences or to tell them about Guiseppe's story. It was to be featured in the Sunday issue of The New York Times in two weeks.

Several times during the next two weeks, I intercepted veiled, mysterious glances from my boss. I had been subdued; but I finished my work, done well and on time. I suspected he was angry with me for not giving Guiseppe's story to him, which I would have done, had it been turned down by more prestigious markets. I had to tell him about the Times acceptance. I couldn't just let him read it in the paper with no warning.

When the story appeared, I was overwhelmed with the response. I got calls from reporters wanting to do interviews with me and with the subjects in the story. There was a call from a movie producer who wanted to turn Guiseppe's war story into a film. I finally left the phone in my apartment disconnected.

When the offer to become a regular feature writer for the New York Times came to me, I took it. I would have been a fool not to. Even Dirk, my giant of a boss, congratulated me; and the staff of Streetside threw a party for me.

On a cold October Saturday, I moved to a brownstone on a side street not far from the Times offices. I loved the old brick building with it's restored original floors and woodwork, the narrow stained glass panel that cast beautiful color on my living room wall and the claw-footed tub in the bathroom.

The only sour note in the music of my new life was my longing for a sandwich from Luigi's. One day at lunchtime I took a cab across town to Luigi's. The ride cost a lot more than my meal. I waited in line, ready to give my order and to ask for news of the family.

"Next." Carmen looked at me as if she had never seen me.

"Hi, Carmen. I want one of those wonderful Italian subs and a large coffee. It's so good to see you! I'm sorry I couldn't reach anyone when Guiseppe...."

"Move on down, please. Next!"

I swallowed my words and moved in line toward the cashier. Luigi handed the wrapped sandwich and coffee to me, told me the cost and gave me my change, all without looking at me one time. Feeling as shunned as a wayward Amish girl, I took my food and left the building.

It was too cold to eat outdoors, so I hailed another taxi and headed back to my new office. I ate a few bites in the car, but I had lost my appetite. I dropped the sandwich into a trashcan on the street and took the coffee with me inside the building.

Late that evening, I answered the telephone, wondering who would call past ten o'clock. "Ms McCoy, this is Carlo Donatelli."

"Oh, Carlo, I'm so glad you called!"

"Are you? I think you will change your mind." His voice was icy. I could hear in his voice nothing of the man who had once kissed me. "Just so there is no misunderstanding, my family wants you to stay away from Luigi's. I wish you had let some one of us, any of us, read that article you sold to the Times. We would have dissuaded you."

"But, Carlo, your grandfather gave me permission to write and to sell it. It was the last conversation we had," I told him. I could hear the plea in my voice, and I didn't like it. I felt that I was being judged unfairly.

"*Listen to me!*" Carlo shouted. "You should not have included the names of my grandfather and the people in his village! That story has put our whole family in peril! In Little Italy there are many Sicilians, some from my grandfather's country, relatives of the man, *you announced to the world, he killed*!

"Ricci has received a death threat with his morning paper. The tires of Johnnie's car have been slashed twice, and the windows of my store display have been shattered. Your ignorance has put us in the middle of a vendetta, and I don't know what the outcome will be! Just stay away from all of us! Do you understand me?"

The phone went dead. I stood there, the dial tone loud in my ear. My heart beat in my throat so hard I couldn't swallow. My knees went weak, and I sank into the nearest chair. Surely Carlo was wrong! How was it possible that a story meant to give honor to a good man could be the beginning of a bloody vendetta against innocent people?

I would ask myself that question for weeks before I got any peace. I kept remembering how I had not pursued the story of Lawrence, the murderous violinist. In my hope to protect his ignorant mother, I had remained silent about his presence and his guilty secret.

Now, in my pride and passion about another man's past, I had unwittingly caused harm, potentially deadly harm, to his descendants. I began to look at my choice of careers with new eyes. I realized the power I wielded with my fingers on the typewriter keys. My motives had been pure, in that I wanted the world to recognize and give honor to a good man, a hero. I hadn't taken the time to count the cost.

From that point on, I looked at all aspects of any story I researched, wrote or reported. I realized that the story was important, but it was only one part of a journalist's purpose. Without considering the human element or the possible effects on the subjects of a story, the journalist dishonors his profession and him/herself. That form of reporting is simply gossip, promoted by egotistic seekers of fame, who cloak themselves in robes of pseudo professionalism.

The next time I went back to my mother's house, I took the photo of Guiseppe with me. I found the album filled with my dad's war pictures, and there it was: the same lion, in pictures taken decades apart. Where Guiseppe's little hand reached to touch the lion's mane, my father leaned against the lion; and his arm fell loosely across its head. His hand rested downward and touched the same spot where Guiseppe's reached upward.

Someone has said that there are no accidents and no coincidences. I don't pretend to know if it's true, but one thing I know: I believe that my meeting with Guiseppe Donatelli occurred for a reason, although I may never completely understand what it is.

I had a copy made of my dad's photo with the stone lion in Naples, and I framed it with the photo of Guiseppe. I look at it often, to remind me that all men who fight for the right principles are connected to each other, that their hearts beat with the same determination to protect the people and the land they love.

Different men, different nationalities, different races, different times.

One brotherhood.

Secrets

M^y first year at the New York Times taught me more about good journalism and cutthroat reporters than all my previous writing years together. The publication employed dozens of people in one capacity or another. As the new kid on the block, I often received some less than challenging assignments; but I did my best on all of them.

I moved into a building closer to the Times offices. For a fee, I could park the Corvette in a nearby underground lot. The apartment, one of many in a renovated brownstone, offered fewer square feet, but was more expensive. Even so, my increased salary more than met my obligations; and I was able to put aside a little money each month. I free-lanced work, too, which took up a lot of my evenings. Occasionally, I went out to dinner with my friends; and we saw some wonderful Broadway shows.

After several months, I stopped perusing the newspapers for unexplained deaths or accidents that involved the Donatelli family. I respected their wishes and never went back to Luigi's Deli. The fact that people I liked and admired had cut me from their lives hurt. At times, I felt as if an inexplicable cloud hovered above me; and then I would remember why.

Eventually, they crossed my mind less and less. I had to accept that I could not change the way the family felt. Nor could I change the circumstances. I stopped berating myself for selling a good story, one of which I was very proud. I thought that Guiseppi would have been proud, too.

In mid-October of that year, nearly to the day I moved from the Bellamy Apartment Building, I received a call from my mother. She chitchatted for a few minutes, but I knew from the tone of her voice she had called for a definite reason.

"What's wrong, Mom?" I asked.

"Well, I'd like to ask a favor of you, Sissy; but I don't want you to feel like you have to do it. I'll understand if you can't."

"Just tell me, Mom."

"Lucy Hanson, my best friend when I was a girl in Missouri, has breast cancer. Evidently, Lucy's cousin has corresponded with my sister all these years. Anyway, Lucy has returned to the Doniphan area; and she wants to see me. She's had both breasts removed, and the doctors have told her that she has only a few weeks to live." My mother took a deep breath.

"I'm sorry, Mom. How can I help?"

"Well...I hadn't told you, but Russell has developed macular degeneration in his eyes. He can't drive."

"Oh, Mom, that's awful!"

"Yes, but that's not why I'm calling, Sissy." She hesitated again. "Honey, is there any chance you could come home and drive me back to Missouri? I'd pay all your expenses and everything. I thought about taking a bus, but then I'd have no way to get around after I got there; and I'm not comfortable driving that distance alone."

I didn't know what to say. Fortunately, I had been with the Times long enough to have a vacation coming. I would approach my superior with the possibility of looking for a story while I was gone. It couldn't hurt.

"When do you want to go, Mom?"

"As soon as possible. Lucy doesn't have much time."

"I don't know how quickly I can get away, but I'll talk to my boss today and see if I can put in for vacation time soon. I'll call you tonight."

"Thanks, Honey. If you can't, don't worry about it. I can always just call Lucy. It won't be like seeing her, face to face; but it would be better than nothing." Whether or not my mother meant to induce guilt had no bearing on the fact that the guilt hit its mark, as surely as if I wore a target.

"Maybe you can find a story among the natives." I grinned ruefully at the woman who gave me assignments. Jennifer Lansing, a tall no-nonsense woman with shoulder-length brown hair, looked at me over her tortoise shell-rimmed glasses. She assured me that the paper could function quite well during my absence, and she suggested that I should search out some local color.

"Would you really run a Missouri story on the pages of the Times?" I asked.

Jennifer shrugged. She took a handful of colorful jellybeans from the wide-mouthed jar on her desk and popped several of them into her mouth. "If I liked it," she said, "and if the story had universal appeal."

"I'll see what I can do," I told her. I had already begun to kick around a few possibilities in my head.

Fall colors in New York State were at their peak when I drove out of the city early on the following Wednesday. All the way to Dixon, I traveled upon highways that were bordered by mountains, hills, rolling slopes and fields of multicolored trees and foliage in every autumnal shade imaginable.

By the time I turned off Symington late that evening, my fingers itched to take up paintbrushes and splash some color onto a canvas, something I hadn't done for a long time. The muse, however, would have to wait. I hoped it wouldn't die of old age.

My mother met me at the door. I put my overnight bag beside the staircase and returned her hearty embrace. A few additional pounds had accumulated upon her once-svelte figure; but at the age of nearly fifty-three, she was still a lovely woman.

"Are you tired, Honey?"

"I'm fine, Mom; but I'm hungry." I picked up the bag and started up the stairs.

"I'll make a sandwich for you," my mother called.

"That would be nice, Mom," I yelled back. "I'll be down in a few minutes." I had spent two nights in my old room the previous December, not long, but long enough to recover the comfortable feeling that old, familiar, dear things wrought.

Quickly, I washed my hands in the bathroom that my brother and I once shared. I hurried down the stairs and into the kitchen to find the warm meatloaf sandwich just as I liked it, smothered with Miracle Whip, onion and tomato. It tasted like home.

I yawned ostentatiously and bid my mother and stepfather an early good night. I was tired. The usual evening rituals occupied my mind until I crawled into bed. I read for a while from one of the half-dozen paperback books I'd brought with me. After reading the same paragraph three times, I gave up and turned out the light. Even after the muted sounds of the television ceased and the last rush of water through the pipes had stilled, I lay awake. Though tired, I was caught up with the memories of home.

By nine o'clock the next morning, my mother and I bid Russell good-bye; and we were on our way back to Missouri. I left the Corvette in her driveway, and we drove Russell's big green Chevrolet. He could no longer drive either of them. The Chevy had ample room for our luggage, as well as being easier to enter and exit. For about fifty miles Mom fretted about leaving her husband; but then her thoughts turned to new photos of her four grandchildren.

To my delight, Mom carried with her new photographs of Beth's little girl, Kathleen Suzanne. The little charmer was already two years old, and I had seen her only twice. The width of the nation separated my sister and me, so we saw each other only at Christmas. Telephone calls, which were many, could never take the place of watching, up close and personal, the amazing transformation of a child from infant to toddler. Beth kept us supplied with current photographs, and Kathy was now able to talk to me on the phone.

The trip with my mother was a first, for we had never traveled, just the two of us. It gave us a chance to concentrate on ourselves, with no interruptions or demands. She asked about my work, and I was able to tell her about a few past assignments and some upcoming ones. I was surprised at the pertinent questions and suggestions she made.

We stopped at rural antique shops and walked through some flea markets. I suggested that we swing south just a bit and drive through Nashville, Tennessee. A fan of country music all her life, she was eager to visit the home of the Grand Ole Opry. We stayed overnight just outside Nashville, and I took her to dinner at the renowned Stockyards restaurant. My mother was like an excited child at the appearance of singer Ernest Tubb, who had come to enjoy a steak.

"I wish I could see the Opry," Mom told me.

"Maybe we can, Mom. Why don't we plan to come back through here on Saturday? I'll call the ticket office and see if we can get tickets." She beamed at the possibility.

When bluegrass icon, Bill Monroe, entered the restaurant, I thought she was going to faint. "Sissy, I can't believe it!" she whispered. "I used to listen to him on the radio when your daddy was overseas! Do you think I could get his autograph?" The woman was shaking with excitement. I laughed.

"Let's wait and see if anyone else approaches him," I suggested. "He might want to eat without being disturbed." I watched the man remove his wide-brimmed white hat and place it on an empty chair at his table. Dressed completely in white, with a mane of white hair, he was the epitome of a southern gentleman, straight from a Tennessee Williams novel.

My mother could scarcely eat her dinner. She sighed with relief when another diner approached the singer and apologetically asked for an autograph, which was graciously given. Mom's blue eyes sparkled like a teenager's. She found a slip of paper in her purse, pushed back her chair and zeroed in on Bill Monroe like a tail gunner in a fighter plane. The man didn't have a chance.

I couldn't believe it when he invited her to sit down, and she did! She left me sitting by myself and ordered dessert at the celebrity's table! I was suddenly in awe of the woman who had given birth to me. She had always been spunky, but I thought she was downright flirtatious with Bill Monroe.

When she rose from his table, he stood and bowed slightly over her outstretched hand. She was so pleased. Her flushed cheeks and the bounce in her step made her look ten years younger.

"Remember me?" I teased.

"Oh, Sissy, he is so *nice*," Mom beamed. On the way back to our motel, she repeated every word the man had said to her. For the moment, the poignant reason for our trip had slipped her mind.

In the upper part of the southern states, as well as the Midwest, October generally offers warm days and cool nights. The second day of our road trip was no exception, for the trees boasted brilliant yellows, oranges, browns and right reds, a spectacular backdrop for the dark green pines and cedars that lined the highways and filled the valleys.

We had followed the splendor from West Virginia to southeastern Missouri; and by the time we reached the boot heel, my mother and I were relaxed and easy in each other's company. I didn't realize how much I needed to get away New York, until I spent a couple of days out of it.

Instead of driving straight to the house where Mom's friend lived, we decided to spend the night in Poplar Bluff, a hilly town about twenty-five miles from Naylor. We checked into a motel on the south side and had an early dinner at a restaurant that promised the best ribs north of Memphis.

By nine o'clock that evening, I had showered, donned pajamas and crawled beneath the sheets. I punched the pillows into my favorite formation and prepared to enjoy another night without the background sounds of the city. Not so my mother. I raised my head to peek at her.

Shiny with Pond's cold cream, her face oozed contentment. Pillows propped behind her, she held an open book on her bent knees. "Russell doesn't like for me to read in bed," she said. "The light keeps him awake. Will the light bother you, Sissy?"

I grinned. "Nope. Read as long as you want," I replied. I squirmed contentedly and closed my eyes. They popped open at a sudden thought. "Mom?"

"Hmmmm?"

"Mom, what about Grandpa Loring? Are you going to see him while we're here?" Complete silence filled the room for the space of several seconds, before her book snapped shut.

"I hadn't planned to."

"Well...do you think maybe we should?" I asked. More silence. "Does Grandpa still live in the same shack? I remember when we drove by there the last time we were down here. I remember Dad saying, 'There's Arthur.' And you said, 'Keep going.' We didn't stop."

With a disgruntled sound, something between a by-word and profanity, something she never used, my mother shut off her light. "I don't want to talk about him, Sissy. Good night." No further conversation took place that night in Room One-forty-three of the Starlight Motel in Poplar Bluff, Missouri.

The next morning brought no mention of my grandfather. We breakfasted, and I turned the car south.

"Where do you plan to stay after you see your friend?" I asked.

"I called Molly before we left, and she wants us to stay at her house."

"She's expecting us, then?"

Mom nodded. I wondered if any of my mother's cousin's children remained in the area. I had heard nothing about any of them for years. I remembered my Uncle Homer and my fear that he would murder us in our sleep the night he had announced he could, if he so chose. As if she knew my thoughts, my mother spoke.

"I haven't heard how Homer is. I suppose Molly might know."

"Mom, there's the turnoff to Doniphan. Would you like to drive through there first?"

"Sure," she said. "Lucy's cousin lives between Doniphan and Naylor, anyway; so it isn't much out of the way." The road wound and unwound, as sinuous as a snake's path. In Doniphan, the Ripley County seat, I turned where my mother told me. Her eyes grew misty when we drove around the courthouse.

"Your dad worked in the three C's camps before we were married, and he helped lay the stonework in the retaining walls around the courthouse. That's where we got our marriage license." I had heard the story before, and Dad had driven us by the courthouse; but this time was different. The stonework he had helped build forty years ago was still there, and he was gone.

We left Doniphan behind and drove the short, curvy distance toward Naylor. A few miles out of town, we approached the village of Oxly. I glanced at my mother. "Would you like to drive through it?"

"Do you mind?"

"No. I'd like to see if I can find the house where Grandma Chinn lived when we rode the train back here to see her." I turned onto one of the graveled streets and drove slowly. There were no more than five or six streets in Oxly, crisscrossed in a small grid.

On the southern most street stood an aged gray building with a high wood porch, stairs at either end. Across the middle of a rusty, screened door, a metal sign advertised orange soda. A vague, faded memory stirred inside my head.

"Mom, I've been inside that old store."

"You remember that?" My mother shook her head. "You were barely two years old!"

"I do. I remember big barrels with stuff in them. Someone held me while they talked to people in the store, and I remember an ice cream cone with two cups, side by side. It was too big for my hands; and some one, Daddy, I think, helped me hold it. Wait a minute! You have a picture of me holding that ice cream cone!"

"Yes, that's where the picture was taken. There was a nickel photo booth inside the store. I can't believe you remember that," Mom smiled. "It was just before we left Missouri. Come to think of it, you weren't quite two years old yet."

"Oh, well. I've always said that I could remember the day I was born," I quipped. My mother laughed.

"I almost believe you!"

I drove up another street, and we found Grandma's house. It looked so small, and the three or four steps up from the sidewalk to the stone path were not at all steep. For just a moment, I fancied that I could see the four-year-old toddler I had been when I had struggled up those steps. They had seemed so tall.

The porch I remembered was still there, but no swing hung from the ceiling. I realized anew what blessings are memories, where flowers remain bright and scented with summer perfume, where loved ones faces are vibrant with life, where laughter never fades. I sent love to my deceased great-grandmother, and we drove out of Oxly. No more than two or three miles down the road, my mother pointed.

"There's Antioch Cemetery. Your grandpa Bannister's house is just about a mile down the road." I glanced at her. Of course, I knew where Grandpa's old house was. Aside from my statement that I remembered the day of my birth, I had no recollections of the inside of the house. I could see Mom's memories in her eyes. "Oh, no!" she exclaimed.

I slowed the car. Where the white farmhouse with the red roof and round attic window had stood was a new, gray and white brick ranch bungalow. I felt a pang of disappointment, both for myself and for my dad and his brothers and sisters who had lived there.

Like my Uncle Sonny, I had secretly nursed the thought of one day buying that house and land. I thought it likely no one in the community gave a hoot that Sissy Bannister had been born in that house. Old timers still referred to it as the old Bannister place, regardless how many different families had owned it during the last thirty-five years. I was glad my dad had not seen the destruction of his boyhood home.

"Oh, I hate that!" my mother declared. "I can still see your dad's mother in her garden, just to the east of the house. She was a good woman, Sissy. She played an old pump organ in the Baptist church for a long time.

"Some kind of conflict erupted there, so she went to a little country Nazarene church, where she also played the organ. No one else could play. She took all her kids to church, and your grandpa went with her, too, for awhile." She laughed. "Your dad and I really didn't like each other much then."

I smiled at her memories. I had heard that particular one many times. Instead of the usual stories told by parents to their children, such as fairy tales and traditional little ditties, my mother told us stories about her childhood and the people who lived in the remote, rural community where she and my dad were born.

Although I met very few of the people in her tales, they became as familiar to me as family members. In time, I knew the names of her school friends more readily than she knew the names of mine.

Sometimes I laughed with her at the antics of her brothers and their friends. Many times I cried at the tragic circumstances she described, for she was born shortly after World War I, during the dreadful influenza epidemic; and there were many tales of woe from that time. Mom never really recovered from the loss of the mother she never knew.

Still talking, my mother hadn't noticed that my mind wandered. I refocused on her words.

"...just down the road from your Grandpa Bannister's house. It burned to the ground a few years ago."

I realized that she was talking about the house where she grew up, a mile straight south of the Bannister house, on a narrow, sometimes graveled road. The soil on this side of Naylor was rocky, the terrain hilly; and anyone who tried to make a living from the poor hillsides had a hard way to go.

Some of the buildings I remembered as a child were gone. Tall trees, a lilac bush or a cluster of perennials, perhaps a well curb, indicated where houses once stood. Broken remnants of a chimney were all that remained of the old Applegate farmhouse, about a mile east of my dad's home place. Pieces of ancient, rusty farm implements, some nearly hidden by tall grass and weeds, had been abandoned, along with the property.

"Turn north at the next road, Sissy." Mom consulted the open letter in her lap. "Lucy says it's the second place on the west side." I followed her directions. Within a few minutes, I pulled off the road and parked in front of the mint green house.

The shotgun style dwelling sat in the center of a small, well-kept yard, enclosed by a wire fence. A tan cocker spaniel ran back and forth along the fence, frantic in his efforts to announce the arrival of strangers. He bared his teeth in an unfriendly snarl, and I decided to wait outside the gate until his owner guaranteed safety.

With that thought, the front door opened. A plump, pleasant-looking woman stepped onto the low porch. "Corky! Stop that! Come here!" The dog barked louder. My mother and I exchanged glances. She was as cautious as I. "Corky!" The woman withdrew something from her pocket and put it to her mouth. A shrill whistle practically pierced our eardrums, and it stopped the dog mid-growl. With a whine of distress, Corky withdrew behind the house.

"Come in, come in! That silly dog just won't mind until I blow this whistle." Our hostess waved us through the gate and up the round concrete stepping-stones to the house. She reached for my mother's hand.

85

"You must be Jackie. Lucy has not stopped telling me tales about the two of you since she learned you were coming." She turned to me. "And you must be Jackie's girl." I nodded. "I'm Hilda Cummings. Well, come on in. Lucy will be thrilled that you've arrived."

I followed my mother inside. The floral interior of the small front room made me blink. Large, white hibiscus-type flowers on a coral background covered the walls. Panels of similar colors in a smaller pattern hung from the windows. The sofa and three upholstered chairs, covered in floral tapestries of varying hues, sat upon an oval, braided rug, formed from rag strips in shades of blues. What should have been a discordant mish-mash was not. The room possessed the charm and warmth of its owner, Miss Hilda Cummings.

"Sit down," she said. "Lucy has been napping, but it's time for her medicine. I'll get her." Hilda bustled down the hall that ran through the length of the house. Mom and I chose chairs across from each other. I watched the anticipation on my mother's face. She fidgeted in her chair, crossed and uncrossed her legs and tapped her fingers nervously on the crocheted doilies that protected the chair arms.

"It's been thirty-five years since Lucy got married and moved from Ripley County," she said. "We were just girls. She started dating Calvin about the time your dad and I were going out." She smiled at her memories. "Lucy and I worked at the canning factory in Naylor, and that's where we got acquainted. We knew each other for less than two years, but she was the best friend I ever had."

"I'd know that voice anywhere."

Mom fairly leapt from her chair. Only a few steps separated her from the frail, fragile woman who leaned on Hilda's arm in the doorway. I watched my mother and her friend embrace. Hilda relinquished her hold on Lucy Hanson and stepped back into the kitchen. I stood quietly and watched the two old friends hold each other at arm's length before they re-embraced.

"Jackie, you don't look much older than when you were eighteen." Lucy's wispy voice gave evidence to how ill she was.

"And you're the same sweet liar you always were!" my mother retorted. They laughed, and I caught a glimpse of the two, fun-loving girls they must have been. For years I had known my parents had lives before I was born, but this was the first flesh-and-blood person from their past who was more than a story to me.

I watched my mother tenderly assist her old friend to the sofa. She sat down beside Lucy, who smiled at me. "I know you're Jackie's daughter," she said. I went to her and held out my hand.

"Yes, I'm Sissy," I said. Lucy laughed softly and took a deep breath.

"Thank goodness, you don't call yourself by the awful name Will and Jackie gave you," she said. She looked at my mother. "Yes, I heard what you named this child, even though I was in Texas when she was born. Lands, Girl, what were you thinking?" I laughed in appreciation, knowing that I had found a kindred spirit. Mom blushed.

"Well, we wanted to honor both our mothers; so we just kind of combined the names and came up with—."

"Don't even say it, Jackie," Lucy commanded. She coughed before she continued. She smiled at me, and I smiled back at the infectious, devilish brown eyes in her wasted face. I could see why my mother held such warm memories of the girl.

"I'm glad to meet you, Mrs. Hanson," I told her. "I'm going to leave you and Mom to catch up, while I take a little sentimental journey of my own. I haven't been here since I was a teenager, but I think I remember the old roads. I'll be back before long, Mom."

"Okay, Honey. Just don't get lost in the boondocks."

"I won't." I turned toward the front door. "Uh, Miss Cummings, will your dog be in the yard?"

"Don't worry, if he is," she called from the kitchen. "He's only upset when people arrive, not when they leave."

I took her at her word and left the yard without being attacked. I turned the car around and headed back the way we'd come. A couple miles down the highway, I turned into the winding lane that led to Antioch cemetery. My last visit to Ripley County had been to attend the funeral of my dad's father, my Grandpa Bannister, who was buried in Antioch. I was fourteen at the time.

For a few minutes, I sat in the car with the windows down. The small, white, Missionary Baptist church on the far west side of the cemetery looked the same as I remembered. A new concrete sidewalk led from the low, single step to the graveled lane. The grounds were deserted in the late October morning.

A moss-covered mausoleum and very old tombstones stood on the north side of the church, among them the graves of my dad's parents and their infant son. I got out of the car and strolled to the Bannister site. As I read Grandpa's name, I could almost smell his cigar and hear his rumble-y chuckle.

I wandered through the cemetery for some time. Many of the names on the stones were familiar to me, although I had never known their owners. Snatches of recalled conversations between my mom and dad held some of those names. I found ancient markers, some so old the engraving was not decipherable. Among the faded ones were those of my great-grandparents, Grandpa Bannister's mother and father, born in the mid-eighteen hundreds.

Nearby, a tall, obelisk stone caught my eye. It held the Bannister name and a short epitaph: "ROBERT – 11 YEARS – FELL ON A PITCHFORK WHILE BALING HAY– 1873." I was struck by the date. One hundred years had passed, and I stood in the exact place where some of my grieving ancestors had stood to mourn the loss of a child. Silence, broken only by the call of birds and the soft whirring of lazy grasshoppers, seemed as eternal as the resting places I honored.

I looked up. Massive oak and hard maple trees, brilliant with fall foliage, cast dappled shade across the thick, green grass. Towering pine trees provided wide areas of brown, pine-needle carpet beneath their low branches. I felt intoxicated by the resin-y scent of ancient cedars that teased the autumn air, hypnotized by the hazy, gauze-like somnolence throughout the grounds.

I glanced at my watch and was surprised at the hour. I hurried down the steep slope to the southwest corner of the cemetery. The grave of my mother's mother was there. I barely remembered it, but it was easy to find. Simple, made of a thin marble slab, her name and dates of birth and death were badly worn on the stone. No more than three or four feet separated her grave from that of Grandpa Loring's third wife, Homer's mother. Her stone was identical to my grandmother's. Something about that didn't seem right.

I glanced at my watch again and hurried up the slope to the car. The crunch of gravel seemed intrusive when I turned the car around. While I had to respond to the call of time and to the needs of others, time had no power in this place; and there were no needs.

My mother dried her tears as we drove away from Miss Hilda Cummings' home. It was a bittersweet time for her. She had been able to reconnect with a dear friend from her youth, but she knew she would never see the woman again. She smiled at me through her tears.

'Thank you for bringing me here, Sissy. I hadn't expected to ever come back."

"You're welcome, Mom. So what do you think? Molly's house, or would you like to drive around the area, see old haunts?"

Mom laughed. "I'm hungry," she said. "Let's see if Naylor has a restaurant."

We ate at the only local watering hole and spent the rest of the day and night at the home of Mom's cousin, Molly. There were lots of "remember when's," and my mother and I shared a bed for the first time since I was a very little girl.

The next morning, we said goodbyes; and I drove toward Poplar Bluff. "Wait, Sissy." My mother placed her hand on my arm. I looked at her. "Go back toward Doniphan." I had not mentioned her father again, but I was certain his shack was our destination. I was right.

I turned south at the old Bannister place. Big, red rock gravel on the narrow road was bad enough; but the washboard effect was murder on the tires and car frame. I slowed to a near crawl. We passed the site where my mother's home once stood. She was strangely silent.

Overhead, the autumn-hued trees made a canopy that should have been lovely; but it made the road look like a dark tunnel. Not even a hint of dappled sunlight broke through. No sky was visible. I could only imagine how dark and oppressive the way must have been, and would still be, on a dark summer night. The treetops would have been so dense no moon or stars could have penetrated them.

Except for a battered, deserted trailer, nearly hidden by wild grapevines, there were no houses along the road.

"There's the pull-off." Mom's voice was little more than a whisper.

"We don't have to do this, Mom," I told her. "I don't know what happened between you and Grandpa, but I know you don't want to see him. We can leave."

"No, I need to see him one more time." She opened the door and stepped onto the rutted space that served as a driveway. "Are you coming with me?"

"Do you want me to?"

"Yes."

I joined her and together we picked our way up the steep, rough incline. Brown weeds and tall grasses brushed our legs, but the overgrown path was passable. Some of the ruts were eight or ten inches deep, softly eroded on the sides. I imagined that they had originally been cut into the ground by wagon wheels, not automobile tires. A row of rusty barbed wire, held together by a pair of torn overall legs, stretched from a crooked post to a tree in the fencerow of the adjoining property.

A few feet behind the fence stood my grandfather Loring's shack. It could have been close to a hundred years old. Foot wide planks, joined together with four-inch wide boards, formed the sides of the shack. The aged wood had acquired the soft, dove gray hue of time, caused by sun, wind and weather. On the roof, sheets of corrugated metal lay beside pieces of wood shingles and rusted tin, stages of roofing at various times.

The only window on the front of the shack, small and four-paned, showed our distorted image as we approached. The heavy door, banded with riveted metal strips, stood ajar. It appeared to be new, and it reminded me of a barricade. Several deep gouges, which had to be from bullets, pockmarked the surface Beyond the open door, I could see a bit of the floor, a mesmerizing sight. It looked like equal parts of decaying wood and dirt. I shuddered at what the rest of the interior must hold.

In a cane-backed chair sat my grandfather, Arthur Loring. He held a newspaper wide open with both hands. Square-rimmed glasses sat atop his long nose. The mid-morning sun created a halo around his snow-white hair, still thick and luxurious, for all his years. He wore high-topped work boots, and bibbed overalls over a long-sleeved white shirt. We stopped about twenty feet from him. My mother cleared her throat.

Startled, the old man raised his head, an expression of naked fear on his lean face. He stood up surprisingly fast for a man in his eighties. He stared at us, no recognition at all in his light blue eyes. I could feel my mother's tension.

"Hi, Poppy," she said. "I'm Jackie, your daughter." I can't describe all the emotions I heard in her words and in her voice—anger, derision, contempt, fear, even a touch of longing. We had not seen Grandpa since he came to our house when we lived in Redbud Grove. I was nine years old at the time.

"Jackie?" he repeated. "Oh, oh, yes. Jackie." He looked at me. "Who are you?"

"I'm Sissy, your granddaughter."

A slow spark of recollection showed in his eyes. He looked from me to my mother and back. He raised one hand and pointed to her. "You have another girl," he said. "Beth."

"And a son," Mom added. "Buddy. We call him Bill now." Grandpa frowned.

"I don't remember him," he said.

"Of course, he would remember only the girls," Mom muttered under her breath.

"Is it Sunday?" Grandpa asked. Mom and I exchanged glances again.

"No," she said. "It's Friday."

"Oh, that's good. I always change my overalls on Sunday. You're so dressed up I thought it might be Sunday." He grinned, and I saw his gold tooth gleam in the sunlight. "Is your man still livin'?"

Mom gasped. I took her arm. "Dad died several years ago," I told him, "in a cold mine explosion."

Grandpa moved his head in a slow nod. "Seems like I recollect something about that," he said. "He was that Bannister boy, wasn't he? Lived up the road?" I tightened my grip on Mom's arm.

"That's right," she said. "The Bannister boy that took me out of your house."

"Mom, maybe we should go," I whispered.

"What about you, Girlie? Do you have a man?" I met my grandfather's smiling eyes. "Pretty thing like you oughta have a man."

"No, Grandpa, I'm not married." A change of subject seemed like a good idea. "How are you? Are you doing all right here?" Grandpa hooked his thumbs in the straps of his overalls and rocked on his feet. His face dropped, and self-pity edged his voice.

"People up here ain't friendly no more," he said. He pointed to his front door. "See that there? Someone shot out a winder one night, so I had Dan put me up one made out-a that acrylic stuff. While he was at it, I had him put me up a good heavy door, too. Good thing I did. Look at all them holes they shot in it. Why, if that door hadn't a-been there, they could-a killed me."

"Someone probably meant to," Mom muttered. I patted her arm.

"Do you know who shot at your house?" I asked. A sly smirk crossed his face and he turned his face three-quarters from me. He cocked his head and slanted his eyes at me.

"Prob'ly some fella thought I was makin' eyes at his woman."

"I don't doubt that one bit," my mother said.

"Well, it gets a mite lonely, not havin' a woman. There ain't many widder-women here. I'd like to find a woman with pretty hair and blue eyes." He shifted that narrowed look at me again, and it raised the hair on the back of my neck. "You'd do," he said.

"What's the matter with you!" My mother's cheeks burned bright red, and her chest heaved in anger. "*She's your granddaughter, for God's sake!*" I put my arms around her shoulders.

"Okay, Mom, let's go. Come on, now." She allowed me to turn her toward the car. Her body trembled.

"Why don't you stay?" my grandfather called. "You could cook us up some dinner, Jackie. It'd be nice to have a woman cook for me. I've got some apples would fry good. They got a few worms, but that don't matter. It's been a long time...." We moved quickly, and his whining words drifted away on the breeze.

"I hate him! I hate him!" Mom's voice choked on her anger.

"It's all right, Mom. We're leaving. You don't have to see him again." Her body still shook when I closed the car door for her. I looked over the top of the car, toward the place I would not see again. Only the peak of the shack's roof was visible.

I turned the car around, thinking that Mom would be ready to shake the dust of her past off her feet, that she would be happy to leave this road without a backward glance. I was wrong. Her home place was no more than a mile north of Grandpa's; and as we neared it, she told me to pull into the driveway.

Obviously a home site, the sunken outline of the foundation was still visible. A tall maple tree grew near the high yard's edge, and several other trees surrounded the empty space. Remnants of a barn and other outbuildings could be seen at the outer boundaries, designated by rotting fence posts and fallen wire.

"It's a pretty place for a house," Mom said. Her cheeks were still rosy, but she spoke calmly. "The house had five rooms and a pantry, a good-sized house for its time. It could have been a happy place. I was almost five the first time I saw it."

"I remember the story, Mom. Grandma Chinn kept you until Grandpa remarried," I said. She nodded. Her voice took on a dream-like quality, and I knew she was drifting back in time. I was afraid of where she was going, for I had just witnessed evidence of evil in my grandfather—an evil she had only hinted at when I was a child.

My mother had often remarked that the story of her life would make a best seller. When I was a little girl, I thought the stories she told of her childhood were often funny, sometimes sad; and I knew she had numerous stepmothers.

Back then, she had selected her stories carefully; but on this day, she left out nothing. With tears and laughter, she put images in my mind that changed the way I thought about my family, my heritage and myself. I have sometimes wished she had not told me. After that day, I would never be the same.

I didn't need to take notes to remember what she told me. At first I tried to write in third person narrative, as any journalist would do; but it didn't have the same impact as first person. Here, as I remember it, as she told it, are portions of my mother's story. I don't have the heart to relate all of it....

When I was a little girl, I often wondered why God didn't let me die with my mother. Better yet, He should have let her live and just taken me. She already had four children, and they certainly needed her, rather than another baby in the house. I could see no good reason why I survived.

Not one household in the rural community where I was born came through the influenza epidemic of 1917-1920 untouched. My grandmother often told me about my twenty-four-year-old mother's last day on earth, the day after I was born. Evidently, one of her cousins had designs on my father at one time. The cousin died of the flu two days before I was born. Grandma said my mother knew she was dying. Grandma quoted her as saying, "At least I don't have to worry that Anna Jane will get Arthur."

As I grew older I recalled that story many times. I always thought it too bad that Anna Jane didn't get the man. My mother could have been spared so much, to say nothing of her children.

The first four and a half years of my life could not have been better for any child. Grandma and Grandpa Chinn, my mother's parents, took me home with them the day my mother died. "I wrapped you in blankets and quilts and walked a mile across the fields," she often told me. I loved to hear about that cold February day, and I never grew tired of the story. I snuggled into her arms, trying to imagine the wintery chill and the frosty ground, thinking how my grandma must have cherished me, the last legacy of her daughter.

I recall only two times that my father came to see me while I lived with my grandparents. He came one day when they were gone. My Aunt Edith, the younger, unmarried daughter, who still lived at home, refused to let my father inside the house. I couldn't understand why. There were no more hospitable people in the area than my "Mommy and Poppy," as I called them. Later, I learned that my father had made unwelcome advances toward his young sister-in-law.

The second time he came, my father held me in his lap and asked which was my favorite color. "Yedder," I told him. Not long afterward, a package of yellow fabric arrived; and from it Mommy made a beautiful dress for me. I wore it the day my world changed forever.

"Your poppy is coming to get you, but don't you cry, Baby," my grandmother said. "You've got a new mommy now, and she's going to make a home for you and your brothers and sister and your poppy. You'll have to call her 'Mommy.' You be a good girl, and mind your poppy. *Don't you cry, Jackie!*"

"I won't cry, Mommy," I said. I didn't, then. I carried my doll, a small baby doll with a porcelain head and soft body. My father placed me on his mule, his only means of transportation, and mounted behind me. The trip back to the house of my birth was taken on the dirt road, not across the field, as my grandmother had carried me from it. It was the first time I had been back to the house where I was born.

My three brothers and a sister stood like stair steps in the front room. They all looked as scared and unhappy as I felt. Jacob, the oldest at thirteen, didn't smile. Neither did James. Almost twelve, his dark brown eyes snapped with anger. Daniel, nine and blue-eyed like Jacob, seemed the least forbidding. Gladys, only two years older than I, was about the same height, but smaller framed. She had the same brown eyes and hair as James.

My brothers had spent the time since our mother's death with three of my father's brothers, and my sister had lived with Aunt Rosa. We were virtual strangers to each other. Only I had lived with grandparents.

"Come in." I turned toward the kind voice of the woman in shadow. She came forward, and I looked into the face of my new Mommy. Augusta Sampson, a tall, handsome woman in her early thirties, had been what the locals called "an old maid" before she married Arthur Loring.

I learned later that she was a woman of property. Her parents had left several acres and a house to her, so she married by choice and not from need. We discovered that Gussie, as my father would call her, was not only kind; she could cook. She made the evening as comfortable for all of us as she could.

My sister and I were to share a bed in one room. The three boys slept together in the second, and the newlyweds shared the third bedroom. In time, we grew used to each other. Gussie, intelligent and hardworking, was more than qualified for the task of rearing five children. It was easy for me to think of her as my mother.

In the fall, after cotton-picking was over, I entered first grade, although I was only five. Every morning Gussie saw that we were dressed in clean clothes. We left the house with neatly combed hair and a stocked lunch bucket. The one room schoolhouse was over a mile away. Our only means of transportation was "shank's pony," as the locals said. That meant we walked.

Life would have been good, had it not been for the constant bickering and arguing between my new mother and my father. He wanted her property, and he would give her no peace until she agreed to deed it to him.

"No, Arthur, I will not." His anger grew with each refusal, and he finally delivered an ultimatum.

"A wife's property and all she owns rightly belongs to her man!" he shouted. "You sign that deed to me, or I'll divorce you!"

Augusta Sampson had lived well for a lot of years before she married Arthur Loring, and she declared that she could live well without him again. One year after their marriage, my father divorced his second wife. We had grown used to the love and care of a good stepmother, and we missed her.

There was no lack of other unmarried women in the area. Within a few months, another woman replaced Gussie. Dora came to the marriage with a two-year-old daughter, a pretty blond, blue-eyed child named Bea. By that time, we were so confused and unsettled we scarcely knew our own names. My sister and I were grateful for a woman's presence, for cooking was not something seven-and-nine-year-olds did well.

As time progressed, circumstances and a genetic mental instability created a stepmother as warped and cruel as any portrayed in fairytales. There she was: barely out of her teens, mother of a two-year-old, responsible for a ready-made family of six more people, immediately pregnant and married to a man who gave her no peace or privacy.

Life for us spiraled downward. The woman resented us. In retrospect, I understand how overwhelmed she must have felt. That said there was no excuse for her unprovoked, unadulterated meanness toward helpless children.

She couldn't or wouldn't cook decent food, but she managed to provide tidbits of good things for her little girl and herself. My sister and I continued to do the laundry as before, with lye soap, hot water and a corrugated washboard. It was next to impossible for us to wring out the heavy overalls and bedding; but together we managed to drape the sopping things over the clothesline.

Dora delighted in tormenting us, in whatever way she could imagine. Instead of calling us one morning, she woke us with several strokes of a hickory switch as we slept. The whipping continued, and large welts formed on our bare arms.

"Get up, you lazy, good-for-nothing little sons-a-bitches!" Thereafter, I managed to be awake and up long before Dora. The first few nights after the whipping, I barely slept, determined to avoid that switch, if at all possible.

Dora seemed to delight in provocation. One evening, to our surprise, she made supper. She even seemed cheerful when she told Gladys and me to set the kitchen table. My father and brothers had been in the fields all day, and they were bone-tired. The meal of sausage, gravy and biscuits wasn't my favorite; but no one turned down food. In the midst of a depression, we were fortunate to have it.

In a voice as sweet as honey, Dora spoke.

"Is it good? Does it have a good flavor? I took the skillet outside and let the dogs lick it clean from breakfast. Then I made sausage and gravy in it. I couldn't eat the slop, but it's good enough for you."

With an oath of rage, James, fourteen by then, jumped from his chair and grabbed the woman. Small for his age, his temper gave him the strength he needed. He wrapped one hand in her hair and pulled her head backward. With the other, he tried to force a spoonful of the awful mixture into her mouth.

"By God, you *will* eat it!" he shouted.

"James! Stop it!" Our father rose and grabbed James' arm. With a viselike hold, he dragged the boy from the house and toward the barn. In terror, we watched through the kitchen window as he shoved the boy against the building. With a doubled fist, he hit his son in the face. "You don't touch my woman!" James spent the night in the barn.

In due time, another daughter was born, a dark-haired, dark-eyed girl, who looked like her mother. They named her Mary. The man of the house declared that the child could not be his, since he had blue eyes; but he had no proof of infidelity.

I thought life couldn't get much worse, but now Gladys and I had the care of a baby added to our duties. Bea now slept with us. Unfortunately, she wet the bed every night, which added more laundry and smell to the overcrowded house. Only a few weeks later, Dora found herself pregnant again; and our lives became indescribable.

Physical slaps and whippings were the norm for any infraction, real or imagined. Dora seemed to delight in carrying out other, subtle cruelties. James' prized leather belt disappeared, and Dora whispered that she had shoved it down a hole in the wall, making sure that it went all the way to the foundation.

One day that summer, my sister and I were set to shelling beans on the porch. There were not many instances of play for us, but we made a game of our task. Gladys slipped a burry bean hull down the front of my dress, and then it was my turn to try to sneak one down her collar. We laughed, two little girls making play of work.

"What are you doing?" Dora screamed and launched out the kitchen door like one of the furies, long switch in hand. Indiscriminately, she lashed out at us. I pitched my pan of beans and ran as fast as I could go to the field, where the boys and our father worked.

I stayed with them the rest of the day, afraid to go back to the house. Filled with dread, there was nothing for me to do but return with them at dusk. For some inexplicable reason, my father ignored Dora's tirade against me. He forbade her to touch me, which didn't sit well with my sister. She had taken the beating for both of us.

I became afraid to eat, for Dora told me that she put poison in the food—sometimes for the boys and sometimes for Arthur's girls, excluding her own, of course. I watched carefully, often eating cold food only after the rest had eaten.

In the meantime, Gladys and I learned to make biscuits and cornbread. Young as we were, we began to cook many of the meals after school. We got the hang of using the wood-fired cook stove, and we turned out some decent food. At least, we didn't have to worry about eating dog drool and poison.

The following October, Dora gave birth to a son, Homer. Like his older sister, Homer had black hair and black eyes; and our father again accused his wife of infidelity. A thinking man would have known better. He never let a night pass without demanding his husbandly privileges.

Unfortunately, the baby's delivery did not go well for Dora. Unable to regain her strength, she seemed to waste away. Aunt Rosa came for the baby boy; and Dora's mother took Bea. On a cold November day, about a month after Homer's birth, one of our neighbors came to the school to get Dan, Gladys and me. Jacob and James no longer attended school.

All the way home, we discussed what could be wrong. "Maybe Dora's sorry she's been so mean to us. Maybe she's going to get well and be good to us," I told Gladys. My sister just looked at me and snorted. Dan didn't say anything. What we found could not have been farther from the truth.

I was nine years old the day Dora Loring died in the same bedroom where our mother had passed away. Bea would not return to our house, and Homer would continue to live with Aunt Rosa, our father's sister. God bless him, I was envious of him for the next ten years of my life.

Had my mother, her relatives or neighbors suspected what was in store for Arthur Loring's children, one or many of them would have surely executed the man before he could have married any unsuspecting girl or woman. Shortly after Dora's death, he insisted that I sleep in his bed, under the pretext that three girls in one bed were too many.

I had always been terrified of him, and I had tried to stay out of his way. Now fear sat on my shoulder every day. When he looked at me, I dropped my eyes and pretended to be invisible. I hated him.

He began to send me alone on chores my sister and I had shared, such as gathering eggs from the hen house. Always afraid and timid, I became even more so, especially in the dark outbuildings by myself. I had reason to fear.

Unlike Gladys, who never seemed to be afraid of anything, I was even hesitant to reach beneath the hens on their nests. One old biddy managed to peck me every time I went near her, and often she drew blood. When my sister stopped gathering eggs, that brown, wicked hen accumulated more eggs than the other hens. I wasn't about to fight her for them.

I finally learned to approach them with a handful of chicken feed. Most of the hens could be persuaded to leave their nests or at least lift off them a bit, enough to allow my hand access to one or two eggs. That spring, the brown hen had more little yellow chicks fluttering around her than the other hens.

The sun never reached the dark recesses of the chicken house. I tried not to look too closely at the corners, where silent, ominous shadows lurked. I had never seen the bogeyman, but I had heard of him. I believed in him whole-heartedly.

The day he grabbed me, I shrieked in terror. I struck out blindly at the arms that wrapped around me from behind. I tore at the groping hands, and eggs flew all over the chicken house. The strength of mind-numbing horror filled my veins, and I broke free of the evil creature. I ran, without looking back, until I reached the house. Only then did I turn to see if the thing pursued me.

All I saw was my father, Poppy, bend his head to avoid hitting the top of the door as he left the chicken house. It was then I learned that there really was a bogeyman, and he lived in my house. He never said a word to me about the many times he abused me; and I didn't tell anyone, not even my sister. Technically, he never raped me. Perhaps even he was too smart for that; but what he did to a child, his own daughter, was criminal, then and now.

Poppy had told me he would have to go to jail if I told anyone, then no one would care for us and we would be completely alone. He told me that I might even have to go to jail, too. I thought I was the only little girl in the world with such a secret.

I wanted to tell Grandma Chinn; but even as young as I was, I knew that she would kill Poppy. Then she would have to go to jail, and there would be no one who cared if I lived or died. No ten-year-old girl is equipped with the ability to discern a lie from the truth, especially from adults who have total control of her life.

I knew that something was terribly wrong with my father. At times I ducked into the pantry when he entered the kitchen. There was always some chore or something that needed rearranged or brought from its depths, anything to avoid his attention.

Afraid of the dark, I tried not to go to the outhouse at night without Gladys. On the evenings she could not be persuaded to go with me, I carried a small, ball peen hammer in one hand. We kept it in the pantry and used it to crack hickory nuts and walnuts.

On one of those nights, as I exited the smelly outhouse, Poppy grabbed me again. Without hesitation, I swung the hammer. I heard the soft thud when it connected with the side of my father's head. He staggered, and I ran. Gladys and I put Mary to bed, and we were under the sheets before Poppy came inside. Shaking, I held the covers to my chin, sure that some horrible punishment was forthcoming. I was afraid he would insist I come to his bed again.

After a time, I heard him in the kitchen. A short while later, he put out the oil lamp and went to bed. As before, he never said a word. The next day I peeked at him surreptitiously, and I was gratified to see the swollen spot and broken skin on his left cheek. He told the boys that one of the mules kicked him. After that, he didn't approach me for a long, long time. I decided to keep the hammer with me.

From the time I was a toddler, my grandma had told me that my mommy was up in heaven. She said I must be good, because Mommy could see me; and she would know if I was bad. So many nights, during those awful times, I looked at the night skies, and I talked to my mother.

Mommy, I'm a good girl. Mommy, why can't you come get me? I want to be in heaven with you. I'm scared, Mommy. I want you to hold me and tell me I'm a good girl. Mommy, why won't you come get me? Why? Why? I can't count the times I cried and had that same one-sided conversation with my deceased mother.

My father insisted that my sister and I dress as girls did when he was young. Shapeless, long, baggy dresses and high-topped shoes were our school clothes. Timid and shy, ashamed of the way Poppy made us dress, I had no friends in school. One day, Charlene Jenkins, who had many brothers, asked me if my brothers ever "bothered" me. Thrilled with her overture of what I assumed was friendship I replied, "No, but my dad used to make me sleep in his bed."

The next day, as my sister and I entered the schoolyard, one of the bigger boys yelled at me. "Hey, Jackie," he called. "What did your dad do when he made you sleep in his bed?" Stunned, I wished with all my heart that the earth would open and swallow me whole. Gladys fought back, but I kept my head down in shame. I have since wondered if any of the children told their parents about me. If so, why did no one come forward to rescue me?

Jacob married a local girl; and James dropped out of school. Dan attended hit and miss, mostly miss; but when he was there, the boys had nothing to say about Poppy. Although Dan hadn't yet graduated, he was sixteen, a man, by local standards.

After I graduated, my teacher insisted that I go to high school. She came to our house and tried her best to convince my father to let me attend school in Naylor, about three miles away. He refused and could not be swayed. My schooling was over.

During those years, our father kept an old fashioned trunk in his room. Metal bands increased its strength, and the heavy hasp had a large keyhole. We were warned to stay away from it, although it was always locked.

The key hung from a nail, placed high on Poppy's bedroom wall. He would say only that the trunk belonged to "his woman." He had not found another woman, but we knew he was constantly on the prowl. We heard about his attempted courtships of various girls and women of the countryside. Fathers and sons would not allow him in their homes. One or two peppered their warnings with birdshot from a shotgun.

One Saturday Gladys and I decided to examine the contents of the mysterious trunk. Poppy had taken James and Dan to the timber with him, and we knew they wouldn't return until evening. We had packed lunch for them early that morning. Mary, who was about five, had been allowed to spend a few days with her little brother, Homer, at Aunt Rosa's house.

We dragged a kitchen chair into the bedroom, and Gladys climbed onto it. She stood on her toes to reach the key, but she could only touch the tip of it. "Hand me that comb on Poppy's dresser," she commanded. I gave her the comb, and she was able to flip the key ring off the nail.

Excited and scared, I knelt beside Gladys while she wrestled with the key in the hasp. Our eyes met silently when we heard the distinct click that meant success. "Open it," I whispered.

"Okay," she whispered back to me. No one could hear us, but fear made us doubly careful. I held my breath as she lifted the heavy lid. Speechless, we stared at the bounty before us. Carefully, Gladys lifted the top bolt of dark blue silk fabric, to reveal several lengths of other beautiful materials.

We were in awe of the lovely things. Poppy still made us wear only the most drab, near shapeless garments, afraid that we would attract some boy's eye. While the other girls in our school had been allowed to wear the styles of the day, we looked like something from the past century. We stared with longing at the dainty pastel prints and heavier, shiny rayons in the trunk.

In the corner, near the bottom of the trunk, we found a package of silk stockings, an unheard of extravagance in depression-torn southeastern Missouri. We dared not open the cellophane, afraid that we would snag the fragile wisps.

Further examination of the contents uncovered a small metal box with a hinged lid. Inside the box were various bejeweled pins and brooches and a long strand of jet beads, shiny black orbs that glistened, even in the dim light of the trunk's interior.

"These things must have cost a lot of money," Gladys speculated. At fourteen, she had a more practical bent than I. Her eyes narrowed. "We should have dresses out of this material. Poppy is saving it for someone he may never get. It should be ours." She fingered a soft pink calico. "I would look good in this." Her hand strayed to a light blue piece. "And this would be yours."

We launched into a prolonged game of make believe, choosing individual fabrics and jewelry. We pretended we were the daughters of someone else, anyone else, and that all these beautiful things belonged to us. The sudden sound of a wagon in the yard jolted us back to reality.

"Hurry! Shut it! Shut it!" I whispered. Quickly, Gladys smoothed the materials into place and closed the lid. There was no time to return the key to its place on the wall. She shoved it into the pocket of her dress, and we carried the chair back to the kitchen.

We barely had time to look busy before the back door opened. "Girls, get a pan of water and a rag. Your brother has cut his leg." Poppy sounded disgusted with James for being hurt. He and Dan supported James between them. They lowered him to a chair and lifted the injured leg to rest on another one.

I gasped at the amount of blood on his pants leg. Poppy took off James' shoe and pulled down his sock. An ugly gash, about midway to his knee, still bled, but not as badly as it had. I was surprised at the tender way Poppy bathed his son's leg. James clinched his teeth, but made no sound of complaint. At seventeen, he was a man.

Poppy went outside and came back with a tin can, half filled with kerosene. He tore off a small piece of rag and soaked it in the liquid, which he then applied to the gash. In the country, it was the accepted method for treating cuts. He bound the wound with a long length of rag and tied the ends.

"You stay here the rest of the day," Poppy told James. "Me and Dan are going back to the timber. Girls, take care of your brother." With that, they left. Gladys and I were caught in the worst kind of dilemma. We looked at each other. What would James, who was the least sympathetic of our brothers, do with our secret?

What options did we have? Tell him we had opened the trunk and would need help replacing the key on its nail? Not tell him and try to return the key? How could we explain dragging a chair back to Poppy's room? Gladys shrugged.

"James, we need help," she said. He stared at her.

"With what?" he demanded. Briefly she explained what we had done and what we needed. Speculation glittered in James' snapping brown eyes. "What's in the trunk?" he asked. We told him. Without a word, he stood and hobbled into Poppy's room. "Bring the chair," he ordered.

Not much taller than we were, James had to stretch to return the key to the nail. I was so grateful I could have hugged him, but that was not even a consideration. The only way he touched either of us was to pull our hair or slap us for some misdeed or other.

"Now you owe me." With James' words, we knew we had exchanged one fear for another. I can't remember how many times he collected on that debt; but whatever he asked us to do, we did, whether it was to shine his shoes, clean his boots, or cook a special food. Should we balk at the blackmail, all he had to do was say three little words: I'll tell Poppy. Anything was better than having Poppy know we had touched his woman's things.

The next few years saw some improvement in our social lives. Gladys and I were allowed to go to church with a group of young people, but never alone with boys. We learned later that Poppy followed us, to be sure we did what we said we would do. He was convinced that every boy we met had designs on us and that we were involved with every one of them.

During that time, the Bannisters sometimes picked us up on the way to church on Sunday mornings. Their new green wagon with the red wheels was the spiffiest thing on the roads, and riding in it sure beat the dusty two-mile walk from our house to Antioch.

Their three older children were married, but they still had six at home. Willis, who was a few months older than I, tormented me every chance he got. One day he threw a baseball at me and knocked me off the fence where I sat with some girls at an impromptu ball game. I didn't like him at all. We called him "that mean old Willis Bannister."

When my sister was sixteen, she met a handsome boy with dark hair that curled on his forehead. He played a guitar, and they were head-over-heels; but she had to keep their relationship from Poppy. I covered for her several times, scared for both of us, should we be found out. When she was seventeen, Gladys eloped with her handsome young man. They moved to another state.

While happy for her escape from the Loring house, I was devastated at the thought of life without her. Not only that, Poppy would no longer allow me to go to church or anywhere by myself. Dan and James, like many young men that decade, had decided to head west. They hopped a freight train, the first of many, and looked for work wherever they could. Occasionally we received a post card, as they could afford it, which wasn't very often. The depression still gripped the country, and jobs were next to impossible to find.

Poppy, left with no slave labor, swore and carried on for several days after the boys' defection. Mary and I were the only ones on whom he could vent, and he did plenty of that. From the day I hit him with the hammer, he had kept his hands off me; but I still caught that ugly, speculative look in his eyes at times. It made me shudder. I was no longer a child, and I knew the evil in his heart. I kept an eye on Mary, too.

Soon after Gladys left, Poppy found another woman. Twenty-four-year-old Lucille married Poppy a few weeks after his pursuit of her began. Pretty in a sleazy kind of way, Lucille didn't cook or clean or wash clothes. She primped and lay around the house until she heard Poppy come home.

Only then did she get off her bed or chair and try to look busy. Poppy couldn't keep his eyes off her. I bit my tongue every time she took a different piece of fabric to the only seamstress in the area. Every month or so, after a particularly noisy night, Poppy presented to her something from his "woman's trunk."

There was satisfaction in knowing that when Lucille left after less than a year, she took with her most, if not all, of the pretty things in that trunk. Poppy would have to start another stash.

I couldn't understand him. He married my mother when he was twenty-eight, and she was sixteen. He was thirty-seven when I was born, and he fathered two more children with Dora. When Lucille left him, he was fifty-four years old; but he continued to be obsessed with girls and women, anything female. By that time, and maybe before, the neighborhood knew who and what Poppy was; but no one, especially his sons and his brothers and sisters, suspected how warped he was.

Close to my sixteenth birthday, my father made a proposition to me. Supper was over, and he sat at the kitchen table while I finished washing and putting away the dishes. We never talked, so I was surprised when he suggested that I sit down.

The lamp cast flickering shadows around the room and on his face, lengthening his nose and chin. He looked like my mental image of the devil. I refused to sit with him.

"What do you want?" I asked. Under the pretext of preparing for breakfast, I raised the heavy lid of the tin-lined box, where we kept ground grains. It was totally mouse proof. I glanced at his face.

"You know, you look more like your mommy than the others do." I nearly gagged at the lie. A picture of my mother had been on the front room wall from the time I had come to the Loring house. Unfortunately, I looked nothing like my mother. Short, like Grandma Chinn, I chose to think I favored her side of the family. "There's something you should know," my father continued. I could see the speculation in his eyes. "You're not mine."

I stared at him. Where had I heard that before? Oh, yes, I remembered. He had said it about practically every one of his children. I didn't even look up. I continued to measure out flour for the next morning's biscuits.

"You're a woman, full-grown, now," he said. "I'll give you fifty dollars to be my woman. No one would know, but it won't matter anyway. We ain't kin." He stood up. It was impossible not to see how affected he was by the thought.

I literally looked through a red haze. I slammed the lid of the chest down hard, wishing his head could be in it. "I wish to the Good Lord I *wasn't* your daughter!" I yelled. "But my mother was a good woman! She had five kids in eight years, and they are all *yours*! That's part of what killed her! I know that, and you know it! Don't you ever, *ever say such a thing again!* And if you ever touch me or suggest…!" I had to stop before I choked on my words. "…I will tell Aunt Rosa and Aunt Lizzie and the sheriff!"

Poppy blinked rapidly. He sat down in his chair. "Aww, you wouldn't put your poor old Poppy in jail," he whined. I glared at him and slammed the mixing bowl on the table. I pointed my finger at him for a long moment before I walked, head high, out of the kitchen.

In my bedroom, I leaned against the door to still my racing heart. Even in the midst of my disgust and revulsion, I felt proud. I had never dared talk back to my father, but I had just stood against him. I would continue to hate him, to revile him, but I didn't think I could ever forgive him.

When I was eighteen, Will Bannister and I discovered each other. Somehow, overnight it seemed, he was the most handsome, sweetest boy in the world. We went together for almost a year before we decided to get married. Before I could marry him, I had to tell him about my father and the way he had molested me.

Infuriated, Will swore like no one I had ever heard, before or since. He wanted to kill Arthur Loring on the spot, and it took a long time for me to convince him otherwise. "You would go to jail, and we could never be together," I told him. He held me as if I were precious and fragile, as I had longed for someone to hold me since I was five years old.

We were married, and the early years were terribly hard, materially; but they were some of the happiest years of our marriage, simply because we were together. Before my children were born, I vowed that no daughter of mine would ever have to endure such a childhood as mine had been. I swore that I would kill any man who touched or molested them in any way, and I meant it....

I don't know how long tears had run down my face. Long before my mother stopped talking, I wanted to put my hands over my ears. I didn't want to know what she just told me. Not knowing what to say, I said nothing for a long time.

"It was a long time ago, Sissy," Mom said. She sounded calm, even serene. Perhaps she felt cleansed with the telling, but I felt raw and dirty. I wanted to purge myself of the Loring blood. "We'd better go, or we won't get very far down the road."

I started the car and turned around in the deserted barnyard. Back at the main road, we turned east, toward Naylor once more. I smiled in the right places and answered with correct phrases; but I felt as if I were in a surreal landscape, where the colors were not quite right, and everything was slightly out of perspective.

Neither of us was hungry, so we skipped lunch and drove all the way to Memphis, where we found a motel near the Mississippi River. After a light supper, Mom was ready to retire; but I was restless.

"I think I'll take a walk," I told her.

"Do you want me to come with you?"

"No. I just need to walk for a little while. I won't be long." I picked up a key but took nothing else with me. The area was well lit, and I had no qualms about a short stroll along the river walk. Ironically, the thought crossed my mind that I was safer there than with my grandfather.

I walked for half an hour before I turned and went back to the motel. I entered the room quietly, just in case my mother was already asleep. She was. I brushed my teeth and slipped out of my clothes. My first thought was that a shower could wait until morning, but I felt so soiled I just had to wash. Quiet tears went down the drain with the hot, soapy water; and I did feel better after I toweled dry. From her bed, Mom snored softly. I stopped and looked down at her.

She seemed younger in sleep. No distress showed on her face, and I hoped her dreams were pleasant. As I gazed at the woman who brought me into the world, I realized there were twenty years of her life I would never be able to comprehend. I didn't know what had kept her sane through the insanity of her childhood.

How had she learned to be a mother, with no woman, no pattern to guide her? I began to understand her love for Grandma Chinn and Aunt Rosa. What little time she spent with them must have been her lifeline.

Physically tired and emotionally bewildered, I crawled into my bed. Positive that I would be unable to sleep, I pulled the smooth sheet over me. I woke to the sound of my mother's voice in the shower. The words of John Denver's "Country Roads" mingled with the water: "... *Country Roads, take me home to the place I belong...West Virginia...*" She sounded happy.

In Nashville, we were able to get tickets to the Grand Ole Opry that night. I shook off the miasma of Mom's revelations enough to enjoy the music and her excitement. I wished my dad could have been the one to experience it with her. He would have loved it, too.

Late the next afternoon, we arrived in Dixon. Mom didn't seem a bit tired, but I was exhausted. After a light supper, I excused myself and went upstairs for the evening. As I closed my bedroom door, I heard my mother begin to tell her husband about the trip. As much as she had enjoyed the reunion with her old friend, the highlight of the journey for her was having dessert with bluegrass singer, Bill Monroe. I shook my head and smiled, in spite of the sadness that lingered in my heart.

The sounds and smells of the city flowed over me with the restorative properties of medicine. I immersed myself in work at the paper; and when Jennifer Lansing asked if I had picked up a story while I was away, I told her my idea. Her eyes lit up.

"Good girl!" she cheered. "Put it together, and we'll see what departments want to fight over it."

I worked on it for several days. The statistics I uncovered angered me. What I had thought was uncommon, an anomaly, proved not to be so. Crimes against children, particularly incest, were not as hidden as the public wanted to believe; but reported cases were the tip of the iceberg. The greatest percentage of these unspeakable abuses was unreported.

Many of the young victims went on to hide their shameful secrets, not realizing the fault was not theirs. Untold pain and anger sometimes warped young lives so badly they turned to substance abuse to deaden the hurt. Some even committed suicide.

There seemed to be a recurring, consistent longing in every victim's heart. When a family member was involved, the betrayal was compounded by mixed feelings. The children wanted to love their families, and confrontation was hard. What they wanted, more than anything, was an apology. They wanted the perpetrator to acknowledge what he had done and to sincerely apologize for it.

When the story hit the stands, telephone messages and letters by the hundreds came to the paper. Jennifer established a hotline to help victims who called, and the newspaper funded the toll free number. It was used daily. That fact helped the darkness that had taken residence inside my head lift away from me. I began to feel better about my heritage.

If my mother, who had lived it, could become the strong, wonderfully loving woman she was, who was I to feel any less worthy? The fact that my grandfather had been born twisted, flawed, misshapen in spirit and soul, had nothing to do with me. My mother and dad had given the best they had to their children, in spite of the deficiencies in their childhoods; and we were better people for their dark experiences.

So I held my head high again, and I regained the sense of pride I had felt in my family connections. Although it was not the same, the secret I carried of Jack's brutality toward me gave me an even closer kinship to my mother, one she didn't suspect.

A childhood question I had filed in my head was finally answered. Mom had once made the remark that she would kill my dad before she would allow him to treat us as her father had treated his children. I remember looking at her with disbelief, wondering how she could say such a thing.

"Mommy! You wouldn't!" I had said. "We have a good daddy. He smokes, and he drinks beer sometimes, though. What did Grandpa do?" She had looked as if she regretted her statement. I remembered that she had clenched her jaw.

"There are much worse things than smoking and drinking a little beer," she said. Skeptical, I couldn't think of anything; but I was only ten. "Maybe, one day, I'll tell you," she said. "Or maybe not."

I understood. I wished I could hug my dad, could smell his cigarettes and, yes, even the musty smell of his occasional beer. I wished I could tell him how proud I was to be his daughter, to thank him for his love and strength.

I'm grateful for the excursion my mother and I took together, for it opened up a whole new world of understanding between us. From that time, when I looked at her, I could see the child she had been. She is a miracle in a woman's body, and it is her strength that made my siblings and me who we are.

I'm glad my mother told me of her secret shame, when she did, how she did, and where she did, in the place where it began and where it ended. I don't think she ever let go of her hatred and disgust for her father, and I can't fault her for that; but I know she finally realized that the shame was his, not hers.

Therein, she finds peace.

Out'a Town By Sundown

After four years of life in the city, I felt quite cosmopolitan and able to deal with just about any situation. I followed the personal safety suggestions. I carried my purse in front of me, never swung it from my arm or shoulder. If I shopped at night, I went to well-lit markets and stores where many customers were visible. I never opened my apartment door to anyone I didn't know, even for deliveries.

When I began my job at the Times, I adopted my initials, C.C., as my first name. It wasn't a far stretch from Sissy, which no longer seemed appropriate, professionally; and there was no way I would allow anyone to know or use my given name. The initials served me well for telephone listing and apartment door tag, too

I became acquainted with some of the residents in the building, one of whom worked in a department store not far from the Times. Sonya Howard and I often walked to work together; but since I spent many afternoons out of the office, we rarely returned home at the same time.

Sonya shared an apartment with Linda Mason, a beautiful brunette with aspirations of stardom on the musical stage. Linda was seldom home in the evenings, so Sonya and I often shared light suppers in our apartments.

I liked her. She reminded me of my high school friend, Delia Brown. Sonya's skin was not ebony black, as Delia's; but her confidant attitude and personality were similar. Something about Sonya's profile made me think of the bust of Nefertiti, ancient Egyptian queen of the Nile, fine-boned and exotic. Her hazel eyes picked up the warm brown tones of her skin, and her curly black lashes needed no mascara.

Sonya wore her dark hair swept straight back from her forehead, which accented her high cheekbones and dramatic eyes. At various times, she wore earrings that matched the gold, silver or ivory hair ornaments in her heavy chignon. She possessed a classic beauty and unique style.

I could understand why, at the age of forty, Sonya was head buyer for a boutique that offered clothing and jewelry from European and Asian markets. Twice a year, she took trips to seek out items from far away places to tempt eclectic New Yorkers. Most of the merchandise was too pricey for me, but there was no dearth of customers at La Palace Boutique. Sonya used her employee discount to great advantage.

I knew she was once married and that she had been divorced for several years. She wasn't forthcoming about her past, and I hadn't pried, in spite of my rampant curiosity. I hoped to learn more about her one day.

"C.C., why don't you do something with your hair?" Sonya often asked me. I sipped coffee from the heavy mug, one from an African collection. In her kitchen, we had just finished a supper of her favorite Mediterranean salad and good bread.

"What do you mean? I wash and comb it every day!" I retorted.

"Yes, but you shouldn't put it in a pony tail all the time! I've never seen it any other way."

I shrugged. "It's easy, and I don't have time to mess with my hair all day. I may be on a boat in the harbor, or rushing around town at any given time. This way, I can run a comb through the pony tail, fluff up my bangs a little, and I'm ready for the next stop."

"They why don't you just cut it short?"

"You sound like my mother," I laughed. "She fussed at me to cut my hair from the time I was fourteen. She never did like it long."

"Long is fine, C.C; but you need some style. Besides, you're too old to wear a pony tail to work."

Ouch! So I was going on thirty-five! My skin was good, and I wore the obligatory blush and a dab of lipstick. I felt that I could hold my own. Still... I swung my ponytail over my shoulder, reached up and pulled the rubber band from my hair. I shook it loose and looked through a long strand at Sonya.

"Is this better?"

She laughed at me. "Not much," she said. She pushed back from the table and stood behind my chair. With her long fingers, she lifted my mop of hair and fiddled with it, fluffing it first one way and then another. "I think you should cut about eight inches off and let it just brush your shoulders. Your hair is so heavy and thick it will hold a good cut. I'll make an appointment for you at the shop next to the Boutique."

I raised my brows. I didn't recall agreeing to a cut. "Uhhhhh, maybe...."

"Maybe, nothing," Sonya interrupted. "I'll make the appointment, and you will keep it, Lady McCoy."

A few days later, I emerged from the hair salon with, not only a new haircut, but new makeup, as well. The ladies in the shop knew their business. I walked with a jauntiness I hadn't felt for a long time. Heads turned when I entered the Times offices, and there were a couple of genuine double takes. My new haircut swung on my shoulders, and my head seemed lighter without the pull of the long ponytail. I had to admit that Sonya was right.

I rounded a corridor and plunged headlong into the arms of a tall, handsome blond Adonis. "Whoa!" He grasped both my arms to keep me from bouncing off him onto the floor. His eyes were so blue they rivaled the Dutch blue of his shirt and matching tie.

"I'm sorry," I breathed.

"I'm not," he said. He smiled. And that's how I met Neal Curry, the architect. He asked if he could take me to lunch as an apology for nearly running me down. Inexplicably, I accepted.

During lunch, I learned that, like Jack, Neal had been a college football player. Unlike Jack, Neal's athletic career had ended with a knee injury that had kept him out of Viet Nam. Fortunately, Neal had maintained his grades and had no trouble graduating with honors.

At forty-three, Neal owned an architecture firm he had founded while in his early thirties. He designed houses for subdivisions, and demand for his company's plans increased every year. Larger companies regularly offered to buy him out, but Neal refused every bid. Neal was a self-made man, used to making decisions, not only in his own behalf, but for others, too.

"I came into the Times to buy some advertising blocks," Neal told me. "My assistant usually takes care of that, but he's out of town. I'll have to give him a bonus for today." Neal watched me over his glass of iced tea. I actually blushed.

"Thank you for lunch," I said as I stood. "I've got to get back to the office." Neal rose, too.

"May I call you?" he asked. I hesitated, and then I looked into those blue eyes.

"Sure," I said.

After lunch, new clothes hovered at the sidelines of my thoughts for the rest of the day. *May as well do it up right*, I thought. Neal Curry took up the center part. It had been a long time since I'd met an interesting man. Not since Carlo Donatelli. My mind told me not to go there.

Sonya agreed to shop with me one evening after work, and we spent a couple of hours in Macy's. Sonya knew how to coordinate and could create several different outfits from a few pieces. She amazed me with her knowledge of accessories and color. By the time we stopped to eat, I was energized with images of the new me.

On our way out of the restaurant, I swung the long strap of my bag onto my shoulder. Before I could react, a man grabbed the bag and started to sprint down the street. He got no more than three or four paces before Sonya overtook him, spun him around with the bag, itself, and chopped him, flat-handed, across his nose. Blood spurted and the man went down. Sonya flipped him onto his back and pulled one of his arms up near his neck.

A uniformed policeman appeared and took possession of the would-be thief. Sonya dusted her hands, much as my mother dusted off flour in her kitchen. A brief interview with the arresting officer resulted in the return of my purse and a request to appear at the hearing. I would be notified.

"Sonya, how did you do that?" In awe of the way she had responded, I could only stare at her. She shrugged.

"I grew up in South Chicago. I had to fight, practically from the day I was born."

"Why?"

"Girls had to learn early-on how to defend themselves, especially me. My mother had this thing for Sonya Henne, the ice skater, so that's where she got my name. In the first place, the gal was white, blond and privileged. I didn't exactly fit the profile, you know? How many black girls do you think there were named Sonya in the Chicago slums in the 'forties?" I laughed with her.

"None but me. Anyway, I decided I wasn't going to be a rape or mugging statistic, and I never was. My three older brothers taught me well." She paused. "One of them was shot and killed in the projects, and another is in prison in Marion, Illinois. The third one is a cop." She winked at me. "Yeah, I know. Who'd a-thought it?"

Suddenly shaky, I suggested we hail a cab. It was several blocks to our building, and my knees felt strange. Sonya agreed. "Come in, and I'll make us a sandwich," I told her.

Sonya made the sandwiches, and she brewed tea while I tried to recover from the tremors that shook me. Surprised and angry at the delayed reaction of my body, I was near tears. I sat on the sofa and concentrated on Sonya, where she moved confidently in my kitchen. I couldn't understand why I acted so wimpy, when it was she who had flown into battle.

She brought me a sandwich of tuna salad, which she whipped up from scratch with whatever was in the refrigerator. She pushed a cup of hot tea, laced with sugar and lemon, into my hands. "Drink," she said. I did; and soon my quivering nerves grew calmer.

"Feel better?"

"Yes, thank you." We ate in companionable silence. "Sonya, when did you leave Chicago? I know you've been with the Boutique for some time, but how did you get from Chicago to there?" Sonya sipped her tea before she answered.

"There were several stops along the way," she told me. She glanced at her watch. "It's eight-thirty, C.C. Maybe you should take a shower and go to bed." I thought about her suggestion for about ten seconds.

"No, I'm fine. I'd like to hear your story."

Sonya grinned. "I don't have a 'story,'" she said. "For a long time, it was just a matter of survival. After my brother was killed, my mother sent me to live with her sister in southern Indiana. Now *that* was an experience. My mother's house in Chicago wasn't much, but it had running water and a bathroom that worked most of the time. Aunt Caroline's house had neither."

"Most of the houses my parents lived in had no plumbing," I told her. "When my dad put a bathroom in our little Redbud Grove house, we thought we had suddenly become royalty. Several of my aunts and uncles lived in southern Illinois, and only one of them had indoor plumbing. It was a treat to go to her house."

Sonya pursed her lips in thought. "You know, it wasn't the lack of modern facilities that bothered me so much. I grew up in a community where everyone looked like me. The storekeepers, clerks, waiters and waitresses, teachers—everybody was black. Not many white people ventured into our streets. Honestly, at that time, I couldn't blame them.

"I wasn't aware of racial prejudice so much until I went to Aunt Caroline's. She lived in the country, about two miles from the nearest little town. She and Uncle Dooley went to town every Saturday afternoon to buy what few groceries they needed. They raised and canned vegetables, and Aunt Caroline kept chickens for eggs and cooking." Sonya grew pensive, and I knew something unpleasant had come to mind.

"Did you like living with them?" I asked.

"They were sweet people, but they weren't totally free to live as they wanted. I can still remember the first time I went shopping with them. Just outside the city limits was a big white sign with black letters, nailed to a post. It said: 'No coloreds after sundown. No exceptions. Law will be enforced.' It was signed by the town sheriff."

I nearly choked on my tea. "You're kidding!"

"No, I'm not. All the restaurants in the city had signs on the front doors, too. 'Whites only.' Seems the citizens would take money from 'the coloreds,' but they didn't want us to eat where they did or breathe the same night air. In the city park, there were separate drinking fountains, too—one for whites and one for coloreds."

Twenty years after the fact, I realized why Mary Grace Foster had asked Lucinda Barnes and me if it were okay for her to drink at the fountain in Redbud Groves' park.

"When I was about twelve or thirteen, I found out that Redbud Grove, where my family lived for almost eight years, had the same law; but I thought it was unique to the town. That was in the early fifties, and I'm sure there were no signs posted then. What year did you move in with your aunt?"

Sonya figured mentally. "I was ten, so it would have been nineteen forty-four. I remember that talk of the war was on everyone's lips, regardless of skin color. There were flags in front of most stores, and banners with a gold star on them in the windows of some houses."

I could feel the same indignation I had felt so many years before, when the sheriff of Redbud Grove had told us about the sundown ordinance. The faces of weary travelers and the broken-down bus, stranded in the park across from our house, came to me with the clarity of yesterday. I told Sonya about the incident. She smiled

"Your cheeks are rosy," she said. "At least you aren't as pale as you were when we first came in. Got your blood pumping, didn't we?"

"Thinking about that day can still make me angry."

Sonya rose from her chair. "I think it's time we called it a night," she said. "I'll help clean the kitchen, and then I'm off for bed."

"Will you tell me more about your childhood at your aunt's house?" I asked.

"Sure, if you want to hear it. I can tell you just how hypocritical some of the townsfolk were in that town." I rinsed the few dishes we had used, and Sonya put away the food. "Good night, C.C." She hugged me. We had never exchanged hugs before, and I enjoyed the warmth of a growing friendship.

I tossed in the bed for a while. The suddenness of the purse snatching and the potential for bodily harm unnerved me, even in the safety of my own place. After a time, I was able to relax; and I found myself excited about Sonya's promise. I smelled a story, and the possibilities were boundless.

The next day I followed up a lead on a story. It took me into vineyard country, a distance from the daily melee of the city. I loved to drive the Corvette where there was little traffic. I put the top down and let the wind blow through my new haircut.

A familiar piano intro on the car radio, tuned to a golden oldies station, sent my fingers in search of the volume dial. I turned up the sound of Fats Domino singing of how he had found his thrill on Blueberry Hill.

The face and memory of someone I had not thought about for years came before me. James-Earl floated pleasantly across the years to lodge in vibrant color in my mind. I smiled. For a time, James-Earl had been one of the most important people in my life.

Old, faded photographs show James-Earl and me lying side by side in a penny arcade booth, both of us dressed in white dresses and bonnets. At that time, there was no fear that frilly clothes might cause a baby boy to become a sissy. Even in those pictures, when we were three months old, his half-closed eyes look as big as soft brown marbles, while my gray-blue frown seems to stare at the world with an "I dare you!" glare.

James-Earl and I played together when we were small children. I liked nothing more than to hear we were going to his house. He had no more toys than Buddy and I; but we made up games and played with discarded tools, bits of broken dishes, long sticks, anything that could help us "make believe."

James-Earl made toy cars from tin cans, with soda pop bottle caps driven into the sides to form wheels. I think he did the hammering, even at the tender age of five. He and Buddy, who could not have been more than three, formed roads with pieces of boards, scoring out houses and gas stations, where they pulled in the cars to "fill 'er up!"

I thought about James-Earl as I sped along the highway, remembering my favorite game, which we had played in an old abandoned jalopy. The mohair upholstery had holes, and portions of rusty springs thrust through the padding. We learned early on to avoid the sharp ends. All remnants of glass windows had long disappeared, and not one mechanical part worked. That didn't stop us from pounding on the

115

middle of the steering wheel, for we made up our own loud "Honk! Honnnnnnk!" Oh, the trips we took in that car!

James-Earl always drove, because in our world, women didn't drive. Women drivers were a yet-unheard-of fact of life in our tiny circle of acquaintances. He couldn't see over the steering wheel any more than I could see over the dash on the passengers' side; but he wielded that wheel with the force of an experienced driver.

We spoke of the good things we were going to buy when we reached our goal of the mom-and-pop store in the nearby town: candy orange slices, with the crystal sugary coating around the gelatinous centers; candy corn; perhaps some licorice sticks, although I didn't like them; grape soda pop that would leave a purple ring around our mouths. Throughout our trips, we chatted in a stilted grown-up manner, imitating our parents. I thought how much fun it would be to have James-Earl beside me in the Corvette.

We played bare-footed in the summers, and one day James-Earl stepped on a piece of broken glass from a discarded soda-pop bottle. His screams of pain brought his older sister, who scooped him into her arms and ran with him to the house. I followed, wide-eyed at the stream of blood that poured from such a little foot. Whereas I would have screamed for my mother, he yelled for his daddy. For some reason, that seemed strange to me; but when I was five years old, many things were unfathomable.

I thought James-Earl was beautiful. Along with those liquid brown eyes, he had curly, dark chestnut hair that fell in short ringlets onto his forehead, unlike my straight, pale yellow strands that swung against my cheeks. Soft freckles, coppery colored against his skin, covered his face, his arms and skinny chest. I often complained to my mother that I wanted "frenkles" like James-Earl. We were so totally opposite in our looks, our personalities, and our manner of speech; but we loved each other.

My dad was drafted into the army and swiftly shipped to Italy. Not only did my mother have no means of transportation for herself and my little brother and me, James-Earl's family moved to a faraway country called California. Too old to be drafted, his father took the family to greener, more productive pastures than those offered by Southern Illinois peach orchards. The loss of my little best friend was more of a blow to me than the absence of my dad, who had been mostly gone to work all the time anyway.

Years passed. Letters were exchanged between our parents, but about the only communication James-Earl and I had were yearly valentines, until we grew too old for that. When we were nine years old, his family made the long trek back to visit relatives in Illinois; and James-Earl and I instantly took up where we had ended. I talked faster than he did, so I ran out of school stories quickly; but I listened with wonder to his tales of the magic land of California, which by then I knew was our most western-reaching state.

Following that visit, James-Earl and I exchanged school pictures yearly. His growth from a sweet boy to a young man was clearly seen in them. When we were seventeen, his family once again came back east over the Christmas school vacation. It was the only time they came to see us in West Virginia. By then, there was a marked difference in our way of life, our likes and dislikes, as well as our looks.

We were juniors in high school, and I had just broken up with Jack McCoy. James-Earl still had his curly hair, his sloe-eyed gaze and freckles; but he was much taller than I, and thin, lanky and a bit swagger-y.

He walked with a loose-legged gait, hands in his jeans pockets, thumbs free. His voice had changed, but he had not lost his slow, soft-spoken manner of speech. I was impressed, in spite of myself. He seemed so worldly. I couldn't wait to introduce him to my friends. Karen Courtney wasn't the only one who had a California cousin!

We went to the skating rink one night. When we entered the hall, the distinctive sound of Fats Domino's "Blueberry Hill," greeted us. Immersed in country music, my parents kept the radio in our house permanently fixed to country stations. The little radio beside my bed, in defiance of the house music rule, played nothing but pop and rock-and-roll, cool tunes. I agreed with James-Earl: Fats Domino was definitely cool; country definitely was not. Thereafter, I could not hear "Blueberry Hill" without thinking of my cousin, James-Earl.

Years later, there I was, in the middle of a two-lane highway in New York, the wind in my hair and Fats Domino on the radio. I began to sing with Fats. I sang to the memory of a sweet boy and the children we were. I sang to the innocence of two little cousins who loved each other...James-Earl and Sissy. In fact, I became so immersed in the song and memories it evoked, I missed my turnoff and had to backtrack three miles.

The lead, which had sent me to the country, resulted in a nice enough story about the local wineries. I had learned how to use a good camera, so I could take my own photos. I was pleased with the article.

My stack of by-line clippings continued to grow, but that longed-for "big" story had not yet come my way. I almost didn't recognize it when it dropped into my lap, practically in full bloom, like a beautiful, dew-kissed fragrant rose.

"Where would you like for me to begin?" Sonya asked. Outside, the streets were blanketed with seven inches of snow; and the city had come to a near standstill. Thankfully, it was a Saturday. The holidays had come and gone with scarcely a dusting, but early February brought a blizzard. Buffalo, with its usual lake effect white out, struggled beneath twenty-four inches of wet snow, with the promise of more to come. Relatively speaking, New Yorkers were lucky.

When I invited Sonya to come down for an early dinner of salad and chili, she accepted. Earlier in the day, I had made a coconut cream pie, a treat I had not concocted for years. It made me think of my Uncle Sonny's wife, Bessie, who was still one of the best cooks in Illinois, perhaps the nation.

Sonya and I chatted easily over the meal. We took our pie and coffee to the living room, where we kicked off our shoes and tucked our feet beneath us on the long, plush sofa, a Christmas gift to myself that year. That's when I asked if she would tell me about her stay with her relatives in Indiana, so many years earlier.

"I don't care where you start," I said. "Do you mind if I take a few notes as we talk?"

She shrugged. "No, although I don't know what I could possibly tell you that you could use."

"Well, we never know." I grinned, thinking of Guiseppe Donatelli. "What was your first impression of your aunt's house?"

"Small, clean, worn." Sonya smiled, her face softened with memory. "That could describe Aunt Caroline, too. She was thin, but wiry, like one of those little terriers that yap all the time, you know? Even her hair was wiry, so she wore a turban when she went to town. Uncle Dooley was just the opposite. He was tall and stocky, strong as a bull ox. He had a fringe of gray hair, but the top of his head was as bald and shiny as a piece of coal.

"The house had four rooms, all the same size. A lean-to on the back had a dirt floor, hard as brick; and that's where Uncle Dooley took off his dirty clothes at night. A bedroom opened off the front room, which also led into the kitchen at the back. The other bedroom was off the kitchen, where the cook stove provided the only heat in the winter. They gave me that bedroom."

"Sounds as if you liked them," I remarked. Sonya nodded.

"They were good to me. They didn't have much, but they shared with me all they had. There's no telling what my life would have been if I'd stayed in Chicago. Aunt Caroline and Uncle Dooley made a difference."

Sonya placed her dessert plate and fork on the coffee table and pulled her legs beneath her on the sofa. She stretched her arm along the back and sighed.

"Would you like more coffee?" I asked. She shook her head.

"No, thanks."

"Tell me about the town," I suggested. "I'm still intrigued with the sundown laws, ordinances, whatever they were called." Sonya laughed.

"The townspeople were serious about that law. A few black families lived in the county, but none were allowed to move into the towns. Of course, they worked as handymen and maids or housekeepers; but they had to be out of town before the sun set."

"Was your uncle a handyman?" I asked. Sonya nodded.

"He called himself a 'tinkerer.' He could fix a lot of things, just about everything except cars. Only the wealthiest could afford cars then. Aunt Caroline was a housekeeper for Thomas Hamilton, the appellate judge. The Hamiltons lived in a house that looked like something in a fairy tale, at least, to me.

"It had a wrap-a-round porch with concrete columns and railings, and there was a turret that extended above the dark roof. The house was white, trimmed with lots of gingerbread and curly-ques in the gables. The trim and the shutters were a dark green, and the house was surrounded with flowering trees and shrubs.

"Sometimes, my uncle helped with the yard and flower gardens, especially when the Hamiltons wanted to throw an outdoor party." Sonya looked at her manicured fingers. "I loved for them to have parties," she said. "Aunt Caroline was allowed to bring leftover food home. That's where I had my first petit fours." She shook her head.

"How did your aunt get back and forth to work? I asked.

"On nice days, she walked. It was nothing to walk two miles to work. When I was twelve, the Hamiltons let me come to the house to help Aunt Caroline. They didn't pay me, but Mrs. Hamilton gave me some of their daughter's discarded dresses. When it snowed and was really cold, she drove us home.

"There was a war on, and gas was rationed. The judge didn't like wasting his precious gasoline on the colored help." Sonya brought up her other leg and clasped her hands around her knee. "You will love this," she said. "One winter Mrs. Hamilton became very ill, and she didn't want my aunt to leave her. So the judge made a big show of putting Aunt Caroline in the back seat and driving her home.

"She told my uncle that she had to go back to the Hamilton's, and he had a fit. He was afraid what the locals would do. There was some klan activity in the area, and they gave no one second chances. Judge Hamilton assured them he would take care of it.

"Well, he did. He drove to the back of the house and smuggled Aunt Caroline into the back door, making sure no one saw her. She stayed up all night with the sick woman. The next morning the judge smuggled her back into the car and took her home, on the pretense that he was driving into the country to pick her up. So poor Aunt Caroline worked three shifts in a row.

"Apparently, no one knew that a colored woman had stayed in their lily-white town overnight. I used to wonder what the klan would have done to the judge if they'd found out that he had smuggled a 'darkie' into town."

"What a hypocrite," I said. A thought occurred to me. "Sonya, where did you go to school?"

"That was the hardest part for me. In Chicago, the schools were not all that good; but there were some teachers who cared about their students. The buildings were run down. In Winslow, no black children were allowed in the schools. I was lucky. Mrs. Hamilton sent books home with Aunt Caroline. I already loved to read, and arithmetic came easily to me.

"I made up my mind to learn everything I could from those books, and there were some wonderful ones. You know what? By the time I went back to Chicago, when I was about sixteen, I was way ahead of my class." Sonya dropped her feet to the floor. "You know what else? I'm going up to my apartment and call my mother. Thanks for feeding me." She blew me a kiss from the door.

For several days I mulled over Sonya's account of the sundown law in an Indiana town. I wondered how widespread the practice had been, or perhaps if it were still acceptable in certain areas. I wanted to know more. The self-proclaimed inventor of the inter net had yet to announce his discovery in nineteen seventy-five, so research took a lot more time and effort.

I decided to take some vacation time and do a hands-on investigation. What I learned in two weeks of travel across the Midwest changed my perspective on freedom in The United States, my understanding of the Civil Rights Movement and the way I looked at the histories of Small Town, America.

As a child, I never questioned why only white people lived in Redbud Grove. It was never an issue to me—not until the busload of people from Alabama had been stranded in the park beside our house. Only then was my social consciousness stirred to awareness.

What I discovered on my quest was that practically every small town in Illinois, Indiana, Missouri, Ohio, Iowa, Oklahoma, even Wisconsin and other northern states enforced the sundown laws. As late as the early sixties, some of them had weathered signs at the town limits, announcing their stand.

Where no signs existed, it was still the policy of motels, some restaurants and other public establishments to refuse service or accommodations to non-white customers. No houses or property would be sold or rented to non-white families. Where sports events, such as football, basketball, track or wrestling matches were held in high schools, coaches whose teams included black members often refused to play those students for their own protection.

There were occasions of riots during and following games where non-white students participated, especially if the all white teams were beaten. Sometimes rocks were thrown at buses and cars transporting integrated teams, and police escorts had to be provided.

The more I learned, the more outraged I became. After my two-week vacation was over, I went back to the Times with what I had found. I was given two more weeks and airfare to San Francisco, where I rented a car and headed east. It was sobering to discover sundown towns in every state from California back to St. Louis, where I boarded another plane to New York.

The newspaper ran a series of articles in several Sunday editions, aptly titled, "Sundown Towns." I had been surprised to learn that the paper had covered a racially tense sports event in Southern Illinois some years earlier, so the Times was no stranger to the subject. Following the publication of the series, mixed reactions poured in to the paper. Some writers were irate in support, and some felt their towns had been unfairly portrayed as bigoted.

At any rate, the story caught the eyes of some influential people. Although it didn't win, it was nominated for the Pulitzer. I finally had my "big story." Shortly afterwards, I resigned from the newspaper.

My freelance work was more than enough to support me, and I liked working from my apartment. Pajamas were much more comfortable than business suits.

One evening in late March, Sonya knocked at my door. She had been more than supportive with my article, and her input and personal observations had been invaluable. Our friendship had deepened, and I trusted her. I knew she felt the same way about me.

"I have news." The door had barely opened before she fairly flew inside. She waved her hands in the air. It would have been impossible to miss the sparkle on her left hand. "I'm engaged!"

I knew she had been seeing someone regularly, but I had no idea how serious she was about her ex-professional football player. The two of them made a striking couple, and heads turned wherever they went.

"So I see," I said. I grabbed her hand. The ring was spectacular. "Wow! How many years did he have to work for this rock?" I asked.

"I'm worth it!" Sonya exclaimed. I listened while she told me their plans. Her fiancé lived in Florida and was an announcer for the Dolphins. They would divide their time between New York and Miami, and she was ecstatic. When she left, the smile remained on my face. I was happy for her.

I leaned against the door and stared at the cream-colored carpet. I *was* happy for her! Everyone deserved to be happy.

I was happy, too. I had been working in a field I loved. I had my own home, well, kind of. I was financially stable for the moment. I was healthy. My family was well, although I rarely saw them. My name was known in the newspaper/magazine world, and I was proud of my contribution to society.

So why were there tears in my eyes?

Why sadness in my heart?

Why?

PART TWO
REDBUD GROVE

The Invitation

I closed the front door of my apartment and dropped the keys onto the foyer table. A cursory glance revealed that the small stack of envelopes I had just taken from the mailbox contained very little of interest: a utility bill, a travel brochure, and a hefty letter from my mother, which I retrieved. Nothing else merited my immediate attention. I hooked my wet umbrella and damp coat upon a wall peg, kicked off my shoes, and collapsed against the soft sofa cushions.

It had been a tiring month, culminating into a hectic day of juggled appointments and meeting with editors. I had met my deadlines, but only barely. I should never have taken on four assignments at the same time; but since I had gone freelance, I couldn't afford to renege on an acceptance of a proposal.

All the extensive articles had turned out well. The magazine editors seemed pleased, and each one had spoken of additional commissioned work. It wouldn't hurt my resume to have pieces in four prominent magazines within weeks of each other. Still, the long hours and little sleep had taken their toll, both mentally and physically. I was tired.

A brief onslaught of early-April sleet pelted the window. I pitied my co-New Yorkers on the street below, even while I was grateful to have arrived home before the rain turned to ice. Thoughts of my sister, beside their sun-drenched swimming pool with her husband and daughter, beckoned like a mirage on a desert isle. I pictured them, enjoying a tall, cool drink in the California sun.

I half grinned at the inappropriate metaphor in my mind. New York City has been called a lot of things, but I don't think desert is one of them. The only sand in the area might be what was spread on the sidewalks to prevent missteps on the icy pavement.

I had promised myself a real vacation, not another story-connected trip. I had been fortunate to do research in England, Italy, Austria and Egypt; but those excursions, if they could be called such, had been limited by time and a tight expense account.

The one trip I had extended into a semblance of a vacation had been to Sicily, the previous summer. I had hired a car in Naples and driven down to the boot tip of Italy, where I had boarded a ferry and crossed the strait. The city of Messina, a jewel in the sun just like Guiseppe Donatelli had described it, had whetted my appetite to see more of the countryside.

I hadn't known the name of Guiseppi's village, but I recognized it the moment I drove the little Italian car into its cobbled streets. As picturesque as a postcard, the narrow thoroughfare wound between two sides of golden-hued shops and stores, bistros and sidewalk markets. Faded signs above some of the shops had caught my attention, one of them at a bakery. "Donatelli's," faded, but still visible, hung above the open door.

My negligible Italian didn't fare well with the town's negligible English; but when I mentioned Guiseppe's name, people had nodded and pointed me in the right direction. High above the town, nearly hidden behind a stand of olive trees, stood Guiseppe's villa. On the slope above the house, I could make out the vineyard that seemed to hug the hillside.

I had parked at the bottom of the hill, content to take pictures and allow Guiseppe's story to echo in my memory. While I stood there, a church bell pealed out the hour. I had turned toward the sound. Around a bend, I could see the top of the village church steeple above the tree line.

The car was well off the street, so I had walked the short distance to the church. Sheltered beneath tall trees and bordered by a low, stone wall, was a cemetery off to one side and behind the church. I had seen nothing to hinder, so I wandered among the markers, some so old the letters were nothing but soft indentations.

A large section was devoted to the Donatelli name. Their history was literally written in stone: Guiseppe's parents, grandparents and great-grandparents, even beyond, as well as his wife and son. The newer one belonged to Guiseppe. I had knelt beside the simple, upright stone that bore the name of a man I had come to know late in his life.

I had shed no tears there for him. His life had been a good one, an admirable one, well lived and productive. Not for anything would I have traded the opportunity to know him. I left the cemetery and went back to my car. For five days, I had driven along the old roads and streets of towns and villages in Sicily.

I had not regretted those days, and it was now time to consider the possibility of another vacation. One thing was certain. My destination would be somewhere warm and balmy, where ice had never touched the ground. Oh, the best laid plans, etc....

As I opened the letter from my mother, I thought about the travel brochures in a desk drawer, just waiting for me to choose a destination from their colorful pages. Perhaps after dinner I would make that choice.

Mom's letter was thicker than usual. When I opened the pages, a newspaper clipping fell out. More than a clipping, it was the whole front page. My heart twisted in surprise. I hadn't seen a copy of that paper since I was a child. The banner read: Redbud Grove Record-Herald. I quickly scanned the paper before I turned to the letter.

Committee Votes to Hold All-School Reunion, stated the headline. I hadn't heard from any of my old friends in Redbud Grove since my sophomore year in high school, in nineteen fifty-five. I did a quick calculation: twenty-two years. My eyes hurried over the page, trying to take in all the information.

The various reunion committees had joined forces. As a result, the town was issuing an invitation to anyone who had ever attended any of the schools, at any time, in Redbud Grove, Illinois, to come to an all school reunion, scheduled for the next Labor Day Weekend. Unless the town had grown substantially, I saw no way it could accommodate so many people. It would take all the motels within a hundred mile radius to house them, depending, of course, on how many nostalgic alumni responded.

I turned to Mom's letter. I skipped through the usual stuff, hoping to find more about the reunion. The letter contained personal news that I skimmed through quickly, planning to reread later.

"...so I thought you would be interested in the reunion. I don't know who sent the paper. The return address just had "Reunion Committee" and a box number. Someone you knew must still have our address. It was sent to you, here in Dixon. Do you think you might go? It would be a good chance to reconnect with your friends. Maybe you could find Sharon and all the girls you knew. What were their names? Melissa,

Sheila, Shirley, Cathy...who else? I can't remember all of them. I've passed the news on to Bill and Beth, but they haven't said whether or not they're interested.

"I'm working part time now. Russ wants to start traveling more, since he's retired. Who knows? I might just retire, too. Well......"

I let the letter fall to my lap. People and places I hadn't thought about for years tumbled through my mind. Through memory's eyes, I saw our little house, the park, my schools, our neighbors, and my friends. A pang of nostalgia shot through me, and I knew that I would return to Redbud Grove, as certain of it as I was that the redbud trees still bloomed there every spring.

The shrill ring of the telephone interrupted my reverie. I thought about not answering. Job related calls wouldn't be likely after business hours. Still...I picked up the receiver.

"Hi, Gorgeous. I'm going to grab a steak at Stephano's—now there's a title for you—would you like to meet me in, say, half-an-hour?" Neal Curry's cheerful invitation irritated more than enticed me. The thought of getting a cab on such a nasty evening didn't appeal to me, but then neither did the sparse contents of my refrigerator.

"Why not?" I answered, "but can we make it forty-five minutes? I need to change."

"Forty-five minutes it is. I'll have a table waiting."

"When are you going to say 'yes'?"

I felt the familiar impatience, topped with irritation, at Neal Curry's question.

"Who said that 'yes' would be my answer?" I countered.

"It's a foregone conclusion, C.C. You know it's just a matter of time before you succumb to my charm, my wit, my fortune." I had to laugh. The quality I liked most in Neal was his sense of humor. "Another thing," he continued. "When are you going to tell me your name? I've known you for a year, and I *still* don't know your name."

"You could always call me 'Sissy', like everyone did before I came to New York; or you can continue to call me C.C., my initials. Take your pick." At the age of thirty-six, I had no more love for my name than I had at the age of six. Not even my many yearbook pictures listed my given name. In college, I had used my first and middle initials, both as signature and name.

"How many times have I asked you to marry me?" Neal had stopped smiling.

"One or two," I replied, still trying to keep the conversation light.

"C.C., I'm serious." I looked at my plate. The muted sounds of conversation, the chimes of crystal glasses, and the background music from the piano bar all seemed louder in the silence at our table. I was beginning to wish I had stayed home and opened a can of soup.

"I know you are, Neal. I care about you – a lot; but I never know where my next assignment or project will take me. I like to travel, and I like my work. I wouldn't be a good wife." I looked into his blue eyes. Neal was a handsome man, rugged, in an outdoorsy way. Tall and tanned, his blond hair held a few strands of silver.

"Why don't you let me be the judge of that?" Neal asked.

"I married once, against my better judgment," I said, "and it was a mistake. I don't think I'm marriage material." I placed my napkin upon the table. "I'm tired, Neal. Thank you for dinner, but I'm going home to a warm robe and a good night's sleep."

"Can't I come with you?" Neal knew the answer before he asked the question, but it didn't stop him from asking.

"Good night, Neal." He stood up and helped me with my coat.

"At least let me take you home."

"No, thanks. I'll get a cab." I kissed his cheek and hurried from the restaurant. I wanted to sink into my bed and sleep until noon the next day, maybe even later. I wasn't in the mood to deal with more pressures from Neal.

Neal's brief marriage to his college sweetheart had produced a son, Ryan, who was now twenty years old. The boy looked like his mother. His dark, brooding countenance showed no resemblance to his father. The few times I had seen Ryan with Neal, the air bristled with undercurrents. I had no desire to be drawn into the power play that would one day lead to an explosion between two domineering men.

In the cab, I rested my head against the seat and closed my eyes. What was it about me that made blond men think me incapable of knowing what was best for me? Unbidden, the thought of Jack appeared. It seemed to me his image had come into my mind more often recently. I thought Neal's controlling demeanor was responsible.

I pushed the thought of Jack aside. If I were going to delve into old memories tonight, they were going to be of Redbud Grove. Perhaps, if

I were lucky, those memories would trigger good dreams, the kind that linger long after waking and create pleasant moments during the day.

When I arrived back home, I locked the door behind me and went straight to my bedroom. I ignored my mother's letter and newspaper article. Tired to the bone, I barely had energy enough to brush my teeth before I crawled into bed. The sheets were cold, but within minutes I was cozy-warm; and I went right to sleep. There were no dreams, at least none that I remembered.

Morning brought bright sunshine that chased away the night's icy rain. I opened the blinds on the street-side windows, allowing the promise of spring to flood my apartment. The original tall windows cast long, golden rays into the room and bounced off picture frames and glass-topped tables.

As I had intended, I'd slept until nearly noon. I padded around in bedroom scuffs and an old terrycloth bathrobe, as I sipped sweet coffee and yawned with lazy pleasure. Only one article was due, but I had two months before deadline. I turned on the television, found nothing I wanted to watch, and pushed the off button. I wandered through the apartment again, made some toast, looked into the refrigerator for something more interesting, which turned out to be butter pecan ice cream.

After three bites I gave up and put the ice cream away. Food wasn't what I wanted. I poured fresh coffee and settled into the couch. From the coffee table, Mom's letter stared up at me. I took the newspaper clipping from the envelope and spread it upon the glass top.

Without skipping one word, I read the whole article. A list of committee members, along with telephone numbers, filled a sidebar. Some of the men's names were familiar, but I recognized none of the women's – married names, no doubt. Another box held a registration form with lines for name, class year, occupation and marital status.

With manicure scissors, I clipped out the form and looked at it for several minutes. I hesitated at the name. What if no one remembered me? I didn't want to sign myself as "Sissy." Defiantly, I made two bold initials, hesitated again, and finished with "McCoy." There. No one would know C. C. McCoy. I could appear at the reunion, check out people and circumstances, and leave without ever making myself known, if I chose to do so.

Quickly, before I could change my mind, I stuffed the form into an envelope, sealed it, stamped it and made a quick trip down to the foyer to put it in the box before the postman arrived. With a huge sigh, I plopped onto the couch one more time. My heart beat fast, as if I had completed a monumental task. In a sense, I suppose I had. I had just taken the first step toward a sentimental journey, twenty-two years into the past.

That done, I made another spontaneous decision. I picked up the telephone.

"Hi, Mom. I have a few days free, and I'd like to come home."

"What's wrong, Sissy?"

"Nothing, Mom. Most of my assignments are finished, and I want to see the dogwoods in bloom. Is it okay if I come home now?"

"Well, sure it is, Honey. You don't have to ask."

"Great, Mom. I'll be there in a few days." I knew that my mother would have questions, probably as soon as I drove into the driveway. Another trip back there so soon after my annual Christmas visit would sound alarm bells in her mother-heart.

The timing was perfect. Spring had already begun to work its magic upon the hillsides. It had been ten years since I'd last seen dogwoods bloom in West Virginia. I had purposely taken the scenic route south of Charleston, through the mountains, so I could see Hawk's Nest again. I stopped at several turnouts, just to see the blooms on the hillsides and deep gorges again. It was more than worth the time.

Like always, my mother met me at the door. She patted my cheek and peered through her glasses, examining my face like she did when I was a child.

"Are you really all right?" she asked again. I put my arms around her.

"I'm fine, Mom, really. I think your letter and the newspaper clipping made me homesick, that's all." I picked up my bag and started up the stairs, while she muttered at the foot of them.

I was glad my mother had found someone to share her life, but I had never completely warmed up to Russell Dunbar. Russell looked even older than his sixty-six years. Ten years Mom's senior, he stood tall, but stoop shouldered. His look of Lincoln became more pronounced as he grew older, and his stoic manner could be disconcerting.

Then again, I might have been somewhat jealous of his daughter, who was my age and lived in Dixon. Andrea had access to the house that had been my home for a long time, and she could drop in anytime to have coffee with my mother. I would have to work on that attitude, for Andrea was devoted to Mom.

"I'll make a pitcher of tea," my mother called.

"That would be nice, Mom," I yelled back. Some things never changed. I arranged my clothes on hangers in the closet, put everything else in dresser drawers and lay down upon the bed, being careful to kick off my shoes first – another unchangeable. I had spent two nights here in December, not long enough. Unsure how long this stay would be, there was no sense of urgency. I already had the comfortable feeling that old, familiar, dear things wrought.

After supper, I bid my mother and stepfather an early good night and yawned ostentatiously. I was tired, but not sleepy. A dozen books waited for me in my luggage, books I had postponed reading for months. Every time I came home, I loved to pull the covers around me and read in my old bed.

I punched a stack of pillows against the headboard and slid into them. I read for a long time, turning pages voraciously. It wasn't until the words began to swim that I closed the book and turned out the bedside lamp.

The room was cool in the darkness. I pulled the top quilt closer around my shoulders, and wiggled into a comfortable position. Thoughts of Great-Grandma Chinn flitted through my drowsy mind while I stroked the worn patchwork quilt that held thousands of stitches made by her gnarled fingers. Sleep came quickly, and morning came too soon.

Like always, I woke to the aroma of coffee. Still half-asleep, I was aware that I was in my old room. An old habit of trying to hold back the morning, as I had done on cold winter days in my teen years, took hold; and I willed myself to return to slumber. It didn't work. The sounds of my mother in the kitchen would not be denied.

"Good morning," my stepfather said. He sat at the kitchen table, in my dad's chair. I tried to amend my thinking. I filled a cup with coffee and sat down at the opposite end of the table.

Not much had changed in the kitchen. Russ had repainted the walls and put in a different floor. Mom still used the same dishes and many of the same pots and pans. I looked at her, noticing changes that would not have been apparent had I seen her every day. Her hair had turned a soft silvery salt and pepper. At fifty-six, her skin showed a few lines and soft wrinkles; but she was still a lovely woman.

"Sissy, are you sure there's nothing wrong?" Mom gnawed away at her worries like a dog with a big, meaty bone. I laughed.

"Mom, I just wanted to see you; and I wanted to see the hills with the dogwood and redbud trees." I paused. "Do you remember how beautiful the redbud trees were in Redbud Grove? I've never seen so many redbud trees anywhere else in the country. Remember the reflections in the river?" My mother smiled.

132

"Sissy, you almost sound homesick." I hadn't realized until she said the words that I *was* homesick! I wanted to see the town again, and our house on Pine Street, and the park, and the monstrous magnolia tree in the Monahan's front yard. I wanted to walk in front of Mrs. Murphy's house and put my foot on her grass, kind of like sticking out my tongue at her. It's amazing how brave I could be when she was no longer there to chase me with her broom.

I wanted to walk along the brick sidewalks that led to the schools I had attended; but more than anything else, I wanted to go inside the house on Pine Street. Like Emily in the Thornton Wilder play, "Our Town," I wanted to live just one day, one unimportant day, in that house, to have my parents, my brother and sister as they were when I was twelve. I had to blink at the thought of it. What I really wanted was to be a child again, just for a day. I smiled at my mother.

"I think you're right, Mom. If I can arrange my schedule, I'll go back to Redbud Grove for the reunion in September. Would you like to go with me?" My mother looked at her husband.

"I don't think so, Honey. Mrs. East is the only person I kept in contact with, and she passed away last year. I doubt that many others would remember me."

I stayed in Dixon for a week and looked up old friends. Karen Courtney and her husband had bought a house only a few blocks from her mother's home. Karen's father, Dave, filled with his beloved mountain dew, had misjudged a mountain curve some years back. He hadn't survived the crash. Karen's oldest daughter, Mona, now almost twenty, was married; and the other two children were well into their teens.

"My cousin, Ginger, has made quite a career for herself," Karen told me.

"Yes, I know." I laughed with delight. "I've seen all her movies, I think. I wonder what it's like to do all those love scenes with such good-looking men. Can you imagine kissing Paul Newman? And Sean Connery?" We reminisced about the days when Ginger had set the boys atwitter at Dixon High. At least I could say I knew her when!

Mom took a few days off work during my stay. We laughed at events that had happened in Redbud Grove, as we told and retold the same old tales that somehow grew more detailed with the repetition.

When I left Dixon, it was with renewed purpose. I intended to work hard all summer and clear my calendar for the weeks before and after Labor Day. I wanted nothing hovering over my head, nothing to distract me when I returned to the place of my childhood. Anticipation at the prospect filled my heart. I was going back to Pine Street, to the park, to the east and west side schools.

To Redbud Grove.

Reunion

On the Saturday morning of Labor Day weekend I took the earliest flight available, and I arrived at O'Hare airport at nine-thirty. It's close to a three hour drive from there to Redbud Grove, depending upon the traffic and weather conditions. The sky could not have been bluer, filled with clouds so puffy and white they looked artificial.

Eager butterflies churned my stomach all the way south on Interstate Fifty-seven. The closer I got to Redbud Grove, the more they fluttered. I didn't know how much change in the town to expect, whether it had maintained the same character or had become a forward-looking community, with no thought of preserving its history.

South of Champaign, I began to watch for familiar farmsteads upon the prairie horizon. I was entering territory my dad had covered on our early evening drives through the countryside. Very few new houses had been erected. Most of the area remained as it had for well over a hundred years—some of the richest, most productive farmland in the United States.

My heart beat faster when I left Tuscola behind. Only seven miles separate it from Redbud Grove. So flat is the land that the water towers in the two towns are visible to each other. Interstate Fifty-seven runs along the east side of the town. As I approached my exit, I kept glancing out the right window of the car, hoping to catch a glimpse of East Side Grade School. I didn't see it.

After exiting the interstate, I took the first street north on Route 133, determined to find the school. It had stood on the northeast corner of town for many decades, butted against farm fields. I knew I couldn't be mistaken about its location.

The school was not there. Where it had stood was a huge, blue steel building that covered the entire block. Not even a blade of grass was left of the schoolyard, where tall, spreading oak trees had once provided shade and play areas. The bleachers and the baseball field, where my dad's team had played every summer, were gone. The only thing that remained of the East Side Grade School grounds was the triangular concrete pad on the southwest corner, where school buses had loaded and unloaded their boisterous cargo. I was so disappointed.

I drove back to the highway. New places of business lined both sides of the street. Mullikin's cafe was gone. A Laundromat occupied the building that had housed a small mom-and-pop grocery store. A wooded area on the north side of the highway, once dark and a little scary, had been cleared. Houses lined both sides of the new paved boulevard that cut through the woods to the first cross street.

I turned north on South Locust and drove past the Cunningham house. The porches were gone, and the once-yellow building had been bricked. It matched the brick on the Catholic Church, which was separated from the Cunningham property by an alley. A sign in the yard announced that the house was now an annex to the church. I wondered where the Cunningham's had relocated. I could not imagine they had left Redbud Grove.

All the other houses looked the same, refurbished here and there, but familiar. More changes awaited me when I reached Main Street. On the corner where the Grab-it-Here grocery had been was a one-story, flat-roofed brick post office. Across the street, in the building that had housed the Ritz Theater, a hardware store reigned. Tall glass showcase windows took the place of theater posters that had announced coming attractions. I was disappointed again.

I turned onto Main and found a parking space in front of what should have been the Sweet Shoppe, next to a corner barbershop. The two buildings had become one, and they formed an Amish themed restaurant called The Dutch Kitchen. I didn't know whether to laugh or cry. Three of the places that had played such a big part in my childhood had been destroyed or replaced. I got out of the car. It was two o'clock, and I had to eat somewhere. It might as well be in the place where I had spent so many fun hours.

The restaurant was crowded, but I saw no familiar faces. Many of the diners must have been alumni, returned for the reunion; but it seemed that Redbud Grove had become a tourist attraction, too. I ordered the special of the day, and I discovered why so many people waited to be served. The food was delicious.

Back in the car, I couldn't decide where I wanted to explore next. For several minutes I watched people come and go. Across the street the pool hall, where my dad spent a lot of evenings with his baseball buddies, still had THE SMOKEHOUSE emblazoned in big white letters on the window. The Record Herald newspaper office, a small department store, and the gray granite bank all looked the same. Some things had not changed.

I crossed the Illinois Central tracks and Route 45, which divided the town into East and West Side. It was the way I had most often walked or rode my bicycle to school, from the sixth through the eighth grades. The street looked much as it had twenty-five years ago, until I came to the site of the West Side Grade School. It was only a huge, empty lot.

Nothing remained except the ghosts of memories and the images of the children we had been. I closed my eyes and conjured up a warm spring day, filled with the laughter and voices of those who had been my friends. Their faces were as fresh in my memory as yesterday, and I hoped with all my heart to see most of them at the reunion. I sighed, opened my eyes and turned around in the nearest driveway.

I had put if off as long as I could, but it was time to visit my old home. I retraced my route past the Dutch Kitchen to Pine Street. I turned south, past the Catholic Church, past the Monahan house where the sprawling magnolia tree, out of place so far north, bloomed every April. The brick street looked much the same. I crossed Route 133 again, and memories overwhelmed me. A scant block from the highway stood the house, now painted white with black shutters.

My dad would have been amazed at the size of the two elm trees he had planted when I was eight years old. They completely shaded the house and lawn and extended across half of Alley Street, between the house and the park. A white sign with red letters was posted in the front yard: FOR SALE. I wrote down the telephone number of the realtor.

I turned onto Alley and pulled into the edge of the park. I felt tears on my face. A range of emotions washed over me, but I couldn't pinpoint one single feeling. Across the street was the Davis house, the Romine house, the Klopfleish house, a vacant lot and the big, brick house once owned by Dutch and Goldie Racer. Straight south of the park stood the two-storied East house, but the East's no longer owned it.

More picnic tables had been added to the grounds, and I saw additional water fountains. The tall poles that held the swings stood in the same place, but other playground equipment had been added: slides and a small merry-go-round. I smiled with pleasure at the trees. Gnarled and so tall that they overspread each other, I couldn't resist getting out of the car to get a closer, hands on look.

I climbed onto the top of a picnic table, as I had so many years ago. I closed my eyes and listened to the sounds of yesterdays that were still inside my head: the soft whirr of a non-motorized lawn mower; the swings' rusty cables; metal roller skates clicking over the cracks in the sidewalk; the zing of cardboard, clothes-pinned to bicycle tire spokes; the smack of a jump rope hitting hard ground, all mingled with the rustling of leaves in the trees and birds in the air.

It didn't feel as if twenty-two years had passed. It felt like yesterday and the day before and the day before that. Even the air smelled the same.

"Sissy? Sissy Bannister?" I opened my eyes and looked into a face, familiar, but different. "Is it really you?"

"Sharon?"

Laughing and crying, we fell into each other's arms. We pulled away, stared into each other's face, and re-embraced.

"What are you doing in the park?" Sharon asked. She joined me on the table.

"I came into town about an hour ago. It just seemed natural to come to the park. Do you still live here?"

"Yes, on the west side. I just left Mother's house, and I decided to drive by your house. I had already passed you, but something about you looked so familiar I just had to stop. You look wonderful!"

"So do you!"

"I guess you came for the reunion?" she asked. I nodded. "I didn't see your name on any of the lists. Did you send in your reservation and bio?"

"Just the registration, but I used my married name: C. C. McCoy."

"Clever girl," she laughed. "Your husband didn't come with you?"

"He was killed in Viet Nam eight years ago."

"Oh, Sissy, I'm so sorry."

"It's okay."

"Where are you staying? Did you find a motel?" I nodded again.

"I'm reserved at a Best Western in Mattoon, but I haven't checked in yet. I should probably do that, so I can get ready for tonight." We stepped off the table. Sharon took a pen and paper from her purse.

"Come by my house, and we can go to the school together. I'll wait for you," she said. I looked at the address.

"Are you married?" I asked. Sharon grinned at me, and I saw the girl that she had been.

"Not any more," she said. "My older daughter is married, but my younger one still lives with me. She's with her dad this weekend. Why don't you just cancel your reservation and stay with me? We can stay up all night and talk as long as we want."

"It won't be an imposition?"

"Of course not. I have three bedrooms and two bathrooms and no one else in the house but me. I'd love for you to stay."

"Okay, I will." I hesitated. "Sharon, are many from our class coming to this reunion?"

"Lots of them."

"Will Lucinda Barnes be here? And Joe Bob Brady?"

"I didn't see Lucinda's name on the list, but Joe Bob is coming. Did you know that he's a Kentucky state senator?"

"No!"

"His data sheet says he's single."

"He hasn't been married all this time?"

"He's been married and has three children. The people in his district must really like him. Divorce isn't very acceptable in some places, especially in politics, and especially in sparsely populated areas. I think the fact that Joe Bob went back to his roots after college helped a lot with his political career." She nudged me on the arm. "What we don't know, we'll ask him tonight."

"Well, let's go to my house. You can follow me, and we'll catch up for a couple hours or so."

Sharon's house was on the west side, in the last block. Route 133 curved northward at the edge of the town before heading west again, and it could be seen from her driveway. Her kitchen window looked onto a flat farm field, brown with soybeans not many weeks from harvest.

I notified the motel that I would not be checking in, but I wanted to keep the reservation I had made for the next four nights. The clerk informed me how inconsiderate I was, since so many people wanted the rooms, what with a high school reunion being held in the area. "If you can rent the room tonight, I don't mind," I told her. "Just be sure it's available to me the following three nights." Her sniff of indignation was audible, but she assured me the room would be mine.

Sharon and I sat in her living room, where we looked at old photographs and yearbooks. I gazed at the faces in her senior annual, and for just a moment I felt bereft. My picture should have been

139

included. The moment passed. I could not regret the years and new friends in Dixon who had made my life so rich.

At six-thirty, Sharon suggested we get ready. "I hope you brought something dazzling," she said, "something to knock their socks off!"

Dazzling wasn't what I had in mind. The most important thing I had learned about clothing and dressing for any occasion was simplicity. The ambiance of dinner and dancing at a school reunion would be different from dinner and dancing in an elegant lounge, but the dress I chose was appropriate for either. A fitted, knee-length white sheath, sleeveless and v-necked, covered well and would be cool in a hot gymnasium, where the event was to be held. Should the evening turn nippy, the short-sleeved matching jacket would feel good. Sonya Howard had taught me well.

White sandals, a plain gold chain necklace and matching hoop earrings were my only accessories. I fluffed my hair with my fingers. Now just below collar length, it was long enough to allow the natural curl to bounce on its own. With a minimum of makeup and a small clutch bag, I was ready for whatever the night might hold.

I opened the bedroom door and took a few steps down the hall before I thought of my camera. A night like tonight would never happen again in just the same way, with the same people, in the same place. How could I not record it? I hurried back to the bedroom and took the smaller camera from the canvas bag, checked the film and quickly changed purses. The drawstring straw was not very glamorous, but it was white and it held the camera and smaller bag.

"I'm sure you remember where the high school is." Sharon said. I nodded. "The new grade school is right beside it. We might as well walk, for we won't be able to find a parking place. Do you mind?"

"No, I don't. My shoes are walk proof." I followed her lead down the sidewalk. Dressed in a not-quite-daring red dress, Sharon looked younger than the thirty-six I knew her to be. The scooped neck and short sleeves set off her petite figure perfectly. Her dark hair curled around her pretty face. We grinned at each other. The last time we'd had a night out together, there had been a curfew.

The weather could not have been more perfect. A soft breeze rustled through the trees, and the scent of ripe field crops rode upon the air. Four blocks from Sharon's house, through the trees I caught a glimpse of the high school's upper story. The new grade school, built of a light brick, stretched along the whole block just north of the high school, which seemed to look down upon the interloper from its lush, green knoll.

The new building centralized the schools, but I felt that the character of the high school had been compromised by the presence of a contemporary structure. Time and progress march on, I told myself; but I didn't have to like it. My views, no doubt, were based upon nostalgia more than the town's needs.

Those pesky butterflies flitted inside my stomach. I took a deep breath. Sharon glanced at me and laughed out loud.

"Sissy, you look a little pale. Are you all right?"

I swallowed hard. "Yes, I think so. It's just been so long. What if no one remembers me?"

"Are you kidding? You were one of the first ones we tried to find," she said. I didn't believe her, but I appreciated her kindness. "Do you want to go through the new school, or would you rather go on to the high school? All the classes from nineteen-fifty to nineteen-seventy are meeting there."

"If you don't mind, I'd like to see the high school again. This new building has nothing to do with me."

"Sure," Sharon said. We passed a group of men and women on the concrete steps leading up to the old school. "Several locals were holding happy hour in their homes at five o'clock. Looks to me like some of the alumni are pretty happy," Sharon laughed.

Tables on both sides of the long corridors held posters with class years on them, some of them multiple years. All the graduation classes were small, a good thing for an all-school reunion, such as this one. We stopped at the table with nineteen fifty-seven through fifty-nine on the poster.

"Hi, Judy. C. C. McCoy and Sharon Bennett," Sharon said. A Judy I didn't know handed each of us a nametag. I slipped mine into my tiny purse. "Do you want to mingle or find our table in the gym?" she asked.

"I think I'd like to sit down," I told her. During the last ten years, I had met with politicians, dignitaries and celebrities of all kinds; but I was more nervous in that school gymnasium than I had been at any of those interviews. So many people milled around, and the noise of dozens of conversations made it difficult to hear anyone clearly.

We found our section, which included four long tables. Some faces I thought I recognized, and I recalled a few names to go with them. I sat at the end of a table, content to watch other uncertain grown-up boys and girls try to find their places. At seven o'clock a tall, lean man approached a microphone on the wide stage at one end of the gym. Deep purple velvet curtains with a big white capital R in the center made an impressive backdrop.

"Ladies and Gentlemen, welcome to the first all-school reunion of Redbud Grove!" Appreciative applause filled the room "We'll begin with the dinner, served, appropriately I think, on the cafeteria trays used by students. If you stragglers would find your tables as quickly as possible, we'll get the dinner underway."

"Is he the principal?" I whispered to Sharon. She nodded. A few latecomers headed for our table. I smiled at two couples as they sat down. I knew the women immediately—Shirley and Cathy, two of the girls who rode out to the Thompson farm with me so many years ago. Quizzically, they smiled at me. Cathy stared at me.

"I know you," she said.

"Yes, you do," I replied. She looked for my nametag.

"You're—you're...."

"Taken any bicycle rides out by the Thompson farm lately?" I asked.

"Sissy! Sissy Bannister! Shirley, it's Sissy!" Cathy squealed. We clasped hands across the table. Suddenly I was no longer nervous. These were some of my childhood friends, and the kinship of youth was still there.

A tall, distinguished looking man, dressed in light trousers and open-collared blue shirt, approached our table. His thick, silvery blond hair, not too short and not too long, accented his tanned face. Silver-rimmed glasses sat atop his slightly crooked nose, and I knew I was looking at Joe Bob Brady. Twenty-two years ago, Lucinda Barnes had told me Joe Bob would be a handsome man. She had been right.

"Hello, Ladies," Joe Bob said. His smile and twinkling blue eyes rested upon each of us, as he glanced at nametags and addressed each person by name—except me. He smiled politely at me and spoke to Sharon. A classic double take brought his eyes back to me. He frowned slightly. "You're not...you *are* Sissy Bannister!" He came around the table, took my hand, and drew me to my feet. He wrapped his arms around me and planted a kiss upon my cheek.

"Hello, Joe Bob. How are you?"

He laughed. "I'm fine, Sissy. It's so good to see you!"

"I understand that you are in politics," I said.

"That's right," Joe Bob smiled. "Who would have thought it?"

I had to laugh. "Not I. Last I heard of you from Sharon, you were the football star of the Purple Riders. I thought you might have gone on to professional sports."

"I did play in college," he said, "but that was all I wanted. I appreciated the scholarship, but I went on to law school, not football." Those at our table joined the food line and moved slowly toward the cafeteria.

There were so many people whose faces were familiar to me. Many of them I could name. The cafeteria line rekindled a near-teenaged spirit among old and new, alike. As soon as the meal was finished and the trays returned to the kitchen, the master of ceremonies announced that a local band would provide music, should anyone care to dance.

The lights dimmed. A spinning silver ball shone above the designated dance area. The person who had set it up must surely have danced in the back room of the Sweet Shoppe at some time in his life.

The band played well. "Rock Around the Clock" exploded from their instruments. The saxophone was as good as any I'd heard. They swung from one fifties melody to another, balancing slow ballads with hardcore rock and roll. I watched couples dance the jitterbug, fox trot, and polka until they were breathless. Many of them must have been dancing together for years, for they moved as one.

When the band took a break, I took one, too. I remembered the way to the restrooms. The granite walls and floors had not changed. A collage of memories formed in my head, of my seventh and eighth grades on the ground floor, of basketball games and talent shows and concerts. I put forth my hand to push open the restroom door and nearly collided with a woman on her way out.

"I'm sorry," I said. I blinked. The woman stared as hard at me as I stared at her. More than a little plump, she had beautiful, creamy skin and green, green eyes. An abundance of dark red hair bounced upon the shoulders of her jade tunic that flowed over matching slacks. She was beautiful. She was Melissa Franklin.

"Melissa," I said. Instant recognition showed in her eyes.

"Sissy." We embraced, right in the middle of the restroom doorway.

"I was afraid you weren't coming," I told her.

"Oh, I'm late, as usual. There's always a crisis with the twins, and tonight was no exception."

"Twins? You have twins?"

"Honey, I have eight-year-old twin boys and a six-year-old daughter. That's the second group. We also have a fourteen-year-old son and a twelve-year-old daughter." Melissa grinned with pride and laughed out loud at my expression of disbelief. "How do you think I got so fat?" she demanded.

"Oh, Melissa, I'm so happy to see you!" I hugged her again. "Fat? Don't you know how beautiful you are?" She shrugged.

"Well, Larry still thinks so, I suppose," she said. "Do you remember Larry Corzine? He was three years ahead of us in school. We've been married for fifteen years, and we live in the house Daddy fixed up when we were kids. Larry's coming by a little later. Reunions are not his favorite sport."

"Of course, I remember Larry, the gorgeous hunk! I can't wait to see your house. I always loved it. Do you remember the day we followed your brother and the Amish girl upstairs, and..." I stopped, appalled at my lack of tack; but Melissa laughed.

"It's all right, Sissy. Sure, I remember that day. There's a lot you don't know about that day, besides Jeff being sent to the west coast. How long are you going to be in town?"

"I'm free all next week," I told her. She linked her arm in mine.

"You'll have to come to the house and meet my family; and then you and I are going to catch up on a lot of years." I forgot about the trip to the bathroom.

We joined the others at our tables. I wanted to speak with Joe Bob, but Laurie Shanafelt, a girl who was two years behind us, clung to his arm like a fly on flypaper in a cow barn. Shortly after the band began to play again, I had my chance. Laurie reluctantly released his arm, with Joe Bob's help. Before I could join him, he came to me. He pulled out the chair beside me and sat down.

"Tell me what wonderful things have happened in your life," he said. The soft Kentucky drawl was still a part of him, but it was a charming, toned-down version.

"Wonderful?" I asked. "There have been some good things, and I like my life. I'm a journalist, freelance, now. I've taken a week's break in order to come back to Redbud Grove. I hear that you are doing well in your home state." Joe Bob shrugged.

"I like politics. I like people, and I think I have something to offer. Tell me more about your writing. Would I have read any of it? I don't recall seeing your name in print."

I opened my bag and withdrew a business card. "This is my byline. My husband was killed in Viet Nam, and I kept his name."

"C. C. McCoy," Joe bob mused. *You are C. C. McCoy?*" I nodded. "You wrote that series about segregation in the fifties? Let me think a minute...one of the articles was about the sundown laws. I remember something about a stranded black family in a town that wouldn't let them stay overnight. Was that *here*?" I nodded again.

"That happened the same night Lucinda's mother was killed," I told him. His eyes narrowed, but he let it pass.

"There were other incidents you mentioned," he continued. "You wrote about some experiences with desegregation in high school and an incident about stopping to help someone with car trouble..."

"I'd rather not get into that now, Joe Bob," I said. "I just want to be Sissy Bannister tonight."

"I understand," he said, "only too well; but I was so impressed with that series. You should have won a Pulitzer." I grinned.

"I was nominated," I said. He shook his head.

"Who would have thought?" he said again.

"Joe Bob, have you ever heard from Lucinda Barnes? Or heard anything about her? I've wondered about her for years." His face sobered instantly.

"No, I haven't; but I've thought about her, too. I even considered hiring an investigator to find her, but I think I was afraid of what he would discover."

"Joe Bob..." I hesitated.

"Don't even ask, Sissy. We had this discussion years ago. Let it go."

"I can't." I whispered

"Sissy, for the love of..." He stopped. I looked at his face. Utter shock and disbelief froze his features. "Oh...my...." His eyes focused on the double doors of the gym, which were about four steps above floor level. I followed his gaze.

In the doorway stood the most striking, sensuously beautiful woman I have ever seen in my entire life, even to this day. Tall and slender, but somehow voluptuous, her short black dress clung to her body in all the right places; but it was not immodest. The garment didn't scream, it *whispered* designer. Her long blond hair gleamed under the lights. Curly now, it still fell like a satiny length of pale yellow silk below her shoulders. With slightly upturned, turquoise blue eyes, the woman surveyed the room.

"Lucinda!" Joe Bob whispered in disbelief. He half rose from his chair, and that's when Lucinda saw him. I had read about magnetism between two people, and I had seen movies in which two people seemed drawn to each other across a crowded room. I had thought it all fiction, until the moment I saw it happen between Joe Bob Brady and Lucinda Barnes.

Slowly, Lucinda descended the stairs as gracefully as if she were floating. Joe Bob stood tall and watched her approach, not taking his eyes from her. I think he stopped breathing. As Lucinda neared the table, Joe Bob moved toward her. For a stunned moment, they just stood there, not touching, not talking, but looking into each other's eyes. I don't know who moved first. It was as if they were drawn together by an invisible force that locked them into an intense embrace. It looked to me as if Joe Bob had no intention of letting her go. Tears stung my eyes. Being a witness to the moment was worth the trip back to Redbud Grove.

"Lucinda." he said. Before he let her go, he moved his hands down her arms and clasped both her hands.

"Joe Bob." Lucinda answered. Her red lips parted in the same perfect smile she had when she was thirteen years old. I remembered it well. Reluctantly, Joe Bob backed away from her

"Are you alone?" he asked. He seemed to hold his breath again, waiting for an answer.

"I am," she said. "My husband died several years ago." Mesmerized by the drama that unfolded before me, I could only sit and watch. Lucinda glanced around the table, nodded politely to some she seemed to recognize, and then she looked at me. I smiled.

"Hello, Lucinda," I said. She knew me the moment our eyes met.

"Sissy," she breathed. "I was hoping you would be here. Can we go outside and talk?" *Was she kidding? Just let someone try to stop me!* Without a backward glance, she turned toward the door. I followed, just as I had followed her when we were children. Like old times, neither of us turned back to look at Joe Bob.

We sat upon the concrete balustrades that lined the steep flight of steps at the front entrance. A cool breeze moved among the evergreens, tall and fragrant where they covered the lower part of the building. I looked at the northeastern sky. The Milky Way spread its wide swath across the heavens, the same view I had watched from my attic bedroom on Pine Street.

"Beautiful, isn't it?" Lucinda said. "It's difficult to believe such a lovely sky can stretch above such rotten people." *Ooh*, I thought. All must not be well with her.

"Not all are rotten, Lucinda," I reminded her.

"You're right," she smiled. "I was thinking about the time I lived here."

"We weren't all bad, were we?"

"No, Sissy. You and your parents were the exception."

"Where have you been all these years?" I asked. "Are you married? Do you have a family?" Without realizing it, I had slipped into my interview mode.

"So many questions. First, tell me about you."

"There's not much to tell," I said. "My family moved to West Virginia right after eighth grade graduation, and..."

"No!" Lucinda exclaimed. "All this time I've envisioned you living right here, married to some Redbud Grove boy you knew all your life."

"No. I got married after two years of college, and my husband went right into the Air Force. He was killed in Viet Nam in nineteen sixty-eight."

"Kids?"

"No."

"Never remarried?"

"No. I finished school, got a degree in journalism, and I live in New York. I worked for a couple of newspapers, but now I'm freelance. Now tell me about you. How did you know about the reunion?" Lucinda took a deep breath. She dropped her eyes, then gave me a rueful grin.

"I'm embarrassed to admit it, but I've subscribed to the Record-Herald for a couple of years."

I laughed at her. "You little hypocrite, you! I thought you had no use for Redbud Grove people." She shrugged.

"Oh, well. You asked about my life." She pursed her lips. "I lived with my grandmother after...after I left here. She died a year or so later, and I was shipped to a great-aunt in Los Angeles. My aunt was okay, I guess. She didn't know me, and she didn't need her life turned upside down by a fifteen-year-old kid. She did the best she could." Lucinda paused and ran her hands through her hair, lifting the long curly strands off her neck.

"Did you live with her through high school?"

"Yes; but as soon as I had that diploma, she wanted me out and on my own. I really didn't blame her. I got a job in a beauty salon, mostly cleaning up and stocking towels, a real go-for job; and I shared an apartment with two other girls. It wasn't much of a place to live, but it was safe.

"The manicurist liked me." Lucinda smiled, remembering. "I mean she really *liked* me, Sissy. She taught me how to do manicures, but I had a hard time keeping her friendship without offending her, if you know what I mean. She wanted to be more than friends." She cast that sideways glance at me, the same one she had used when she'd told me what I baby I was so many years ago. "It's a different world out there, Sissy. You wouldn't believe the propositions that were presented to me." Again, the sideways glance. "I took one of them."

I think Lucinda meant to shock me; but when I laughed, *she* looked shocked. She stared at me, full-face, before she chuckled. We couldn't stop. It had been so long since I had laughed like that with someone who knew me as well as, or better than I knew myself. It felt good.

"So who was he and what was the proposition?" I asked.

"His name was Malcolm Overstreet. He owned a modeling agency a few blocks from the salon, and he was a regular client of Brandy, the manicurist. He came in one day when Brandy was letting me work at her station. The first thing he said was, 'How would you like to be a model?' I laughed at him."

"I would have, too. That line is as old as sex."

"He came back the next day and the next and the next, until Brandy convinced me the guy was for real. I went to his office, signed a contract, and he put me to work."

"You're a model?" I asked. "Why haven't I seen you in magazines or anything?"

"Sissy, I haven't modeled for years! I was eighteen back then, and thin enough to suit the camera. Most of my work was contracted for teen magazines."

"What are you doing now?"

"I learned everything I could about the business, and I saved every cent I didn't need to live. After three years, I could no longer pass as a teenager. I had enough money to lease a small office, so I formed my own modeling agency. Malcolm wasn't happy about it, but he came around." Lucinda paused for a long moment. "I married him."

"Huh?" I hadn't seen that one coming.

"Malcolm was a sweet man, close to fifty when I met him. He looked and acted much younger, and he was good to me. After five years, he made another proposition to me. He asked me to marry him."

"Did you love him, Lucinda?" I asked.

"After a while, I did. He was ill, Sissy. Routine blood work found something that called for further testing, and he was diagnosed with pancreatic cancer. He had only a few weeks to live. He wanted me to marry him. He told me that if I lived with him until his death, he would leave his modeling agency to me. Everything else would go to his two children, but the agency would be mine. I thought about it for a day or two, and then I told him I would marry him."

I didn't know what to say, so I said nothing. Lucinda's story sounded so crass, even calculating. I felt a twinge of disappointment. She laughed. Her eyes actually twinkled.

"Sissy, Sissy," she said. "You still don't live in the real world, do you? Yes, it sounds as if I married Malcolm for what he could do for me. I admit that was part of it, but I cared about him from the beginning. Before he died, I could honestly tell him that I loved him, for I did. He treated me better than anyone else in the world—except you, Sissy. You were the only true friend I had from the time I moved here until I met Malcolm."

"What about Joe Bob?" I couldn't resist asking.

"Yes, Lucinda, what about Joe Bob?"

Neither of us had heard him approach. As one, we turned and watched the handsome man come toward us. He looked so casual, both hands in his pants pockets, strolling slowly, as if he hadn't a care in the world. His eyes said differently, readable even in the soft light that filtered through the windows.

"May I join you?"

"Of course," Lucinda replied. He withdrew his hands from his pockets and folded his arms across his chest as he sat down beside Lucinda. The three us sat silently for several moments, bound together by long-kept secrets of one horrible night, almost twenty-three years in the past.

"When we were kids, you and Sissy were my best friends, Joe Bob. I was just telling Sissy that no one else ever cared about me like the two of you did. You both saved my life, literally."

"Lucinda, don't…"

"Joseph Robert Brady, I think it's time Sissy knows what happened that night." Joe Bob faced Lucinda. He grasped both her hands and raised them to his lips.

"Lucinda, please don't. It doesn't matter any longer. It's over."

"My dear man, it will never be over for me. I've just learned to live with it." Lucinda leaned forward and pressed a soft, gentle kiss upon the lips of the boy who had adored her. From the looks of things, the man still did.

"You don't owe me anything, Lucinda," I told her. "I've thought about you for years, wondering where and how you were, hoping that you had a good life. Now I know that you have, and that's all I need to know."

"Just listen, Sissy." She glanced all around. With a rueful smile she said, "I don't think Sheriff Murphy is hiding around the corner. I'm not sure he believed our story, Joe Bob."

"Lucinda…" In resignation, Joe Bob bowed his head; but he still clung to Lucinda's fingers.

"Do you remember that Sunday, Sissy? We had gone to a movie in the afternoon, and you wanted me to stay at your house that night. You were worried I would be alone with Al Pitts."

"I remember, Lucinda."

"You were right to be worried, and I should have listened to you. Al was drunk. I think that's the only reason I was able to shove him off me. He would have raped me, maybe even killed me if he'd been a little more sober. After Al hit me, I ran barefooted to your house."

"Lucinda, do you have any idea how many times I've wished I had dragged you into the house and woke my parents?" I asked her. She shook her head.

"It wouldn't have changed anything," she said. "Al would have run away, and nothing would have been done. I was just the daughter of the town whore. No one cared."

"Yes, Lucinda, many people cared. There were some good people in Redbud Grove back then, and I'm sure there still are." Lucinda shrugged.

"Did you know I took your dad's golf club that night? It was leaning against the side of the house. When you went back inside to get some clothes for me, I moved it to the front corner. I picked it up on my way back home.

"Al wasn't there when I got back. I thought perhaps he was gone permanently; but I was glad I had that club. I still remember the way it felt in my hands." A far away, dreamy quality softened her voice. "I locked my bedroom door and put the club on the bed beside me, just in case Al came back; which he did.

"I was almost asleep when I heard him turn the door knob. He swore and kicked it in. The force of his lunge threw him across the bed, but I managed to grab the club and run into the living room. If he hadn't been so drunk, I probably wouldn't have had a chance. He was furious.

"He came out of the bedroom, roaring like an animal, telling me what he was going to do to me. When he reached out to grab me, I swung the club. I think I hit his arm, and he was even more furious. I closed my eyes and swung that club back and forth as hard as I could. He screamed, and I kept swinging."

"Lucinda, stop! You don't have to go on!" Joe Bob's hoarse, anguished whisper tore at my heart; but it was as if Lucinda didn't hear him.

"Al finally fell. I leaned against the couch, but I held onto the club like a baseball bat. I was afraid he'd get up again." Lucinda paused.

"That's when I saw my mom," she whispered. She cleared her throat. When she spoke again, her voice was steady and strong.

"She was lying behind the couch, twisted and bloody. There was a big gash on one side of her face, and her head was bashed in." Lucinda looked at me. "Do you remember Al's ring? The ruby eyes on the snake?" I nodded.

"I remember."

"You're confused, Lucinda." Joe Bob broke in. "You didn't see your mother until after I got there." He turned to me. "Al killed Lucinda's mother, Sissy. He cut her face with that ring when he hit her, and then he broke her neck."

"Joe…" Joe Bob placed one finger across Lucinda's lips.

"I saw them through the window when I ran up the sidewalk," Joe Bob said. "Al fell before I could open the door, and that's when I saw Lucinda's mom on the floor."

"Oh, Lucinda." Heartsick, I could only put my arm around her shoulders, offering what little comfort my touch could give.

"I took the ring from Al's finger and told Lucinda to throw it in the river. I told her to run and to hide somewhere safe, until I could get to her. Then I made up the story about the two men and a possible robbery attempt." Joe Bob and Lucinda stared into each other's eyes.

"The ring was slippery with blood. I almost dropped it." Still calm, Lucinda sounded as if she were telling a story about someone else. "His blood spattered all over me and the furniture and the walls."

"Lucinda was in shock, Sissy. I think we both were. I told her what we would tell the police, and I sent her to hide near the river. I guess that's when she ran to your house and hid in the garage. You found her the next night," Joe Bob continued. "That's it, Sissy. That's what happened." I nodded.

"Why didn't you tell me that day at the river?" I asked him. "The day you threw Al's ring into the water, remember?" He nodded. "You wanted me to think that *you* had killed both of them."

Joe Bob actually grinned. "Well, I wanted you to wonder. If you didn't know for certain, you couldn't tell anyone."

"I wouldn't have told anyway." For a moment, I felt as indignant as if the horrible events had just taken place.

"It doesn't matter." Lucinda smiled at both of us. She placed an arm around each of us and drew our heads together. She kissed my cheek and then Joe Bob's. "Sissy, do you mind if Joe Bob and I take a walk around the campus?"

"Of course not. I'm going to sit here and look at the stars, maybe make a wish or two before I go back inside." I grinned at my own words. "Will I see you both later?"

"Count on it." Joe Bob Brady may have been a politician, but I believed him. I watched them out of sight, feeling as if one weight had been lifted and another dropped onto my shoulders. Relief that Lucinda had apparently come to terms with the tragedy vied with the horror I knew she had carried for such a long time.

I glanced up at the star-filled sky. I focused on one big bright star, perhaps a planet. It wasn't the first I had seen that night, but with all my might I whispered one wish:

Serenity for Lucinda.

Reconnections

I stood and stretched my arms. A slow fifties melody wafted into the September night. Reluctant to rejoin the crowd inside, I moved to the music, willing away the conjured images Lucinda's words had created. The band played an old Nat King Cole song, telling me to "pretend."

For a moment I closed my eyes and "pretended" that I was fourteen years old again, in the old Sweet Shoppe, dancing in the arms of Victor Delacourt. I had always been good at pretending. Pretense and fantasy were two of my childhood companions.

Inside the building were more people I wanted to see. So far I had spoken with only a few, and I was curious about many. I had caught brief glimpses of teachers I recognized. Once brisk and vibrant, they had aged noticeably. That saddened me.

"May I have this dance?" Embarrassed at being caught dancing by myself, I turned to see who witnessed my performance. In silhouette against the light, the man's features were not discernible. "Do you still like to slow dance to Nat?" I frowned in concentration. I knew that voice.

"I don't know," I told the man. "I haven't 'danced to Nat' for a long time."

"Oh, come on, Sissy. I bet you still remember how." He came into the light. For just a moment, I thought he was a hallucination. I closed my eyes tightly. "Sissy Bannister, all grown up."

"Victor." His name floated from my throat, along with my breath. While I stood in stupid silence, Victor Delacourt walked slowly to me, put one arm around my waist, and placed my left hand upon his shoulder. As easily and naturally as breathing, he moved me across the concrete; but I swear it felt like moving on smooth, warm satin.

We were both taller. My eyes were level with his mouth, dangerously so. It had been a long time since I'd been at a loss for words. The area in my brain that controlled my speech had suddenly turned to mush, while all my other senses were in overdrive. I inhaled him, wondering how I could have remembered his scent all these years.

The tobacco smell was not detectable; but that wonderful, subtle pheromone thing emanated from him, as elusive as mist on a mountain. I moved closer to him, and his arm tightened, just a little. His breath moved the hair at my temples. I closed my eyes. Just as it had when I was fourteen-and-a-half years old, my heart picked up the cadence that beat: *Victor, Victor, Victor.*

At forty, Victor Delacourt moved with the grace of the eighteen-year-old boy I remembered; but his body felt harder, more muscular. The dim light from the windows revealed no silver in his black hair. His eyes, dark as midnight, still sparkled with life and humor. Something smoldered in their depths, not fire, but the promise of flame. He looked like an Italian cliché, the embodiment of sensuous masculinity.

It wasn't until later that I remembered all the questions I should have been asking as we danced: Are you married? Do you have children? Where have you been all these years? Do you still play your guitar professionally? How long were you in Elvis Presley's band? How did you get into that band? Where do you live now? *Why does my body still call out to you?*

"I looked for you, Sissy," he said. I smiled. "After I saw you at that concert in Charleston, I looked for Bannisters in the phone book. Only two were listed in the Charleston area, and they didn't include you."

"We lived in Dixon, about fifty miles from Charleston," I told him. *He had looked for me!* "We moved there right after my eighth grade graduation."

"I knew you had moved. I checked out your house by the park the first time I came back to visit my aunt. She didn't know your family, so she had no clue where you had gone. I wasn't about to ask around town for a kid...would have totally ruined my image." He struck a pose, supposedly cool. *He had looked for me!*

"You were what, about sixteen at the Elvis show?" I nodded. "Who was the guy with you? He looked older."

"He was, a little. His name was Jackson McCoy. I married him about four years later." Victor moved slightly away from me. "Jack died in Viet Nam," I told him. I had spoken those words many times that evening. Victor was the first not to reply that he was sorry. He pulled me closer. Subtlety had not been his strong suit when he was younger; it still wasn't.

"Do you have children?"

"No. Do you?"

"I have an eighteen-year-old son. He lives with his mother, to whom I was briefly married. She was a pretty girl who thought guitar players were sexy. When Elvis went into the army, our band broke up. So did my marriage. It seems I'm not much better than my dad was at fatherhood." *He's not married!* My heart did a joyous flip-flop.

"Do you still play guitar?"

"Mostly for my own pleasure. I don't sing much either, but I write songs; and I sometimes play with a band in...where I live." *Was that an evasion?*

"What have you written?"

"Well, there are ballads recorded by country singers. Some soft rock pieces hit the charts, too. 'Stay a Little Longer' and 'Firestorm' and 'Only Then' all did pretty well."

"You wrote 'Only Then'? For real? The words are so corny, Victor; but the melody is beautiful!" Victor put his mouth close to my ear, and I shivered when he began to sing. I'm sure my mother sang lull-a-byes to me when I was a baby, but no one else had ever sung to me. I forgot how corny-country the words were.

The sound of Victor's voice close to my ear, singing a song of undying devotion, should have been silly; but it wasn't. It sounded as if the words were meant only for me. I began to wonder if I was in a dream, and then Victor laughed.

"Are you suitably impressed?" he asked.

"Am I now supposed to melt into your arms, possibly swoon?" I managed to assume the same bantering tone as Victor. Not for anything would I let him know how he affected me.

"That would be nice," he said. "Let's take a walk." He took my hand and led me down the steps. We followed the same course Lucinda and Joe Bob had taken, but they were nowhere in sight.

"How did you know I was out here?" I asked.

"I went to your class section to see if you had come."

"You were looking for me?"

"Sissy Bannister, I've been looking for you, in one way or another, ever since I left this town twenty-two years ago." I stopped in my tracks. I couldn't tell if Victor were teasing or if he meant what he said. I laughed.

"Come on, Victor. What are you talking about?"

"I remember our date, Sissy. Do you? I was furious with you for making a fool of me, but I never forgot you. As I got older, I was angrier with myself. I really was a fool, a teenaged, hormone-driven fool. At least now I can apologize for making such as ass of myself." The last thing I had expected from Victor Delacourt was an apology. He tugged my hand, and we resumed our walk.

"You no longer smoke," I said. "When did you quit?"

"Several years ago. I was with Elvis when my dad was diagnosed with lung cancer. He died within a year. We never did get along, but no one should have to die like that. I couldn't remember a time when there wasn't a cigarette in his hand or in his mouth. I decided I could do without them. I don't see my son often, but I can say he's never seen me smoke."

"I'm sorry about your dad, Victor. My dad died, too, a few months before I got married. He smoked, too, mostly a pipe; but that didn't contribute to his death. He died in a coal mine explosion just outside Dixon."

"That's rough. I'm sorry, Sissy"

"Do you still need beer to have a good time?"

"What?"

"When I was in the car with you that night, you complained about the lack of beer. You were only eighteen, Victor." For a moment, he was quiet. My heart dropped, remembering Jack's addiction.

"Well, I do still like an occasional drink; but I don't drink a lot. Most of the really stupid decisions I've made were when I was under the influence, as they say."

I was appalled at the sense of disappointment I felt. It shouldn't have mattered to me how often, or how much, Victor Delacourt drank. Yet, it did.

We walked across the football field, bright with floodlights. A soft breeze tossed my hair. He squeezed my hand, and I shivered. I think the touch of his hand contributed more goose bumps than the cool air. Had I been a child, I would probably have pinched myself.

"How long will you be in town?" Victor asked.

"A few days. Then I have to go back to work."

"Where would that be?"

"New York."

Victor stared at me. "Where in New York?" he asked.

"New York City. I live in a Brownstone apartment not far from Central Park."

"Where and when do you fly back, assuming that you flew?" he asked.

"Next Friday at one o'clock, TWA, out of O'Hare."

"Good," he said. "I'm staying with my aunt for a few days. Would you have dinner with me one night?"

"Dinner would be nice. Is the Dairy Queen still here?" Victor laughed.

"I'll spring for more than ice cream," he said. "My aunt told me that the Embassy is quite good. Maybe we can go there, or I can make reservations somewhere in Champaign."

"Just call me at Sharon's. She was kind enough to offer me a room in her house. I should probably go inside and see if she's ready to go home." We turned back toward the school, hand-in-hand.

"Have you kept in touch with Sharon all these years?"

"Actually, no. After we moved, Sharon and I exchanged letters for some time, but then we lost touch. Cathy, Sheila and Georgia corresponded with me for a while, too. It's difficult to maintain a long distance friendship. Lives go different directions, families increase—we just don't take the time."

"How did you find out about the reunion?"

"Someone sent a newspaper article to my mother last spring."

"My aunt notified me," Victor told me. "I timed my visit with her around the reunion."

"Is your mother still in Chicago?" I asked.

"Yes. She remarried several years ago. My step dad is okay, I guess. He doesn't like me much, and I'm not crazy about him. It's better for all of us if I stay away, so I call her often."

"Do you still live there?"

"I'm not far from there," he said. Again, he sounded evasive; but I let it go. We retraced our steps back to the school.

Finished with music from the fifties, the band played tunes recorded by The Mamas and the Papas, Fleetwood Mac, Janice Joplin and other musicians from the sixties and newer things in the early seventies. The dance floor was filled with couples, some still young and supple, some not. Back at our table, Joe Bob sat with Lucinda. His arm rested lightly across the back of her chair, and they both seemed at ease.

Melissa's husband had joined her, but Sharon was nowhere in sight. Victor spoke to everyone, shook hands with Joe Bob, and then politely kissed my cheek.

"I'll call you at Sharon's tomorrow. I assume she's in the phone book," he said.

"Not too early," I cautioned him. "We plan to sleep late." He squeezed my hand, waved to the group and went back to his class section at the far end of the gym. I sat down at the table; and for the next hour I caught up with other classmates.

Lyle and Larry both owned farms near Redbud Grove. Norman taught in the high school, and Bert still lived in the area. Several classmates lived in nearby towns. I was surprised to learn how many who lived in or close to Redbud Grove chose not to attend school reunions there.

Pat Monahan and his older and younger brothers continued to work in the Thomas Monahan Company, founded by their grandfather, the first Thomas Monahan, in nineteen twenty-two. I had always known that the Monahan boys' father, also named Thomas, had been associated with the company; but I hadn't realized that three of his four sons would continue the tradition. I suspected that some of the next generation would do the same.

Rosalie and Glenn, two of the class, were married to each other and lived in Redbud Grove. Doug and Georgia, also classmates and high school sweethearts, lived outside St. Louis. Talk about shared memories!

I listened to those who had gone through high school together reminisce about school trips and proms, championship football and basketball games, and all those other events that had taken place without me. That was the moment I realized, like Thomas Wolfe, you really can't go home again.

The memories I shared with this group were from a younger, innocent time, before dating and matchmaking and teenage angst. For the most part, I was glad. I could look at all the men I had known as boys, and there was not one moment of embarrassment. With the exception of Jimmy, in the second grade, only one Redbud Grove boy had kissed me—Victor, the bad boy, who had been sent to the small town as punishment he considered exile.

I was suddenly tired. It had been a long day, filled with emotional ups and downs more draining than physical work. I wasn't alone. When the band stopped playing, Sharon wound her way among the dancers and joined us. "Whew! I haven't moved that much since the last high school dance; and you know how long that's been! Sissy, if it's okay with you, I'm about ready to call it a night!"

"I'm ready to go any time you are, Sharon."

"Sissy, I have a room in Champaign through Tuesday night," Lucinda said. "Could we meet somewhere one afternoon? I'd like to spend some time with you."

"I'd love to, Lucinda. I'm going to Melissa's for lunch Monday, but I could meet you on Tuesday."

"Good. Meet me at the picnic table in the park."

I didn't have to ask which table. At the door, I looked back at people of all ages who had walked the same old wood floors and played on the same school playgrounds I did. Taught by most of the same teachers, from the same books, in the same classrooms, we had a common, unbreakable bond.

We loved Redbud Grove and our memories of it. A few had resided here all their lives; but most, like me, had returned with the hope of recapturing, if only for an evening, a sense of golden-hued days and years of childhood.

I hoped that each one would go to their beds with happy recollections of good days filled with sunshine and laughter, summer showers and bare feet in warm puddles, best friends and wonderful teachers.

God bless us all.

Wonderland

Victor called at eight o'clock the next morning. I didn't hear the phone, but Sharon stumbled groggily into the guest bedroom to wake me.

"For Pete's sake, Sissy, couldn't he wait until the sun came up to call!?" she grumbled. I raised my head from beneath the pillow and opened one eye.

"Sharon, I hate to break it to you, but the sun is up. You'll have to open your eyes to see it." She shielded her eyes with her hand and squinted at me.

"Oh." She motioned me to follow her, and I picked up the phone in the living room.

"I told you we were going to sleep in," I muttered into the mouthpiece. The sound of Victor's chuckle brought me to an instant state of complete consciousness.

"It's a beautiful morning, Sissy. Instead of dinner tonight, why don't you spend the whole day with me? We can have breakfast at the Dutch Kitchen and get reacquainted with the countryside." The thought of a whole day with Victor Delacourt made me breathless. "Sissy? Did you fall asleep on me?"

"No, no, I'm awake!"

"I'll pick you up in half an hour. West Jefferson, right?" He hung up the phone. Half an hour! I tossed the receiver in the general direction of the phone and ran into the bathroom.

"Sharon, he'll be here in thirty minutes! Would you please find the pair of white slacks and a light blue knit top in my suitcase? I've got to shower!" I heard her grumble something that I hoped was affirmative.

With five minutes to spare, freshly bathed, shampooed and blown-dry, I stepped into sandals and sat down to wait for Victor. I felt like the fourteen-year-old I had been the night I met him at the Sweet Shoppe. Impulsively, I called to Sharon, who was grumbling at her coffee pot in the kitchen. "Hey, Sharon, can I borrow a red lipstick?"

It became very quiet in the kitchen. With a big grin on my face, I looked down at my red toenails. I wiggled them while I waited for a response from Sharon, which didn't take long. She peeked around the corner at me.

"For a minute there, you scared me," she said. "I thought you had reverted to childhood." She laughed at me. "Yeah, I remember that night. You came to my house wearing your girlie pink lipstick and a red tee shirt. I tossed my red one to you and you smeared it all over your mouth. You looked like a hooker."

"I did not! Besides neither one of us would have known what a hooker looked like," I retorted.

"Sure we did—like Lucinda's mom."

"Sharon!"

"Well, it's the truth. I'm sorry for what happened to her, and I wish that Lucinda hadn't been raised like she was; but the man who was killed with Mrs. Barnes wasn't the first one she had monkey-ed around with here in Redbud Grove."

"What are you talking about? I never heard anything about other men."

"We wouldn't have, Sissy. I heard my mom and a neighbor discussing possible suspects after Lucinda was sent to Oklahoma. You wouldn't believe me if I told you some of the names. Evidently, more than one of the locals had visited with Daisy. Whoever Joe Bob saw that night could have been someone that lived here." I squirmed at the direction our conversation had taken.

"Don't tell me. I don't want to know. Leave me some of my illusions. Daisy, huh? I never did know her first name. It fits, somehow. She was a very pretty woman," I mused.

"Oh, yeah, she was pretty, but not nearly as beautiful as Lucinda."

Much as I still liked and trusted Sharon, I couldn't tell her what had really happened. Joe Bob's career could be hurt, and Lucinda might possibly have to answer to local authorities. I didn't think what she had done could be construed as murder. She had acted in self-defense; and

Al Pitts had viciously killed Daisy Barnes. Still, there was no statute of limitations on murder.

"There's Victor." I rose and picked up my shoulder bag. "I have no idea where we're going or when I'll be back," I said, "but I'll pick up my things and stay at the motel tonight. See you later." I gave her a quick hug and went out the door to meet Victor.

He got out of his car to greet me. He looked so good! Jeans and a white pullover knit shirt revealed just how fit and muscular he was. Daylight confirmed that his black hair held no gray. The skin on his freshly shaved face stretched smooth and taut over his wonderful cheekbones. He looked tanned and healthy and delicious enough to eat.

Victor opened the car door for me. I caught the scarcely concealed appreciative appraisal he gave my legs when I swung them inside the car. Hmmm. I exhaled, only then aware I had been holding my breath. I couldn't wait to discover what the day would hold.

Breakfast must have been good, but I don't remember what we ate. We laughed and talked and stared at each other like two kids on a first date. We drank two pots of coffee. I didn't need the caffeine, for I was already wired enough to fly. It was close to ten-thirty when we left the restaurant.

Victor pulled onto Main Street and headed east. As we neared the First Baptist Church, I touched his arm. "Victor, could we go inside the church? Look. A few people are just now going in. Do you mind?"

"Not at all. I haven't been to church for years. Think it will help me?"

"It couldn't hurt!"

Those annoying butterflies started to dance inside my stomach again. Only a few concrete steps led to the door; but with each one, years seemed to drop away from me. I was ten years old again, dressed in my homemade Sunday best, shoes shined, hair barrette in place, ready for Sunday school.

The vestibule seemed to have shrunk. I felt like Alice in Wonderland, suddenly grown taller. Victor and I slipped into a back pew. Until he handed a handkerchief to me, I didn't know tears had begun to slip down my cheeks. Through moist eyes, I examined the sanctuary, which, like the vestibule, had shrunk. Red carpet runners covered the aisles, but the rest of the hardwood floor looked the same. It seemed a shorter distance from the back of the church to the raised platform, where the same pulpit stood.

Behind the pulpit, red velvet curtains were pulled across the baptistery, where I had been baptized at the age of eleven. I grinned at the memory. The pastor had instructed me to hold my breath when I went under, and he had held a white handkerchief across my mouth and nose.

It didn't matter. Somehow, I managed to draw in water; and I came up gasping and coughing so hard I gagged and nearly threw up on the pastor. I think he was happy for the Sunday school teacher to assist me out of the water.

To the left of the platform was a small choir loft, where the children's choir often sang. During one performance, my little sister, about three years old at the time, had lain in the floor and thrown a kicking, screaming temper tantrum.

At nine, I was totally embarrassed. I had desperately tried to upright her, until Miss Ghere, the director/librarian, told me to leave her alone, which had further embarrassed me. I ran my fingers along the pew in front of me. They were the same ones in which I had squirmed as a child, and they had been lovingly cared for over the years.

I glanced at the congregation, voices raised in familiar hymns, hands holding the same worn hymnals. The book in my hands could well be one I had held over twenty years ago. Carefully, I returned the book to the slot on the back of pew in front of us.

"Let's go," I whispered to Victor. He didn't question. We slipped quietly from the pew before the hymn ended. We didn't speak until we were back in the car. "I'm sorry," I told him. "I guess I didn't expect to feel so...so..."

"Sad?" Victor supplied.

"Exactly. The years I spent here were wonderful, but I had my mom and dad and my brother and sister. I didn't realize that time and people we love are temporary, that the years would disappear like fog in the wind." He took my hand and brought it to his lips.

"I understand," he said; and I knew he did. "Is there any other place in town you would like to see?"

I thought for a moment.

"The river. Let's drive down by the waterfront." Victor put the car in gear, and we continued eastward.

River Street hadn't changed much. Some of the more dilapidated houses had been torn down, and other small dwellings rose on the sites. Additional wharves had been added at the end of the street.

"That's where Lucinda's house stood." I pointed to a vacant lot. All traces of the violence-filled house had disappeared. That was probably a good thing. We parked near the wharf and strolled to the water's edge. An attempt had been made to beautify the area, somewhat successfully. Concrete urns overflowed with bright petunias, and several benches offered comfortable places to sit and watch the flow of the river.

At the end of the wharf, a weathered staircase led down to the water's edge and meandered for several yards among the willows, river birches and redbud trees.

"I want to show you something," I told Victor. It felt as natural as sunshine when I reached for his hand. To have mine enfolded into his warm grasp felt better than I wanted. I led him along the walkway until it ended, and then we strolled along a beaten path, away from River Street.

"The summer I was about ten or so, some of my friends and I decided we would learn how to swim along this bank. We stripped down to our underwear and splashed for a couple of hours one afternoon. Of course, we got muddy and stained; so we made up a story about playing in dirt at Shirley's house. Our mothers would have grounded us forever if they'd known we'd been in the river. So the next time, we took off all our clothes!" I laughed, remembering; and Victor laughed with me.

"I can see you now," he said. I blushed at the twinkle in his black eyes. We perched upon a huge tree root that extended from the bank into the water. Victor straddled it and pulled me into the sheltering support of his body. I leaned against him. He crisscrossed his arms around my midriff and held me securely. I sighed with contentment and rested my head in the hollow between his neck and shoulder. If I had turned my head just a little, I could have kissed his neck. The thought was so tempting I almost did it.

"This is nice," Victor said. His breath stirred my hair, as well as every other cell in my body. "I don't think I ever came down here." *And I thought he meant that holding me was nice!* "I bet the trees on the other shore are beautiful in the fall."

"Oh, Victor, you should see them in the spring!" I exclaimed. "That whole river bank is filled with redbud blooms, and the reflections just take your breath away!" I turned my head up to look at him, and I was a goner. His eyes captured mine and held as tightly as steel bonds would have. I stared into their dark depths. My heart jumped and raced when his lashes lowered to my mouth.

"Sissy Bannister, *you* take my breath away," he whispered. I knew he was going to kiss me. I still remembered what his kisses had been like when I was fourteen; but I wasn't prepared for the overwhelming rush of fire and longing caused by the touch of his mouth upon mine.

Something within me called to him, and he answered, as no other boy or man had ever done. I knew it was foolish, but I shut out all thought of anything except the moment. It didn't matter that I knew no more about Victor today than I did that night over twenty years ago.

I turned toward him and put my arms around his neck. Without embarrassment or hesitation, I kissed him back, thoroughly and completely. There was no tomorrow, only the yesterday that had held Victor, and the today that held us both.

"Sissy, Sissy…" he breathed against my cheek. He buried his face in my shoulder, and I could feel his heartbeat against my chest. At least I think it was his. It could have been mine. We clung to each other for a long time, savoring the moment, the river, even the tree root that held us.

He relaxed his hold upon me and raised his head. "You taste the same," he said. "How is it possible that I still remember the taste of you?" A wry grin twisted his beautiful mouth. "You were practically a child, which I didn't know at the time; but you still feel and taste the same." He leaned toward me and lightly ran his tongue along the outline of my lips. I shivered, and he laughed.

"Do you remember the last thing I said to you that night?" he asked.

"You told me I would really be something when I grew up." I tilted my head. "Am I? Am I 'really something?'"

Victor threw back his head and laughed, a delightfully deep, outrageously masculine laugh. "You know you are!" he accused. "We'd better get out of these woods before you become more of a nymph than you already are." He threw one leg over the root and rose to his feet. Before I could stand, he lifted me in his arms and stood me upon the ground.

"Let's take a ride through Amish country," he said.

We headed west, out of Redbud Grove. Only a few miles from the city limits, we drove into an area that was like entering a time warp, transported back one hundred and fifty years. The extensive farms held by the Amish looked exactly as I remembered. Many fields of corn had turned brown and would be ready for harvest soon. Dairy cattle dotted the pasturelands.

Any given homestead looked like a bucolic landscape painted by a master. Windmills, clotheslines and outbuildings clustered around each rambling farmhouse, some of which had wings built on to accommodate aging parents.

The rich loam of central Illinois often produces the highest yields of corn and soybeans in the country, and the Amish fields are among some of the best. How they accomplish such high yields with only horses, steam and manpower is amazing.

Unlike most of the organized Christian denominations, Amish worship services are not always held on Sundays and not in churches. They gather in homes or barns, perhaps once or twice a month, sometimes more often. No electric poles or lines connect the outside world to Amish homes. No cars or trucks are parked in the graveled driveways, unless Mennonite friends come to call. Traditional black buggies and horses provide the only means of transportation.

"Victor, slow down!" He wasn't driving fast, but he immediately slowed the car to a crawl.

"What is it?" he asked.

"There! Look at that man!" I pointed to a tall young man dressed in traditional black trousers and suspenders that crossed the back of his blue shirt. He looked at us and raised his hand in a polite wave before he disappeared into an outbuilding not far from the road. It was unusual that he wore no hat, and his auburn hair and short beard, an indication that he was married, shone like a banner in the bright sunlight. He was the image of Jeffrey Franklin, Melissa's older brother.

"What about him?" Victor frowned in concentration.

"That's Jeff Franklin's son! I *know* it! He looks just like Jeff!"

"Sissy, what are you talking about?" Victor picked up speed, and I turned around in the seat on the chance that the red-haired man had come out of the barn. I didn't see him. My thoughts raced in all directions. Uppermost in my mind were questions about Melissa's family, whether or not they knew about this man. Living in such a small community, how could they not?

"Victor, when I was twelve, Melissa Franklin and I were best friends. I was at her house often, even stayed overnight several times that summer. You know that big, refurbished Victorian house on the east side?" Victor nodded. "An Amish girl worked for the Franklins, a beautiful girl with dark hair and creamy skin and a great figure.... Stop drooling, Victor!" He grinned at me.

"Melissa's brother, Jeff, was eighteen or nineteen. He was home from college for the summer, and he was crazy about the girl. Her name was Rebecca. One day Melissa and I followed them up to the third story, Jeff's suite. Yes, I know. Disgusting that a kid would have such a place to live, isn't it?"

"I was thinking how rotten if was of you and Melissa to spy on them!" Victor laughed.

"We were curious! Actually, it was Melissa's idea. I was afraid we'd get caught, and Jeff would be furious with us. Anyway, through the walls, we heard the argument. Rebecca came running down the stairs with Jeff right behind her. She had just told him that she was going to get married to an Amish widower, who had two children; and Jeff was trying to change her mind..." I stopped to take a breath.

"Sissy, are you telling me that the Amish girl gave birth to a Franklin heir?"

"Well, yes, I guess I am."

"Come on, Sissy, that doesn't make sense."

"Victor, I saw the baby. I saw an Amish family get out of their buggy in front of the little department store, next to the Sweet Shoppe...the...the...the Dutch Kitchen, now. The woman was Rebecca, and I could tell she was already pregnant again. Victor, she was carrying a baby, about eight or nine months old. The wind blew the blanket away from its head, and I saw a mop of red hair and big brown eyes, just like Jeff's. Victor, I *know* that baby was Jeff Franklin's!"

"The baby could have been her husband's, Sissy," Victor reasoned.

"No. They got married in September. If the baby had belonged to Rebecca's husband, it couldn't have been born until June, at the earliest. That baby was at least eight or nine months old, a big baby; and Rebecca was already five, possibly six months pregnant again. You do the math!"

"Okay... but I bet even some Amish babies are a bit, uh, premature." Curiosity filled Victor's eyes when he looked at me. "So what are you going to do with your supposition?"

I slumped in my seat. "Nothing," I said. "It's not any of my business, but I'm just so full of questions." Victor kept driving while I mulled over the Franklins. I wasn't prepared when he turned the car into what looked like the middle of a cornfield. "Where are you going?" I asked. He just grinned and kept driving slowly along the right-of-way between fields. Within seconds, the car was engulfed, completely hidden among the tall cornstalks.

"This isn't...it *is* the place you took me that night!" I punched Victor's arm, and he started to laugh.

"Well, I thought we should at least take a look at the location of our memorable first date," he said.

"It wasn't a date! You didn't even pay for my movie ticket! All you wanted to do was neck with a new girl! You were a...a..."

"Creep?"

"Yes!"

"Lech?"

"Yes!"

"Jerk?"

"Yes!"

"Cradle robber?"

"Yes!"

"Did you like being kissed by me?"

"Yes!" I bit my lower lip. Victor's slow smile softened his eyes.

"Then or today?" he asked. I dropped my head. He took my chin in his hand and turned my head toward him. "Look at me, Sissy." I swallowed hard before I raised my eyes to his. "Then or today?"

"Both," I whispered, "but, Victor..." He kissed me again, not deep or demanding, just very, very sweet.

"I'm not trying to seduce you, Sissy. I just wanted to revisit this place." He took my hands in his. "I wasn't kidding about trying to find you. Even after my divorce, when I was dating other women, I wondered where you were and what kind of life you were living. I've never been able to forget you." He kissed my fingers.

"The reason I wanted to spend the day with you is that I have to go back to Chicago this evening. My mother called last night. Her only remaining brother is coming to see her tomorrow, and she wants me to see him, or him to see me." I felt a sickening surge of disappointment. I turned away.

"Sissy, I'm sorry. I'd like to spend more time with you, but I just can't right now."

"It's all right, Victor," I laughed. "Maybe we'll keep in touch. You can always call me at my apartment in New York sometime." I pulled away from him. "You'd probably better take me back to Sharon's. I need to gather my things and find my motel in Mattoon."

"Sissy..."

"Let's go, Victor." There was no room in my voice for discussion. The ride back to Redbud Grove was much like the first one I had taken with Victor. The difference was that, this time, I was the disappointed one. "Don't get out," I told him, when we pulled into Sharon's driveway. He didn't listen.

I grabbed my purse and walked quickly toward her front door. Victor caught me in two strides. He grasped my shoulders and shook me, just a little. I looked up to discover that he was grinning! Grinning!

He kissed my indignant mouth, once, twice, three times. By the third one, I softened considerably.

"I *will* call you," he whispered. "I got your address from the reunion records." I think I believed him. I *wanted* to believe him. For most of my life, he had lingered inside my head and in my dreams.

Now that I had seen him, touched him, kissed him, the thought of never seeing him again made my chest heavy. He was the first boy to kiss me, my dream lover, the phantom image on my wedding day, the boy I never forgot.

He was Victor.

The Whirlwind

From my motel room on Monday morning, I called Melissa Franklin Corzine. She invited me for lunch at her house, and I could hardly wait to enter the big Victorian her father had restored when Melissa and I were children. She told me to come at noon, so I had time to fill.

I drove north on Locust Street, past Dr. Fishel's office and several other old Victorian style houses, some desperately in need of repair. One of them, painted a dark, oppressive blue, triggered a memory. I parked in front of the house and stared at the decaying front porch.

It had been years since I'd thought about the witch's house; but there it was, much scarier looking than it had been when I was ten. There I sat, alone in a rental car, unable to stop the chuckles that came up from my throat.

Like watching a movie, I could picture Sharon, Shirley, Cathy and me as we had sneaked up to the side window of that house, determined to see what kind of spells the witch, Cora Parker, cast on her victims. At the memory of the town butcher in his drawers and how Cora had "disfigured" him, I laughed, loud and long.

Still chuckling, I drove on, before someone reported the crazy woman parked in front of a dilapidated house, laughing her head off. I made a mental note to record the story so I would not forget again.

Across an abandoned set of railroad tracks stood the old foundry, the factory that had drawn my dad to Redbud Grove so many years ago. I hadn't realized how small it was. I remembered the place as quite large. The buildings were made of metal, and what looked like sheets of tin covered the roof. I could only imagine how cold it must have been in the winter, even while the laborers worked with molten iron. Respect for my father's occupation grew exponentially.

It looked deserted. Tall grass grew along the limited parking space, and it looked as if no one made an effort to keep the place neat. There was no indication that another company had ever used it.

Back on East Main, I passed the library, another important planned stop on my itinerary. Thankfully, it looked just like it had when I got my first library card, at the age of eight. More images of Miss Ghere, the librarian/Baptist Sunday school teacher, spun through my mind. It was amazing how kind and how grim she could be, depending upon the situation. I decided to learn where and how the stately lady fared, and I planned a long visit inside the walls of what had provided my summertime day care.

"Come in!" Melissa greeted me with a hearty hug. She answered my knock on the back door immediately, so I knew she had expected me to come there. I couldn't recall a time I had entered her house any other way. "I probably should have invited you for tomorrow. I forgot that school would be out Labor Day."

"Don't be silly," I told her. "I was hoping to meet your children." The words were scarcely out of my mouth when two identical boys, blessed with the Franklin auburn hair, and a little girl, a petite version of Melissa, burst into the kitchen. "Keith! Karl! Lori! We have company! Behave yourselves! Say hello to..." Melissa looked at me. "What is your last name?"

I grinned. "McCoy," I said.

"Like in 'the real?'" she grinned back.

"No, like in 'the Hatfields and...'"

"Oh!" We laughed as we had when we were twelve. "Say hello to Mrs. McCoy."

"Hello, Mrs. McCoy." Keith, Karl and Lori, in unison, made me feel matronly.

"Patty and Kevin are with friend's." While she maintained a running conversation, Melissa made sandwiches for her lively crew. She poured milk, patted them on their heads, sat them in the nook and directed me to the sunroom, where she had set a lovely table for two. Salads, club sandwiches and iced tea awaited us; and I thoroughly enjoyed the delightful lunch.

"Sissy, do you mind if I ask about your husband?"

"What do you want to know?"

"How did you meet him? When were you married? What was he like? Were you happy?"

"In high school. When I was twenty. Wealthy, charming and abusive. In the beginning. His name was Jackson McCoy. He was named after his mother's family."

Melissa pursed her lips. "O-kay," she said, drawing it out as she rolled the information around in her head. "That pretty much covers it, I guess." She narrowed her green eyes and cocked her head to one side. "Are you happy now? Is there anyone else in your life? Someone you are serious about? Do you like what you do? How are your brother and sister?"

I laughed. "Yes. Yes. No. Yes. My sister lives in California, and my brother lives in Charleston, West Virginia. Beth has a little girl, and Bill has three boys. They are all very happy. Anything else, before we get down to you, your family and Jeff?" Melissa's green eyes twinkled.

"Oh, there's lots more questions," she said, "but I promised I would tell you about Jeff's checkered past...and his son." *Aha, so I was right!*

"Does Jeff live in Redbud Grove?"

"No," she told me. "He came back for a short time, but he hasn't been here since my dad died, five years ago."

"What about your mother?"

Melissa's mouth tightened. "Mother lives in Champaign. She left Dad when he brought..." She stopped. "I'm getting ahead of myself. Let me check on the kids while I bring in dessert. Then I'll tell you the whole sordid saga of the Franklins."

While Melissa returned to the kitchen, I examined the room. It had been redecorated, of course, probably more than once. The original woodwork in the house had been stripped and brought back to its natural finish; but in the sunroom, it was now painted white.

Soft yellow walls reflected light from the six windows, curtained with drawn-back strips of white gauzy fabric. An Oriental rug, in muted shades of antique gold, rusts and blue, lay beneath the glass-topped wicker table. Plump cushions, covered with dark gold linen, gave the white wicker furniture just the right touch. Matching place mats and napkins, complete with white, woven wood napkin rings, completed the magazine-perfect room.

"I hope you like fresh peach crisp," Melissa said. She carried a tray on which sat a white ceramic coffee server, two cups and two huge bowls of peach dessert, swimming in cream. "I know, I know," she grimaced. "I still love sweets."

"I didn't say anything," I laughed, "but I do remember how you loved cookies!"

The dessert was as delicious as Melissa's laughter. I knew I would not let this renewed friendship slip away again.

"I know I should get serious about getting my weight down," Melissa sighed. "I've been blaming it on baby weight ever since my oldest child was born! That just won't cut it any longer. But you know what?" she grinned wickedly and took another bite of peach crisp.

"What?"

"Larry always says, 'The softer the cushion, the better the pushin'." She winked at me, and we giggled like the teenage girls we used to be.

"Now I remember why I liked you so much." We finished the dessert. I was so full, I all but groaned.

"Okay," Melissa sighed. "On to the promised story." She winked at me again. "Maybe you can put it in a book or something," she said, "but you'd have to change the names. Jeff would probably kill you."

As Melissa began to speak, I leaned back in the soft cushions and let the prepetual movie in my mind play out the drama as she described it. Like most life chronicles, it truly was stranger than fiction....

Howard Franklin shoved the heavy drawer on the right side of his massive mahogany desk. It closed with a loud crack that echoed against the hard surfaces of the room. Ordinarily, he took time to admire the dark wood paneled walls and brown leather furniture. He had chosen every piece himself, from the long, overstuffed sofa and matching club chair, to the Audubon prints and original Remington paintings.

A slow-burning fire crackled in the original brick fireplace. It felt good against the chill of an early fall evening. Flickering flames cast undulating shadows on the walls and sent bright shafts of light off copper urns and gold-toned picture frames. The room reflected the taste and wealth of its owner.

The big man scowled at a picture on his desk. The handsome young man in the photograph smiled at the world, confident with his standing in it. He looked like his father. His thick, auburn-y chestnut hair appeared dark in the black-and-white picture. The elder Franklin's hair, just as thick and luxurious, had begun to gray at the temples. He didn't mind. He felt it lent an air of distinction.

Thirty when Jeffrey was born, Howard had denied his son nothing in the way of material things. He had assumed the boy would follow in his footsteps, would be the same strong leader of men and productivity, perhaps even assume the head position at Petro, Howard's own domain.

At the moment, he wished he had taken a more hands-on approach to fatherhood, instead of relegating most of the responsibility to his wife, Jeannine.

Howard thought about his wife, a woman of sophistication and style. He felt he had made a good choice in her, for she provided all a man in his position could wish: beauty, of course, but more than that. She exuded confidence in the way she moved, with the graceful fluidity of a dancer.

Jeannine ran the house as he ran Petro. She delegated menial jobs to her ever-changing staff of housekeeper and cook; and she hired additional help when they hosted dinner parties for board members and majority stockholders. For a long time, Howard had no complaints with the way she managed the house and their son and daughter.

Jeff seemed destined for greatness. Howard felt affection for his daughter, Melissa; but he had no aspirations for the plump, sometimes precocious, girl. No doubt, she would marry well and produce some children, which was all he expected of her.

At first, he had lauded Jeannine's decision to employ members of the Amish community. The young women were dependable, thorough and immaculate; and the food they prepared was second to none. Howard's many dinner guests left the big Victorian house with full bellies and praises for the chefs, who were long gone before the meal was finished. Jeannine had personally trained two local young women to serve. She feared that the Amish would be a distraction.

All went well until Jeannine hired that dark-haired Yoder girl. For two years after Rebecca Yoder left his household, Howard fumed with anger and disappoint. He had expected Jeff to sow some wild oats, so to speak; but he hadn't expected the sowing to take place in his own house.

Howard never got over the humiliation he felt the night Samuel Yoder came calling. The Amish man had driven his horse and black buggy into the driveway and right up to the back door. Yoder had been respectful enough, but Howard's sense of empowerment took a beating from the dignified words of a man to whom he felt superior.

When Jeannine had come to tell him who wished to speak with him, Howard had been curious, but not concerned. He had simply instructed his wife to escort their visitor into his office. He had stood and extended his hand, not surprised at the strong grip of the farmer.

Dressed in traditional Amish manner, the man wore a dark blue shirt beneath suspenders that held up black trousers. His long, black beard indicated that he had been married for a number of years; and his equally dark eyes gazed without guile into Howard's lighter brown ones.

"Mr. Franklin, I am Samuel Yoder. My family and my community hope you will stop your son from more visits to my home. Not wanted are his attentions to my daughter They are not good and have much distress and embarrassment caused her. You will see to this, yah?"

Howard floundered in ignorance of his son's actions. He stared at his uninvited guest, a man as tall as he, but with the thick arms and legs of one well acquainted with hard, physical labor. Speechless, he watched Yoder turn his wide-brimmed black hat in gnarled hands, the only indication of nervousness.

"Mr. Yoder, I know nothing about this incident; but I can assure you, if my son has conducted himself in such a manner, I will see that it doesn't happen again."

Samuel nodded in acknowledgement and turned to leave. "Thank you." Howard saw him to the door, where Samuel again nodded and placed his hat upon his head. Without a backward glance, he climbed into the buggy and clicked to his horse. "Gee-up," he said; and the animal clip-clopped down the driveway. Howard's growing anger became rage when he saw the huge pile of the horse's calling card, steam still rising, on the pristine white of the concrete.

"Jeffrey! Jeffrey, get down here!" The confrontation that had taken place between father and son had left both of them shaken. Jeff had been banished to a university in California the following day. As Howard had hoped and expected, Jeff soon forgot his infatuation with the Amish girl.

Unfortunately, Jeff found and married a California girl when he was still a junior in college. The girl's father owned a successful real estate company; and along with his daughter, he offered Jeff a position the young man could not refuse. Jeff forgot his obligation to Franklin family matters. Howard never forgave him.

Howard leaned back in his leather chair and swiveled it toward the windows behind him. He took satisfaction in the grounds that surrounded the refurbished house. He had managed to reproduce a piece of old world charm at the edge of an Illinois prairie town. Through the trees, he could see the Embarras River, where it flowed peacefully between its banks.

He contemplated the scene for several minutes before he picked up his telephone and dialed a memorized number. He spoke tersely into the receiver. "I want you to get someone to watch the Samuel Yoder farm in the Amish settlement. Don't be obvious about it. I want pictures of a

176

child who lives there. He's about three years old and has dark red hair." He listened for a moment. "I know they don't want their pictures taken! Don't let them see you take the pictures! Just take them!" He slammed down the receiver.

Howard and his wife had successfully managed to put a positive spin on Jeff's decision to leave the University of Illinois in favor of California's Berkley. Neither of them had mentioned the Amish girl or Jeff's involvement with her. Howard had not even thought about her until he saw a young Amish woman on Main Street, only days before he made the phone call.

With each hand, the woman led a toddler. The bigger one, about three years old, was a stocky little boy who walked with firm steps on the brick sidewalk. When the wind caught his small black hat and blew it off, exposing a thatch of auburn hair, Howard stopped in his tracks. His breath caught in his throat. Regardless of the boy's attire, at that moment Howard Franklin knew he was looking at his grandson.

The following years led to changes, as years do. Without telling another soul, not even his son or his wife, Howard Franklin amassed a collection of photographs. Periodically, he retrieved them from the desk drawer he kept locked when he was away from his home office. Only one key opened that drawer, and it hid among many others on Howard's key ring.

The pictures, all in color, had been taken with the most current cameras at any given time. Remarkable close-ups, the result of zoom lenses, chronicled the growth of Rebecca Yoder Martin's son. Howard learned that the boy's name was Adam. His growing attachment to the child became a near obsession.

In the photographs, Adam left boyhood behind. Howard could spread out the pictures and see changes from year to year. When Adam was fourteen, Ethan Martin, the man he had known as his father, was killed in a buggy accident. The badly injured horse involved had to be destroyed.

Howard, pseudo-sympathetic as he was for the Martin family, could not help but think the unfortunate event could play in his favor. As he had watched the boy grow, Howard had researched everything he could find on the Amish way of life. What he found excited him beyond belief.

He discovered that when Amish young people reach the age of eighteen, they have the option to participate in *Rumspringa*, a period of time wherein they are allowed to try the things of the world. Nothing is withheld from them. They may even move away, if they choose.

Howard Franklin decided then and there that he would approach his grandson at that time. He would invite Adam into the Franklin home and teach him all the things a Franklin heir would need to know. Fully confident in his ability to sway the young man, Howard did not contemplate any other outcome.

When the appointed year arrived, Jeff was nearly thirty-nine and had been married to the California girl for eighteen years. They had two daughters, ages fifteen and eight. Melissa, married to a Redbud Grove boy and living on the west side of town for ten years, had two children.

Howard had no constraints about denying his wife or his son knowledge of the son born to the Amish girl, Rebecca. He gave no thought to Melissa's approval or disapproval. It simply didn't matter to him. He felt his only problem lay in approaching the Martin family.

Unfortunately, Howard had not allowed for his wife's reaction to his decision. He had assumed she would follow whatever path he chose, as she had always done. He could not have been more wrong.

"Do you seriously think you are going to bring that Amish girl's son into this house?" Jeannine demanded. "How can you even consider such a thing?"

"The boy is Jeff's son."

"How do you know that?"

"Jeannine, all you have to do is *look* at him! He's the image of Jeff!"

"Where have you seen him?" she demanded.

Howard unlocked the drawer and spread the photographs across the top of his desk. "I've had these taken for several years. *Look* at him, Jeannine! He is our first grandson!"

Jeannine glanced at the pictures. At the age of sixty-three, Jeannine had few lines in her face. No one could have guessed her age, for she worked hard at maintaining what she felt was her best asset—her looks. At great expense, her hairdresser in Champaign prevented any hint of silver in Jeannine's once naturally blond hair; and Jeannine still possessed the figure of the eighteen-year-old girl she had been when she married Howard.

The stony set of her jaw and the coldness in her blue eyes destroyed the illusion of youth. *"You cannot bring that boy here, and you cannot acknowledge him! What would people think? We would be the laughingstock of the county! I won't have people pointing and suggesting that Jeff consorted with an Amish girl!"*

"Consorted?" Howard laughed. "Well, he certainly did, if that's what you prefer to call it. I call it getting a little..."

"How *dare* you speak to me like that? How can you be so crude?" Jeannine screamed at her husband."

"Well, if you prefer, we could let people think the boy is mine. After all, I lived here, too, when he was conceived."

Following Jeannine's gasp of shock, silence prevailed in the room. With a cry of rage, surprising in one who hated unpleasantness, she swept the stack of pictures from the desk onto the floor. "Do what you wish," she told her husband. "I won't be here to witness or sanction any of it." She turned and strode from the room, her back as straight and stiff as any Bethlehem steel rod.

Rebecca Martin removed the quilt block from her lap and rose to answer the knock at her front door. The tall man on her porch stood outlined against the early May sun, and she could not see his face clearly. "Good morning," she said.

"Good morning, Mrs. Martin. You may remember me. I'm Howard Franklin, and you once worked for my wife in our home." Howard smiled at the young woman, who was as lovely at thirty-five as she had been at sixteen, perhaps more so.

"Oh," she breathed. She raised one hand to her chest, clenched to still her shaking fingers. "Yes, Mr. Franklin. How are you?"

"Quite well, thank you. May I come in? There's a matter I would like to discuss with you."

Rebecca glanced over her shoulder. "My daughter is in the kitchen," she said. "For a moment let me see to her, please?"

"Of course. I'll wait here, if that's all right."

The woman nodded and softly closed the door. She swallowed hard before she went to the kitchen, where her eight-year-old daughter hand-stirred cake batter. Heat radiated from the big wood cook stove, but Rebecca shivered in its warmth. From a wall peg, she took down a black cape and draped it around her shoulders.

"Mama, are you cold?"

"Anne, there is someone on the porch to see. Right back I will be."

"Yes, Mama," the girl answered. She raised dark lashes and gave her mother a smile. Rebecca smiled in return, her heart full of love for this child, born only a few weeks after the death of her husband. It had been a hard time, but caring for the baby girl had truly been for her a gift from God.

Dread now in her soul, Rebecca walked into the brisk April morning to learn what brought Howard Franklin to her door. She tried not to display the fear that crawled over her spirit like spiders.

"Mrs. Martin, I'll come right to the point," Howard began. "You have a son, Adam. I have reason to believe that my son, Jeffrey, is the boy's father." He watched the blood drain from Rebecca's perfectly oval face. She seemed to stagger a bit before she backed against a wood bench and sat down.

"Why are you here, Mr. Franklin?"

"I understand your community has a practice called '*Rumspringa*,' which allows your young people to live in the outside world for a year. Is this true?"

"Yes," Rebecca whispered.

"I propose that you allow young Adam to live with me during that time. As a Franklin heir, he has the right to know his paternal family and to get acquainted with our way of life. Naturally, I would support his needs and desires while he is with me; and he would be safe." Rebecca looked at her hands, twisted in her black apron. They seemed even whiter against the dark material. She cleared her throat.

"Adam does not know..."

"I'm sorry, Mrs. Martin. I couldn't hear you."

Rebecca raised her head. "Adam does not know this thing," she said. "Ethan was good to us, to me; and he made not one difference between his older sons and Adam. Ethan died before our daughter came. Dishonored his name should not be." Her voice grew stronger. "If you agree not to tell him of his mother's shame, I will talk to Adam about your offer. He must decide."

Howard had not expected this. The whole point of bringing the boy into his house was to groom him, to mold him into the man Jeff was not. It had been his intention to tell the boy. He thought for a moment.

"If Adam fits well into our way of life, after a period of time, I must tell him his true heritage. If, however, he decides to return to the Amish community, I will say nothing to him of his parentage."

Rebecca stared up at the man who had just made her worst fear a reality. She turned her head to gaze at the newly plowed fields beyond the road in front of her house. She gazed at the flowerbeds she and her daughter had dug, and she thought of the seeds they had carefully harvested from last year's blooms. She loved her home, her children, her life.

Once more, a Franklin man was about to destroy her peaceful world. She closed her eyes in silent supplication, bowed her head for a moment and found her voice.

"I'll tell Adam of your interest," she said. "If his wish it is to partake of *Rumspringa*, he will come to you." Rebecca drew her cloak closer around her body in an effort to stop the chill that swept through her soul. It seemed her sin of so many years ago was not to go unpunished. She wished with her whole being that only she would have to pay, but she remembered the power and determination of the Franklins.

'Thank you, Mrs. Martin." Howard nodded to her before he turned sharply and walked like a young man to his car. Rebecca thought he looked very pleased, and her heart trembled for her son. At the gate, Howard turned back. "Mrs. Martin, I'll return in seven days. You won't have to notify me." He nodded and climbed into his car.

Since Adam's birth, Rebecca saw Jeff every time she looked at her son. Except for his mouth and the shape of his chin, his face was the image of Jeff Franklin. There was nothing she could do, except pray for her son.

Although Mr. Franklin had promised not to tell Adam, she knew Adam's innate intelligence would make the connection the first time he saw a picture of Jeff. She had seen the many family photographs in the Franklin house. Mentally, she drew back from the accusation she feared would one day be in Adam's eyes.

Rebecca wondered what retribution, if any, would come her way, should Adam choose to leave. There had been no meeting, no discussion, no protocol followed with her arbitrary decision. Adam couldn't know that his mother feared Howard Franklin's power more than the bishops, those in charge of the morals and conduct of her community.

Whatever retribution came her way, she would live with the consequences. Her overriding concern was for the safety and well being of her son. If he chose to live with the Franklins, her constant prayer would be that Adam would soon tire of their way of life and return to the people and the God of his mother.

Adam Martin lay in the hayloft of his deceased father's barn, but he should have been in the field with his older brothers. Spring planting, already well under way, didn't wait for a young man to decide his future. It must be done when the ground was ready and the weather was right.

The spring this year was glorious, warm and mild, with just the right amount of rain to soften the earth without flooding it.

Warm breezes blew through the open loft door, tall enough to allow a man to stand in the open space and pull heavy hay and straw bales through it. From the adjoining field, Adam could hear Seth, his oldest brother, call to the big black draft horses that pulled the hand-held plow.

From the tool shed beside the barn came the sound of steel against a sharpening wheel, powered by the foot of his other brother, Simon. The whine of the grinding stone grated on Adam's nerves, already stretched tightly. One moment he knew what he wanted. The next, he wasn't sure.

Adam thought about Abigail Shrock, the daughter of Ansel, three farms across the way. She was a pretty girl, fair-skinned, with a sprinkling of freckles across her pert little nose. At sixteen, she was of an age to be courted; and Adam had the inclination. If he chose *Rumspringa*, Abigail might decide on someone else. Adam frowned.

Some of his friends had already made their decisions. During the last three years, most of his eligible friends chose to remain in their homes and continue the way of life they had always known. Only two boys decided to take advantage of *Rumspringa*. They had already left their parents' homes, one to Chicago, the other to the west coast.

When his mother first mentioned Mr. Franklin's offer to him, Adam was intrigued with the notion of living like the people in Redbud Grove. He had seen the way town girls looked at him, some with disdain, some with interest. He wondered how they would treat him if and when he appeared in English clothing. His heart quickened at the possibilities.

"Ouch!" Something hard struck Adam's forehead.

"Gotcha!" Levi, only a year younger than Adam, peered at him from the top of the ladder. He held another corncob in his hand, ready to repeat the attack on his older brother. He ducked as Adam retrieved and threw the cob, barely avoiding the well-aimed missile.

"Seth sent me to get you. He wants you to relieve him on the plow," Levi said. "Simon needs Seth."

"I can help Simon," Adam said. Levi shrugged.

"You'd better go to Seth. He said he hadn't seen you all day."

"Adam!"

He sat up at the sound of his mother's voice. Adam looked through the loft opening. A long black car was parked beside the mailbox, and a tall man leaned nonchalantly against the door. Adam scooted around

Levi and swung quickly down the ladder. He brushed the telltale straw from his clothing.

"Tell Simon I'll be there as soon as I see what Mother wants."

"Adam!" his mother called again. He hurried through the barn and exited from the back.

"I'm coming, Mother!" He stopped at the backyard pump. He splashed water onto his face and dried with the towel that hung from a post for that purpose. He slowed his run to a dignified walk as he approached the front yard.

"Adam, this is Mr. Howard Franklin, from Redbud Grove. He wants to speak with you." His mother, usually friendly to everyone, seemed strangely subdued. She folded her hands in front of her apron and looked at the man, who was anything but subdued. A quiet excitement emanated from him. Adam felt that he had seen the man before, but he knew it wasn't likely.

"Hello, Adam." Howard extended his hand, and Adam took it. Adam knew he was being examined. "I'm sure your mother has told you who I am."

Adam nodded.

"I've seen you around Redbud Grove several times, and you seem like a bright, intelligent young man. I understand that you are at a crossroads, so to speak, and I would like to offer you a proposition."

Adam looked at his mother, who fixed her blue eyes upon his face. He raised his eyebrows, a silent question. She nodded. He turned back to the man.

"Are you considering *Rumspringa*?"

"How do you know about that?" Adam asked. Howard Franklin smiled.

"I've lived near this Amish community most of my life," he said. "I'm acquainted with many of your beliefs and practices." He looked at the silent woman. "In fact, your mother worked in my house when she was a bit younger than you. She made quite an impression on my family with her abilities and sweet manner. Her contribution to us is one of the reasons for my interest in you." His mother drew in her breath.

"If you wish to take a year away from this way of life, I'm offering my home to you. You may live in my house, partake of anything you want and I will support you. I'll even arrange for you to have a job where I work, if you wish. I'll supply you with a car, clothes, money and anything else you might desire. There is only one condition."

Adam's head spun with the possibilities. Nothing he had considered came close to what this stranger offered. He glanced again at his mother.

Everything about her was as familiar to him as his own breath, from her white prayer cap to the tips of her plain, black, laced shoes. He had never spent a day out of her presence.

"What is the condition?" he asked.

"That you do not return to this farm and that you have no contact with anyone in the Amish community until the year is over. If, at any time, you break that condition, I'll withdraw my support; and you will have to fend for yourself." Howard looked at his watch. "You have twenty-four hours to decide. I'll come back tomorrow at the same time, and you can give me your answer." He nodded to Adam's mother. Without a backward glance, he got into his car and drove away.

Adam looked after the car until it disappeared, and still he stared down the road. The sounds of the farm in springtime continued in the air: the clucking of hens, a boastful rooster's crow, bees in the honeysuckle that grew along a fence, the gee and haw of his brother directing the plow horses in the field. It was so much a part of his daily life—and sometimes, so very boring.

Behind him, Adam heard his mother open the door and enter the house. Still he stood, contemplating the life he knew and the life he might know. Twenty-four hours. He could think about all the possibilities for twenty-four hours. He went back to the barn and climbed the ladder to the loft. The hay smelled just as it did when he left, only minutes ago; but it seemed like hours.

"Adam!" The sound of Seth's voice reached him from the field. On his way down the ladder, it crossed his mind that this might be the last time he had to run when his older brother called.

Before dawn the next morning, Rebecca Martin served her family a full breakfast, just as she had done since she was seventeen. Simon said the blessing before they began to eat, but the usual chatter and daily planning were missing. Rebecca asked the question no one else would voice.

"What do you want to do, Adam?"

"I don't want to hurt you, Mother," said the boy. "I love you and my brothers and sister, but I know that Seth and Simon will take care of you, just like they always have since Papa died. Levi can take my place. I want to know what life is like in town. I'm going to take Mr. Franklin's offer."

A great sadness fell upon Rebecca's face, but she didn't cry. Adam's brothers rose from the table and left the house. He looked at Anne. She sat with her head bowed, but she didn't speak. For a moment, Adam felt that he had been shunned.

"You have that right, Adam," Rebecca said. "We will miss you, and we will pray for you."

"What should I take?" he asked. He couldn't hide his excitement, although he tried to control it, for his mother's sake. In spite of herself, Rebecca smiled.

"Nothing but what you wear," she said. "Mr. Franklin will see that you have town clothes."

Adam went upstairs to his room. It held two twin beds, one for him and one for Levi. They had been inseparable, like, yet unlike each other. Adam thought he would miss his younger brother more than anyone else. He sat on the bed and contemplated his life as he never had before, but he had made up his mind.

When Howard Franklin parked his big black Oldsmobile in front of the Martin's house, Adam stood beside his mother on the front porch. No other family members were visible. Howard watched as Adam put his arms around his mother, who briefly clung to the boy as if she would never let him go.

"Good-bye, Adam." Rebecca pulled away.

"Good-by, Mother. I love you."

"Go, Adam!" The anguish came out as anger, a reaction Adam had never seen in his mother.

"Adam, wait!" The front door burst open. Anne flung himself into Adam's arms. "I wish you wouldn't go!" she sobbed. Adam hugged her tightly.

"Anne! Let your brother go! He has the right. The Lord will keep him safe." Rebecca drew her daughter into her arms and held her while Adam hurried across the lawn toward the car. "Come inside," she said. Before Howard could pull away, Rebecca led the girl into the house and closed the door. When Adam looked back, not one member of his family was visible.

Adam would never forget his first view of the Franklin house. He had been to Redbud Grove many times, but his trips had always been with family members to grocery or hardware stores. Sightseeing excursions through town were not common occurrences for the plain people. He had rarely ridden in automobiles and never driven one.

"Come inside, Adam," Howard told him. He opened the back door, which led into the spacious kitchen. Howard led the way up the back staircase to the second landing. From there, he took a third, shorter set of stairs, which led to a smaller landing, decorated in red and white. The landing formed a cozy reading area, complete with winged back chairs and many lamps.

Indicating that Adam should follow, Howard led the way through the single door, into a combination bedroom sitting room. It took up the remainder of the third floor. Tall windows stretched across the north and south walls and filled the room with light. A pair of armchairs flanked a long sofa, separated from the sleeping area.

"This was my son's room before he left for college," Howard said. "He seemed to enjoy it very much, so I thought you might also like it." He watched the boy's eyes as they flew from one object to another.

"It's very big," Adam remarked. He thought of the room he shared with his brother, Levi. In it were a wardrobe, two straight chairs, and two twin beds, covered with handmade quilts. It wasn't big enough to accommodate anything else.

Adam looked at the full bed, covered with a thick comforter in dark shades of blue, dramatic against the off white carpet that covered the floor. Matching lamps stood on the side tables, and books filled floor to ceiling shelves on the whole east wall. A would-be avid reader, his mouth practically watered at the sight of so many books.

"What do you think, Adam? Will you be all right staying in this loft apartment? If you don't like it, we'll find a room for you on the second floor."

"This is fine, thank you," Adam nearly stumbled over his words. "It's a very nice room." His words sounded inadequate in his own ears.

Howard opened yet another door, and Adam followed him into a full bathroom. Unusual at the time of the house's remodel, Howard had commissioned a walk-in shower, as well as a full bathtub. He crossed the tiled floor and slid open a pocket door to reveal a large closet. He indicated the row of clothing: slacks, shirts, suits and blue jeans. Shoes lined a shelf, and there was lots of drawer space.

"I think you might find something here to fit you for now," Howard said. "Tomorrow we can shop for more up to date things, and you may pick what you want. I'll leave you to explore. Go anywhere in the house you wish. Everything is open to you, except my office. That door will be closed." Howard turned away. "Oh, there's food in the refrigerator; so make whatever you want for lunch. I'll be back sometime after five o'clock."

Adam listened to his benefactor's steps go down the first flight of stairs. He crossed to the windows and watched the black car disappear down the winding driveway. Only then did he gingerly sit on the bed, bounce a little and smile at the softness of the comforter. He caught a glimpse of himself in the mirror and stared at the familiar reflection. His clothes looked utterly out of place.

He hurried to the bathroom and stripped his homemade shirt and trousers from his body. It took only moments for him to figure out the cold and hot water faucets in the shower. For the first time in his life, he enjoyed the luxury of abundant hot water, sweet-smelling shampoo and soap that was not made of lye and wood ash. He smiled with the pure sensuality of creature comforts.

When the picture of his mother and the rest of his extended family edged into his mind, he turned the faucet on full force and washed away the images. The siren call of freedom, wealth and unimaginable experiences that awaited him sounded sweetly in his ear. He was going to enjoy *Rumspringa.*

The following weeks of summer proved to be all Adam Martin could desire. Howard took him to Champaign, where he bought a complete wardrobe of new clothing, shoes, even a stylish haircut for the boy. He was surprised that the new hairstyle detracted from Adam's resemblance to Jeffrey, which suited him just fine.

At the end of the first month, Howard presented Adam with a set of keys to a new Mustang, as red as a winter sunset. Howard came home earlier and earlier in the evenings, and he spent this extra free time teaching Adam how to drive. Adam was a quick study, and he got the feel of the wheel in record time.

Adam passed his driver's exam and took to the road with the exuberance of any teenager in nineteen seventy-one. He tuned the car radio to music he liked, and it wasn't hymns. Howard asked only one thing of him: Adam was not to tell anyone of his Amish ties. Howard introduced him as a nephew, and no one questioned the relationship.

The only person Howard could not fool was his daughter, Melissa, who came by the house at her father's invitation. The current housekeeper had refrigerated a light lunch, which Howard set on the kitchen table.

When Melissa entered the house, Howard tried to tell her a partial truth with the introduction. "Melissa, this is Adam Martin. I'm sure you remember Rebecca Yoder, the young Amish girl who worked for your mother one summer? This is her son, and he'll be staying with us while he takes some time away from the Amish way of life, a practice called *Rumspringa.* While Adam is with us, he'll be presented as your cousin, so as not to create uncomfortable questions for him."

"Hello, Adam. I'm happy to meet you." Melissa stopped staring at Adam long enough to offer her hand and a smile. "I hope you enjoy your stay here." Rarely at a loss for words, Melissa sat at the table and ate with her father and her nephew. She asked Adam general questions, without touching on his personal life; and lunch appeared to be a pleasant meal for all three.

Dad, may I speak with you in your office? There's a matter I need to discuss with you." Without waiting for a reply, Melissa turned and crossed the hall and sitting room toward the closed door of her father's inner sanctum. The door was locked.

"Just a moment, Melissa," her father stated. He selected a key from the ring and allowed his daughter to precede him.

"Dad, what are you thinking? That boy is the image of Jeff, and I know he's Jeff's son! Is this why mother left you?" Howard moved to the chair behind his desk.

"Lower your voice," he ordered. The genial host had disappeared, and the in-total-control father she had always known appeared in full force. "I know the boy is Jeff's son, but he doesn't. As of now, only you, I and his mother know."

"What about Mother?" Melissa asked.

"She guessed."

"So that *is* why she moved out. She told me you and she had a disagreement, so she moved to Champaign until you come to your senses."

"That's close enough to the truth, I suppose. Melissa, I have an agreement with Rebecca. I agreed not to tell Adam of his true parentage, and she promised not to stop his living with me for a year—or until Adam decides to embrace the Amish way of life forever."

"What if he goes back home? Are you going to tell him then?" A speculative gleam shone in Howard's brown eyes.

"I don't know," he said.

"What about the pictures of Jeff you have all over the house? All Adam has to do is see one of them, and he'll reach his own conclusion," Melissa pressed.

"I took them down. They're locked in the file cabinets," Howard explained. Melissa shook her head.

"Dad, you're playing with Adam's life. It's true he's your grandson, but that doesn't mean he'll want to be a Franklin. Jeff isn't too keen about it." Melissa's cheeks flushed in frustration and embarrassment. She knew she had gone too far with her father.

"It was good of you to come by, Melissa." The tone of dismissal was the same one Howard used with his employees. He rose from his chair and circled the desk. He opened the door and stood aside for his daughter to exit the office. "Next time, you might want to bring Kevin and Patricia. I think they would enjoy meeting Adam."

Melissa hurried through the house. She gathered her purse and keys and smiled warmly at Adam, who sat patiently at the table. She couldn't help but notice that Adam had barely touched his dessert of key lime pie. "The pie isn't as good as the ones your mother makes, is it?"

Adam actually blushed and ducked his head for a moment. "No," he answered.

"Good-bye, Melissa," Howard spoke from the doorway.

"'Bye, Dad. I hope your new project works out well for you. I think your blueprints have a lot of miscalculations that need to be adjusted. Otherwise, it doesn't have a prayer of succeeding. See you later, Adam." The back door didn't exactly slam, but it came close.

It was just a matter of time before the girls in Redbud Grove heard of the new boy in town. It would have been hard to miss the handsome lad in the bright red Mustang. Adam struck up conversations with people at gas stations, cafes, even department stores. His new appearance gave him confidence, for he no longer felt different.

At an early age, he had learned not to react to rude questions from tourists. Although it became more difficult as he approached puberty, he walked away from would-be confrontations with town bullies. Those occurrences had been rare, for his trips to town had been few and far between.

After the Sweet Shoppe became a restaurant, there were few places left for young people to meet. The Dairy Queen was popular on summer nights, and Adam's new social life debuted just as summer began. The graduating high school class contained some very pretty girls, and most of them were intrigued with Howard Franklin's visiting nephew.

Adam soon found himself in great demand among both boys and girls of the town. Not one person recognized him as a member of the Amish community. He was careful to use town talk. It wouldn't do for him to slip and twist around verbs and nouns, common among those who are used to speaking Amish German.

Available to drive to a party with carloads of other people, Adam enjoyed taking a girl and one other couple more than going with a group. Summer seemed to melt away with the hot days and warm nights, filled with new sensations and relationships.

During the colder months of autumn, graduates who didn't leave for college gathered at various hangouts in Mattoon, to the south, or Tuscola, to the north. Sometimes a carload of teenagers drove to Champaign, where many restaurants and bars catered to the college crowd. It was there that Adam tasted his first alcoholic drink, bought for him by a college student. He didn't especially care for it.

Melissa invited them to her house for Thanksgiving. She was warm to Adam, and he enjoyed her son and daughter. Before dinner, Melissa's husband, Larry, asked a blessing on the food and gave thanks for their family. An unbidden lump formed in Adam's throat, for he could picture his mother, brothers and sister sharing their meal at a table with one empty chair. He swallowed hard, and the moment passed.

Two weeks later, Howard invited Adam to take a trip. "Adam, how would you like to go to Hawaii for Christmas this year?" Howard asked. "Melissa and her children are spending the holiday with her husband's parents, and Jeff won't be coming. What do you think?" Adam's mind whirled with the thought. *Hawaii? For Christmas?* He thought of the simple observations of Christmas he had always known.

"I don't know what to say," he told his benefactor. "I never dreamed of seeing such a place."

Howard chuckled. "It's a veritable paradise," he said. "I'll make reservations, and we can leave a few days before Christmas. We'll take only an overnight bag. I hate dealing with luggage. It's summer all year round in the islands. We can buy everything we need right there, and I'll have it shipped back here when we're ready to come home. You'll have a good time, Son." Howard clapped the boy's shoulder, an affectionate gesture that came more easily with his grandson than it had with his son.

"Thank you, Mr. Franklin," Adam grinned. "I mean, Uncle Howard." Subterfuge had been alien to Adam before he became of part of town life. Now, not only was he living in the manner of the world, his relationship with the man who made it possible was a total lie. At times, he felt as if he were in the middle of a dream, that he would wake and find himself in the room he shared with his brother.

Adam was too excited to be scared. With wide eyes, he examined the airplane's interior. He listened to the pre-flight instructions carefully, and he had a moment's pause at the mention of seat cushions as life preservers. His heart accelerated at the same rate as the plane's engines on takeoff.

On the flight from Chicago to Los Angeles, he watched the ground from his window seat, exclaiming at the sights below him. In LAX, he watched, with awe, the constant ebb and flow of thousands of people. He had thought Champaign was a big city, but Los Angeles was beyond his comprehension. So many people milled around in as many directions, and the noise was constant.

Their first class seats to Honolulu far surpassed the coach accommodation on the flight from Chicago. A superb lunch was served, and drinks of all kinds were available for the asking. Howard used the time to look at papers in his brief case before he took a long nap. After the first hour of watching the Pacific Ocean through clouds, Adam dozed, too.

He dreamed of his new home in the beautiful Victorian house. It was as if he floated from room to room, where he touched all the beautiful things and ran his hand over shiny wood tables. He seemed to float upward, toward his loft; but his mother stood at the top of the stairs, preventing him access.

"What are you doing, Mother? You don't belong here."

"Neither do you, Son. Come home. Come home, before it's too late."

"I like it here, Mother. It's a wonderful place. Just look at the bathrooms and the lights and my car. Mother, you must see my car."

"Adam, please come home now. Adam. Adam...."

"Wake up, Adam. Through the window you can see Pearl Harbor. Look." Howard pointed to the memorial. Disoriented, Adam blinked wordlessly at the place where so many young American servicemen lost their lives, long before he was born. The color of the water had changed from deep, bottomless blue, to shades of green: emerald, teal, aquamarine and turquoise.

Long, rolling waves, some tipped with foam, rushed to the white, glistening sands of the beaches. Adam caught glimpses of tall palm trees and boulevards as the plane descended, and excitement caused him to tremble with anticipation. He glanced at Howard, who smiled with what looked like satisfaction.

For his whole life, Adam would look back at those ten days with a sense of wonder. From the moment he stepped off the plane, he felt as if he had landed in another world. Even the air was different, sweet with flowers and an essence he could not name. It smelled freshly washed. *If rainbows had a scent*, he thought, *this would be it.*

Their suite at the resort had a sitting room with an ocean view. The two bedrooms both had a television, wet bar and bathroom. Although the flight had been long and Adam had been up since very early morning, he was too excited to rest. A softening of the blue sky with the faintest hint of purple spoke of the coming night, but the beaches still held many worshippers of sand and sea.

"Is it alright if I go down to the water?" Adam asked.

"Sure, go ahead. Don't you think you might be a bit over dressed?"

Adam looked down at his clothes. He had carried his overcoat folded over his arm when he left the plane; but he still wore warm casual pants and a long sleeved shirt, comfortable attire for Illinois in winter.

"Oh, I guess I am."

Howard laughed. "Don't worry. Let me change, and we'll hit some of the shops in the hotel. You can change into the new things as we buy them, and then we'll go to dinner. It will still be twilight on the beach, and you can explore all you want." He laughed. "I'm betting jet lag will catch up with you as soon as you eat."

Howard was right. By the time dessert arrived at their table, Adam's eyes began to grow heavy. After the meal, they took the elevator to their fifteenth floor suite. Shortly thereafter, Adam barely shed his new shorts and cotton shirt before he collapsed onto the softest bed he had ever known. Through the open window, he drew in deep breaths of the balmy sea air, filled with the scent of orchids and rainbows. Sleep came quickly.

Over the next few days, Adam's itinerary was filled with a combination of intoxicants found only in the Hawaiian Islands. Howard spent most of his daytime hours in his room with his briefcase and the telephone, but he made sure that Adam had as many of the island's pleasures as possible.

Whale watching took up most of one day. Instead of the usual tourist vessels, Howard booked a passage on an exclusive yacht, which catered to a limited number of passengers. Binoculars, as well as lunch, were provided; and the deeply cushioned seats and long benches allowed those on board to view the illusive whales, should they be spotted, in comfort.

Couples comprised most of the travelers, but a few strikingly beautiful young women made the voyage. Clad in a bikini, topped with a semi-sheer white cover-up, one of the girls smiled brightly at Adam as the yacht headed for open water. Like any young, red-blooded eighteen-year-old male, Amish or not, Adam responded.

"Hi," she said. "I'm Tiffany." She extended her hand, which Adam took.

"Hi. I'm Adam." Adam took Tiffany's slender fingers but was afraid to apply much pressure. She was a slim, near fragile-looking girl, with long brown hair and deep blue eyes.

Adam could hardly raise his eyes from her mouth. His experience with kissing, newly acquired, had not yet included such a voluptuous, delicious looking mouth. Tiffany's smile exposed the whitest, most perfect teeth Adam had ever seen. She drove away any lingering half thought of Abigail he might have nurtured.

For the hour it took the yacht to reach reported whale water, he and Tiffany sat together in a cozy cushioned corner on the upper deck. She dazzled him so completely he forgot why he was on a boat miles away from the beaches of Honolulu.

"Thar she blows!" In response to the cry from the pilot, excited chatter erupted on both decks.

"Look!" Tiffany pointed. She threw her arm around Adam's waist, and they rushed to the nearest rail. About two hundred feet from the boat, a huge gray breached and appeared to hang in the air for a breathless second before he sank back into the ocean. Spontaneous applause and shouts of admiration echoed across the decks.

"There's another one! Look! Look!" Adam's arm circled Tiffany's shoulder, and he pulled her closely against his side. She hugged his waist with both arms and squealed with delight. "Look, Adam, it's a pair!" A smaller gray breached beside the first one in graceful movements as beautiful as ballet.

Adam didn't know what excited him most, the spectacular appearance of the two whales or the nearness of the beautiful girl in his arms. When the grays disappeared beneath the foam, he was fairly certain the girl took precedence.

"Folks, I've been steering vessels in these waters for twelve years," announced the pilot, "and this is the first time I've ever seen such a sight! Someone on this ship must lead a charmed life, for this is something to write home about!" At the moment, Adam felt that the charmed life was his.

For another three hours, the yacht cruised the waters in search of additional whales; but none appeared. Adam didn't mind. He wished the boat could stay out as long as possible. He and Tiffany reclaimed their corner and sat close together as the pilot revved the engines and turned the vessel toward shore. He cleared his throat, unsure exactly how to go about the next move

"Do you have plans tonight?" he asked.

"Nothing special," Tiffany replied.

"Would you have supper, uh, dinner with me? I mean, if you don't have to be with your parents or anything." *Dolt! She may not be with her parents! She may be with friends or something!* Tiffany laughed, and Adam blushed.

"I would love to have dinner with you," she said.

"My, uh, uncle and I are at the Hilton. The restaurant is nice, if you'd like to eat there. Where are you staying?"

"Not far from your hotel," she replied. "Why don't I meet you at the Hilton's restaurant at eight o'clock? Maybe we can take a walk on the beach after dinner."

Adam thought his heart would leap from his chest. It was going so much easier than he anticipated. He couldn't believe that such a lovely girl would be so approachable. Hoping not to appear too obvious, he glanced at the golden skin of Tiffany's slender, beautiful legs below the translucent beach robe, which showed a tantalizing outline of her body, without being brazen.

Too soon for Adam, the yacht dropped anchor; and the shuttle skiff appeared to return the passengers to shore. He was disappointed when Tiffany joined the other two young women and walked away with them on the boardwalk. She turned and waved to him, and his spirits lifted accordingly.

"What should I wear?" Adam, fresh from his shower and wrapped in a towel, stood before the open closet in his room. Howard chuckled.

"It's the girl who's supposed to worry about that," he said. "It's very casual here, but you don't want to look like a tourist at dinner. Wear those light slacks and the tan short-sleeved shirt. You don't need a tie."

Adam stood in the hotel lobby and waited for Tiffany to appear. Several times he glanced at his gold wristwatch, a Christmas gift from Howard. The minute hand seemed stuck or barely moving; but as it crawled closer to eight o'clock, he worried that Tiffany wouldn't come.

He raised his head from another watch check, and there she stood. His chest tightened at the sight of her. Dressed in a white sundress with tiny straps, her skin looked like golden-touched ivory. Her shiny brown hair touched her shoulders and gleamed in the soft light of the lobby. Adam tried to take in every inch of her at once, but it seemed impossible. Even the small sequined bag she carried caught and reflected beams of light.

Tiffany's high-heeled white sandals clicked lightly on the marble floor as she approached him. Adam's heart seemed to beat in cadence with her steps, and he swallowed hard.

"I hope I'm not late," Tiffany said.

"No. No, you're not. Late." Adam felt as if any semblance of social skills he may have developed had deserted him, but the gorgeous creature seemed not to notice.

"Good," she said. "I assume you have reservations?"

"Oh, yes. Yes, we do. My uncle is waiting for us at our table." Adam nearly trembled when Tiffany took his arm. He wasn't sure which one of them led the way to the dining room.

Through a Tiffany-filled haze, Adam ate what he ordered; but he was never able to remember the food. He watched her charm Howard, the waiter, the busboy and, he was certain, every man and boy in the dining room. From his perspective, Tiffany was the most beautiful girl in the hotel, on the island, in the world.

"Adam, I hope you young people will excuse me. I have a late night appointment on the other side of the city, so I won't be back until very late." He glanced at his watch. "I may even stay overnight. If I'm not back by midnight, don't look for me. Tiffany, it was delightful to meet you. Adam, you and the young lady have a good evening."

Howard nodded and left the dining room. Adam saw him speak to the maitre'd and knew that the dinner would be charged to Howard's account. He tried not to think too much about the amount of money being lavished on him. It was beyond his comprehension, but he enjoyed the benefits.

"Do you still want to walk along the beach?" he asked Tiffany.

Ruefully, she looked at the wisps of shoes on her bare feet. "I suppose I could go barefooted," she said. Amazed at his boldness, Adam made a suggestion.

"We could go up to our suite. It has a big balcony, so we could watch the moonlight on the water from there." Tiffany considered for the space of three seconds.

"That would be so nice," she said.

In the elevator, Adam pushed the button for floor fifteen and tried not to appear as nervous as he felt. His mouth, dry as parchment, caused his tongue to stick to his teeth. He fumbled with the key at the door, but managed to open it on the third try.

"This is lovely," Tiffany exclaimed as she wandered around the sitting room. She touched the bamboo box on the glass-topped cocktail table. "Which way to the powder room?" she asked.

"Mine is off the bedroom, through that door," Adam directed.

"I'll be right back." Tiffany smiled at him. Adam opened the balcony doors and took a deep breath of the sweet night air. He crossed the tiled floor and braced both arms against the waist-high concrete railing.

A three-quarter moon appeared just above the ocean's horizon, and its reflection cast a pathway of gold all the way to shore. The murmur of the rushing waves blended with balmy, flower-scented breezes—earth, wind and water, joined in a symphony unlike any music Adam had ever heard. Even fronds of the potted palms on the balcony brushed against each other, an additional instrument in nature's star-lit serenade.

"How lovely it is here." Adam sensed Tiffany's presence before she spoke. The jasmine of her perfume belonged with the sensuality of the night. She rested her head lightly against Adam's arm and entwined her fingers with his. Her hand felt warm.

"I've never seen anything like this before," Adam said. "I couldn't imagine how big the ocean is. I can't, even now, while I'm looking at it." He drew his eyes from the sea and looked down at Tiffany. In the moonlight, Adam thought her face took on the aspect of everything beautiful. His pulse quickened at the sight of her. She raised her head.

As if drawn to a magnet, Adam lowered his head and brushed her mouth with his. Tiffany responded in a way that made Adam's head spin. Her lips parted, and she kissed him as he had never been kissed. During the weeks he'd lived in the Franklin house, Adam had kissed a few girls; but this was a whole other planet.

"Adam," she breathed against his mouth. "Adam, make love to me." The boy knew he must be dreaming. In the first place, what she asked of him was forbidden until marriage. In the second, she was too beautiful to want a near-red-haired Amish boy. In the third, he was inexperienced and afraid. "Adam." Tiffany's voice became a husky whisper. Thoughts one, two and three dissolved like a sliver of ice on hot metal.

Adam experienced no clear thought until much later. He woke in his bed among a mass of twisted sheets, embarrassed to find that he was naked beneath the linens. He ran his hand through his hair and glanced around the moonlit room. There was no sign of Tiffany. He drew on his trousers and pushed open the bathroom door. The room was empty.

Puzzled and oddly relieved, he looked through the silent sitting room. A faint light showed beneath Howard's bedroom door, and Adam felt a moment of panic. Had the man come in while Tiffany was there? Had a light been left on, without Adam's noticing earlier? Could Tiffany be inside that room? Adam knocked softly, but there was no answer.

He opened the door. A draft from the open window blew a small piece of paper from the nightstand onto the floor. Adam bent to retrieve it and replace it against the lamp. He didn't mean to read it, but he saw his name in the text. Curious, he held it to the light.

Mr. Franklin, I have done as you requested. Adam is a happy boy tonight. You can send the rest of my money to my hotel, addressed to me. You know where it is. The clerk delivers personally.

Xxx's and Ooo's......Tiffany

Adam sat on the bed and reread the note several times. He felt the blood drain from this face. What he feared just could not be possible. Tiffany was too beautiful, too refined to even consider.... Surely Howard Franklin was not a man to buy a woman, not for anyone, certainly not for a boy he hardly knew.

Adam put his head in his hands. Disgust toward Tiffany and Howard filled him; but most of all, he was disgusted with himself. He put the note on the nightstand and left Howard's room, carefully closing the door. He hurried to his bathroom and turned on the shower. All his life he had dealt with cow manure, horse dung, chickens and all manner of filth; but never before had he ever felt so dirty. Head bowed, he stood beneath the stream of water for a long time.

Finished in the bathroom, he left the light on and shuffled toward his bed. The complimentary mint still lay on the nightstand, along with a sheet of hotel stationery he had not noticed. When he picked up the note, he caught a whiff of Tiffany's perfume, a subtle, expensive scent. In elegant script were two words: Call me! An island number, in bold numerals, followed. Adam tore the note into tiny pieces and tossed them into the wastebasket.

The clock on the bed stand pointed to three when Adam heard Howard come into the suite. The man scarcely made a sound, not even when he closed his bedroom door. Adam lay awake during what was left of the morning hours. He watched the approach of a rosy dawn above the water; but it seemed artificial to him, even tainted. Adam felt years older than when he left the prairie.

During the remainder of their stay, Adam acquiesced to Howard's suggestions. He smiled in the right places, laughed at Howard's stories and was the epitome of a happy tourist. There had been no mention of Tiffany until the day before the flight home.

"What happened to that pretty girl who had dinner with us the other night? Tiffany, wasn't it? I thought you might see her again. Did you get her telephone number?" Howard seemed genuinely interested.

"She gave her number to me," Adam said, "but there's no reason to call. She lives here, and I don't."

"I thought you liked her," Howard pressed. Adam shrugged.

"She was pretty." Wisely, Howard dropped the subject of Tiffany.

The flight back to the mainland was uneventful. Like a jaded traveler, Adam slept during most of the trip. In Los Angeles, they discovered that airports in the Midwest were closed, due to snow and ice storms. It could be as many as six to eight hours before air travel would begin.

"Come on, Son," Howard said. "Since we have such a long wait, you should see some of this city." The suggestion piqued Adam's interest in spite of himself. Howard flagged a taxi and instructed the driver to hit the main tourist spots. For two hours, Howard kept the cab on his payroll, driving through the palm tree lined boulevards where rich, famous and infamous celebrities lived.

Some owned sprawling estates, while others' domains were less ostentatious. All were behind high, wrought iron fences, some with gate attendants. "Are they keeping people out or themselves in?" asked Adam.

"Both, I think," Howard laughed. "We'd better go back to the airport," he told the driver. "Weather can change rapidly in the Midwest." They had arrived in California at five o'clock, and they should have reached Chicago before eleven, Central time.

It was still three hours before they were able to board a plane for O'Hare. The plane circled for an hour after they reached Chicago. When they were finally cleared for landing, it was a scary, bumpy ride. Ice could not be completely removed from the runways, and the city streets and highways were hazardous.

Even Howard Franklin was unable to locate a nearby, vacant hotel room; so he and Adam spent the rest of the night with other unhappy, stranded passengers. The roads were just too treacherous.

Early the next morning, Howard and Adam had coffee and a leisurely breakfast. It was nearly noon before they could take a shuttle to the parking lot. They had to brush off several inches of snow from Howard's car and scrape away a heavy layer of ice from the windows. Howard used a cigarette lighter to thaw out the door handles, and both men sighed with relief when they finally crawled into the cold car.

One lane on each side of Interstate Fifty-seven was passable, although still snow-packed and icy. Adam thought Howard drove too fast. At times, he felt the car slide in the frozen ruts, but he didn't voice his uneasiness. After all, his driving experience was next to nothing, compared with the older man's.

As they neared Champaign-Urbana, Howard spoke of his plans for Adam to enroll at the University of Illinois's spring semester. Although Adam had not attended high school, Howard assured him that his innate intelligence and abilities would be sufficient to get him admitted. Adam said nothing.

"Don't you want to go to college?" Howard pressed.

"I don't think so," Adam murmured.

"You won't have to worry about finances, Adam. I'll take care of everything. You simply must attend college, because you can't get anywhere in today's world without a degree. I'm sure there are any number of subjects that will interest you."

"No," Adam answered. Howard took a quick look at Adam's profile.

"What do you mean, 'No?'" he demanded.

"I mean, 'No, thank you.'"

"You're turning down the chance to make something of your life? A chance to go places and see the world? To become anything but a farmer?" Howard's voice rose with each additional demand.

"Mr. Franklin, I think I've seen all of the world I need to see. I want to go home."

Howard Franklin's face grew flushed. His breath quickened at the same pace as the speedometer on his car. Adam tightened his grip on the hand rest. "Mr. Franklin, I'm grateful to you for your hospitality and your generosity to me." He shook his head. "I'm just not suited for your way of life."

"Well, I'll say one thing for you! You're as stupid as your father is!" Howard shouted.

"My father?" Puzzled, Adam looked at Howard, who jerked the steering wheel and sped into the passing lane. The back tires fishtailed, but Howard passed a slower car successfully. Through narrowed eyes, he glanced at Adam.

"That's right, your father! You look a lot like him, you know. You got that thatch of hair from him, and he got it from me! It's about the only thing he did get!"

Adam blinked his eyes. He truly did feel stupid, for nothing Howard said made any sense. Howard spoke as if Adam's father was still alive, but Ethan Martin died when Adam was little more than a child.

"What's the matter, Boy? Haven't you figured it out yet?" Howard stared fully at the befuddled boy beside him. "Your father is my son, Jeffrey Franklin! Your mother is the little Amish slut that worked in my house and seduced my son! *You, you ungrateful little bastard, are my grandson! And you're going to do more with your life than live on that farm with cows and chickens!*"

"Mr. Franklin, look out!" Too late, the angry man turned his eyes ahead. The car strayed again into the passing lane, headed directly toward the concrete overpass columns. Howard braked hard, which threw the car into a deadly spin. The massive column seemed to rush at the car, which smashed into it, driver's side foremost. The last thing Adam remembered was the sensation of flying through the air, and then there was darkness.

Alien sounds and sensations seemed to float above and around him. Voices murmured; bell sounds dinged from far away, and someone coughed. He tried to move his legs, but one was too heavy. His sides hurt when he breathed. He told his left arm to move, but it would not.

"Adam? Adam, can you hear me?" A soft, insistent voice called to him. "Time to wake up it is, Adam." *I am awake.* "Open your eyes, Adam." *I'm too tired.* "Adam, can you squeeze my hand?" *Not now. I'm still tired.*

"His vital signs and neural responses are good, Mrs. Martin," a strange voice said. "Nurses will be monitoring him throughout the night. I'll check on him before I leave the hospital. You should get some rest, too."

"Thank you, Doctor Wells." He knew that voice, but what was his mother doing here? Where was here? Why did his head hurt so? He heard a slight beep, and sounds began to fade away....

With a great effort, Adam opened his eyes. The room was filled with bright light, so he closed them. He heard a faint, constant beeping sound, as regular as a heartbeat. It still hurt to breathe, so he took tiny little breaths, until he forgot and tried to take a big one. He groaned.

"Adam, are you awake?" his mother spoke softly. He opened his eyes, just a slit; and he saw his mother's face. She looked so beautifully familiar. Tears filled Adam's eyes.

"Mama," he whispered. "So much I missed you."

"Shhhh, Adam. No talk. Just rest." He felt her cool hand against his forehead, and he closed his eyes in gratitude. He knew that everything would be all right.

The next time Adam opened his eyes, his mind was clearer. Although he had never before been inside one, he knew he was in a hospital. The window was dark, so night had fallen. He just didn't know which night. He had lost all sense of time.

"So you are finally awake." Adam tried to turn his head toward the voice, but it hurt too much. "Don't overdo. I can move. You can't." The pretty face of Melissa, Howard's daughter, came into view. "Your mother went for some coffee. She hasn't left since you were brought here."

"How long?" Adam was surprised that his voice was little more than a whisper.

"Five days. You took a really nasty bump to the head. It's a good thing it's so hard."

"What else?"

"Well, let's see. You have one broken leg, several broken ribs, a cracked collarbone and a dislocated shoulder. You were unconscious until last night. Aside from all that, you're fine. It's a good thing you landed in a huge snowdrift, or you could have really been hurt." Adam grinned at Melissa's wry attempt at humor.

"What happened?" he asked. Melissa's face sobered instantly.

"There was an accident," she told him. "You and my dad were in a car crash."

"There was ice," Adam said. Melissa nodded.

"Yes, Dad skidded on the ice and hit an overpass support."

"How is he?"

"Adam, my dad didn't survive the crash." A single tear ran down her face, and she brushed it away. "He died instantly. His funeral was yesterday. My brother came home for the service." Melissa's green eyes searched Adam's face. "Jeff and I both have warm memories of your mother, Rebecca, from the time she worked for my family, when I was a child."

Adam turned his head away.

"I told Jeffrey that our father had invited you to spend your year of *Rumspringa* at his house. He was surprised, as I was; but Dad was always doing something out of the ordinary. Jeff will be here only until the will is read, and then he's going back to California."

Slowly, Adam turned back to Melissa. "You know, don't you?"

"Know what?"

"About me."

"I know that you are lucky to be alive," Melissa answered. Her gaze didn't waver as she looked directly into Adam's brown eyes. "With your head all bandaged like that, you look like a mummy. It's a shame these pretty nurse's aides can't see your gorgeous hair." She chuckled briefly, before she continued.

"Adam, you have nothing to worry about, except getting well again. If you wish, after you recover, you're free to live in Dad's house, as before." Melissa rose. "I know he enjoyed having you there."

Adam started to shake his head, but the motion brought pain. "No, thank you," he told Melissa. "I want to go home." He raised his eyes to the window.

"I understand," Melissa said. She approached Adam's bed. Gently, she took his right hand in hers. "Adam, if you ever need anything, anything at all, you can always come to me. Adam, look at me." After a moment, Adam shifted his gaze to her.

"I don't want anything from the Franklins," he said. He had been a boy the first time he saw Melissa, only a few short months ago. Today he was a man. Melissa nodded.

"May I come visit you again while you're in the hospital?"

"If you wish," Adam told her. Melissa gently squeezed his hand and left the room....

"Melissa, how do you know what your father told Adam the day of the accident?" I asked. She filled our coffee cups and leaned back in the wicker chair.

"Adam was in the hospital for several days," she said. "I went back every afternoon, and he finally started to talk to me. I often picked up Rebecca and took her up to Carle Hospital. She didn't have to depend on neighbors; and I convinced her that I was going anyway. It was easier for her.

"Her daughter got sick one day, and Rebecca couldn't go. That's the day Adam told me what my dad said to him. Sissy, it made me so mad I wanted to dig him up and beat on him."

"Melissa!"

"Well, it's true. How could he have talked to Adam like that? His own grandson! That hateful, controlling attitude is what drove Jeff away. He hasn't come home for years because of the way Dad treated him. When Jeff married the girl in California, he also got a father-in-law who is good to him."

"What about your mother? Did she come back here after your dad died?"

"Oh, no! She wanted nothing more to do with this house. She took what Dad had left her in the will, and she never looked back. Speaking of which, you haven't asked about my dad's will. Aren't you curious?"

"Well, now that you mention it..."

"That's the best part. Dad left this house and grounds to me. He left a third of his liquid assets to Mother. The rest of his estate was divided between Jeff and me, with a couple of exceptions. He left my children and Jeff's acknowledged children ten thousand dollars each. The only other person named in the will was Adam Martin, which confused Jeff, to say the least."

"You didn't tell him Adam was his son?" I asked.

"No. Adam made me promise not to. Dad left five thousand shares of Petro stock to Adam, to be used for his education or to buy additional farm ground, whichever Adam chose. Adam was still in the hospital when I told him about the legacy."

"What did he say?"

"At first, he wanted nothing to do with it. So I didn't push."

I knew Melissa was dying to tell me more. She practically bounced on her chair, willing me to ask.

"So what did he do, Melissa?"

"Well, it seems there was a girl named Abigail on the neighboring farm. Adam liked her a lot. When he returned to the fold, so to speak, and after a time of penitence, he courted the girl. A year later, they were married.

"Unfortunately, the two older Martin boys were married first and had dibs on the family farm. The original house had been doubled in size, so it holds the two older brothers and their families. Rebecca, Levi and Anne were moved to the smaller house, built for older parents. Yeah, Rebecca was all of thirty-seven! She's only forty now, young enough to remarry, if she chooses. Of course, there'd have to be another Amish widower."

"You are incorrigible," I told my grinning friend. "What did Adam do?" I asked, but I already had a good idea.

"He came to me," Melissa absolutely beamed. "My *nephew* came to me! He wanted to know if he could sell the stock and buy ground with it, which of course, he could; and he did! His neighbors helped him build a house on the property, which already had an old home site on it."

"And that's the red-haired Amish man I saw yesterday! I knew it! He had a short beard, so I knew he had to be married!"

"Yep," Melissa grinned. She sounded just like she did when we were children. "Adam and Abigail have a two-year-old son, Thomas, another little boy with this Franklin mop of hair." She flipped her hand through her curls. "Which makes Jeff a grandfather," she laughed. "I hope Adam will allow me to tell Jeff about him and his son some day."

I helped Melissa clear the table. For a while we sat in the sitting room, where Rebecca had let down her long, dark hair for Melissa and me, almost twenty-five years ago. I thought about Mr. Franklin, who was so seldom at home with his family in those days. I remembered Melissa's mother, so fashionable and proper.

"Melissa, what about your mother? What did she do during all this drama?" Melissa's face changed completely. The smile left her pretty face.

"Mother remained above all of it. She attended the funeral and took her place as the widow. Afterward, she began to travel. She has been on cruises to every available country from every available continent's port. She winters where it's warm and summers where it's cool. We rarely see her."

"I'm sorry, Melissa."

"You know how she always was, Sissy. She hated anything 'unpleasant.'" I nodded. I did remember.

The children came into the room, and I felt I had taken up more than my share of their mother's Labor Day. Melissa and I exchanged hugs, and we promised to stay in touch, a promise I meant to keep.

I went to the motel in Mattoon and took a long shower. That evening I ordered a pizza delivered to my room; and I sat on the bed, cross-legged, as I ate it and watched a sappy movie on television.

After I went to bed, I lay awake a long time, thinking of the handsome Jeff Franklin and the son he would likely never know. Somewhere from the back of my mind came a Bible verse that had stuck there, along with other Bible school memorizations. I couldn't recall all of the text or where it was; but it said: "Those who sow the wind shall reap the whirlwind."

I certainly didn't sit in judgment of Rebecca Yoder Martin. I thought about the human race, as a whole, and the choices we make, especially when we are young and inexperienced. It's doubtful that many people, if any, have not sown to the wind at some time in life.

My choices had not always been in my own best interests. Some had been downright foolhardy when I was a girl. Many were just silly. Except for marrying Jack, I didn't feel that I had made a truly horrendous life choice, as yet. Still, there is always room for error.

And I was still young.

Relatively.

Three-twenty South Pine

The next morning, I called the realtor who had the listing for my old home in Redbud Grove. I made an appointment for one o'clock. That would give me plenty of time for my meeting with Lucinda Barnes at two. I took a leisurely bath, skipped breakfast and enjoyed a lazy morning.

I thought about the past three days. It felt more like a month. It was amazing what I had learned in such a short time. The two most important mysteries from my childhood had already been resolved, and I still had four days of my vacation time left.

On the way to Redbud Grove, I decided to see if I could get an earlier flight back home. After some time with Lucinda this afternoon, I would try to contact Sharon later in the evening.

Once again I went to the Dutch Kitchen for lunch. While I waited for my order, I explored the larger dining area. The walls were lined with paintings, many of them quite good. On closer examination, I discovered that my third grade teacher, Fern Covalt Knauss, was the artist.

Many old photographs, some dated near the turn of the century, were also displayed. Sports teams, mayors and other elected officials of the town, as well as former teachers stared from the walls. A photograph of the city, taken in the nineteen-twenties, didn't look much different from nineteen seventy-six. The same brick streets and many of the same store facades were the same.

I topped off my salad and iced tea with a piece of the restaurant's specialty, shoo fly pie. Rich beyond belief, a few bites were more than enough. Ruefully, I thought of the extra walks I would have to take when I got back to New York.

I left the restaurant and stood on the sidewalk at the intersection of Main and Locust, streets I had walked hundreds of times. Home. That's when a sense of disorientation hit me. This town still felt like home to me. Home was also a red-roofed house in Dixon, West Virginia.

The places and towns where I had lived with Jack had never been "home," but my apartment in New York had more of myself in it than any other place. So, where, exactly, did I belong? I shook off a sudden vertigo and hurried to my rental car. I put my head on the steering wheel until the sensation passed before I started the car and drove south on Locust.

I turned onto Alley, and on a whim, I parked the car in the exact spot my dad used to park before he built the garage. I got out and walked to the front of the house, just as the agent arrived. For a moment, I felt a tiny bit of guilt for taking his time, for I knew I wasn't going to buy the house.

"Hello. I'm Dale Atkinson." He literally unfolded himself from the car. I frowned in concentration as he brought his long legs to where I stood, beside the red pump in the front yard.

"I remember you," I said. "You played basketball for the Riders, sometime in the, ah…late forties?" He blinked in surprise.

"Yes, I did," he replied. "I'm afraid I don't recall…"

I laughed. "You wouldn't. I was about nine or ten, but I remember all the talk about that tall Atkinson kid on the basketball team. My dad took us to one of your games at the high school. I'm C.C. McCoy, better known here as Sissy Bannister." I pointed to the house. "This is where my family lived when I was a child."

"Then you are on a sentimental journey?" he asked. I nodded. "Did you attend the reunion?" I nodded again.

"Yes, it was wonderful to see so many old friends."

"Well, let's see if your house is as you remember it." The sidewalk seemed so narrow and not nearly as long as when I learned to skate on it. The front step was the same. I waited while Dale unlocked and pushed open the front door. He stood aside and allowed me to enter first.

For a moment I couldn't catch my breath. I had stepped into a time warp and instantly traveled backward into nineteen forty-seven. The walls had been painted, and the flooring was different; but the original woodwork had not been replaced.

To my right, a door opened into a small bedroom, at one time shared by my brother, sister and me. Another door, cut out of the wall by my dad, led from that room onto the attic stairs landing. Unbelievably, it was still framed with the woodwork Dad had copied from the other doors in the house. The second bedroom, once shared by my parents, opened from the landing, also.

"Do you want to walk through the house?" Dale asked. I shook myself. My feet seemed frozen to the spot.

"Yes." My husky voice cracked, and I cleared my throat. "Yes." Silently, I moved through the first bedroom and stood at the bottom of the attic stairs. Absolutely nothing had been changed. The original stairs, left uncovered while we lived there, were still bare. The treads were the same, old, uncovered wood.

I looked up. At the top of the stairs, the brick chimney still half blocked access to the attic floor. I started up the steps, amazed how narrow the passage seemed. I swung around the chimney, and there were the two rooms Dad had partitioned off for my brother and me. My memories eyes saw the bed, where it had rested beside the window. The hundreds of nights I spent there, staring dreamily at the sky, flashed through my mind.

"Are you okay up there?" Dave called.

"Yes, I'll be right down." I took one last look before I went downstairs. I peeked into the laundry and bathroom that opened on the north side of the landing. Like everything else about the house, it seemed minute. Six or seven steps took me through my parent's room and into the kitchen.

That's where I almost came undone. Echoes of voices, from baby to childish to teenager to Mom and Dad, of friends and neighbors, of laughter, those raised in anger and frustration—hit me all at once. I heard and saw my brother and me squabbling as we washed and dried dishes at the corner sink. I saw the phantom table where the five of us ate. This one room was bigger than I remembered, actually the largest room in the house.

I looked at the back door, and I felt myself grow smaller. Once again, I shuddered at the memory of my angry father. *No, I don't want to remember that!* I moved, to break the moment. I walked across the kitchen, back to the living room where we had entered.

Happy thoughts emerged, of the Christmas trees we decorated; of the upright ebony piano in the corner, which now stood against a wall in the Dixon house; of the play table where I did my grade school homework; of Dad's big rocker, where he propped up his feet against the massive heater in the winters; my little sister playing with her dolls; my brother poring over some experiment; my mother, picking through tiny quilt pieces; it was all so dear. I wanted to wrap my arms around the memories and make them real, to close my eyes and relive five minutes of one ordinary day. I could almost….almost….

"Ms. McCoy, are you alright?"

I shook my head at my own fancies. "Yes, I'm fine," I reassured Dale Atkinson. "I just spent some very real moments in my past." I looked up at him, which was quite a distance. "This house is the last place where my family lived, intact. My dad died seven years after we moved from here; and I will always, *always* treasure this house and the time we spent in it."

"I'm glad I could show it to you," he said. "I don't suppose you're interested in buying it?" For a moment, I was so tempted. I thought about the possibilities, but then I realized it wasn't actually the house I wanted. It was the past.

I wanted to look out the front door and see Shirley or Tom or Susan Romine bound out their front door, or perhaps see Mrs. Davis, arms folded, sitting on her front porch on a hot afternoon. I wanted to play in the park with the neighborhood kids, Sharon Bennett and Mary Alcorn, or ride my bicycle around the perimeter, or roller skate along the broken sidewalks; but I had already experienced those things, and I could never relive them.

"I thought that I might, and for a moment or two I considered it." I told him. He locked the door behind us, and walked to his car. We exchanged waves as he drove up Pine Street, and I watched him out of sight.

"Hey! What took you so long?" I looked toward the park. Cross-legged, in blue jeans and a tank top, sat Lucinda Barnes on the picnic table.

"I know where you can get a good deal, if you'd like to buy a house," I told her.

"Not in this town." She didn't try to hide or soften the disdain in her voice. "You and Joe Bob are the only good memories I have of this place." I scooted onto the tabletop beside her. We took up only a bit more space than we had when we were thirteen. We sat in companionable silence, each of us lost in private thoughts.

I wrapped my arms around my knees, as I had done hundreds, even thousands of times when I was a child. A head turn to my left gave me a view of Mrs. East's house. Straight ahead, the whole park was visible, bordered by Locust Street, where nothing had changed, except ownership of certain residences. Lucinda sat on my right, and beyond her was my house.

"I half expect my mother to open the back door to call me in or tell me to do or not to do something," I said. Lucinda chuckled.

"I loved your mother," she said, "but she had a voice that could be heard all the way to Main Street."

"She still does, given motive." Silence filled several moments.

"Did you find the ring?"

Surprised at the way she jumped right into the past, I looked at Lucinda.

"By accident," I replied. "Several weeks after you left, my dad decided to clean his golf clubs and store them for the winter. When he took the clubs from the bag and turned it upside down in the back yard, something hit the concrete and bounced onto the grass. I'll never forget how the sun struck the ruby eyes of the snake on that ring. I stepped on it and pushed it into the grass. I told my dad it was a little rock."

"Did he believe you?" Lucinda asked. "You weren't a very good liar, as I recall."

"That's what my mom always told me," I laughed, "but it didn't keep me from trying. Actually, it was about that time I decided the truth was the best way to go."

I turned fully toward Lucinda. "If we had just gone inside and told my parents how Al had hit you that night, he would have been arrested. He wouldn't have killed your mother, and..."

"Oh, Sissy," she breathed. Lucinda slanted that mocking, blue-eyed glance at me, the one she had used every time I'd said something incredibly stupid when we were kids. She shook her head. "I don't think you're a bit better at discerning lies than you are at telling them. Did you actually believe Joe Bob's version of the story?"

"Well, sure," I stammered. "Why wouldn't I? He has no reason to lie to me, does he?" Lucinda half smiled and shook her head again.

"Sissy, Sissy. You were the best friend I ever had, before, during and after I left Redbud Grove. In all the years since, I have never trusted anyone like I trusted you." Lucinda looked at my house for a long moment. "I can still see the golf club, where I stood it against the corner there."

"Lucinda, at first I wished I had taken the club into the garage, instead of leaning it against the house that night. Remember how we sat in the swing in the back yard? How I stubbed my toe on it and complained about Buddy being so careless with Dad's clubs?" Lucinda nodded. "After a while, though, I realized that the golf club probably saved your life. Al could have killed you, as well as your mother."

"Sissy." Lucinda faced me. She took both my hands in hers and looked into my eyes. "Sissy, Al didn't kill my mother. I did."

I felt as if everything in my body grew cold. In the late summer air, every sound seemed isolated: birds' songs in the trees above us; individual cars along the streets; the autumnal call of a distant crow; a barking dog on Locust Street. I was tempted to shake my head, for I surely had not heard correctly.

"I...don't understand." Well, that was certainly the understatement of the year. "Joe Bob said that Al killed her."

"Joe Bob Brady did what he always did—he protected me. He saw the whole thing when he came onto the porch. Most of what he...we... told you is true. Al, vicious and bloody drunk, broke down my bedroom door and came after me. I hit him with the club and got as far as the living room before he caught me. I shut my eyes and started swinging that club, blindly, back and forth, even after I heard the cursing stop and something fall."

Lucinda spoke matter-of-factly, as if she told a story about someone else; but her body gave her away. She trembled, and I saw goose bumps on her bare arms. She still clasped my hands, and hers were suddenly icy.

"When I opened my eyes, Al was slumped, half on the couch, half on the floor. Joe Bob had just come into the house. He didn't say anything. He bent down behind the couch for a few seconds, before he came to me. He took the club from me and grabbed an old quilt that was folded on the couch. I just stood there, while he wrapped it around me and led me to a chair.

"Then he went back behind the couch. He told me to stay in the chair, but I wanted to be closer to him; so I walked around Al. That's when I saw my mother."

Lucinda stopped talking. She swallowed hard and looked down at our joined hands. "With Al's swearing and my screams, I didn't hear my mom come into the house. I can't imagine what she must have thought, but I'm sure she was running. She must have been scared to death." Tears spilled from Lucinda's beautiful eyes and rolled slowly down her face.

"While I was swinging that club, it connected with my mom's head; and I killed her, Sissy. I killed my mother." I squeezed her hand.

She raised her eyes to mine, and I drew her to me. It was awkward, but we hugged each other. Our cheeks touched, and our tears mingled on the same table where we had met the night that tragedy changed the course of Lucinda's life.

"It was an accident, Lucinda. You didn't mean to hurt your mother. Al Pitts was responsible for all of it. People would have understood."

"Joe Bob and I didn't think so," she said. She withdrew her hands and brushed away the tears from her face. "Sorry. I haven't cried about it for years. Anyway, Joe Bob didn't take the ring from Al's finger. I did. I don't know why. Maybe I just wanted to destroy it, like I destroyed him. That's when Joe Bob told me to hide somewhere. He was going to tell the police he saw the fight and that I had already run away, that I had been beaten, too.

"The only thing I did differently was to hide in your garage. It was the safest place I could think of; but I forgot to throw the ring in the river, like I meant to. So I dropped it into your dad's golf bag. I thought I could come back sometime and get it, then throw it into the river.

"I didn't know I would be packed off to Oklahoma so quickly. I guess I thought I'd be able to stay in Redbud Grove." Lucinda shot a quick glance at me. "Maybe even at your house." I smiled.

"You know, I bet my mom and dad would have let you, if the idea had been pitched to them. Mom always liked you."

Lucinda nodded. "I know she did," she said. "I was so envious of you back then. You had everything I didn't. Remember the night I stayed all night with you? We slept in your bed upstairs, beside the window. I felt so safe there."

"Yeah," I laughed, in spite of the tears drying on my cheeks. "Safe and crowded! That bed was pretty small."

"Small, yes; but it was one of the best nights in my life, Sissy. I won't ever forget how good your parents were to me, especially that awful night. Your dad was so mad. Next time you see them, be sure to tell them how much they meant to me."

"Lucinda, my dad died several years ago, when he was only forty-one. You may remember hearing about a coalmine explosion in West Virginia back then. He didn't work there, but he was one of the men killed in the mine."

"Oh. Oh, Sissy, I didn't know."

"Well, there's so much we have to catch up on," I told her. We both turned to watch the car that pulled up on the road between the park and my house. "Oh, no!" I wailed, in mock dismay. "It's Joe Bob Brady! Why can't he ever leave us alone?"

That quickly, Lucinda and I became the thirteen-year-old girls we had been so long ago, when Joe Bob magically appeared wherever Lucinda happened to be. I guess he still had his radar honed in on her.

"Stop whining, Sissy! Didn't I tell you that Joe Bob Brady would be a handsome man when he grew up?"

"Yes, you did; and he is." We watched the tall, ruggedly good-looking man approach.

"Hi, Girls," he said. We both returned his greeting, but Joe Bob had eyes only for Lucinda. He stopped beside her and propped one foot on the bench. "Do you have plans for the rest of the day? I'd like to take you to dinner." His eyes shifted to me, politely.

"Thanks," I said, "but I've got a few places to visit. I plan to leave tomorrow, if I can get a flight out of Chicago." I stepped off the table and took a business card from my purse. "Lucinda, don't lose this. Call me when you get back home, and we'll do some more catching up." I hugged her quickly and turned away. "Joe Bob, it's been wonderful to see you. Good luck with the next election, or whatever your next goal is. I'm sure you will be successful with it."

"Goodbye, Sissy," he said. "Keep up the good writing. Next time you'll get that Pulitzer."

"From your lips to God's ear," I laughed, on the way to my car. "'Bye!" I waved as I drove off, but I watched through the rear view mirror as Joe Bob climbed onto the table beside Lucinda, just like old times.

I had a strong feeling that Joe Bob Brady and Lucinda would never be far from each other again. I had no idea how they would work it out; but some things are just meant to be, regardless of time or space or circumstance. I felt good about them. The picnic table had been a great place to sit and work out problems when we were children. For the moment, all was well beside the once-yellow little house.

At three-twenty South Pine.

Beside the park.

Fool's Gold

Still smiling at the image of Lucinda and Joe Bob on the park bench, I drove up Locust Street to Main, and from there, east, to the library. On either side of the tall flight of concrete steps were dark spruce trees that reached half way up the high windows. I parked on the west side, in the designated area that accommodated no more than three cars at a time.

My heart beat with anticipation as I approached the stairs. Indentations on the steps from the thousands of feet during the past seventy-five years were deeper than I remembered. I recalled the dozens of times my friends and I had jumped sideways up and down those stairs: two up, one down, all the way up to the landing and back down to the sidewalk.

The spruces hid a four-inch concrete ledge across the front of the building, about six feet above the ground. While we had waited for the library to open at two o'clock every summer afternoon during the six weeks of reading club, we took turns daring each other to walk the width of the wall on that ledge.

It was scary to step carefully sideways, hands brushing along the rough surface, our heels pressed against the building, until we reached the projecting corner stones. That was where we had to decide whether to reverse, still facing forward, or turn around and tiptoe back to safety. I always faced outward, my heels solidly placed on the ledge. I was adventurous, but not foolhardy, most of the time anyway.

If we were really brave, we maneuvered around the corner and continued along the ledge to the wing. I tried that only once. My foot slipped; and for a breathless moment, I had visions of my nine-year-old body, flattened on the green grass beside the library.

I pushed open the heavy door as I had hundreds of times and took another step backward in time. In the foyer, the same black and white mosaic tiles welcomed my much older feet. I inhaled deeply as I opened the inner door. The aroma of old and new books, old and new times, felt good in my lungs.

The check out desk I remembered divided the librarian's office from the rest of the first floor. No one entered her domain, through the door on the east side, without her permission. The only missing part was Miss Ghere. I had half expected her to greet me.

To my right stood the statue of David, still sporting his sword and his fig leaf. He seemed shorter, all over smaller, than I remembered. His leaf no longer fooled me.

"Hello. May I help you?"

Literally lost in the 'forties and 'fifties, I hadn't heard the young woman approach. She had come from my left, the research and reference room that contained heavy mahogany tables and leather-covered chairs. The walls were lined with shelves and magazine stands that once held back issues of National Geographic magazines. My friends and I had often browsed through them, looking for pictures of naked natives, which, of course, we found.

We had gazed at the pictures with innocent curiosity, intrigued with the notion of wearing no clothes. Melissa had once made the remark that she wouldn't want to see Mr. Pritchard without his clothes, which had sent Cathy and me into near-hysterical giggles. At that time, Mr. Pritchard was the art teacher. To call him portly would have been a compliment.

"Shhhhhh," Miss Ghere had admonished us from the checkout desk. We had clapped our hands over out mouths to smother our laughter, but I doubt that Miss Ghere was fooled. I suspect she grinned at us behind her hand.

"I would just like to look around, if you don't mind. I used to live here, in Redbud Grove. Actually, I practically lived in the library during the summers." I held out my hand. "I'm C.C. McCoy, Bannister, when I lived here."

"Did you come back for the reunion?"

"Yes, I did. Are you the librarian?"

"Assistant. Mrs. Williams, the librarian, had to run an errand. Did you want to see her?"

"No. Miss Ghere was librarian when I spent so many hours here. One year my brother and I, along with Art Beasley, a boy between our ages, read the optimum number of books allowed, two per day, six days a week, for the six week period. Miss Ghere had us come to the library the following week to take our pictures."

"You know, I think I've seen those pictures somewhere in the library. While you browse, I'll see if I can find them." She went behind the desk and began to look through a file drawer, while I sauntered into the main fiction section. It seemed so small.

I ran my fingers along a row of books, pulling out familiar titles. A copy of <u>Gone With the Wind</u> caught my eye. I opened it, and I remembered the day Miss Ghere allowed me to check out the book for my mother. I was only ten at the time, and Miss Ghere would never have let me take home such a book without a note from Mom, which I had. Worn and dog-eared, it was the same copy that had held my mother enthralled.

I dropped to one knee and looked through the bottom shelf, the one I had decided to rearrange one afternoon. The books had looked uneven to me, so I realigned them, according to height. I had gone to the desk and informed Miss Ghere what I had done. An expression of disbelief on her face, she had moved more quickly than I thought possible. Always stately and self-contained, Miss Ghere had never seemed to hurry toward anything, with the exception of that afternoon.

"Oh, no, Sissy!" she had exclaimed. "Books are arranged according to the Dewey Decimal System. Look." She knelt on her knees and showed me the numbers on the spines, something I never forgot. It's a wonder she didn't banish me from the library.

"I found the picture."

I rose and took the photo the woman held out to me. In glorious black and white, it showed the image of an eleven-year-old girl and a nine-year-old boy, both frowning into the afternoon sun. They held large construction paper triangles with a long string of six additional, smaller triangles dangling from it. On the small triangles were titles of the books read each week during the summer of nineteen fifty-one.

"Oh, yes," I sighed. "My brother and I in our claim to fame. Thank you for finding this." I returned the picture to her. That intermittent sadness of the last three days swept over me; and my throat swelled with unshed tears. It seemed to be my day for weepy nostalgia.

"I must go," I said. "Thank you for your time." I turned and fled, leaving the assistant librarian with the picture in her outstretched hand. I made it to the car before the tears came. I don't know why that particular moment brought them. It was if all the memories from all the years culminated into one big collage, a moving mural of times, places and people, most of which were gone or changed.

My moment of tears in the First Baptist Church seemed nothing compared to this day's cascade. Again I thought of Emily in the play, "Our Town." She had been right. To relive one ordinary day, in an ordinary life, in an ordinary town was too painful to endure.

When I could see again, I drove out of Redbud Grove the quickest way possible, south to Route 133, east to I-57 and south to my motel in Mattoon. There I called the airline and booked a noon flight for the following day. By seven o'clock the next evening, I was ensconced in my apartment, shoes off, pajamas on, and safely back in the present. I didn't know when, if ever, I would return to Redbud Grove.

The flight back to New York gave me a couple of hours to contemplate my life. The days in Redbud Grove had been good for me, in that it gave me new perspective on the present. I suppose it's natural to look back at roads not taken, romances not pursued, friendships left in limbo and any manner of issues not resolved.

For me, the only issue left dangling was how I felt about Victor. In reality, I didn't know him. He had seemed genuinely interested in me, and he remembered more about me than I could have imagined. I had always thought that men didn't remember girls from their past, especially teeny-boppers. He had said he would call me. Well, time would tell.

During the next two weeks, I worked with a renewed energy and enthusiasm. Ideas for articles and storylines seemed to leap from my head to my fingers. I couldn't type fast enough. I even outlined a novel I had been thinking about for a long time. The reunion sometimes crossed my mind, and I thought about the people with whom I had reconnected; but my perspective was sound. No more crying jags for me.

I wrote notes to Sharon, Melissa and Lucinda. I suggested that each of them should come for a visit to New York. All three replied that they would love to do so, and I looked forward to sharing my present day life with them. Totally immersed in a project one afternoon, I impatiently answered my apartment's buzzer.

"Yes?"

"May I come up?" I stared at the intercom. "Sissy? I know you're there. May I come up?"

I tried to swallow, but my mouth suddenly felt as dry as Tucson in the summer. I blinked, stupidly. I knew the voice, but its presence in my apartment didn't compute. "I'm here." *That was brilliant. Of course I was here.*

"Are you going to let me in?"

"Well, I'm not sure."

"Would you rather I go?"

"No!" I buzzed open the downstairs door and made a dash for the bathroom, where I ran a comb through my hair, checked to see if my deodorant was working, swished mouth wash through and around my teeth and tucked my tee shirt into my jeans. Make-up? No time.

When he knocked at the door, I took a deep breath and counted to ten. I forced myself to walk slowly and to stand perfectly still for another few seconds before I turned the knob.

"Hi." Victor Delacourt greeted me with his slow, too-sexy smile. Without permission, my heart double thumped. It seemed to stop momentarily before it began to beat at an alarming, unsustainable pace. I took another deep breath.

"Hi." It was all I could think to say.

His grin grew wider. "How long do you want me to stand in the hall?"

"Oh, come in." I stepped aside.

"Well, okay, since I was in the neighborhood...."

I laughed, and he drew me into his arms as naturally as if he had been doing so for years. He wrapped his arms totally around me and hugged me tightly. My arms crossed around his back, and we rocked back and forth like children. He broke the hug and placed his hands on my shoulders.

"What are you doing here? How did you find me? Why didn't you call and let me know you were coming to New York? Would you like something to drink?"

"Let me answer your last question first. I would love something cold."

"Iced tea? I never have liquor in the place."

"Iced tea is fine."

I slipped from his hands and gestured toward the sofa. "Sit down, and I'll bring it." Instead, Victor began a slow stroll through my living room.

"This is nice, Sissy. How long have you lived here?"

My hands trembled, and I sloshed tea on the counter when I tried to pour it into the ice-filled glasses. "About two years. I moved here right after I started to work for the Times. I like it a lot." I placed the drinks on the glass-topped coffee table and sat down in the chair beside the sofa. I was shaking too much to sit anywhere else. He might have lounged beside me, and it would have been too embarrassing, should my trembling body shake the couch.

Instead of joining me, Victor continued his tour of my living room. He stopped in front of Willow's painting of the lodge. "Wow," he said softly. "What a great place this must be." He leaned closer to the canvas. "I don't see a signature, but it must be an original."

"It is."

"Who's the artist?"

"Willow Thornhill. Maybe I'll tell you about her one day." *Uh-oh. That sounded as if I expected a long-term connection.*

"I'll look forward to it. The smaller one is by the same artist?"

"Yes." My monosyllabic answers sounded inane to my own ears.

He moved along the wall, quoting titles from among my collection of books on the shelves. "You read a lot. Interesting subjects you choose—poetry, archeology, music, world religions, modern art, art composition." He looked at me. "Are you an artist, too?"

"I love to paint, but I haven't for quite some time. Willow taught me a lot, but mostly she made me aware how little I knew about painting."

"The painter of these pictures?" He pointed to Willow's canvases.

"Yes."

"Hmmmm, there are some pretty racy novels here, too, from the covers."

I was much too old to blush, but I came close. "I like to stay current," I quipped. He laughed and sat on the couch cushion nearest to me. I watched him pick up his glass and take a long swallow of the amber liquid. I found everything about him pleasing, from his dark hair to the tips of his suede loafers, black, of course.

Without being too obvious, I hoped, I admired the sheen of his royal blue shirt, opened at his throat, tucked neatly into fitted, black pants. He should have been on the cover of a European fashion magazine. I dropped my eyes as he lowered his glass.

"What are you doing here?" I asked. Casually, he placed one foot atop his knee and leaned against the back of the sofa. *Easy, Girl. He looks too comfortable there.*

"Would you believe me if I told you I live in Brooklyn?"

"No."

"Well, I do. For a couple of years, I lived in Memphis, and in Nashville for a while. I've lived in different places here in New York for, oh, close to ten years. I like where I am now."

My mind became mush—again. How was it possible that Victor Delacourt had been in the same city as I all that time, and I didn't *feel* him here? We could have been on the same streets, in the same restaurants, on the same flight back to Redbud Grove! Why didn't he tell me the day we spent together?

"Why didn't you tell me that day in Redbud Grove?" The words instantly followed the thought.

"I almost did, but I thought how great it would be to surprise you, hopefully a pleasant surprise." He smiled at me over his glass. He was just too handsome. I caught a glimpse of my reflection in a gilded wall mirror, and I flushed.

"Oh, well. You show up looking like a...a...like *that*, and catch me in jeans and a ratty tee shirt. Surprise!" I stood and threw out my arms, drama queen personified. "You might have called or some..."

Before I could finish the word, Victor stood and pulled me into his arms. There was nothing gentle about it. "Shut up," he growled. He took total possession of my mouth. There's just no other way to describe the way he kissed me. Before he was through, I was as weak-kneed as I had been the first time I had felt his touch. The only difference between that fourteen-year-old girl and the thirty-six-year-old woman was time.

"Shut up," Victor whispered again against my mouth. "You look beautiful. Beautiful." He interspersed his words with long, slow kisses that numbed my mind and threatened to incinerate the rest of me. Somehow, we were on the couch; and I was on his lap. I didn't remember moving.

His hands were warm on my back, suddenly on my skin, beneath the ratty tee shirt. *How'd that happen?* "Sissy," he breathed against my throat. *Déjà vu.* I wriggled out of his grasp and stood up. I was flustered, aroused, embarrassed and angry.

"Enough! I'm not the green, stupid little girl I once was; and I'm not at a school reunion, high on old memories, like I was a couple of weeks ago!" I backed away from him and turned away to tuck my shirt into my jeans, where it should have stayed.

Victor laughed. He actually laughed. "No, but you're the same, spit-fire-y girl I remember."

"I'm not a girl, Victor!"

"Now don't get huffy on me. It's obvious that you're a woman, *all* woman. I'm sorry, Sissy. I guess I responded like an eighteen-year-old,

219

but that's how you make me feel. You just look so much like you did all those years ago, sexy jeans and all." He rose, and I backed away from him.

"Sure I do." Sarcasm dripped and formed a puddle on the floor. "I know we got up close and personal in Redbud Grove, but...but...you can't just come into my home and...and...think I'll just take up where... where...and I really don't know you...." Nothing I said was coming out right. I stuttered and stammered and finally stopped.

"I'm sorry." The smile left Victor's face. "I apologize for being such a jerk. This is not what I intended, truly." I wanted to believe him.

"I'm not easy, Victor."

"I never thought you were. I shouldn't have pushed."

"I haven't been...close...to anyone since, well, not for a long time."

"Will you let me start over? Would you go to dinner with me this evening? I promise to be on my best behavior." His face was serious, but his black eyes sparkled. "I won't even ask if I can come up afterwards." Then he smiled.

"We-e-l-l-l," I hedged.

"Please?"

I met him at a small restaurant ten blocks from my building. Fontana's served a variety of cuisines, and it was close enough for me to walk to and from, should I desire. It was cool for late September, so I took a cab.

I deliberately dressed down, which made me feel more in charge. Dark brown slacks with matching sweater and leather boots suited me just fine. I added a gold chain and gold earrings at the last minute and wore very little makeup.

I had ambivalent feelings about Victor being on my turf, and I needed to feel as strong and in control as I had ever since Jack died. Victor, the distant dream-lover, was totally different from Victor, the flesh and blood man—in my territory.

In Redbud Grove, I had reacted to him as I had twenty-plus years ago, holding nothing back. I couldn't completely blame him for any expectations he might have now; but in New York I was C.C. McCoy, a strong, independent woman, not Sissy Bannister, the kid. If Victor didn't like it, he could go away.

Filled with resolve, I entered the restaurant with my head high. Victor waited at the bar, a short glass in his hand. He saw me and placed a bill on the bar before he came toward me. I watched his eyes travel from my head to my boots to my eyes. I could almost hear and see his thoughts: *So she covered herself up...as if that makes a difference.*

"You look beautiful," he said. I glanced at his glass, and he lifted it close to my nose. "Club soda."

"You don't have to answer to me," I told him. "You're in charge of your own vices. By the way, how many do you have?"

I thought I saw something flicker in his eyes, but it was gone so quickly I credited the dim lighting. "Only beautiful women," he quipped. *Wrong answer, Victor.* He took my arm, and the maitre 'd led us to a table.

Victor had donned a black jacket that matched his slacks, and I think every female eye in the place focused on him. He scarcely took his eyes off me, which flattered and disconcerted at the same time.

Determined to hide the maddening attraction I felt, I answered his questions about my life, my job, my friends and my family. At times, I had to look away from his eyes or be lost in them. He seemed as determined to undermine my resolve as I was to maintain it, and I had the feeling he knew exactly what I felt every minute. A burning edge was a dangerous place to stay balanced, but the fire had such a mesmerizing glow.

Soft music, soft lighting and soft glances made it difficult for me to stay focused on anything but the nearness of Victor Delacourt. More than once, a sense of unreality nearly convinced me I was in a dream, that my alarm buzzer would sound any moment to blast me back to reality.

"Would you like to order dessert?"

"Hmmm?"

"Dessert?"

"Not unless you would like something," I managed.

"How about some strawberries, maybe some chocolate fondue?" he suggested. *Oh, Man! How could he know my decadent weakness?*

"You couldn't know how much I love strawberries! And chocolate? The combination should be illegal."

"Hello, Sissy."

I looked up and nearly choked on my water. Carlo Donatelli stood beside our table. He inclined his head to Victor, who rose from his chair.

"Carlo, I-I'm surprised to see you. It's been a long time."

"Yes, it has." Carlo glanced at Victor.

"Oh, I'm sorry. Victor, this is Carlo Donatelli. Carlo, Victor Delacourt." The two men shook hands, each seeming to take the other's measure. Except for the difference in height, they could have been related. Both had thick dark hair and black eyes and wonderful olive-toned skin. Both of them looked like an ad for a glorious vacation in Italy. Carlo, at six-foot four or so, had the advantage of height over Victor; but then he looked down a bit on most men.

The waiter approached with our chocolate and strawberries, and Carlo stepped away from the table. "I didn't mean to interrupt your dinner, Sissy. I just wanted to say hello."

"Carlo, wait. Is your family okay? Carmen? Giovanni? Is all well with you?"

"Yes, Sissy, we are fine. Apparently, whoever committed those small acts of terrorism grew tired of the game. There have been no other incidents. I'm glad I saw you.

"I've been meaning to call. I speak for all the Donatelli's when I ask you to come back to Luigi's. I apologize for the way I spoke to you the last time we talked. The family wants you to know that the article you did on my grandfather was good. We sent copies to people in his town in Sicily, and we are proud of the way you told Grandpapa's story."

I smiled at him, relieved more than words could say. I rose and held out my hand. Carlo took it, pulled me toward him and kissed me on each cheek.

"Thank you so much. I think about your wonderful family often, and I've missed Luigi's food."

"If you ever need anything, *Cara Mia,* don't hesitate to call me." Carlo bent and kissed my hand, nodded to Victor and walked away. I stared after him until Victor cleared his throat.

"Who is that?" There was an edge in his voice, a displeased edge.

"He's the son of a Sicilian immigrant. I did a story on his grandfather a few years ago. When it was published, the whole family was placed in potential danger. I haven't seen any of them, until just now."

"He's a good-looking dude. Did he have a thing for you?"

I laughed. Did I detect a note of jealousy? "No, not really. We didn't know each other very long. The last time we spoke, he was furious with me. He told me to stay away from him and his family, even the restaurant his father ran; and he meant it." In spite of my words, I felt a touch of regret over Carlo. In another time, we might have had a chance to build something good.

Victor picked up a perfect strawberry and dipped it into the warm chocolate. He held it out to me. I leaned forward and took a bite of the luscious fruit, which left a trail of sticky juice down my chin. Victor caught it with his finger and popped it into his mouth. "Sweet," he said.

"Ummm," I purred; and I took the remainder of the berry from his hand. "Get your own."

"Greedy."

"I am," I conceded. "I don't share strawberries."

We bantered over dessert until it was gone; and by then, it was later than I realized. Victor signaled for the check and asked the waiter to call a cab for us. On the way back to my building, we spoke very little.

"Wait for me," he told the driver.

"You don't have to see me to the door," I laughed. "I've been coming home alone for a long time."

"Of course I do. I always see a lady to her door."

"And how many ladies have there been?" I teased. He didn't answer. I couldn't decide if that were a good or a bad thing. At my door upstairs, Victor took my key and unlocked the door. He pushed it open and stood aside.

"Good night, Sissy. I hope you enjoyed the evening as much as I have." He sounded very polite, and I stared at him, puzzled.

"Of course I enjoyed it."

"Can we do it again sometime?"

"If you wish," I countered.

"I wish." He leaned forward and kissed my cheek. "Good night, Sissy. Sweet dreams." With that, he turned and quickly disappeared down the stairs. I closed the door, leaned against it and pondered the sudden change in Victor's manner. After a moment, I grinned at an unlikely thought.

Was he jealous of Carlo? Was it possible my phantom dream-lover had old-fashioned courting in mind? If so, I'd wager he wouldn't be able to restrain his true personality indefinitely.

The next few weeks were anything but boring. Flowers might arrive from Victor one day, and then I wouldn't hear from him for four or five. He took me to restaurants all over the city, from pizza parlors to nightclubs. One night he took me ballroom dancing to a club in New Jersey. The next time it was to a diner, where we actually did the jitterbug. He never held me too tightly; and he never gave me anything but totally unsatisfying, chaste kisses. He was holding up better than I was!

I even asked for his phone number one evening over dinner. From his wallet he took a card and handed it to me. "This is my office number. If I'm not there, the receptionist will know where to find me."

"What about your home phone?"

"It's an unlisted number, but I'm in the process of getting it changed. There's no service there at all now. As soon as it's worked out, I'll give the number to you."

"Why is it unlisted? Don't you want business people to contact you?"

"Only at the office," he said. "It's the only way I can avoid untalented, persistent, want-to-be singer/songwriters."

"I see." I tucked his card into my purse.

✳ ✳ ✳

I loved Octobers. The sky was bluer, the air crisper and cleaner, and my energy levels soared. By the middle of the month, all my assignments and projects were complete; and I wanted to take a long drive into Vermont, maybe Maine. The fall colors were just past peak, which meant a bit less traffic and tourists on the road.

At dinner that night, I asked Victor if he would like to go with me. He stared. "Who are you, and what did you do with my date? Are you serious?"

"Yes, I am. There are dozens of little bed and breakfast inns, and there should be fewer tourists. I'm going to go in my little red Corvette, with or without you. I thought you might like to see the leaves, and I'm sure the inns will have more than one room available. Have you ever been in that part of the northeast?" He shook his head.

"I'd love to go. Let me check my schedule, and I'll let you know first thing in the morning."

"Okay."

"Ummm, about those rooms..."

"Don't push your luck," I warned.

At the door that evening, Victor annihilated his false inhibitions. He took me into his arms and kissed me, like a famished man set before a feast. I clung to him, as hungry as he was. Both of us trembled when he let me go. "If you back out on me, I may kill you," he whispered. He rested his forehead against mine. I chuckled.

"If I back out, I may kill myself," I joked. He drew me close and began to sing in my ear:

"Oh my darlin,' Oh my darlin,' Oh my darlin' Clementine...."

"You remembered?"

"How could I forget," he asked. "You're the only Clementine I've ever known."

"Well, don't ever use it again," I ordered. "Only the government and I know what the C. C. stands for, at least in this state. I don't think my mother even remembers my name any more.

"Can you imagine what a field day the kids in my classes would have had with my name? A few of my older cousins, those ten or twelve years older, used to tease me unmercifully. By the time I was school age, they were grown; and the younger ones have only known me as Sissy.

"Then there was Clem Kadiddlehopper, Red Skelton's alter ego. I used to dread discovery after he came on the scene."

Victor leaned forward and kissed me again. "Aw, come on. I bet you would have made a cute little Kadiddlehopper," he laughed. I frowned. "Okay, you win. When do we leave?"

"Tomorrow afternoon, if you can make it."

"I won't have to look at my calendar," he breathed. "I'll be here at noon, so I can ride in your little red car."

The next morning, I got a call from a publisher in Delaware, asking if I could drop by the office to look at some last minute editing. Irritated, I looked at the clock. It would be mid-afternoon before I could complete the job and be back at my apartment. I agreed, not very graciously.

Quickly, I threw into a suitcase the clothing I had laid out last night. I kept a toiletries bag fully stocked for quick business trips, and I tossed it into the same case. I would put it in the car when I left for the publisher's.

I dialed Victor's office and was told he would not be available for a few days. On a whim, I looked for his name in the telephone book. I knew it was a waste of time. I had no reason to believe his name would be listed there. Among the many Delacourts was one with the initials, V.P.

Oh well, it was probably a little old widow named Vera Pauline or something. I dialed it anyway.

"Hello?"

"Oh, I'm sorry," I told the woman who answered. "I must have the wrong number."

"Who are you calling?" Her voice reminded me of whiskey-voiced country singers, sultry and deep. She sounded nothing like a little old widow.

"I'm trying to reach the Victor Delacourt residence. I'm sorry I bothered you."

"This is it," the voice said. "How can I help you?"

"Is Victor available?"

"I'm sorry, he isn't. He's already gone. He'll be out of town for a few days, meeting with his song-writing crew. May I take a message?"

"To whom am I speaking?" I asked.

"This is his wife, Dottie."

It seemed like eons before I could speak, but it was only seconds. "No, no message." I started to hang up. "On second thought, there is a message, if you don't mind. Just tell him that Clementine called. Thanks." I broke the connection.

Like an automaton, I walked to the garage to get my car. It was nearly noon when I reached the publisher's office, but it took only a few minutes to go over the editing with him. From there I headed north on the closest interstate. Everything I needed was in the car.

I drove for five hours before I noticed a rustic sign announcing that the Pine Place Country Inn had vacancies. I pulled onto a tree-lined, winding road that led to a large, picturesque two-storied house. A covered veranda boasted rocking chairs and some wicker loveseats. Pots of frost-tipped flowers were still pretty; and the border of chrysanthemums, in various shades, was lovely against the crimson maples and pine trees.

One space remained in the parking lot. Apparently, other followers of the autumn colors hoped to avoid a few tourists, too. I parked and carried my bag inside, where I took the one available room. I listened attentively to the woman behind the desk. She continued to smile as she told me breakfast, lunch and dinner hours.

"I'm afraid you've missed dinner this evening, but there's always food in the kitchen. You're welcome to find a snack, if you wish."

"Thank you. I might do that a little later."

"Would you like a wake-up call?" she asked.

"No, thank you. I may sleep until noon."

"That would be perfectly fine. We want you to be comfortable during your visit with us. How many nights do you intend to stay?"

"Two, I think." I paid her for the two nights, and she gave me directions to my room on the second floor. The big farmhouse had been decorated in the style of a hundred years ago, with distinct Victorian embellishments. Large hurricane lamps with glass globes stood on various tables. Guests sat on mohair and velvet covered overstuffed sofas and chairs. Some leaned back comfortably, their feet crossed on footstools covered with needlepoint or tapestry.

The stairs creaked as I went up, to be expected in such an old house. I pushed open the door of room number four and discovered a small sanctuary. It was lovely. A featherbed topped the four-poster, and it was as soft as it looked. The lace dust ruffle and floral counterpane in cream, yellow and soft rose looked like something from a decorator magazine.

In the brick fireplace, a slow fire burned, shedding the only light in the deepening dusk. I think it was probably also the source of heat, for I could see no radiator or vents. The quilt rack, on which three handmade quilts were draped, may have been there for more than atmosphere.

A maple occasional table stood in front of the window, and two rose tapestry upholstered chairs sat on either side of it. On one wall, an old-fashioned antiqued armoire was the only closet. Across from it, a small chest held a water pitcher and basin, shaded in rose and sage green, a very old set.

I placed my clothes in the armoire and chest before I checked out the bathroom. The tub was half-sized with claw feet, and there was barely room for the stool and a pedestal sink below an oval mirror. It was like stepping back to the previous century.

The whole room screamed romance, but I refused to think. I washed my face and joined the other guests downstairs, where three of them joined me in the kitchen. They discovered leftover apple crisp, so that and a glass of milk was my supper. After a few bites, my throat tightened; and I couldn't swallow more.

Sometime around midnight, the first crack appeared in my façade. Another crack began, followed by yet another, until every last bit of shell was gone; and what remained was as raw and new as a freshly hatched chick, wet and weak, vulnerable and hungry.

Throughout the early morning hours, I discovered truths about myself, about dreams and fantasies, about life and reality. I felt like the worst fool who ever drew breath. At first, a sense of betrayal was uppermost; but I finally had to admit that Victor owed me nothing. In truth, I had gone to the reunion in hopes that he would be there, if not actually looking for him.

In spite of the devoted attentions of Neal Curry, the potential companionship of Carlo Donatelli, and other men who had expressed an interest in me, I had been a solitary person for years. I had harbored adolescent illusions about Victor for over twenty of those years. It wasn't his fault.

The "bad boy" persona of his rebellious youth had deteriorated into a totally selfish, untrustworthy man. One thing was certain: The golden aura I had envisioned around Victor had faded away, and all that was left were rusty fragments. I would not be fooled again.

I finally fell asleep and didn't wake until midmorning. Breakfast was well over, so I wandered into the kitchen in search of coffee. I chatted with the cook while I sat at a service table, hot cup in hand. She told me what to expect for lunch and dinner, and both sounded good. I was hungry.

I enjoyed the rest of the day and evening, more than I expected. I spent more time with the cook, and from her I learned which routes to take and what to expect in the way of accommodations up the road.

"It won't be many days before a heavy frost will pretty much take away the color, you know," she said. "Better make the most of what you have left." Her words rang in my ears for the next two days, while I wound around and through the forested hillsides. By the time I was ready to head back to New York, I knew what I was going to do. I was going to make the most of what I had left.

It didn't take long to find someone to sublease my apartment. I agreed to sell most of my furniture to him. There was no employer to notify, a beautiful aspect of being self-employed. The last thing I composed, before I packed my typewriter, was my resume.

I compiled clippings, photographs and tear sheets of my published articles and stories, all of which resulted in what I thought was an impressive body of work. I packaged and sent the resume to Charleston, West Virginia's major newspaper.

Address changes to magazines and periodicals didn't take long to do. I used that same afternoon to send another letter to Lucinda in California, Sharon and Melissa in Redbud Grove, and one to Penny in Nebraska, telling them of my change in plans.

Within a few days, my furniture and personal things were packed and shipped to my mother's address. The phone rang as I stood in the middle of my kitchen. Victor had called many times; but when I recognized his voice, I had broken the connection. He hadn't called for several days.

"Hello." For a moment, no one answered me.

"Are you going to hang up on me again?" Butterflies no longer troubled me when I heard his voice.

"What do you want, Victor?"

"I want to explain."

"There's nothing to explain. I acted like the fool you must have thought I was. I never really knew you, but I had imagined you to be someone different than who you are."

"I thought you were playing the hard-to-get game, Sissy," he said. "I didn't expect you to be the same little girl I spent one evening with when we were kids. You've been married. You've been around."

"So you thought I was just playing hard to get?" I asked.

"Sure. You proved me right when you invited me to 'look at leaves.' How many leaves do you think we'd have seen?" He laughed, but it wasn't a happy sound.

"You should have told me you're married."

"Oh, come on, *Clementine!* What difference does it make?"

"That question proves you don't know me at all. It makes a huge difference. Do you really have a son?" I asked.

"Yes, I do."

"How many times have you been married?" He was quiet for a bit. "Three, but..."

"Goodbye, Victor. My condolences go to your wives." I hung up the receiver. The click sounded solid to me, like a closing door.

Here it was another November. On the drive back to Dixon, I remembered what my mother had once said about how she hated Novembers, that so many tragic things had happened in the Novembers of her life. I could recall many of them, myself

This November, however, was going to be different. My soul-searching had revealed to me how little I had in my life that mattered. Sonya had been my only close friend during the more than six years I lived in New York. Except for Beth, my family lived in the Charleston area. The high school and college friends with whom I was still connected lived there, too, again with one exception, Penny Olson.

If it hadn't been so cold, I would have put down the top of the car and let the wind blow in my hair all the way back to Dixon. Eagerness rode beside me on the leather seats, and excitement pressed my foot on the accelerator much too hard. I made the drive in record time, taking those curves faster than I ever had.

Snow had fallen near Hawk's Nest. The pines were as beautiful as ever, and I looked at them with a new appreciation. I had always loved West Virginia, but it seemed practically new to me. With a rueful grin, I realized the state was the same. It was I who had changed.

By late afternoon, I drove into Dixon's city limits. I smiled all the way to the red-roofed house on Symington. In the driveway, I sat for a moment, anticipating my mother's questions and her look of anxiety and fear that all was not well with her firstborn, as she so often called me. My smile became a wide grin.

I got out of the car and dragged my suitcase from the trunk. With a happy heart in my chest and no burden on my back, I opened the screened door. I knocked briefly before I threw open the white front door and entered my mother's house.

"Mo-m-m-m!" I called.

"I'm home!"

PART THREE
HEART'S HOME

Ephiphany

My stepfather thought I had lost my mind. I'm fairly certain my mother thought the same thing, although she was subtler in her reaction.

"Honey, what's wrong?"

"Nothing, Mom," I told her. "I've made some changes in my life, and this is my first stop along the way." She and her husband exchanged glances, and I could see speculation on both their faces. I put my case on the floor and took off my coat.

"Did you quit your job?" Russell demanded. I had never been able to make him understand that I didn't need a boss in order to support myself. He had thought me certifiable when I resigned from the Times.

Born on a farm in nineteen ten, Russell had lived through the historical stock market crash of twenty-nine, which had precipitated the great depression during the nineteen-thirties and early forties. It was an era when one was fortunate to have any kind of work, and one did not quit a paying job. Russell thought self-employment was another form of laziness, risky at best. "Are you out of money? Is that why you came home?"

I didn't know whether I wanted to laugh or hit him. Since I planned to sleep in his (uh-uh, my *mother's*) house that night, I chose to laugh. "None of the above, Russell. I want to live closer to my family. Since more of you live here than anywhere else, here is where I choose to be. Bill's boys scarcely know me, and I miss all of you. I'm going to try coercing Beth to come home more often, as well."

Mom unclenched her fist in relief and hurried to my side. She wrapped her arms around me. "Well, it's a good thing I keep your room ready. Are you hungry?" I hugged her again. I was surprised she had waited so long to ask.

"I love you, Mom! What's in the ice box?"

"Sissy, we haven't had an ice box since we left Redbud Grove! Oh, speaking of which! Did you go to the reunion in September?"

"Yes, I did; and you won't believe all I have to tell you about those Redbud Grove people!" My mother and I walked arm in arm into the kitchen, where I knew something good would be in the refrigerator.

While I ate warmed-up spaghetti, rich with Mom's homemade sauce, I told her about the Franklins and most of what I had learned about people she once knew.

"Was Lucinda Barnes there?" she asked. Surprised, I raised my eyebrows.

"You remember Lucinda?"

"Well, of course, I do. Your dad and I would have taken her in if it had been possible. That poor child. I know I probably shouldn't say it, but the best thing her mother ever did for her was to get herself killed!"

"Mom!"

"Well, it's true. God only knows what that girl went through all her life." *Oh, Mama, if you only knew.*

"Lucinda was at the reunion, Mom. She has had a good life, and you can't imagine how beautiful she is. She asked about you and Daddy, and she was saddened to learn he passed away." I paused. "We are going to stay in touch. I've already let her know I've left New York." I laughed. "It wouldn't surprise me if she moved to Kentucky." I updated her about Joe Bob, and I told her I thought the two of them would eventually get together, maybe even get married.

"Are any of the boys you used to know single?" *Gosh, Mom. I just gave you credit for subtlety.*

"Yes. Allen Hastings has been divorced twice. Leroy Maxedon came on a motorcycle, and he's still looking. He asked me out." Guilelessly, I looked into my mother's blue eyes. "Actually, three or four, some single, some not, asked me out." I hid my smile in a forkful of spaghetti that would have made the Donatelli's jealous.

"Sissy! Are you serious?"

"Only a little, Mom!" I laughed. I had no inclination to tell her about Victor. I looked at the clock on the kitchen stove. "I'm really beat, Mom. Do you mind if I go on up to bed?"

"Of course not, Honey."

I picked up my dishes and took them to the sink, where I rinsed and stacked them, as I had been taught. There was no dishwasher. "You don't have to do that, Sissy. I'll take care of it."

"I know, Mom." I hugged her and kissed her cheek. "Good night. I love you."

"Good night, Sissy," she murmured. I could feel her eyes on my back all the way to the stairs.

After breakfast the next morning, I drove into Charleston. The gold-covered dome of the state Capitol Building gleamed in the November sun, and I was reminded anew how beautiful it is. Interstate highways wound through and around the city, moving a heavy volume of traffic away from the downtown streets. Still, the thriving metropolis buzzed with activity; and parking places were difficult to find in the business section.

I finally found one three blocks from my destination and zipped quickly into the space. A brisk, pre-winter breeze lifted my hair. I buttoned my coat and pulled the collar close to my face, but the chill was nothing like the frigid blasts I had experienced in New York.

I turned into the building that housed The Charleston Gazette and handed my card to the receptionist at the front desk. By the time I left the editor's office, two hours later, I had been hired as a contributing/roving/features/special reporter. An office was available when I wanted to use it; but I was free to work wherever I wished, as long as required pieces were on time and print-ready.

My next stop was at a realty company a few doors from the newspaper. I told an agent what I wanted, and she had several places to show me. None of the apartments were suitable, but I fell in love with a two-bedroom house in a residential area. I hadn't lived in a house for over eight years, not since Jack died.

There was nothing fancy about the place. Slightly rectangle, it had a bedroom and long living room in front. The living room opened into a real kitchen, with a window that looked onto the small back yard. A short hall at the other end of the kitchen led to another bedroom and bath.

Neat and spotless, I could have moved into it immediately. The monthly rent was less than half what I paid for my last apartment. If I could have reached the movers at that moment, I would have told them to bring what furniture I had kept directly to the house; and I would have spent the night.

Back at the realtor's office, I supplied references, signed a six-month lease, and wrote a check for first and last month's rent. With a new sense of who I was and where I wanted to be, I drove out of Charleston and pointed the car back to Dixon.

During supper that night, I told Mom and Russell what I had done, fully prepared for a barrage of questions from my mother and disapproval from her husband. They didn't disappoint me.

"I don't know why you couldn't find a place here in Dixon, close to your mother," Russell stated. "Then you'd be here when we need you."

"Does your new house have a yard you can fence? You might like to get a dog, maybe another Schnauzer, like Sophie," my mother suggested.

"Doesn't your daughter still live here in Dixon?" I asked Russell. "I understood that she looks in on you regularly." He continued to eat without answering me. "There is a yard, Mom; but I don't plan to get a dog, not for a long time, anyway." Russell had little to say from that point, but my mother kept me busy with predictable questions and suggestions.

After supper, I called Karen Courtney Smith. For the last few years, our only communication had been the seasonal Christmas card. I knew that her daughter had graduated from high school over a year ago, but it was difficult for me to imagine the little girl as an adult.

Life happened so suddenly. Many of my high school friends were parents of grown and nearly grown children, while I had none. One or two who had married right out of high school were already grandparents. The thought boggled my mind.

"Hi, Karen. How are you?" For a moment, the line was quiet.

"Sissy? Sissy, is that you?" Karen fairly screamed into the phone.

"'Fraid so." I chuckled.

"Where are you?"

"I'm at my mother's house."

"What are you doing in town? Is your mom all right?"

"Everything and everyone is fine," I laughed. "I'm hoping you can have lunch with me tomorrow."

"Sure. Where and when?"

"You choose."

"I'll pick you up, and we'll drive out to Franky's, a new place east of town, just off the interstate. Is twelve okay?"

"I'll be ready. Can't wait to see you," I told her.

Karen arrived in a restored nineteen fifty-seven Chevrolet, as shiny and bright as when it was new. The chrome sparkled against the turquoise and white finish, and I knew that her husband, Matt, had perfected his craft.

After the first few strained moments, Karen and I fell into the familiar pattern of give and take we had developed in our teen years. Over lunch in the new restaurant, we caught up on each other's lives; and then we moved on to mutual acquaintances.

"Did you know that Lilly Faye has moved back to her home in the mountains?" I shook my head, and Karen continued. "She no longer tours. She and her husband have built a fabulous place on the hill above her 'tabernacle.' You'll have to drive up and see it, Sissy. It's built of pine logs and walls of glass that look across the valley." Karen grinned. "Maybe you should call on her." I raised my eyebrows.

"The last time I saw Lilly Faye, she scared me to death. I don't think I want to get any closer to her than I was then."

"She's not so bad," Karen said. "I see her occasionally, in the grocery store or the library, sometimes at the Diamonds Department Store."

"Does she have children?"

"No, she doesn't." Karen grinned again, the way she used to just before she said something she thought would shock me. "How could she have children, Sissy? Can you imagine Lilly Faye doing the dirty deed of procreation? Come on! She's too holy for such a carnal act." I had to laugh with her, which wasn't very charitable of either of us. I felt like fifteen again...almost.

"What about the rest of the gang? Do you ever see Beverly or Rowena? Gary, Donnie, Wes? Last I heard, Jerry Davis and his wife were in Hawaii, I think."

"Rowena is in California, and Beverly is still in Dixon. I haven't seen the guys for a long time. Why don't we see if we can round up the ones still here and have a party or something? Are you game?"

I thought about it for a minute. My reunion with old friends only weeks ago had brought about this life-change for me. Was I ready for another? "Sure," I said. "Why not?" I could think of no one in Dixon, either past or present, with the power to change anything for me now or in the future. We agreed to postpone our mini-reunion until after New Year's.

For the first time since I married Jack, the holidays were not rushed moments filled with rehashed memories. I spent a leisurely Thanksgiving with Mom and Russell, but Christmas was three days of celebration. My mother and Russell agreed not to mention my change of address until the whole family gathered. I wasn't nervous about it, but I would rather tell the story one time.

The week before Christmas, Russell tackled his yearly job of decorating. Lights and tinsel dangled from every possible surface, and the outdoors resembled a downtown department store's window. He looked at every tree in every lot in Dixon before he chose a fragrant Norwegian spruce. He had to bring in a ladder to reach the upper branches; but when he was finished with the lights and decorations, the tree was spectacular.

My sister and her husband flew back from California the day before Christmas Eve. I hadn't seen them for a couple of years, and I could hardly wait to hug her. Although they flew out of Palm Springs early in the day, they had to make two plane changes. It was after dark when the front door burst open and Beth called out, "Merry Christmas, Everyone!"

In the kitchen, Mom and I raced each other to the dining room, where we collided in a group hug that threatened to annihilate all three of us. I smiled into the sweet face of my baby sister, as beautiful as ever. No matter how old we might become, when I looked at her, I would always see first the baby, followed by all the stages of her growth, to gorgeous adulthood, all in a microsecond.

"Oh, Sissy, it's so good to be home!" I knew what she meant. We let go of each other and repeated the hugging process with Eric. In the doorway stood five-year-old Kathleen Suzanne, one of the most beautiful children I had ever seen. She had Beth's dark, curly hair and blue eyes, but she resembled Eric more than her mother.

"Hello," I said. I knelt on one knee, close, but not touching her. "You might not remember me, but I know who you are. I'm your mommy's sister."

"I know. You're my Aunt Sissy. You read <u>Green Eggs and Ham</u> to me last time we were here."

"I did," I nodded. "I think the book is still in my room upstairs. Maybe we can read it later?" A smile touched her rosy mouth, and she nodded. Her shyness totally disappeared. That Dr. Suess could work magic every time.

We spent most of the next day in the kitchen. With big eyes, Kathy sat at the table and watched two generations of women work magic with ordinary ingredients, from sugar cookies to yeast breads, pecan pies to coconut cake.

"Can I help?" Before the words had died on Kathy's lips, her grandmother had slipped an apron over the child's head. Soon the little girl was dusted with flour and dotted with batter. I grew still as I watched her. Longing for a child of my own twisted my heart.

Lazy snowflakes began to fall in mid-afternoon. Kathy, who had never experienced a white Christmas, squealed with delight. All of us donned warm coats and hats and joined her in the back yard, where she lifted her face and opened her mouth. She giggled with pure joy at the melting flakes on her tongue. Snow continued into the evening hours, and I was as excited as I knew the four children would be.

Santa Claus visited the white house on Symington Street that night. Soft morning light had begun to filter through my bedroom curtains when I heard the floorboards creak outside my door. Kathy had agreed to sleep in her Uncle Bill's old room, as long as the doors could be open.

"Kathy, has Santa Claus come yet?" I called softly to her. She peeked around the doorframe of my room, and her eyes looked like big blue marbles in a sea of white.

"I don't know," she whispered. "Can we go look?"

"Of course, we can." I threw back the quilts, reached for my robe and shoved my feet into house slippers. Together, Kathy and I tiptoed down the stairs.

"Oh, Aunt Sissy, look!" A virtual fairyland had taken up residence in the living room. A two-storied white castle, complete with turrets and what looked like leaded glass windows, stood beside the tree. Kathy's cries of delight brought the rest of the family, disheveled hair, yawns and all, into the living room.

Quietly, my mother slipped into the kitchen and plugged in the coffee pot. While Kathy discovered more gifts and opened packages, we enjoyed coffee and sweet companionship for another hour. By the time we had made and eaten Mom's version of a continental breakfast, it was mid-morning.

We were scarcely dressed and the Christmas turkey barely in the oven when the front door opened, and the air fairly erupted with Bannister boys. My brother's two older boys, Willie and David, now eleven and nine, reluctantly allowed me to hug them; but at seven, John hugged fiercely, growling like a bear while he squeezed my neck. I loved it.

Bill and Lainie barely had time to kick off snowy boots at the door before Beth and I descended upon them. We merrily hugged each other in a near version of ring-around-the-rosy, laughing and twirling like the children who left us for the packages that waited beneath the tree.

The rest of the day was glorious, filled with boisterous children, laid-back (for the day) parents, proud grandparents, good food, family and fun. It truly felt like home to me for the first time since my dad died, and the thought of him brought a smile to my heart.

Merry Christmas, Daddy.

Eye Of The Storm

The furniture I had kept arrived at my new address shortly after New Year's, and I moved into the house the same night. The slower paced life in Charleston soothed my citified soul like balm on raw skin. True, my house was in a suburban area, away from the business part of town. Charleston is a large city and is the capitol of West Virginia. It's just smaller than New York City.

The nights in my mother's house had prepared me for the quiet evenings. Although I didn't visit much with my brother and his family, just knowing they lived on the other side of town was an added blessing. All in all, I felt as if I had entered a peaceful, undemanding phase of my life. I went to the Gazette office two or three days a week, and I worked on freelance pieces as I chose.

You know that old saying about the "lull before the storm?" There's a reason those old adages are repeated from generation to generation. Truth lies at the heart of them.

In February, I observed my thirty-seventh birthday. My mind knew it was thirty-seven, but internally I felt no older than I had at twenty or at any of the birthdays that followed. The usual cards and phone calls arrived, and I was the usual pleasant recipient. In spite of my protestations, my mother included a check in her card. With other errands to run anyway, I decided to stop at the bank, where I had opened a new account, and deposit the check.

"Hello, Ms. McCoy. How are you today?" The teller, as always, was pleasant.

"Fine, thank you." I pushed the check and a deposit slip beneath the iron grillwork toward her. Unlike some of the newer buildings, the bank's interior had not been updated or remodeled since it was built in the first quarter of the century.

"Is it still snowing?"

"No. The sun was beginning to peek through the clouds when I came inside. I hope we have an early spring this year. I can't wait to see the dogwoods bloom," I told her.

"My Dear, I agree with you. I love dogwoods, too; but I have a request. No, don't turn around!" The man behind me stepped closer to me than I liked. "Just keep smiling sweetly at the teller; and you, Ma'am, smile back."

"I'll be with you in a moment, Sir," the teller replied politely. She reached into a drawer, and that's when I felt something hard against my ribcage.

"Take your hand out of the drawer, please. That's fine. We can't have you pushing the alarm button, now, can we? I would hate to put a hole in this lovely lady's side, but I'll do it if you don't do exactly what I tell you."

The man stood so close to me, it must have looked as if we were together. "What are you doing?" I asked.

"Why, Darlin,' I'm robbing this bank; and you're going to help me." Casually, he raised an over-sized attaché case and slowly pushed it toward the teller. "Fill that with fifties and twenties out of the drawers, no big stuff; and make it the un-banded stacks."

"Yes, Sir," the teller said. I admired the calm expression on her face, but her hands trembled. I don't remember my first thoughts at that moment. Probably disbelief, numbness and fear, but my overriding emotion was anger.

"You won't get away with this," I told him. Anyone watching would think I spoke to the teller.

"You bet I will," the man said. "I've done it many times. So far, no one has caused a scene; and no one's been hurt. Don't you be the first to screw it up." He jabbed the hard thing into my flesh, to emphasize each word. He drew in his breath. "You smell good."

He nuzzled my hair. Repulsed, I turned my head to the side. His breath was heavily scented with mint, not unpleasant; but I would never feel the same about mint mouthwash again.

The man stepped even closer to me. Through my coat I could feel his body press against my back. Incredibly, he was aroused. Disgust mingled with the anger that swept from my head to my feet. Limited as my range of vision was, I could see customers at teller stations on either side of me. No one glanced our way.

"Maybe I'll just take you with me," the man murmured. I had not yet seen his face, but I knew that he was tall and muscular. There was no way to determine his age. My eyes traveled from the teller, who grew more nervous by the moment, to the man who sat at the ornate desk, well behind all of the clerks.

I willed him to look up, but he continued his conversation on the phone. I cleared my throat, loudly. The hard thing pressed deeper into my side. I refused to think that it was truly a gun. It could be anything, I told myself—a stick, a soda bottle, maybe even a toy gun.

On the other hand, Idiot, it could be a forty-five or a big nine-millimeter. Are you willing to risk it?

The saner part of my mind prevailed, and I exhaled a big sigh. If the criminal had done this before, as he said, he didn't want to hurt anyone. His goal was to escape with as much money as his case could hold.

"Put your wallet on the counter," he told me. Slowly, I did as he said. *So he's going to rob me, too! What a sweetheart!* "Show me your pictures." *What? Why does he want to see my pictures?* I flipped open the wallet to the plastic holders that held photos of my brother and sister and their families.

"How nice," he said. "No husband? No children?"

I didn't answer, and he nudged me with what was feeling more like a gun all the time. "No."

"I didn't think so. I've watched you for some time, now. I haven't seen a guy around, but one never knows."

He pushed me tightly against the counter. The teller struggled to close the case, but it finally snapped; and she carefully pushed it across the counter. Unbelievably, the man pressed his mouth against the side of my neck before he moved away from me. "I'll be seeing you," he whispered. "Don't turn around. You just keep doing your business with the teller there. I'd hate to kill you before we've been properly introduced; but I'll do it, if you make me." He stepped away from me.

The teller and I locked eyes, both of us afraid to make the wrong move. "Is he gone?" I whispered.

"Not yet. He's at one of the service counters, like he's looking at the brochures. He's picked up one and seems to be looking through it."

I picked up my wallet and slipped it into my purse. "Now?"

"He's looking at us. Now he's turning and he's going out the door. He's gone!" She reached beneath the counter, and immediately an alarm sounded. I turned, hoping to catch a glimpse of the man, but he was already out of sight.

"What did he look like?" I demanded of the teller. "Describe him to me!"

"I-I don't know! He's tall; and he wore one of those nice felt hats, you know, like businessmen sometimes wear in the winter. He kept moving behind your head, with his face kind of down. I think he had dark hair, but not much of it showed."

"What kind of coat?"

"Dark brown, nice, long, a nice winter coat."

"What about his hands? Rings?"

"I only saw his left hand, and there was no ring on it. It looked really clean, even manicured."

"Thanks," I told her. She had begun to look a little pale, but I wanted as much information as I could get before she talked to everyone else. By George, I had an eyewitness story for the next issue of the Gazette! It was only later that the impact of the bank robber's words hit me. He had been watching me!

After the mandatory interviews with the police, I hurried to my office to write the story. It appeared on the front page of the Gazette the following day, complete with a byline. Everything I wrote about the man was as uncomplimentary and ugly as I could make it. I didn't let the fact that I hadn't seen his face deter me.

The man had not lied. Over the course of a year, he had taken close to a million dollars. He hit banks all the way from Huntington, Point Pleasant and Charleston, to Martinsburg, Richmond and Norfolk, Virginia. So far, he had chosen larger cities. I learned later that the Dixon banks hired more security guards, just in case the bandit chose smaller ones.

Of course, I had to warn my parents and my brother about the story, which led to admonitions and advice. From my mother: "Sissy, you've got to come home! You can't stay there by yourself!" From my brother: "Way to go, Sis! Can't you stay out of trouble anywhere? Why don't you find a man and get married? Give you something to do and keep you out of trouble."

I assured them I was fine, that I would lock all the windows and doors and not open to strangers. I was skittish for a while. All the shades in my house were pulled before dark; and I attached inside bolts to the front and back doors, even the one that led into the garage.

I took second looks at every man I met on the street, in restaurants, the grocery store, the newspaper office, even drivers in cars beside me, as I drove to and from work.

Cameras had just been installed in the bank, but the technology was not yet the best. The pictures of the man were not helpful. His face was in shadow from the brim of his hat. He had kept his face down on his way in and out of the bank. Apparently, he had been able to carry out one more successful robbery. The local banks tightened up security throughout the city, a classic case of closing the barn door after the horse was stolen, I thought.

A few days later, I was asked to come to the police station to look at a lineup of suspects. I knew the men could not see me, where I stood behind the glass; but it was still intimidating. Unfortunately, I could not identify any one. I had told the police I had not seen the robber, but I felt I would recognize his voice. They had each man repeat the words I had reported, but it was useless. None sounded even remotely similar. No one was more disappointed than I.

Spring arrived. I took every opportunity I could find to drive into the mountains. Karen arranged a lunch date with as many of our friends as she could find, and we met at Hawk's Nest, still one of my favorite places. We laughed and talked and reminisced about school days and wondered aloud about classmates with whom we were no longer in touch.

"Hey, have you guys seen Mark Watson lately?"

"No."

"Yes! He was cute in high school, but now he's downright gorgeous!"

"Is he dating yet?"

"I don't think so. It's been, what, three or four years since his wife died?"

"Oh, at least. I haven't seen him with anyone else. He's devoted to his daughters. No one can fault him there."

I listened to the speculation about Mark, and my mind wandered, as it was prone to do whenever I thought about him, back to our one "date." It would be nice to see him again.

"I saw him once, when I was at my mom's house for Christmas, oh, five or six years ago," I told them. "His daughters were five, I think, sweet little things."

"It couldn't have been more than a year or so later that his wife died."

I looked across the gulch. Hundreds of feet below, a railroad track followed the course of the river, winding along the base of the mountains. The slopes were beautiful with soft color and new life, harbingers of the summer to come. An eagle soared above it all; and I watched his flight, wondering how the scene must appear from his view.

"Where did you go, Sissy?" Rowena asked. She waved her hand in front of my face.

"Oh, just wool-gathering, I guess." After I left the girls, Mark Watson wasn't far from my thoughts for the rest of the day. It was strange that I remembered the way his blue eyes danced and how his dark, curly lashes had swept downward when he looked at me. Strange, indeed.

My days at the Charleston Gazette were not as demanding as the New York Times. After my assignments were turned in, I often went home to work on pieces for magazines and proposals. They paid more than the paper, but I liked working for a smaller periodical. I worked on the novel I had outlined, and I was happy with the concept.

All seemed well until the day a detective from the Charleston Police Department came to the office. "Ms. McCoy, we think the man who held you at gunpoint in the bank could be a real threat to you."

My mouth ached with the effort not to utter the sarcastic words that formed inside it. In the first interview, I had told them what the man had said to me in the bank, every word. My eyes must have conveyed the message, anyway. Detective Hayes cleared his throat.

"Ma'am, he has used other women as a shield in those robberies, as he did you. Three of those women have since been... assaulted in their own homes, and one of them was severely beaten. The connection was made just recently, and we wanted to warn you right away."

I looked into his weary eyes. "By 'assaulted,' you mean the women were raped?" I asked. He dropped his gaze.

"Yes, Ma'am. We don't have the man power to give you round-the-clock protection, but we will drive by your house several times during the day and night until the guy is apprehended."

"Thank you, Detective. I appreciate it."

"Call us if you feel the least bit threatened, any time, day or night."

"Oh, trust me. I will." I leaned back in my chair and watched the detective walk away. I tapped my cheek with the eraser end of a pencil in contemplation for several seconds. I could always go to my mother's house, but I didn't want to do that. I was no longer a child, and I valued my independence.

I could get a dog or a gun. The gun was the cleaner of the two, and it would allow me more freedom. Handguns were foreign to me. My dad had owned a rifle and a shotgun, for hunting; but I had never handled them.

I opted for neither. Instead, I went to a hardware store and bought deadbolts for all the doors in my house. Then I bought a heavy baseball bat.

I spoke to the landlord about putting in window alarms. When I offered to pay for them, he agreed. After those were installed, I decided I had made my home as safe as possible. I had not yet figured out what to do about the rest of the city.

Much as I had poured over the grainy photos from the bank's camera, I could see no recognizable features or any way to identify the gun-wielding figure. I did have a greater sense of well being when I saw police cars make random runs past my house. In time, I began to relax a bit.

The neighbors to my left, Bert and Evelyn Thomas, both worked at the chemical plant on the Kanawha River. Their four grown children lived out of state. Close to retirement, they looked forward to a life with no interruptions from alarm or time clocks.

"We don't take vacations for fun," Evelyn told me one day. "When the kids were growing up, we couldn't afford trips, and now we take turns visiting them and their children."

The Thomas house and lawn were well kept, and a kidney-shaped flower garden near the street was filled with a colorful blend of blooms. Foxglove and delphiniums vied with lupine and columbine in the center, while a mix of annuals outlined the whole garden. Various shaped rocks contained the plantings.

Bert and Evelyn were an inspiration to me. One beautiful Saturday in early June, I decided to place big flowerpots on the front porch. I had never planted flowers or thought about gardening in my adult life. I discovered that I liked the feel of potting soil and the scent of petunias, snapdragons and marigolds.

With a great deal of satisfaction, I placed my gloved hands on my hips and stood back to survey the effect. Though small, the white house with its dark gray shutters and roof were a perfect background for my bright splashes of color.

I asked the landlord if I could paint the front door, and he agreed. I just didn't tell him I painted it dark red. I thought the effect was stunning.

"Hi," Evelyn called to me. "Your pots are lovely."

"Thanks. I like them a lot."

"Could we ask a favor of you?"

"Sure."

"Would you mind keeping an eye on our house for a few days?"

"Are you going to take a fun trip this time?"

"Well, yes and no. Our youngest daughter just had her first baby, our third grandson. We're going to Atlanta to see them, but we plan to be home by Thursday."

"I'd be happy to keep watch. Do you have interior plants that need watered? Anything else you want done?"

"Well, yes, if you don't mind. Come on over, and I'll show you."

I agreed to water the plants, check locks on the windows and doors and take in their mail and daily newspaper. It made me feel like a real neighbor. I knew that Bert and Evelyn would do the same for me.

Wednesday, I worked late at my office. By the time I finished editing, the janitorial crew had begun cleanup on the main floor. I waved goodnight and practically trudged into the parking lot. Mentally I inventoried my refrigerator and decided to drive through a McDonald's.

I nibbled on the fries as I drove home, and they were nearly gone by the time I drove into my garage. I was so tired I was tempted not to pick up my neighbor's mail until morning. I reconsidered and with a sigh, I placed my purse, my keys and food sack on the hood of my car and made a quick run next door.

It took no more than ten minutes to unlock their door and make a cursory check of the house. All looked in order. I was halfway out of their house when the shrill sound of an alarm filled the warm, night air. I stumbled back inside, relocked the door and ran to the telephone. Until the police arrived, the receiver stayed in my hand. I was, finally, well and thoroughly afraid.

"Ms. McCoy, you can come out now." I pulled a curtain aside just enough to see the glint on the badge before I opened the door. Someone had silenced the alarm, and all the lights were on in my house. "Would you like to tell me why your garage door was open and your purse left on the car?"

Embarrassed and shame-faced, I told the policeman what I had done and why. I offered no excuses, for I had none.

"Ma'am, we patrol this street at various times every night, because we feel you are at risk here. We can't be one hundred percent sure this attempted break-in was done by the same guy that robbed the bank, but it's a pretty good guess it's the same one.

"It looks like he's staked out your house, and you practically issued an invitation to him tonight. Now he knows the place is alarmed, but that won't stop him. He'll probably look for other opportunities; and the sad part is, neither you nor we have a valid description."

"What should I do?"

"Go somewhere else tonight, or what's left of it. I doubt that he's still around, but he could be parked on a side street or hidden in someone's shrubbery. Is there somewhere you can go?"

I thought of my brother, but I didn't want to put him or his family at risk. "I can check into a hotel downtown."

The officer nodded. "That's probably as safe as you can be. We'll wait while you get what you need. Someone will be out to dust for fingerprints, but you can take your car. I'm sure the guy wore gloves."

My purse seemed intact, and the McDonald's sack was undisturbed; but my keys were gone. My shoulders sagged with the knowledge that the intruder now had access to my house, my car, the newspaper office and my mother's house. Chagrined and embarrassed beyond belief, I had to tell the officer.

"Do you have an extra key for your car?" he asked. He was gracious enough not to tell me how stupid I had been.

"Yes, and I also have another key to the house. I can change the locks again, but what about the Gazette building?"

"Ma'am, I can't help you with that. You'll have to take it up with your employer." He began to sound impatient, and I didn't blame him.

"I'll get a change of clothing and be right out," I told him. I carried out more than that. First, I grabbed Willow Thornhill's paintings. It took four trips to get all I wanted, but there was no way I would leave work in progress or things I treasured to the eyes and hands of a stalker. He might not come back, but he had the means; and he had proven he had the inclination.

The two patrol cars didn't leave until I backed out of the garage and headed down the street toward the business section. I took a room on an upper floor of a downtown hotel, and I asked for a bellboy to help carry my things. He raised an eyebrow, but he didn't question when I handed the paintings to him.

"Don't ask," I told him. He merely smiled and accepted my tip at the door of my room. There I was in a hotel at ten o'clock, tired, hungry, scared, and getting angrier by the moment. *How dare anyone try to take away the strength, the independence, the very* **right** *I had earned to live my life as I saw fit!*

I looked at the hotel menu, picked up the telephone and called the front desk. "Is it too late to order room service? No? Then I'd like to have a fruit and cheese plate, crackers and iced tea sent up, please." When it arrived, I practically pounced on the food; and I enjoyed every bite, all the while trying to develop a plan to bring down the well-dressed bandit.

At midnight I wedged the desk chair under the door handle and went to bed. I didn't think anyone would risk coming to the hotel; but just in case the guy had followed me, I was taking no chances.

The next morning I went to the Charleston Police Department and offered to be bait. "If this guy is watching me, and apparently he is, it's reasonable to assume he would follow me to Dixon. He probably knows where my mother lives, as well as my brother. Wouldn't it also be reasonable to think he might be tempted to rob a bank in Dixon if I'm in it?"

Detective Charles Douglas, who had graciously agreed to see me, tapped his desk with a pencil before he stuck it behind his ear. Around fifty, painfully thin, he had the look of a man who had seen more of life's bad stuff than was good for him. His light eyes drooped at the outer corners, and an interesting scar zigzagged across his chin.

"Ms. McCoy, you have no idea what danger you could be in. From what you and the other victims have told us, this guy talks like a gentleman while he's committing these crimes, both at the banks and in the women's homes. Keep in mind that he nearly killed one of them."

My heart rate accelerated, but I couldn't back down. The most priceless gift Jackson McCoy ever gave me was the determination that no one would ever again make me afraid to live in my own home. Whoever this criminal was, he was not going to intimidate me much longer, not if I could help set him up.

It took some hard talk to convince them. In the first place, I was a civilian; in the second place, I was a *woman* civilian; so what could I possibly know about police work? It was only after I declared that I would do it on my own that they agreed to give it a try.

The Gazette manager was not happy about changing the locks to the offices, but getting first crack at another potential front page story soothed his bruised indignation. I gave him my account of the previous night's events, and then I got into my car and drove to my mother's house. I wanted her to see that I was okay before she read an account in the paper.

"Mom, I'm fine. The police think the intruder might be the same guy who robbed the bank, so we're taking precautions."

"Well, Sissy, you're going to stay with us. That's all there is to it, so don't even try to argue with me!" My mother's mouth took on that rigid, you-might-as-well-hush straight line I remembered from my childhood. Her set mouth had meant business, whether it had been a denial of permission or the administering of medicine that tasted like horse pucky. There was no quarter given, and I didn't expect any now.

"Actually, Mom, I would like to stay with you for a few days. The police think it's a good idea, too." I kept a straight face while hers softened in victory.

"You know, I'm pretty good with my shotgun," my stepfather offered. "I used to be a crack shot." I tried not to shudder at the thought of Russell, whose eyesight continued to deteriorate, trying to aim a gun at anything.

"Thanks, Russell; but I don't think that will be necessary. The break-in at my house could just have been a random act. Everything will be fine." There was no need to tell him about my keys or that his houseguest had volunteered to become a target.

Like most banks, Dixon National closed at three every afternoon. I waited until two-thirty to enter the shiny, brown granite building. There were ten banking stations in the lobby, but only two had tellers. Five customers waited in the bank. None of them fit the limited description of the person I sought.

A man dressed in work clothes bent over a brochure table, laboriously filling out a form. Two elderly women sat in wing-backed chairs, happily chatting to each other. Another man waited behind a woman at one station, so I got in line behind the man at the other. Dressed in light khaki pants and a white knit shirt, the tall fellow got my attention. From the back, he looked good, fit, without an ounce of unnecessary bulk.

I waited patiently for him to complete his business. I looked into my purse for the check I needed; and in the next moment, I was nearly knocked to the floor. For a moment, I was terrified that the bandit had found me.

"Oh, I'm so sorry!" The man grabbed my arms to keep me upright. "I didn't know anyone was behind me...Sissy? Sissy Bannister?"

Well, if the guy knew me as Sissy, he probably wasn't an enemy. I raised my eyes and stared into the incredibly blue gaze of Mark Watson. I don't know which one of us was more surprised.

"Mark? What are you doing here?"

"Sissy, what are you doing here?" Spontaneously, he threw his arms around me and gave me the most incredible hug. I clung to him as tightly as he held me. It's hard to put into words what I felt. Three come to mind: safe, welcome, remembered. When Mark loosened his hold, he ran his hands down my arms and squeezed my fingers.

"You are beautiful," he smiled.

"Thank you. So are you."

We laughed with abandon, right there in the middle of Dixon National Bank at near closing time. I forgot why I was there. I stood with my hands in his, looking up at him; and I had to agree with my friends. Mark Watson was truly gorgeous.

"Would you like to get some coffee? Or something cold?" he asked.

"Yes, I would."

"Ma'am, did you need to make a transaction here at the bank?" the grinning teller asked.

"Oh, no," I replied. "I can take care of it tomorrow." On our way out, we stood aside for a man who pushed open the inner door. I gave him a cursory glance, noting that he was attractive and very debonair in his white linen suit and light, Panama straw hat. I looked at him twice. Our eyes met briefly, and he gave me a polite smile, nodded, and thanked us for holding the door.

"Let's go to Dooby's," Mark suggested.

"Wonderful."

He took my arm, and guided me to his car, a dark blue, four-door Lincoln. The leather seats were hot from the sun, but the air conditioner soon had the interior comfortable.

"I certainly never expected to see you," Mark told me. "Someone mentioned they thought you were back in the area, but I didn't believe it. Are you on a long visit? Is your mother well?"

"Mom is fine. I was just suddenly tired of New York, and I wanted to come home. I can write in Charleston as well as in the big city. Maybe I needed to reconnect with family and old friends."

"I'm glad, Sissy. I can't remember the last time I was this happy to see someone."

"Me, too." We exchanged glances. I dropped my eyes, and in the beverage holder I saw a package of breath mints. Mints. My mind spiraled backwards. Mints! "Mark, turn around! We've got to go back to the bank!"

"Why? Did you lose something?"

"No, but the man who came in as we were leaving smelled like mints! Strong mints! Mark, we've got to go back!" He looked as if he just realized he had a crazy woman in his car. "I'll explain, but I've got to go back!"

Mark checked his rearview and did a u-turn in the middle of the street. Horns honked and drivers yelled, but he completed the maneuver. The car skidded to a halt outside the bank entrance, and I flung open the door. "Sissy, wait!" Mark called. I could hear his steps behind me. I tugged on the bank's door, but we were too late. It was locked. The bell in the Catholic Church tower just down the street sounded it's first of three peals.

"It's closed." I leaned my forehead against the glass door. "It was the bank robber. I know it."

Mark put his hand on my shoulder and turned me toward him. "Sissy, what's going on? What robber?" While we stood in front of the bank, I told him all of it. I even told him how I planned to open an account in Dixon National today, how I hoped to draw the man out where the police would be waiting.

"I didn't count on his being here, not so soon. He had to have followed me from Charleston. I expected him to do that, but I thought he would want to check out the bank before he followed me into it."

"How do you know he hasn't already done that?"

"You mean for a hold-up?"

"Why not?"

"He's only hit bigger banks in larger cities," I explained.

Mark looked at his watch. "Sissy, I've got to pick up the girls. Why don't you come with me? I can't leave you alone now. Come on. You'll like them."

"Should I take my car?"

"No. Make sure it's locked, and I'll bring you back for it later."

"The creep has a set of keys to my car," I told him. "Locking it won't keep him out of it, if he wants in."

"All the more reason for you to come with me." I didn't disagree.

I learned that the twins were on a swim team, and they trained every day in the public pool. Twenty-year-old memories assailed me as we approached the fence that surrounded the concrete deck. "I used to come here with Karen Courtney. Gosh, Mark, I haven't been swimming for years."

"Would you like to come back one evening while you're here?" he asked.

"I would." I was surprised how appealing that sounded. I waited while Mark went to get his girls. I recognized them right away when the swim team climbed from the water. Thin and blond, they were twice the age they had been when I last saw them. I had never seen twins so identical. Melissa Franklin's boys had looked alike, but not as much as Mark's girls.

I watched the trio approach the car. Mark turned from one to the other, like a ping-pong ball, as they vied for his attention. I thought that the three of them were the most beautiful people in Dixon.

"Girls, this is Mrs. McCoy..."

"Oh, please, Mark. They can call me Sissy."

"I remember you," said Alyssa. "You were at Dooby's a long time ago."

Not to be outdone, Clarice stated, "I remember you, too. Are you coming with us?"

"I invited Sissy to go to Dooby's with us," Mark told her.

"Okay. Can we get strawberry milk shakes?"

"Won't that spoil your supper?" he teased.

"Come on, Mark," I chided. "I intend to have a strawberry shake with a double dollop of whipped cream; and I can't have it if you won't let the girl's have one, too."

Mark grinned at me. "Well, I see I'm completely outnumbered. Strawberry milkshakes, it is."

The banter between the girls in the back seat of the car was like sweet music to me. They maintained a chattering marathon about their afternoon, arguing over who swam the most laps and who was faster. I recalled the way my siblings and I had fussed at each other when my dad took us for evening drives into Amish country, near Redbud Grove. It was a good memory.

Inside Dooby's front door, I stopped in shock. Never had I dreamed it might change. A bright new floor replaced the worn tiles I remembered. The old, round, white soda shop tables and chairs were gone. Square, red-topped tables, trimmed with chrome took their place; and red vinyl booths lined the walls.

Mirrors stretched across the wall behind the counter, and new menus were wedged between the napkin holders and salt-and-pepper shakers on the tables. The only familiar thing in the place was the Wurlitzer jukebox on the far wall.

"Wow," I murmured.

"I know," Mark commiserated. "The new look kind of ruined the atmosphere, didn't it?" He briefly hugged my shoulders. I briefly melted.

For the duration of the milkshakes, I forgot why I came to Dixon. Entirely captivated by Mark and his daughters, I gazed from one to the other, content to bask in their company. The first drugstore yodel from Clarice's glass brought me back to reality. The rest of us joined in the rude noises, and we laughed all the way to the car.

"Are you coming home with us?" Alyssa asked.

"No, Honey, I'm not. Your dad is only taking me to get my car," I told her. On the ride to the bank parking lot, the girls asked questions. Mark grinned at me as he answered "yes" and "no" in the right places.

"Sissy and I went to high school together," he told them.

"Yes, we did. One time he took me to a picnic at his grandpa's house in the hills; and we walked up to the spring and sipped cider from a cup in the cider house."

Mark took his eyes from the road long enough to give me a quizzical glance. "You remember that?"

"It's one of my very favorite memories. There have been times when I would have given anything to be back there, listening to your aunt sing, watching your grandpa chew on his twig."

"Do you mean great-grandpa Watson?" Alyssa asked. I decided that she must be the more precocious of the two.

"Yes. I think he was a nice man," I answered.

"He died," she stated. My eyes flew to Mark.

"He was one hundred years old," he said. "Grandpa just didn't wake up one morning. He never missed a day going up to the spring behind his house, and I think he probably always stopped for a sip from the cider cup. One of my cousins kept it filled for him." He glanced at me again. "We live there now."

"No! How wonderful for all of you!" I could think of nothing more delightful.

Mark laughed. "The house is a lot different from when you saw it. Grandpa left it to me, but I did nothing with it until a couple of years ago. Grandpa's house stood empty while Terri was so ill."

"What do you do, Mark? Do you work here in Dixon?"

"My official job is at the chemical plant in Charleston. I won't bore you with details, but I work with the mathematical compositions of the different solutions and 'potions.' The plant is currently devising computer programs, and eventually everything will be computerized. It's the coming thing, you know." He grinned at me, and something turned over inside my chest.

"So you really are brilliant in math," I quipped. He raised his eyebrows. "I remember that you got a full scholarship in mathematics."

"You remember that, too?" he asked. He seemed pleased.

He pulled into the bank's lot and parked beside my car. It seemed undisturbed. Mark got out and checked all four tires, even opened both of the Corvette's doors and looked at everything. "I think it's okay," he said.

"Thank you so much," I told him. I held out my hand to him. He took it, looked down at our clasped hands, looked at my face and pulled me into his arms. The hug was gentle, sweet; and I felt tears well into my eyes.

"I'm so glad you came home, Sissy," he said. I was embarrassed to look at him, but he raised my chin with one hand. I blinked rapidly, but a few tears trickled down my cheeks. He rubbed them away with his thumb. "Why the tears?"

I laughed nervously. "I don't know, Mark. Seeing you, being with you after so many years and so many hurts just seems so...so..." I floundered.

"Right?" he murmured. I nodded and looked into his eyes. Such warm blue eyes, with the sooty lashes I remembered; soft, brown hair that still fell across one side of his forehead; a straight nose and nearly square jaw—in short, a face full of strength and determination. I had never kissed his mouth, but it looked entirely kissable, firm and soft at the same time.

"What are you thinking?" he asked. I smiled.

"Maybe I'll tell you sometime."

"Daddy, it's hot in here! Can we go home now?" From Mark's car, the girls spoke with one voice.

"I'm coming," Mark told them. "Before I take the girls home, I'm going to follow you to Symington. Don't argue, just get in your car." I did as he said. His big blue vehicle in my rear view mirror was more comforting than I could have imagined.

The moment I went into my mother's house, I called the Charleston Police Department and told them about the man in the bank. I described him, even down to a tiny scar I had noticed on his right cheek. A good journalist/writer notices details, sometimes unconsciously.

I remembered that his eyes were hazel, beneath dark brows. What bit of hair I saw below his hat was dark; and although clean-shaven, his beard stubble was dark, too. I stumbled over how handsome the man was; but criminals aren't all dirty, ugly and sullen. Titles are not tattooed across their foreheads, telling the world they are rapists, murderers, robbers, thieves and embezzlers.

"Ms. McCoy, there's no proof at all that this is our man," the detective told me. "He could simply be a client who arrived late, as you did. Speaking of which, why were you in the Dixon bank today? I thought you banked at Charleston."

"I do." I hesitated. "I wanted to check out the exits. It's been twenty years since I was inside the building, and it's been completely remodeled. I deliberately waited until closing time, since the bank in Charleston was full when he robbed it. The more people inside a target bank, the better, I would think. There's less chance of someone noticing a man who is, supposedly, standing close to his wife." I didn't mention that I completely forgot to examine the exits, nor that I had been distracted by a big, handsome, blue-eyed former classmate.

"Perhaps. If you haven't blown our crack at him, maybe he'll be there tomorrow. Maybe he'll think you no longer feel safe in the Charleston bank. Can you tell me anything else about the man?"

"Yes. His breath practically exuded mint. I should have caught it right away, but I was...distracted." A heavy sigh came across the lines.

"I guess he doesn't want to offend his mark. The Dixon PD will have two plainclothesmen in the bank when it opens tomorrow. Would you please just stay inside your mother's house tonight? Play cards or something." They line went dead. *Goodbye to you, too.*

I did as the good detective suggested. After supper, Mom, Russell and I played cards until nine-thirty. I didn't tell them of the upcoming plan to catch my stalker. I knew my mother felt as if she was once again protecting one of her chicks, and there was no need to add to her worry. Instead, I told her about running into Mark Watson.

"How nice," she said. "He's a good boy." *Nothing boyish about him, Mom.* "I saw him often when his wife was in the hospital, especially toward the end of her life. Mark stayed with her as much as he could. He seemed devoted to her. I think Terri's mother kept the twins most of the time during those days."

"I met his daughters today, too."

"You did?" When she twisted her mouth in speculation, I threw in my hand, yawned and announced that I was headed for bed. The wheels in my mother's matchmaking head had begun to turn, so I did what I had done as a teenager when I didn't want to face her. I fled to the relative safety of my upstairs bedroom.

A summer storm, complete with thunder and lightning, hovered over Dixon the next day. Mom rose early. She had volunteered to fill the seven-to-three shift for a vacationing nurse at the hospital I offered to take her, but she declined a ride in the Corvette. I tried not to pace. The longer it rained, the more nervous I became. At ten-thirty, I called Detective Douglas in Charleston and was told he was not in the office.

"Can you please tell me where I can reach him?"

"I'm sorry, I can't."

The man didn't sound sorry at all.

"This is C.C. McCoy. I would really like to talk to him."

"Just a minute." There was a murmur in the background, and someone else came on the line.

"Ms. McCoy, Detective Douglas left early this morning. Someone was supposed to notify you that he would be in Dixon all day. I guess we dropped the ball here."

"Thank you." *Dropped the ball? Really? Do you think?* I heaved a huge sigh and replaced the receiver. I shuddered at the chill that suddenly encompassed my body. Much as I didn't want to admit it, I was scared. A dozen scenarios played in my mind: What if the man stuck a gun in my ribs again? What if the cops couldn't stop him? What if he dragged me out with him? What if I couldn't get away?

Worse: What if he didn't show up, and I had to continue to live with his invisible presence? What if he just broke into my house one night? What if he raped and/or murdered me? None of the possibilities were acceptable. All I could do was hope the police were where they said they would be.

I dressed in a sleeveless white blouse and comfortable navy slacks. Opting for speed over style, I pushed my feet into socks and tennis shoes, just in case I needed to run. I didn't like the possibilities in my head.

My reflection in the mirror looked normal. My hair had grown some since Sonya had made me get it cut shorter. It brushed just below my shoulders again; and sometimes I used it to veil the side of my face, mostly when I wanted to avoid interruptions at work. I brushed a bit of eye shadow over my lids, flicked blush over my cheekbones and dabbed some gloss on my lips. I was as ready as I was going to be.

In my throat, a nervous lump rose that refused to be swallowed. I kept trying, all the way down the switchbacks. The rain had slowed to a drizzle, and the mountains were misty above the valley. At the end of Symington, I paused long enough to gaze upward at the slopes. It made me think of my untouched oil paints, and I vowed to myself that I would unpack them when this miserable business was finished.

Somewhere between my mother's house and Main Street, I realized how much I loved this town. Redbud Grove had been the home of my childhood. Dixon had not only been my home throughout my teen years and young adulthood; it was still the home I came to, the place where the essence of my dad remained, the kitchen where my mother still cooked the foods I loved, the comfort I sought when I needed it. Home.

Cars, pickup trucks and vans filled the bank's parking lot. Three vehicles followed me in, and we circled in competition for an empty space. I waited while a white-haired lady slowly backed her ancient Cadillac from a spot, and I zipped the Corvette into it.

All over the lot, I saw elderly men and women, many of them with umbrellas, enter and exit the bank, and it dawned upon me that it was the first of the month—social security check time. I scanned the lot; but I saw no one I recognized. Again I tried to swallow the lump, unsuccessfully; and I opened the car door.

Inside the bank, long lines formed at each teller's window. Casually, I glanced around the large lobby. Snatches of conversations could be heard. It somewhat reminded me, on a much smaller scale, of an airport terminal. Wing-backed chairs and matching loveseats formed three or four conversation areas, all of which were filled.

I joined the smallest line. My purse strap hooked into the crook of my arm and dangled against my hip. As nonchalant as possible, I continually moved my eyes over the faces around me, smiling, nodding, polite and serene. Many of them smiled back, but a few blinked and looked away. None seemed threatening, and not one man resembled the one I sought.

Relieved and disappointed, I reached the teller without incident. She placed forms in front of me, which I signed and then wrote a check from my account in Charleston to open a new account in Dixon. She thanked me, I thanked her, and I turned to leave.

"Oh, no!" someone cried. "I just heard on the radio that Elvis Presley has died!" The bank grew totally silent. I glanced at the teller, who looked as stunned as I felt.

"Maybe it's just a rumor."

"No, I heard it myself!"

"Well, Elvis can't possibly be dead. That's all there is to it. He's too young."

Shock registered on the faces inside the lobby. I felt sick. The memory of the young Elvis I had seen when I was sixteen, when his hair still had lighter glints, when he still had the smooth face of a boy, flashed into my head.

Hushed conversations gradually picked up. A lobby filled with people, who were mostly strangers to each other, discovered a common bond. However individuals felt about Elvis Presley, the young man who changed forever the sound and face of music in the world, they would remember him.

For a few minutes, I forgot why I stood in the midst of these people. I was one who had been a teenager when Elvis burst like a rocket upon the music scene. Karen Courtney and I had been two of his most avid fans, and we had collected every one of those little forty-five rpm records Elvis recorded in the 'fifties. They still remained in cardboard boxes stored somewhere in my mother's house.

I felt as if I had lost someone I actually knew, and I wasn't alone in that feeling. Two women, older than I—younger than my mother, followed me outside. Tears actually fell down the face of one.

"I was at the concert Elvis gave in Charleston, just before he went into the army," she said. "He was so young and vibrant, and he was on the verge of holding the world in his hand."

"A group of my friends and I also attended that concert," I told her. We stood beneath the awning and conversed for a few minutes, hoping the rain would stop. We wished each other well, and the two of them ran for their cars, sharing an umbrella. I wished I had carried one.

Still dry beneath the awning, I looked up at the leaden skies. There was nothing to do but run for it. My plan to flush out our quarry had not worked. I didn't know if I were happy or sad about that. The death of Elvis had nearly wiped it from my mind.

I took my keys from my purse and splashed through the puddles toward my car. I fumbled at the lock, and the key ring slipped from my fingers. "Rats!" I muttered and stooped to retrieve them. I saw his reflection in my car window when I stood up.

"Hello, Ms. C.C. McCoy. You look mighty fetching in your wet shirt." He wore a brimmed hat, but it didn't conceal the way his hazel eyes traveled down my body. His courteous voice couldn't hide the evil in his soul, and the skin all over my body felt too tight. "Now don't do anything foolish, like draw attention to us." He opened the passenger side of the car next to mine. "Would you be so kind as to get inside?" The handgun he displayed looked very big. "That's right. Smile as if you are glad to see me."

I couldn't smile. All I could do was follow his orders and hope that the Dixon and the Charleston Police forces were watching. My safety, if not my life, depended upon them. Ruefully, I realized that, except for an attempted purse snatching, in New York I had never been in the peril I was right here, in my own hometown.

"Move over, Darlin.' For the moment, I'm afraid you must drive. Do please forgive my lack of manners."

He moved next to me, and I had no choice but to scoot beneath the steering wheel. I glanced at his face. He smiled, and I caught the scent of mint on his breath. His features were picture-perfect-handsome, but his green/brown eyes were as frigid as the South Pole.

"You have led me on a merry chase, you know. Your first article in the Gazette caught my attention months ago, so I decided to find you. It wasn't difficult; and I enjoyed watching you, worshipping from afar, so to speak." He laughed. "Imagine my surprise when you entered the very bank I had planned to, ah, 'borrow' from. Now that was, indeed, serendipitous." He sounded so pleased with himself.

"Why me?" I asked. He chuckled and playfully waved the gun, a wicked-looking black thing, with lots of chrome on it.

"Now, Sissy...may I call you 'Sissy?' I overheard that young man you were with yesterday call you that. From outside, you both seemed very surprised to see each other. Who is he? An old friend? An old lover?" He sounded less pleased. "Start the car, Sissy. Why you? Talented young women fascinate me."

"I'm not that talented. I just write."

"Oh, you are too modest. I read your article on the sundown towns. Nice, very nice."

I wanted to gag. "Where am I going?" I asked.

"You will drive where I tell you to drive, turn when I tell you and stop when I tell you. I've followed you in your little red car enough to know you are an excellent driver—a little on the fast side, but that can be exciting. Slowly, now. Don't draw attention. Turn left."

Frantically, I looked both ways, hoping to catch a glimpse of flashing red lights and uniformed drivers. I pulled into the flow of traffic, and three cars followed me. Hopefully, I watched them in the rear view. The first one turned at the first light, and the second one pulled into a grocery store lot. Other cars joined the lane, and I lost sight of the third car. My heart sank. I felt like the worst kind of idiot, the most ignorant, stupid, asinine fool ever born.

From my side vision, I saw him glance periodically behind us. Evidently, he was as watchful as I, but for different reasons. Rain continued to fall, and the wipers swished smoothly against the windshield. It was a great car, a white two-door Bonneville that still smelled new, bought, no doubt, with some bank's money.

"Nice car," I said, surprised that I sounded almost natural.

"Thank you. I'm pleased that you like it." He sounded so polite, so *normal.* "Turn right at the next light." I didn't slow enough for the turn, and the tires skidded on the pavement. He swore and pointed the gun at me. "I hope you didn't do that on purpose, Sissy." His words were as polite as ever, but anger lay beneath them.

"I drive a small car," I told him. "This one is harder for me to handle in the rain." I swallowed.

"You are a very bright young woman, much smarter than all the others. You surprised me with the alarms, you know. None of the others thought of that. They didn't make the connection, but you did."

"Actually, I didn't. Detective Douglas, of the Charleston PD put it together. He warned me. You give me too much credit. There's nothing special about me, at all."

He laughed. "Oh, but there is. I've watched you when you had no clue. So many times I could have reached out and touched you."

"Where?"

"Just about everywhere you go. I've placed ads with your paper and watched you while the other girl took down the copy. I have eaten only a table or two from you in restaurants. I know which dry cleaner you use, which department store you shop and what you buy there.

"I know what brand of toothpaste and shampoo you use. And laundry soap. And body cream. And lingerie." His voice deepened. I looked full at him.

"You can't know all that!"

"Oh, but I do, Sissy. I've even watched you while you sleep."

My heart lurched. He had been in my house! Before the bank robbery, he had been in my house! My hands tightened on the steering wheel, and my foot lowered on the accelerator. The car responded like the fine machine it was. I clenched my jaw in anger.

"Slow down, Sissy." He didn't raise his voice, but he raised the gun. "Believe me when I tell you that I will shoot you. Slow down now."

"Why? You mean to kill me anyway. If I wreck the car, I might get you, too!" The speedometer climbed to fifty, fifty-five, sixty. We were headed out of town, and the traffic had thinned considerably. I passed a pickup truck and swerved back into my lane, with little time to spare from the oncoming bus.

"Sissy, I have no intention of killing you. I want to spend some time with you, get to know you on a more—personal level; but I don't want you dead. Slow down!" He cocked the pistol and pressed it against my side. Now I knew where that proverbial rock and a hard place met.

With only moments to weigh the options, I relaxed my foot. The car slowed to fifty, forty-five. He un-cocked the gun, but kept it against me. He shifted his weight and looked behind us again.

"Turn left at the crossroads and make a sharp right. Do it very carefully, Sissy."

I did as he said. The sharp right was nothing but a graveled road that wound upward into brush and tall pines. It looked more like a logging trail than a road, barely wide enough for the big car to avoid low-hanging branches.

Okay, I reasoned. If he truly means not to kill me, I'll take my chances. One thing was certain in my mind. If I survived whatever the next few minutes or hours held, I would make it my life's goal to put his ass, along with the rest of his miserable body, in a prison so deep, he would never see the sun again...if I didn't kill him first. I didn't know I was capable of such cold, focused anger. My jaw clenched with it, so tightly it hurt.

"Good girl," he said. With the gun, he waved toward what looked like no more than a dirt lane. I drove onto it, and the tires spun in the muddy ruts. "Stop. There's no need to bury it. I'll get it out later." He leaned toward me and took the keys. "It's just a short walk to our cabin, Darlin.' How nice that the rain has stopped. You may get out of the car now."

He leveled the gun at me. "No, not through that door. Slide toward me." I did as he said, and he actually took my hand to help me out through the passenger door. I withdrew it as quickly as possibly, and he chuckled. "You will learn to appreciate my touch," he promised. He motioned with the gun for me to walk ahead of him. "I like to watch you move," he murmured.

Tall grass and brush grew thickly along the lane. I tried to stay on the patchy grass, but my shoes were soon covered with mud. Our feet make sucking sounds as we lifted them from the mud. I was surprised that such a fastidious dresser would even consider coming to this place. He seemed to read my thoughts.

"I'm sorry for the mess," he apologized. "The rain was an unpleasant surprise. Don't fret. We can clean up in the cabin." The whole scenario took on a sense of unreality to me. How in the world did I get here? Only a few weeks ago, I was immersed in the business of choosing new furniture, making new contacts, totally happy with a new location and job.

"There it is. Our own little honeymoon cabin."

I lifted my head. About fifty feet ahead, nearly hidden in a mass of errant kudzu vines, stood what once must have been a lovely log cabin. It looked sturdy, but there were no signs of recent habitation. I stopped. *How strange. I didn't know kudzu grew at all in West Virginia.*

He stepped close to me. Although he didn't touch me, I could feel him. A hint of mint wafted over my shoulder, and I turned my head in the opposite direction. I had always associated the scent of mint with good things: Christmas candy, chewing gum, peppermint sticks, and chocolate mint ice cream. Now it made me nauseous.

"Go ahead, Sweetheart. The steps are sound, and we can leave our muddy shoes on the porch. It's quite nice inside." When I didn't move, he nudged me with the gun. Fear and anger battled inside me; but for the moment, fear had an edge.

Once on the porch, he transferred the pistol to his left hand. With his right, he took a key from his jacket pocket. A shiny new knob and deadbolt lock on the door told me how well he had planned his moves. The door opened smoothly, without a hint of hesitation or creak.

"Ah," he said. "Home, sweet home."

The place looked like a movie set, staged in the center, with no substance on the perimeters. In front of the wide, stone fireplace, a shaggy white rug stretched the full width and beyond. A mattress, covered with some kind of tapestry, lay beside the rug. I shuddered.

"Now, now," he soothed. "Don't get ahead of me. I won't rush you... much. There's a screen to protect your modesty." He pointed with the gun toward a folding screen across one corner of the room. "You will find suitable attire there."

"If you think I'm going to..."

"Oh, yes, I do think you're going to." He shrugged out of the same white linen jacket, now damp, he had worn the day before and carefully draped it along the back of a straight chair, one of three at a small matching table. Only then did I see the bottle of wine and two glasses.

He unbuttoned the top buttons of his shirt, without once taking his eyes from mine. I turned away when he continued with the buttons. I searched the walls for any kind of makeshift weapon, fireplace tools, wood, anything.

"Step behind the screen and get ready for our romantic afternoon, Sissy." He put his hands on my shoulders and gave me a little push toward the screen. "It would be better if you do this without my help." Beneath his courteous words, I could hear the cold steel of leashed cruelty. I sensed that I wouldn't have a prayer if and when he unleashed it.

I went behind the screen and held tightly to the hope that someone would come charging in on a white stallion to rescue me; but I would settle for a thin, droopy-eyed man with an assault rifle. In truth, I'd welcome someone on a pogo stick, anything to distract this lunatic long enough for me to dive through one of the windows, glass and all, like the heroes and heroines did on television.

"I've waited long enough for you, Sissy. Don't make me wait any longer."

I heard the sound of a cork popping, and I knew he had opened the wine bottle. It clinked against a glass, followed by the rush of liquid. The rustle of fabric followed, and I fought the wave of nausea that threatened to recycle the pancakes I'd eaten at breakfast. Slowly, I stepped out of my slacks and slipped my blouse from my shoulders. No way was I going to remove anything else.

I picked up the silky white dressing gown he had draped across the fourth straight chair of the set. The gown was a lovely thing, more translucent than sheer, suitable for a bride on her honeymoon. I shrugged into it and ran a hand through my rain-curled hair.

"Come out now, Sissy. I've gone to a lot of trouble for you. Your predecessors were not so pampered. Actually, I'm glad your alarms forced me to plan something special for you. The anticipation has been exquisite."

I held the robe closed, took a deep breath and stepped around the screen. At first, I kept my eyes on the window beyond him, dreading what I might see. My heart lurched with hope when I thought I saw a shadow of movement. I caught my lower lip with my teeth at the realization that it was probably the wind in the vines.

I glanced at the table. Beside the wine bottle was his gun, but he was much closer to it than I was. I could not possibly reach it before he did.

"Ah, yes, you are even lovelier than I imagined, all flushed and modest."

It was then that I looked at him. I could not believe it. From somewhere he had produced an old fashioned smoking jacket, the kind worn by now-deceased actors in old movies. It was made of dark red jacquard trimmed with black satin lapels and cuffs. I stared. He looked totally ridiculous, bare legs shining beneath the jacket. I wanted to laugh.

I was consumed with the need to laugh. There he stood in his lust and his movie-set garb, with no idea how pathetic he looked. I hiccupped, and he blinked. I hiccupped again. Helplessly, I started to laugh.

"What are you doing?" he demanded. I slapped my hand over my mouth and tried to stop the laughter; but it would not be suppressed. I howled with it, open-mouthed and loudly. "Stop it!" he shouted.

I couldn't stop. He grabbed my shoulders and shook me, and still I laughed. Tears ran down my face with the force of my hysteria while I literally laughed in the man's face. He shook me harder.

"What's the matter with you?" he screamed. "Stop it! I said stop it!"

He slapped me, and that's when I screamed. I continued to scream at the top of my lungs. I drew in sweet air and expelled it with the unexpressed rage I still carried from the abusive years with Jack.

"Shut up! Shut up!"

He slapped me again. I hit him back, which was not the wisest move I'd ever made. He held me with one hand and slapped my face from side to side with the other. His courteous words became a string of enraged curses that escalated with each blow to my face and head.

Still I screamed. I screamed until the sound of it echoed in my own ears. His hands moved to my throat and squeezed, and I knew that I was going to die right there, in a sorry cabin, killed by a maniac with a romance fetish. My dying wish was that I'd taken some pointers on fighting from Sonya, my streetwise friend who would not know how I died.

I didn't hear the door burst open, but I heard the gunshot. The man took his hands away so quickly I fell to the floor. For a moment, I thought I had been shot; but the only pain I felt was in my head, my face and my tortured throat. Air had never tasted sweeter.

"Don't move!" someone said. So I didn't, well, only slightly—enough to draw the silky material tightly around me. I peeked through the mess of my hair. The room seemed filled with dark uniforms and drawn weapons, all pointed to the silly-looking man in the smoking jacket.

Who needed a warrior on a white horse? My rescuers were beautiful, slow-talking, West Virginia patrolmen. At the moment I would have married any or all of them. I felt a gentle tug on my forearm as someone helped me to my feet.

"Miss, are your clothes here?" he asked. Through eyes that were quickly becoming slits, I looked at him and nodded. I pointed to the screen. "Would you like to get dressed?" I nodded.

Through the hinged cracks in the screen, I watched the angry, nearly naked man, whose name I did not know, thoroughly subdued and humiliated. "Would you please just let me put my pants on?" he begged. One of the officers tossed the trousers to him. It hurt my face too much to grin, but the sight of my would-be rapist, trying to pull up his pants with shackled hands, went a long way toward restoring my peace of mind.

To say I was a reluctant celebrity was an understatement, but there was nothing I could do about the publicity. Dixon had another nine-day-wonder in the news, and my byline was printed under the headlines of the Charleston Gazette: **LOCAL JOURNALIST HELPS APPREHEND ALLEDGED BANK ROBBER/RAPIST IN DIXON.** Photographs of my swollen mouth and black eyes were less than flattering. The editor was ecstatic.

The joint efforts of the two police forces had worked beautifully. The third car I had seen pull out from the bank lot was one of four unmarked cars. They had kept Quentin Morley's car in sight as I drove it out of town. The only hitch had come when I panicked and passed the pickup truck. They had lost sight of the car when I rounded a bend.

They caught a glimpse of the white Bonneville when I turned off the highway, but they missed it when I made the sharp right onto the graveled road. They had driven a few miles past it before they backtracked and noticed fresh tire tracks in the muddy gravel.

The team had carefully approached the cabin. They had waded through the tall, wet grasses to the back of it; and that's when I'd seen the moving vines. One of the men saw me through the window.

My laughter had given them pause, but my screams gave them the cover they needed to break through the door. The atmosphere at the station when I gave my statement was not exactly light-hearted, but there were a few chuckles when I described my reaction to Morley's attire.

"Your laughter threw him off," Captain Pearson, Dixon's police chief, told me. "He thrived on fear and intimidation, and you apparently had neither."

"Oh, yes, I did! I was scared witless; but I was just plain mad, too."

"Well, I think your laughter probably saved you a great deal of suffering, if not your life. Possibly that, too. He came close to killing his last victim. You're a lucky young woman."

"Yes, Sir, I am. Thank you so much."

From the police station, they took me to the hospital, in spite of my resistance. As luck would have it, my mother was in the ER when two burly policemen escorted me inside. By that time, my mouth had become so swollen I could barely speak.

"Sissy! Dear God, Sissy! What happened to you?"

"I aw right, Ma. Jus a li'l bruise..." I don't know what happened then. My knees gave way, and they told me later that I just kind of melted onto the floor. I woke up in a clean white bed, totally at the mercy and control of my mother, which was all right with me. I wanted to smile, but it hurt too much; so I went back to sleep.

I slept through the night and most of the next morning, due, I suspect, to some chemical help. When I opened my eyes, the first thing I saw was the handsome face of Mark Watson. After my initial joy at his presence, my next thought was how horrendous I must appear to him.

"Hi," he said softly. He picked up my hand and held it gently between both of his.

"Hi."

"You look awful."

"Thanks."

"You're welcome. You know, if you had given me a clue day before yesterday, as to what you planned to do, I would have stopped you."

"Oh, yeah?"

"Yeah. The afternoon we spent together was just about the happiest day I've had for a long, long time. When I heard what happened yesterday, I felt like I'd been kicked in the stomach. I called your house, and your stepfather told me you were here. By the time I got here, you were asleep; and they wouldn't let me see you."

My insides became all warm and gooey. "You ca' to see 'e las' nigh'?" Through my swollen mouth, the words may not all have been clear, but he understood me.

"I did. Sissy, that summer right after high school, I wanted to spend more time with you. I really liked you. You had broken up with Jack, but we were both going to different schools; and I wasn't ready to be tied down. You weren't either, if I remember." I nodded.

"You righ'," I told him.

"I was disappointed when I heard you had married Jack, after all."

Mark lifted my hand to his lips before he gently released it. I could have happily killed my mother when she bustled into the room. Her starched white uniform fairly crackled.

"Hello, Mark," she said. "I think the doctor is going to allow Sissy to come home this afternoon, but only if she promises to take it easy for a few days. Would it be too much to ask you to drive her home?" I changed my mind about killing her.

"I'd be happy to," Mark told her.

If my face hadn't hurt so much, I would have grinned from ear to ear.

There was no trial. Quentin Morley pled guilty to ten counts of armed robbery, eleven counts of aggravated battery and ten counts of forcible rape and assault. The Charleston PD were surprised by the number of unreported rape victims who came forward after Morley's arrest. If he ever got out of prison, he would be too old to go to the bathroom by himself. I thought that was fair.

My bruises and lumps healed, and once again I felt safe in the hills of beautiful West Virginia. Sometimes, dreams disturbed my slumber, but only momentarily. Mark found it convenient to drop by my house in Charleston on occasion, many occasions, actually. We laughed easily together. We spent hours talking about the past, about the present and, eventually, the future; but he had not yet kissed me.

One cool October evening after a movie, I invited him in for coffee. He leaned against the counter while I spooned grounds into the filter, but suddenly he was behind me. He wrapped his arms around my waist and turned me toward him. Without a word, he leaned down; and I lifted my face to his.

When he kissed me, I kissed him back; and I felt as if I had come home. There were no residual thoughts of any other man, not Jack, not Carlo, not Neal, not Victor. There was nothing but Mark's soft mouth, moving against mine; and it was the sweetest, most satisfying sensation I had ever known.

"Sissy," he breathed. He leaned his forehead against mine and wrapped his arms tightly around me, so close I could feel his heart beat.

"Sissy, this may sound crazy to you; but will you marry me?" Those pesky tears sprang to my eyes again.

"Mark, this may sound crazy to you, too; but...yes."

"No doubts?"

"None."

"Good."

"When?"

"Tomorrow?"

"Okay."

"Ummmmmm."

"Uh, Mark? What about the girls? Will they be okay with us getting married?"

"Yes."

"How do you know?"

"I already told them."

"You what?!"

"I told them."

"But...but...you just asked me."

"Shut up and kiss me," he said.

So I did.

And Heaven, Too

My eyes popped open. I stared at the ceiling for a moment, looked at the walls on either side of my bedroom... head back to the center of the pillow for another look at the ceiling. The room seemed fine. *Okay, so what is different?* I glanced at the bedside clock.

Wow! Eight o'clock, the time I'm supposed to be at my desk. I threw back the sheet and ran to the bathroom. My face in the mirror didn't seem right. I looked...younger or something. The knowledge was right there. It waited in my eyes. All I had to do was look closer at the replica of my dad's gray-blues.

Happiness. It was unadulterated happiness. I smiled at the woman in the glass, and she smiled back at me. "We're engaged," I whispered. I watched the mirrored lips move, and then I twirled in several little circles. "We're engaged!" I shouted.

While I showered and brushed my teeth, I relived every moment of my time with Mark the night before. Like true friendships allow, Mark and I had picked up where we had ended, following graduation. It was as if everything had been leading us to the present moment. All we had to do was let it happen.

The phone rang. The towel slipped from my wet head as I ran into the bedroom and plunged onto the bed. I grabbed the phone on the fourth ring. "Hello."

"Hello yourself. You had me worried," Mark told me.

"Why?" I flopped to my back and smiled at the ceiling.

"Because you weren't at your office yet. They told me you are never late. Is everything all right?"

"Yes, I just overslept; and I've been playing in the bathroom."

I could imagine the look on Mark's face as he realized he had just become engaged to marry a lunatic. A glance at the clock told me how crazy I was. It was just short of nine. I had been cavorting in the bathroom for nearly an hour.

"So why were you worried about me?"

"Oh, I don't know. Maybe because you have a tendency to become involved in dangerous schemes, one of which put you in a hospital a while back. Maybe because it took nearly twenty years for you to come back into my life." He paused. "Maybe because I love you, and I can't stand the thought of being without you."

The last "maybe" got me. Intense happiness swept through me. "Oh, Mark." I took a deep breath. "I love you, too." It had been a long, long time since I'd uttered those words to anyone except my mother, my sister, my brother and their children.

"Have you told your mother yet?"

"No, I've been savoring the taste, like dark chocolate on my tongue. You know, the smooth, creamy kind that just lingers there, waiting for you to swallow it?" He grew quiet; and when he spoke again, his voice was husky.

"Woman, how soon can we get married?" It was my turn to be silent. At just the thought of becoming Mark's wife, his lover, his darling, my heart went crazier than I acted in the bathroom.

"I have nothing on my calendar."

"Then how about I bring you an engagement ring tonight, and we can announce to your family and mine that we're going to elope?"

"Mark? Ummm...I don't need an engagement ring. I think I'd rather have a gold wedding band."

"I sense a story there," he mused.

"The ring Jack gave me was huge, and it always felt like a lead weight on my hand. I love the thought of a simple band."

"That's good enough for me."

Late that afternoon, Mark picked me up on his way home from the chemical plant. My heart quickened at the sight of him. He had tossed his suit jacket into the back of the car and loosened his tie. While I watched from the living room window, he jerked off the tie and tossed it into the car, too. He unbuttoned the top few buttons of his shirt. *Oooh, I want to do that.*

I whispered to myself, "I could go for a good elopement about now." I opened the front door and met him in the middle of the stone path. His arms felt so good around me, and my arms fit perfectly around his back. I didn't care what Bert and Evelyn or the whole neighborhood thought.

I had been kissed soundly and well, but no other man's kiss had touched more than the physical. In Mark's arms, I felt complete, whole and cherished. He made me aware of another plane, the center of who and what I was, a spiritual connection I had never before experienced. Of course, the physical side was off the charts, too!

"Are you ready for the fireworks?" he asked.

"Ready? I thought we had just created some." I kissed the tip of his manly nose. I loved his laugh.

"Oh, Sissy, I'm so happy for you!" My mother enveloped me with her hug, and then she turned to Mark. "You are so right for my daughter! Oh, this is just perfect! Perfect!" Mark winked at me over her head.

"I think so, too, Mrs. Dunbar."

"When are you getting married?" Mom asked. Mark's daughters stood on either side of me.

"Daddy, can we get married in our church? Then Clarice and I could be bridesmaids."

"Yeah, Daddy, can we?" Clarice and Alyssa wound their arms through mine. Alyssa looked up at me. "Can we, please, Sissy?" Helplessly, I met Mark's eyes.

"Girl's, we were kind of planning..."

"Mark, it's okay. It would make them happy," I told him. A ceremony in Mark's church seemed fitting to me. For several Sundays, I had attended with him and the girls; and I liked it. The congregation of the Methodist Church on Walnut Street was filled with people I had known in my teens, many of our former classmates. Sitting next to Mark there on Sunday mornings felt right.

"Whatever you want, Sissy," Mark said; and I knew he was pleased. It was unbelievable how much pleasing him pleased me.

That's how, on a frosty Saturday evening in mid-November of nineteen seventy-seven, I found myself standing beside my brother in the vestibule of the Methodist church. Bill had agreed to escort me down the aisle.

"Are you sure you want to do this, Sis? Do you really love this guy?"

I turned to my little brother, who would always be Buddy to me; and I smiled at him.

"I love Mark so much, it takes away my breath. I love him so much, I can't stand the thought of life without him. I love him so much..."

"Okay, okay, I get it. You convinced me."

The music began. I held my brother's arm and floated toward the most handsome, most desirable, most delicious man in the world. I wore a simple, medium blue dinner suit and carried white lilies.

Dressed in identical lighter blue dresses, Alyssa and Clarice preceded me toward their father. Usually so animated they sometimes bordered on giddy, the girls walked with sober dignity and grace. I loved them already.

I burned every moment of the candlelight ceremony in my mind and heart. Mark looked into my eyes as he repeated the vows, and I didn't blink when I gazed into his as I said mine. The old traditional words bound us to each other tighter than steel bands ever could. I had not even heard them when I married Jack.

"You may kiss your bride."

Mark swept me into his arms, bent me backward and planted a deep, resounding smack on my mouth. The congregation applauded, but then Mark kissed me with an unimaginable gentleness. "I love you," he whispered.

"I love you," I whispered back.

In a shower of rice and good wishes, we exited the church. Someone had painted Mark's car with hearts and our names and silly sentiments. It should have been much beneath our dignity, but I thought it looked beautiful.

Alyssa and Clarice waved to us, both their lovely faces aglow. While Mark and I took a few days for a short honeymoon, they would stay with their maternal grandparents, who were supportive of our marriage. We drove from the church to a hotel in Huntington, where Mark had booked a suite.

There are no words to describe our wedding night and all the nights that followed. We had both been through the red-hot lust of extreme youth, the kind that doesn't last. We had both loved and lost, and we had both experienced sorrow and heartache.

The passion between us was on a different level. I clung to him, on a precipice so high I was dizzy. Mark murmured to me, sweet, husky, wordless sounds of love. He touched me and I touched him with a new awareness, a new discovery of what real love between a man and a woman should and can be.

In a solitary moment, I learned what joyful passion is. Many years ago, someone described that moment as "the little death." They were wrong. For me and for Mark, it was and is a rebirth, a celebration of who we are together, an indescribable oneness. I did, indeed, feel reborn.

During that week, we made love, we talked for hours, we made plans, we discussed the possibility of children. I even told him that my given name is Clementine Carole, and he won my heart anew by not singing "Oh, My Darling Clementine." We couldn't wait for night to come, and we were thrilled with each new dawn.

I gave up my rented house in Charleston, not exactly a hardship. The day Mark carried me over the threshold of his grandfather's remodeled house was another beginning. I was the first woman to live in the new part of the house. Instead of building outward, he had built upward—a whole new story with a deck that walked onto the hillside behind and above the house.

He had opened up the lower story, creating a spacious kitchen, dining room and living area. An ample powder room fit nicely beneath the stairwell, and a laundry room filled what once was the back porch. Three bedrooms shared a large bath upstairs, and the master bedroom and bath looked onto the upper deck. It was a lovely house.

Alyssa and Clarice had their own rooms, with twin beds in each one. Most of the time they slept in one room, maintaining a closeness that lasted all their lives. I rarely heard a disagreement between them.

My real life began the day I married Mark Watson. I thanked God for him then, and I have every day since. I cannot imagine a life without him.

While I was in high school, I read a book by an author, whose name I think is Ben Ames Williams. The story followed a woman through horrendous circumstances, including prison, physical hardship, travel from one country to another, until she finally met and married a good man. The name of the book is <u>All This And Heaven, Too</u>.

At the time I read it, I was too young to understand all the implications. Since then, I've heard the title used sarcastically, even flippantly. Today I understand what the title and the book mean.

For the believer, heaven awaits at the end of life, whatever the circumstances. For the believer who is blessed with someone to love and is loved in return, heaven is simply icing on an already wonderful cake. We spread our arms and encompass "all this," our earthly paradise, while "heaven, too," waits over the hill.

Passion, joy and heaven, too.

EPILOGUE: Afterglow

When my son, Alexander Scott, was placed in my arms exactly one year from the day Mark and I were married, I thought my heart would explode with joy. Even then, Alex looked like his father. I didn't think it was possible to be happier.

Two years later, just shy of my fortieth birthday, I gave birth to our daughter, Rene Lynette. While Mark and I gazed at her and made those silly, sweet sounds parents make to a new baby, she opened her eyes. She had the Bannister steely-blue gaze of her grandfather. *Oh, Dad, I wish you could see her and my little boy.*

The years flew so quickly, it was like being on a merry-go-round that constantly ran faster. There were school projects, ballgames and parties for Alyssa and Clarice at the same time we dealt with diapers, potty training and kindergarten with Alex and Rene.

I was not a young mother. Most of the mothers of my children's classmates were in their twenties and thirties, while I was mid-and-upper forties. It didn't bother me in the least, but there were times I caught wondering glances from the young things.

After Alex and Rene entered school, I found time to write again. It isn't strange that I turned to stories for children. Before they could walk, I had begun to read to them. As they became toddlers, I made up stories and often included them as characters within the tales. They loved it.

It seemed natural that I would write those stories; and from there it followed that I would illustrate them, too. Nothing I had written during my so-called career meant more to me than those colorful children's books. The illustrations are on the whimsical side, filled with unlikely renderings of animals, fairies and such. In time, I began to write seriously again, but not until Alex and Rene were older

Overnight, it seemed, the twins were in college. The younger children were in high school. About that time, Clarice married her college sweetheart; and suddenly Mark and I were grandparents. Alyssa became a teacher. She was able to find a position in a Dixon grade school, and she actually taught her sister's children, as well as her half-brother and sister.

Alex went from college into the Air Force. Due to my history, it wasn't what I would have chosen for him; but he had always been fascinated with aviation. He longed to be a pilot, and there was nothing I could do to dissuade him. Today he is a pilot for a major airline, so he was right to follow his heart.

He and his wife, Sandy, live near Atlanta, in a magnificent, restored Southern home, set among magnolias and willow trees. Their two-year-old son, Gregory, and a Golden retriever named Lucky, romp together on the lush, green lawn.

Rene, our baby, is almost as fine an artist as Willow Thornhill was. Like her willful mother, Rene went to New York, where she studied with some of the best art instructors. She has won many awards, and her paintings sell well in various galleries along the east coast, quite an accomplishment for a young woman not yet thirty. As yet, she shows no inclination toward marriage.

Mark and I took our first trip to Europe together the year after Rene left home for college. It was in Ireland that I discovered my writing voice again. Our plane flew over it on the way to London; and when I first saw the emerald green island rise from the sea, something caught in my chest.

The feeling only escalated when I saw the misty slopes from the ground. Old stone ruins of cottages and castles spoke to me in a language of the heart, and it seemed that I had been there at another time. I don't know if memories can be passed genetically, but even the scents and sounds seemed familiar to me. The musical Irish brogue sounded sweet to my ears. Characters leapt into my mind, full-blown. Before we left Ireland, I had outlined a plot and storyline in my laptop, a bargain at any price. That book, Bridget's Castle, was the first of a series set in the Emerald Isle.

My stepfather died a few years ago. He was nearly ninety. My mother, now eighty-seven, continues to live in the white house with the red roof on Symington Street. Still fiercely independent, she enjoys her grandchildren and, thanks to my brother's prolific boys, seven great-grandchildren.

Bill and Lainie moved closer to Dixon after their boys grew up and got married. Mark and I see them often, and we've traveled throughout the country together. Red-haired Lainie pretty well keeps Bill in line.

My sweet little sister cannot be persuaded to leave sunny Southern California. She and Eric move among the more conservative of the Hollywood set. Eric has written and produced several somewhat successful screenplays, and I suspect it's just a matter of time before he does one of those blockbusters.

When Beth's daughter, Kathy, was ten, another little girl, Debra Kristin, completed their family. Beth recently retired from fulltime teaching, but she continues to work with college professor candidates. When the university calls, she can't say no. Her two daughters have given her and Eric five grandchildren, all of whom Beth adores.

All in all, the three Bannister kids from Redbud Grove are happy and content with their lives. It's been quite a journey for all of us, most of it probably not much different from the rest of the country. I love that we continue to nurture each other.

My Redbud Grove friends and I correspond and see each other when we can. About ten years after the first reunion I attended, Melissa Franklin called to tell me her brother, Jeff, had been told that Adam Martin was his son. Rebecca, while only in her early forties, died in her sleep one winter night. It was then that Adam asked Melissa to notify Jeff. Melissa told me that Jeff came back to Redbud Grove often, and he and his son have developed a good relationship.

"I attended the burial service for Rebecca Martin," Melissa told me. "Adam came to the house to invite me. Although there was sadness, there was a great sense of acceptance. The casket was a plain, pine box, much like what we've seen in old western movies. The men seemed stoic, but many of the women shed tears of sorrow. I think Rebecca was well-loved and respected."

"It sounds like you and Adam are close, Melissa."

"We are, Sissy. He's my nephew, the only one I'll ever have here."

I was wrong about Lucinda Barnes and Joe Bob Brady.

"Sissy, the secrets we both carried from what happened in my mom's house were too much for us," Lucinda told me in a long telephone conversation. Less than two years after they met at the reunion, she broke the connection with Joe Bob. "Joe Bob was up for re-election, and I knew his opponents would zero in on me."

"How did he feel about it?"

"He tried valiantly to convince me that it wouldn't matter; but I knew it did. I commuted back and forth from the west coast to Louisville for about three months."

"Did you, uh, live together?" I asked. Lucinda had laughed.

"Well, yes, my little Puritan friend; we did. That part was great, but it wasn't enough. He won his election, and I hear he has higher aspirations. He also has a lady friend, a nice widow, with the right political affiliation."

"So you're happy?"

"Happy?" she had repeated. "Content, is a better word, I think. I love what I do, and the weather is always fantastic. You should bring your sweet Mark and stay out here for awhile."

Eventually, Mark and I did see Lucinda when we went to visit my sister. Lucinda was as beautiful as ever. I knew that, like Mae West, she would not age until she was close to a hundred, bless her. All I ever wanted for Lucinda was peace, and I think she found it.

As for Sharon Bennett, we chat occasionally, but we are in constant touch on the inter net these days. She spends winters in Florida, and she talks about moving there permanently. I don't believe she ever will. Her children and grandchildren are much too important to her. When we talk, it's as if we just pick up where we left the last conversation.

I saw Victor Delacourt on a television awards program a few years ago. One of his many hit songs received a top award. His once muscular body looked soft, and his belly had a tendency to lap over his belt. Deep lines dented his forehead, and his jaw line sagged.

Signs of too many indulgences were apparent on his face. Instead of charming, he looked decadent. In his thank-you speech, following his acceptance of the award, he mentioned his wife; and her name wasn't Dottie. I could only speculate how many times he had been married. Again, I thanked God for opening my eyes before I became so entangled with Victor Delacourt I couldn't get out unscathed.

I can't decide which season I love most in Dixon. In the spring, I set up an easel on the front porch and paint the dogwoods and redbuds and dainty greens that line the mountainside across the valley. I'm too busy with Mark in summer to paint; but when the color begins to change in the autumn, I'm back on the porch with paints and canvasses.

If I simply had to choose one season as my favorite, it would probably be the white stillness of winter. Mark and I love to bundle up in warm clothing and walk up the high slope behind the house. Starkly black against the snow, the trees are in silhouette, even in the daytime.

The mountain spring never freezes. It bubbles and chirps, and I am again reminded of the first time Mark brought me up the hill to see it. We often carry a lidded container and stop at the cider house before we go home. I think the cider is the most delicious then, icy cold from the wood spigot. I suspect there's enough alcohol in it to prevent it from freezing, but I'm not going to investigate too closely.

We always take some back to the house, where I heat it and add a stick of cinnamon to our mugs. We sit in front of the expanse of windows on the house's upper level, and together we watch the sun fall behind the mountains. I think it's the most beautiful place on earth.

On snowy days, I sometimes paint snow scenes—when I'm not tucked into a chair near the fireplace, lap quilt and book in my lap. Yes, I think winter is my favorite.

Mark's hair has turned a lovely shade of silver, with only a bit of the dark brown left. It grows a little farther back on his forehead now, but his brilliant blue eyes have not faded. Looking at him can still make my heart flutter. That poet who said so many years ago, "Grow old along with me. The best is yet to be," knew his stuff.

Do I have regrets? Of course I do; but the choices and the mistakes I made are what brought me to this moment, where I am today. For that reason, I would not change a thing, except to have my dad be able to see who and what his children and grandchildren are. I think he would be pleased.

The Bannister saga continues with the little people, those who carry the name and those who do not. They rank uppermost in my daily thank you to God. On Sunday mornings, when Mark and I sit in the Methodist church together, I realize how blessed we are, how blessed I am. Barely a Sunday goes by that I'm not reminded of the words from the book I read all those years ago:

"All this, and heaven, too." Icing on my cake, a very, very sweet one.

Do I still wish on a star now and then? Not often. When Mark and I sit on the upper deck on warm summer evenings, I love to lay my head back and look at the sky.

I always sigh with pleasure at the moment just past twilight, when most of the sky has turned to purple, with lavender and pink at the horizon. I sometimes experience a moment of sadness, for I know that another precious day is gone from our allotted number.

The first star seems to magically appear in the very spot where my eyes are focused. Of course, it could be that after all these years, my eyes know where to look. As for wishing on it, I don't. There's nothing more I want. I would be content to spend the next thousand years exactly as I am, Mark's wife, his companion, his lover (yes, still!), his best friend, as he is mine.

If I could wish for anything, it would be for time to slow down, for the fast-flying days to decelerate by half. I know I'm not the first to think it, and I certainly won't be the last. So I enjoy every day to the fullest, trying to fill each one with good things, faces of people I love and moments of passion and joy.

What more could I possibly ask?

Here on this earth.

With Mark.

Author's Note

And so we come to the end of Sissy's story. Living through it with her has been a hoot. I'm a bit torn about the conclusion of the series. On one hand, I'm glad to get on with other writing projects. On the other, I'm sorry that Sissy Bannister will no longer be my constant companion. She often surprised me with the directions her story took, and I have no idea where some of the characters came from.

As previously stated, most of the three books are fiction. The first two chapters in Starlight, Starbright... are totally true. After that, the lines of distinction between truth and fiction begin to blur. The character in the chapter, JULIE KITCHEN, is based upon a woman I remember from my early childhood; but the circumstances of the storyline are totally fiction.

The little lady in MRS. MURPHY'S LAW actually lived up the street from me in "Redbud Grove." Her story is as I and many other children of the town remember it. She was quite a gal. GRANDMA CHINN really was my great-grandmother, exactly as I described her. THE GRANDPAS were also as my grandfathers really were, but the laxative story is fiction. Sorry, Girls, but the Victor Delacourt character is also total fiction and based upon no one person.

Now retired USAF Colonel Jerry Davis is another matter. He didn't live in West Virginia, but he was my friend in the first grade, he really did give me a black eye, and he really did do the "chest measuring" with his eyes when we were in the eighth grade. After living all over the world with the Air Force, Jerry has come back to his grandfather's farm to retire, where he and his lovely wife, Marilyn, have built a "new, old-fashioned" farmhouse beside a small lake. He is, literally, my oldest friend, given the number of years we have known each other. We live no more than ten miles apart, and we visit often.

Sissy's Uncle Sonny is really my Uncle Sonny. Everything in the books about him is true, and some of the little personal things in the book are based upon incidents with him and my brother, sister and me. He left a big family and a wonderful heritage to his children and his many, many nieces and nephews.

Some stories in <u>Wish I May, Wish I Might...</u> , are fictionalized accounts of only bits of truth. Again, the line between truth and fiction has become difficult for me to identify. It might be a scrap of something read in an old newspaper that triggers my imagination, and a new story chapter magically appears.

My family has never lived in West Virginia, and my father didn't die in a coal mine. However, Sissy's dad passed away at the same age as mine, in a hospital, with a tracheotomy, his young family nearby. That chapter was the most difficult to write, and sometimes the words on the computer blurred with my tears.

From my heart, I thank my mother. I admire her bravery and strength, for she has wanted to tell the world her story ever since I can remember. The events described by Sissy's mother are only a part of those my mother has told me. Like Sissy, I didn't have the heart to tell it all. My mother is a wonderful example of rising above one's upbringing to become a magnificent human being. "I used to want to climb to the highest hill and scream to the world what my life was like as a child," she told me during our discussion about her chapter. After I wrote it, I sent a copy to her; for I would not print it without her approval, which she gave.

Many thanks also go to my brother and sister, upon whom "Buddy/ Bill" and "Bethy/Beth" are based. Most of the childhood stories about them are true; and I have used them with permission, however reluctantly granted. They are outstanding human beings, and I love both of them very much.

Should the reader have any questions about a particular story or character, please feel free to contact me at bjlogger2@aol.com. I welcome your comments. I am always available to speak at book clubs, libraries, book signings or other events. Thank you so much for your kind compliments on the Starlight Trilogy, and thank you for coming along for the ride!

Gratefully,
Barbara Elliott Carpenter
www.barbaraelliottcarpenter.com

Printed in the United States
96226LV00003B/127-153/A